EVERYMAN, I will go with thee,

and be thy guide,

In thy most need to go by thy side

GEORGE ELIOT

(pseudonym of Mary Ann (or Marian) Evans)

Born at Arbury Farm, in the parish of Chilvers Coton, Warwickshire, November 1819. Translated Strauss (1846) and Feuerbach (1854); assistant editor of John Chapman's *Westminster Review*, 1851–3; began writing fiction in 1856; lived with George Henry Lewes from 1854 till his death in 1879; married John Walter Cross (twenty years her junior) in May 1880, and died seven months later, on 22nd December 1880.

GEORGE ELIOT

Middlemarch

IN TWO VOLUMES · VOLUME TWO

INTRODUCTION BY
GERALD BULLETT

DENT: LONDON
EVERYMAN'S LIBRARY
DUTTON: NEW YORK

CONTENTS

VOLUME TWO

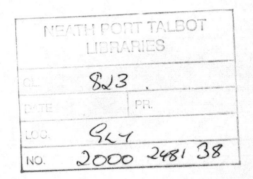

BOOK V

THE DEAD HAND

CHAPTER XLIII

This figure hath high price : 'twas wrought with love
Ages ago in finest ivory ;
Nought modish in it, pure and noble lines
Of generous womanhood that fits all time.
That too is costly ware ; majolica
Of deft design, to please a lordly eye :
The smile, you see, is perfect—wonderful
As mere Faience ! a table ornament
To suit the richest mounting.

DOROTHEA seldom left home without her husband, but she did occasionally drive into Middlemarch alone, on little errands of shopping or charity such as occur to every lady of any wealth when she lives within three miles of a town. Two days after that scene in the Yew-Tree Walk, she determined to use such an opportunity in order if possible to see Lydgate, and learn from him whether her husband had really felt any depressing change of symptoms which he was concealing from her, and whether he had insisted on knowing the utmost about himself. She felt almost guilty in asking for knowledge about him from another, but the dread of being without it—the dread of that ignorance which would make her unjust or hard—overcame every scruple. That there had been some crisis in her husband's mind she was certain : he had the very next day begun a new method of arranging his notes, and had associated her quite newly in carrying out his plan. Poor Dorothea needed to lay up stores of patience.

It was about four o'clock when she drove to Lydgate's house in Lowick Gate, wishing, in her immediate doubt of finding him at home, that she had written beforehand. And he was not at home.

" Is Mrs. Lydgate at home ? " said Dorothea, who had never,

that she knew of, seen Rosamond, but now remembered the fact of the marriage. Yes, Mrs. Lydgate was at home.

" I will go in and speak to her, if she will allow me. Will you ask her if she can see me—see Mrs. Casaubon, for a few minutes?"

When the servant had gone to deliver that message, Dorothea could hear sounds of music through an open window—a few notes from a man's voice and then a piano bursting into roulades. But the roulades broke off suddenly, and then the servant came back saying that Mrs. Lydgate would be happy to see Mrs. Casaubon.

When the drawing-room door opened and Dorothea entered, there was a sort of contrast not infrequent in country life when the habits of the different ranks were less blent than now. Let those who know, tell us exactly what stuff it was that Dorothea wore in those days of mild autumn—that thin white woollen stuff soft to the touch and soft to the eye. It always seemed to have been lately washed, and to smell of the sweet hedges— was always in the shape of a pelisse with sleeves hanging all out of the fashion. Yet if she had entered before a still audience as Imogene or Cato's daughter, the dress might have seemed right enough : the grace and dignity were in her limbs and neck ; and about her simply parted hair and candid eyes the large round poke which was then in the fate of women, seemed no more odd as a head-dress than the gold trencher we call a halo. By the present audience of two persons, no dramatic heroine could have been expected with more interest than Mrs. Casaubon. To Rosamond she was one of those county divinities not mixing with Middlemarch mortality, whose slightest marks of manner or appearance were worthy of her study ; moreover, Rosamond was not without satisfaction that Mrs. Casaubon should have an opportunity of studying *her*. What is the use of being exquisite if you are not seen by the best judges ? and since Rosamond had received the highest compliments at Sir Godwin Lydgate's, she felt quite confident of the impression she must make on people of good birth. Dorothea put out her hand with her usual simple kindness, and looked admiringly at Lydgate's lovely bride—aware that there was a gentleman standing at a distance, but seeing him merely as a coated figure at a wide angle. The gentleman was too much occupied with the presence of the one woman to reflect on the contrast between the two—a contrast that would certainly have been striking to a calm observer. They were both tall, and their eyes were on a level ; but imagine Rosamond's infantine blondness and wondrous crown of hair-plaits, with her pale-blue dress of a fit and fashion so perfect that no dressmaker could look at it without emotion, a large embroidered collar which it was to be hoped all beholders would know the price of, her small hands duly set off with rings, and that controlled self-consciousness of manner which is the expensive substitute for simplicity.

"Thank you very much for allowing me to interrupt you," said Dorothea, immediately. "I am anxious to see Mr. Lydgate, if possible, before I go home, and I hoped that you might possibly tell me where I could find him, or even allow me to wait for him, if you expect him soon."

"He is at the New Hospital," said Rosamond; "I am not sure how soon he will come home. But I can send for him."

"Will you let me go and fetch him?" said Will Ladislaw, coming forward. He had already taken up his hat before Dorothea entered. She coloured with surprise, but put out her hand with a smile of unmistakable pleasure, saying—

"I did not know it was you: I had no thought of seeing you here."

"May I go to the Hospital and tell Mr. Lydgate that you wish to see him?" said Will.

"It would be quicker to send the carriage for him," said Dorothea, "if you will be kind enough to give the message to the coachman."

Will was moving to the door when Dorothea, whose mind had flashed in an instant over many connected memories, turned quickly and said, "I will go myself, thank you. I wish to lose no time before getting home again. I will drive to the Hospital and see Mr. Lydgate there. Pray excuse me, Mrs. Lydgate. I am very much obliged to you."

Her mind was evidently arrested by some sudden thought, and she left the room hardly conscious of what was immediately around her—hardly conscious that Will opened the door for her and offered her his arm to lead her to the carriage. She took the arm but said nothing. Will was feeling rather vexed and miserable, and found nothing to say on his side. He handed her into the carriage in silence, they said good-bye, and Dorothea drove away.

In the five minutes' drive to the Hospital she had time for some reflections that were quite new to her. Her decision to go, and her preoccupation in leaving the room, had come from the sudden sense that there would be a sort of deception in her voluntarily allowing any further intercourse between herself and Will which she was unable to mention to her husband, and already her errand in seeking Lydgate was a matter of concealment. That was all that had been explicitly in her mind; but she had been urged also by a vague discomfort. Now that she was alone in her drive, she heard the notes of the man's voice and the accompanying piano, which she had not noted much at the time, returning on her inward sense; and she found herself thinking with some wonder that Will Ladislaw was passing his time with Mrs. Lydgate in her husband's absence. And then she could not help remembering that he had passed some time with her under like circumstances, so why should there be any unfitness in the fact? But Will was Mr. Casaubon's relative, and one towards whom she was bound to show kindness. Still there had been signs which perhaps she ought to have understood as implying that Mr. Casaubon did not like his cousin's visits during his own absence. " Perhaps I have been mistaken in many things," said poor Dorothea to herself, while the tears came rolling and she had to dry them quickly. She felt confusedly unhappy, and the image of Will which had been so clear to her before was mysteriously spoiled. But the carriage stopped at the gate of the Hospital. She was soon walking round the grass plots with Lydgate, and her feelings recovered the strong bent which had made her seek for this interview.

Will Ladislaw, meanwhile, was mortified, and knew the reason of it clearly enough. His chances of meeting Dorothea were rare; and here for the first time there had come a chance which had set him at a disadvantage. It was not only, as it had been hitherto, that she was not supremely occupied with him, but that she had seen him under circumstances in which he might appear not to be supremely occupied with her. He felt thrust to a new distance from her, amongst the circles of Middlemarchers who made no part of her life. But that was not his fault : of course, since he had taken his lodgings in the town, he had been making as many acquaintances as he could, his position requiring that he should know everybody and everything. Lydgate was really better worth knowing than any one else in the neighbourhood, and he happened to have a wife who was musical and altogether worth calling upon. Here was the whole history of the situation in which Diana had descended too unexpectedly on her worshipper. It was mortifying. Will was conscious that he should not have been at Middlemarch but for Dorothea; and yet his position there was threatening to divide him from her with

those barriers of habitual sentiment which are more fatal to the
persistence of mutual interest than all the distance between
Rome and Britain. Prejudices about rank and status were
easy enough to defy in the form of a tyrannical letter from Mr.
Casaubon ; but prejudices, like odorous bodies, have a double
existence both solid and subtle—solid as the pyramids, subtle as
the twentieth echo of an echo, or as the memory of hyacinths
which once scented the darkness. And Will was of a temperament to feel keenly the presence of subtleties : a man of
clumsier perceptions would not have felt, as he did, that for the
first time some sense of unfitness in perfect freedom with him
had sprung up in Dorothea's mind, and that their silence, as he
conducted her to the carriage, had had a chill in it. Perhaps
Casaubon, in his hatred and jealousy, had been insisting to
Dorothea that Will had slid below her socially. Confound
Casaubon !

Will re-entered the drawing-room, took up his hat, and looking
irritated as he advanced towards Mrs. Lydgate, who had seated
herself at her work-table, said—

" It is always fatal to have music or poetry interrupted.
May I come another day and just finish about the rendering of
' Lungi dal caro bene ' ? "

" I shall be happy to be taught," said Rosamond. " But I
am sure you admit that the interruption was a very beautiful one.
I quite envy your acquaintance with Mrs. Casaubon. Is she
very clever ? She looks as if she were."

" Really, I never thought about it," said Will, sulkily.

" That is just the answer Tertius gave me, when I first asked
him if she were handsome. What is it that you gentlemen are
thinking of when you are with Mrs. Casaubon ? "

" Herself," said Will, not indisposed to provoke the charming
Mrs. Lydgate. " When one sees a perfect woman, one never
thinks of her attributes—one is conscious of her presence."

" I shall be jealous when Tertius goes to Lowick," said Rosamond, dimpling, and speaking with aëry lightness. " He will
come back and think nothing of me."

" That does not seem to have been the effect on Lydgate
hitherto. Mrs. Casaubon is too unlike other women for them
to be compared with her."

" You are a devout worshipper, I perceive. You often see
her, I suppose."

" No," said Will, almost pettishly. " Worship is usually a
matter of theory rather than of practice. But I am practising

it to excess just at this moment—I must really tear myself away."

"Pray come again some evening : Mr. Lydgate will like to hear the music, and I cannot enjoy it so well without him."

When her husband was at home again, Rosamond said, standing in front of him and holding his coat-collar with both her hands, " Mr. Ladislaw was here singing with me when Mrs. Casaubon came in. He seemed vexed. Do you think he disliked her seeing him at our house ? Surely your position is more than equal to his—whatever may be his relation to the Casaubons."

"No, no ; it must be something else if he were really vexed. Ladislaw is a sort of gypsy ; he thinks nothing of leather and prunella."

"Music apart, he is not always very agreeable. Do you like him ? "

"Yes : I think he is a good fellow : rather miscellaneous and *bric-à-brac*, but likable."

"Do you know, I think he adores Mrs. Casaubon."

"Poor devil ! " said Lydgate, smiling and pinching his wife's ears.

Rosamond felt herself beginning to know a great deal of the world, especially in discovering—what when she was in her unmarried girlhood had been inconceivable to her except as a dim tragedy in bygone costumes—that women, even after marriage, might make conquests and enslave men. At that time young ladies in the country, even when educated at Mrs. Lemon's, read little French literature later than Racine, and public prints had not cast their present magnificent illumination over the scandals of life. Still, vanity, with a woman's whole mind and day to work in, can construct abundantly on slight hints, especially on such a hint as the possibility of indefinite conquests. How delightful to make captives from the throne of marriage with a husband as crown-prince by your side—himself in fact a subject—while the captives look up for ever hopeless, losing their rest probably, and if their appetite too, so much the better ! But Rosamond's romance turned at present chiefly on her crownprince, and it was enough to enjoy his assured subjection. When he said, " Poor devil ! " she asked, with playful curiosity—

"Why so ? "

"Why, what can a man do when he takes to adoring one of you mermaids ? He only neglects his work and runs up bills."

"I am sure you do not neglect your work. You are always at

the Hospital, or seeing poor patients, or thinking about some doctor's quarrel ; and then at home you always want to pore over your microscope and phials.   Confess you like those things better than me."

"Haven't you ambition enough to wish that your husband should be something better than a Middlemarch doctor ? " said Lydgate, letting his hands fall on to his wife's shoulders, and looking at her with affectionate gravity.   "I shall make you learn my favourite bit from an old poet—

> ' Why should our pride make such a stir to be
> And be forgot ?   What good is like to this,
> To do worthy the writing, and to write
> Worthy the reading and the world's delight ? '

What I want, Rosy, is to do worthy the writing,—and to write out myself what I have done.   A man must work, to do that, my pet."

"Of course, I wish you to make discoveries : no one could more wish you to attain a high position in some better place than Middlemarch.   You cannot say that I have ever tried to hinder you from working.   But we cannot live like hermits.   You are not discontented with me, Tertius ? "

"No, dear, no.   I am too entirely contented."

"But what did Mrs. Casaubon want to say to you ? "

"Merely to ask about her husband's health.   But I think she is going to be splendid to our New Hospital : I think she will give us two hundred a-year."

CHAPTER XLIV

> I would not creep along the coast, but steer
> Out in mid-sea, by guidance of the stars.

WHEN Dorothea, walking round the laurel-planted plots of the New Hospital with Lydgate, had learned from him that there were no signs of change in Mr. Casaubon's bodily condition beyond the mental sign of anxiety to know the truth about his illness, she was silent for a few moments, wondering whether she had said or done anything to rouse this new anxiety. Lydgate, not willing to let slip an opportunity of furthering a favourite purpose, ventured to say—

"I don't know whether your or Mr. Casaubon's attention has

been drawn to the needs of our New Hospital. Circumstances have made it seem rather egotistic in me to urge the subject ; but that is not my fault ; it is because there is a fight being made against it by the other medical men. I think you are generally interested in such things, for I remember that when I first had the pleasure of seeing you at Tipton Grange before your marriage you were asking me some questions about the way in which the health of the poor was affected by their miserable housing."

"Yes, indeed," said Dorothea, brightening. "I shall be quite grateful to you if you will tell me how I can help to make things a little better. Everything of that sort has slipped away from me since I have been married. I mean," she said, after a moment's hesitation, "that the people in our village are tolerably comfortable, and my mind has been too much taken up for me to inquire further. But here—in such a place as Middlemarch—there must be a great deal to be done."

"There is everything to be done," said Lydgate, with abrupt energy. "And this Hospital is a capital piece of work, due entirely to Mr. Bulstrode's exertions, and in a great degree to his money. But one man can't do everything in a scheme of this sort. Of course he looked forward to help. And now there's a mean, petty feud set up against the thing in the town, by certain persons who want to make it a failure."

"What can be their reasons ? " said Dorothea, with *naïve* surprise.

"Chiefly Mr. Bulstrode's unpopularity, to begin with. Half the town would almost take trouble for the sake of thwarting him. In this stupid world most people never consider that a thing is good to be done unless it is done by their own set. I had no connection with Bulstrode before I came here. I look at him quite impartially, and I see that he has some notions— that he has set things on foot—which I can turn to good public purpose. If a fair number of the better educated men went to work with the belief that their observations might contribute to the reform of medical doctrine and practice, we should soon see a change for the better. That's my point of view. I hold that by refusing to work with Mr. Bulstrode I should be turning my back on an opportunity of making my profession more generally serviceable."

"I quite agree with you," said Dorothea, at once fascinated by the situation sketched in Lydgate's words. "But what is there against Mr. Bulstrode ? I know that my uncle is friendly with him."

" People don't like his religious tone," said Lydgate, breaking off there.

" That is all the stronger reason for despising such an opposition," said Dorothea, looking at the affairs of Middlemarch by the light of the great persecutions.

" To put the matter quite fairly, they have other objections to him :—he is masterful and rather unsociable, and he is concerned with trade, which has complaints of its own that I know nothing about. But what has that to do with the question whether it would not be a fine thing to establish here a more valuable hospital than any they have in the county ? The immediate motive to the opposition, however, is the fact that Bulstrode has put the medical direction into my hands. Of course I am glad of that. It gives me an opportunity of doing some good work,—and I am aware that I have to justify his choice of me. But the consequence is, that the whole profession in Middlemarch have set themselves tooth and nail against the Hospital, and not only refuse to co-operate themselves, but try to blacken the whole affair and hinder subscriptions."

" How very petty ! " exclaimed Dorothea, indignantly.

" I suppose one must expect to fight one's way : there is hardly anything to be done without it. And the ignorance of people about here is stupendous. I don't lay claim to anything else than having used some opportunities which have not come within everybody's reach ; but there is no stifling the offence of being young, and a new-comer, and happening to know something more than the old inhabitants. Still, if I believe that I can set going a better method of treatment—if I believe that I can pursue certain observations and inquiries which may be a lasting benefit to medical practice, I should be a base truckler if I allowed any consideration of personal comfort to hinder me. And the course is all the clearer from there being no salary in question to put my persistence in an equivocal light."

" I am glad you have told me this, Mr. Lydgate," said Dorothea, cordially. " I feel sure I can help a little. I have some money, and don't know what to do with it—that is often an uncomfortable thought to me. I am sure I can spare two hundred a-year for a grand purpose like this. How happy you must be, to know things that you feel sure will do great good ! I wish I could awake with that knowledge every morning. There seems to be so much trouble taken that one can hardly see the good of ! "

There was a melancholy cadence in Dorothea's voice as she spoke these last words. But she presently added, more cheerfully, " Pray come to Lowick and tell us more of this. I will mention the subject to Mr. Casaubon. I must hasten home now."

She did mention it that evening, and said that she should like to subscribe two hundred a-year—she had seven hundred a-year as the equivalent of her own fortune, settled on her at her marriage. Mr. Casaubon made no objection beyond a passing remark that the sum might be disproportionate in relation to other good objects, but when Dorothea in her ignorance resisted that suggestion, he acquiesced. He did not care himself about spending money, and was not reluctant to give it. If he ever felt keenly any question of money it was through the medium of another passion than the love of material property.

Dorothea told him that she had seen Lydgate, and recited the gist of her conversation with him about the Hospital. Mr. Casaubon did not question her further, but he felt sure that she had wished to know what had passed between Lydgate and himself. " She knows that I know," said the ever-restless voice within ; but that increase of tacit knowledge only thrust further off any confidence between them. He distrusted her affection ; and what loneliness is more lonely than distrust ?

CHAPTER XLV

" It is the humour of many heads to extol the days of their forefathers, and declaim against the wickedness of times present. Which notwithstanding they cannot handsomely do, without the borrowed help and satire of times past ; condemning the vices of their own times, by the expressions of vices in times which they commend, which cannot but argue the community of vice in both. Horace, therefore, Juvenal, and Persius, were no prophets, although their lines did seem to indigitate and point at our times."—SIR THOMAS BROWNE : *Pseudodoxia Epidemica.*

THAT opposition to the New Fever Hospital which Lydgate had sketched to Dorothea was, like other oppositions, to be viewed in many different lights. He regarded it as a mixture of jealousy and dunder-headed prejudice. Mr. Bulstrode saw in it not only medical jealousy but a determination to thwart himself, prompted mainly by a hatred of that vital religion of which he had striven to be an effectual lay representative—a hatred which certainly found pretexts apart from religion such as were only too easy to find in the entanglements of human action. These might be called the ministerial views. But oppositions have the

illimitable range of objections at command, which need never
stop short at the boundary of knowledge, but can draw for ever
on the vasts of ignorance.   What the opposition in Middlemarch
said about the New Hospital and its administration had certainly
a great deal of echo in it, for heaven has taken care that everybody shall not be an originator ; but there were differences
which represented every social shade between the polished
moderation of Dr. Minchin and the trenchant assertion of Mrs.
Dollop, the landlady of the Tankard in Slaughter Lane.

Mrs. Dollop became more and more convinced by her own
asseveration, that Doctor Lydgate meant to let the people die in
the Hospital, if not to poison them, for the sake of cutting them
up without saying by your leave or with your leave ; for it was
a known " fac " that he had wanted to cut up Mrs. Goby, as
respectable a woman as any in Parley Street, who had money
in trust before her marriage—a poor tale for a doctor, who if
he was good for anything should know what was the matter
with you before you died, and not want to pry into your inside
after you were gone.   If that was not reason, Mrs. Dollop wished
to know what was ; but there was a prevalent feeling in her
audience that her opinion was a bulwark, and that if it were
overthrown there would be no limits to the cutting-up of bodies,
as had been well seen in Burke and Hare with their pitch-
plaisters—such a hanging business as that was not wanted in
Middlemarch !

And let it not be supposed that opinion at the Tankard in
Slaughter Lane was unimportant to the medical profession :
that old authentic public-house—the original Tankard known
by the name of Dollop's—was the resort of a great Benefit
Club, which had some months before put to the vote whether
its long-standing medical man, " Doctor Gambit," should not
be cashiered in favour of " this Doctor Lydgate," who was capable of performing the most astonishing cures, and rescuing people
altogether given up by other practitioners.   But the balance had
been turned against Lydgate by two members, who for some
private reasons held that this power of resuscitating persons as
good as dead was an equivocal recommendation, and might
interfere with providential favours.   In the course of the year,
however, there had been a change in the public sentiment, of
which the unanimity at Dollop's was an index.

A good deal more than a year ago, before anything was known
of Lydgate's skill, the judgments on it had naturally been divided, depending on a sense of likelihood, situated perhaps in the

pit of the stomach or in the pineal gland, and differing in its verdicts, but not the less valuable as a guide in the total deficit of evidence. Patients who had chronic diseases or whose lives had long been worn threadbare, like old Featherstone's, had been at once inclined to try him ; also, many who did not like paying their doctor's bills, thought agreeably of opening an account with a new doctor and sending for him without stint if the children's temper wanted a dose, occasions when the old practitioners were often crusty ; and all persons thus inclined to employ Lydgate held it likely that he was clever. Some considered that he might do more than others " where there was liver ; "—at least there would be no harm in getting a few bottles of " stuff " from him, since if these proved useless it would still be possible to return to the Purifying Pills, which kept you alive, if they did not remove the yellowness. But these were people of minor importance. Good Middlemarch families were of course not going to change their doctor without reason shown ; and everybody who had employed Mr. Peacock did not feel obliged to accept a new man merely in the character of his successor, objecting that he was " not likely to be equal to Peacock."

But Lydgate had not been long in the town before there were particulars enough reported of him to breed much more specific expectations and to intensify differences into partisanship ; some of the particulars being of that impressive order of which the significance is entirely hidden, like a statistical amount without a standard of comparison, but with a note of exclamation at the end. The cubic feet of oxygen yearly swallowed by a full-grown man—what a shudder they might have created in some Middlemarch circles ! " Oxygen ! nobody knows what that may be—is it any wonder the cholera has got to Dantzic ? And yet there are people who say quarantine is no good ! "

One of the facts quickly rumoured was that Lydgate did not dispense drugs. This was offensive both to the physicians whose exclusive distinction seemed infringed on, and to the surgeon-apothecaries with whom he ranged himself ; and only a little while before, they might have counted on having the law on their side against a man who without calling himself a London-made M.D. dared to ask for pay except as a charge on drugs. But Lydgate had not been experienced enough to foresee that his new course would be even more offensive to the laity ; and to Mr. Mawmsey, an important grocer in the Top Market, who, though not one of his patients, questioned him

in an affable manner on the subject, he was injudicious enough
to give a hasty popular explanation of his reasons, pointing
out to Mr. Mawmsey that it must lower the character of practitioners, and be a constant injury to the public, if their only mode
of getting paid for their work was by their making out long bills
for draughts, boluses, and mixtures.

"It is in that way that hard-working medical men may come
to be almost as mischievous as quacks," said Lydgate, rather
thoughtlessly. "To get their own bread they must overdose
the king's lieges ; and that's a bad sort of treason, Mr. Mawmsey
—undermines the constitution in a fatal way."

Mr. Mawmsey was not only an overseer (it was about a
question of outdoor pay that he was having an interview with
Lydgate), he was also asthmatic and had an increasing family :
thus, from a medical point of view, as well as from his own, he
was an important man ; indeed, an exceptional grocer, whose
hair was arranged in a flame-like pyramid, and whose retail
deference was of the cordial, encouraging kind—jocosely
complimentary, and with a certain considerate abstinence from
letting out the full force of his mind. It was Mr. Mawmsey's
friendly jocoseness in questioning him which had set the tone
of Lydgate's reply. But let the wise be warned against too
great readiness at explanation : it multiplies the sources of
mistake, lengthening the sum for reckoners sure to go wrong.

Lydgate smiled as he ended his speech, putting his foot into
the stirrup, and Mr. Mawmsey laughed more than he would
have done if he had known who the king's lieges were, giving his
"Good morning, sir, good morning, sir," with the air of one who
saw everything clearly enough. But in truth his views were
perturbed. For years he had been paying bills with strictly-
made items, so that for every half-crown and eighteenpence he
was certain something measurable had been delivered. He had
done this with satisfaction, including it among his responsi-
bilities as a husband and father, and regarding a longer bill
than usual as a dignity worth mentioning. Moreover, in
addition to the massive benefit of the drugs to "self and family,"
he had enjoyed the pleasure of forming an acute judgment as
to their immediate effects, so as to give an intelligent statement
for the guidance of Mr. Gambit—a practitioner just a little
lower in status than Wrench or Toller, and especially esteemed
as an accoucheur, of whose ability Mr. Mawmsey had the poorest
opinion on all other points, but in doctoring, he was wont to
say in an undertone, he placed Gambit above any of them.

Here were deeper reasons than the superficial talk of a new man, which appeared still flimsier in the drawing-room over the shop, when they were recited to Mrs. Mawmsey, a woman accustomed to be made much of as a fertile mother,—generally under attendance more or less frequent from Mr. Gambit, and occasionally having attacks which required Dr. Minchin.

" Does this Mr. Lydgate mean to say there is no use in taking medicine ? " said Mrs. Mawmsey, who was slightly given to drawling. " I should like him to tell me how I could bear up at Fair time, if I didn't take strengthening medicine for a month beforehand. Think of what I have to provide for calling customers, my dear ! "—here Mrs. Mawmsey turned to an intimate female friend who sat by—" a large veal pie—a stuffed fillet—a round of beef—ham, tongue, *et cetera*, *et* cetera ! But what keeps me up best is the pink mixture, not the brown. I wonder, Mr. Mawmsey, with *your* experience, you could have patience to listen. *I* should have told him at once that I knew a little better than that."

" No, no, no," said Mr. Mawmsey ; " I was not going to tell him my opinion. Hear everything and judge for yourself is my motto. But he didn't know who he was talking to. I was not to be turned on *his* finger. People often pretend to tell me things, when they might as well say, ' Mawmsey, you're a fool.' But I smile at it : I humour everybody's weak place. If physic had done harm to self and family, I should have found it out by this time."

The next day Mr. Gambit was told that Lydgate went about saying physic was of no use.

" Indeed ! " said he, lifting his eyebrows with cautious surprise. (He was a stout husky man with a large ring on his fourth finger.) " How will he cure his patients, then ? "

" That is what *I* say," returned Mrs. Mawmsey, who habitually gave weight to her speech by loading her pronouns. " Does *he* suppose that people will pay him only to come and sit with them and go away again ? "

Mrs. Mawmsey had had a great deal of sitting from Mr. Gambit, including very full accounts of his own habits of body and other affairs ; but of course he knew there was no innuendo in her remark, since his spare time and personal narrative had never been charged for. So he replied, humorously—

" Well, Lydgate is a good-looking young fellow, you know."

" Not one that *I* would employ," said Mrs. Mawmsey. " *Others* may do as they please."

Hence Mr. Gambit could go away from the chief grocer's without fear of rivalry, but not without a sense that Lydgate was one of those hypocrites who try to discredit others by advertising their own honesty, and that it might be worth some people's while to show him up. Mr. Gambit, however, had a satisfactory practice, much pervaded by the smells of retail trading which suggested the reduction of cash payments to a balance. And he did not think it worth his while to show Lydgate up until he knew how. He had not indeed great resources of education, and had had to work his own way against a good deal of professional contempt ; but he made none the worse accoucheur for calling the breathing apparatus " longs."

Other medical men felt themselves more capable. Mr. Toller shared the highest practice in the town and belonged to an old Middlemarch family : there were Tollers in the law and everything else above the line of retail trade. Unlike our irascible friend Wrench, he had the easiest way in the world of taking things which might be supposed to annoy him, being a well-bred, quietly facetious man, who kept a good house, was very fond of a little sporting when he could get it, very friendly with Mr. Hawley, and hostile to Mr. Bulstrode. It may seem odd that with such pleasant habits he should have been given to the heroic treatment, bleeding and blistering and starving his patients, with a dispassionate disregard to his personal example ; but the incongruity favoured the opinion of his ability among his patients, who commonly observed that Mr. Toller had lazy manners, but his treatment was as active as you could desire :— no man, said they, carried more seriousness into his profession : he was a little slow in coming, but when he came, he *did* something. He was a great favourite in his own circle, and whatever he implied to any one's disadvantage told doubly from his careless ironical tone.

He naturally got tired of smiling and saying, " Ah ! " when he was told that Mr. Peacock's successor did not mean to dispense medicines ; and Mr. Hackbutt one day mentioning it over the wine at a dinner-party, Mr. Toller said, laughingly, " Dibbitts will get rid of his stale drugs, then. I'm fond of little Dibbitts— I'm glad he's in luck."

" I see your meaning, Toller," said Mr Hackbutt, " and I am entirely of your opinion. I shall take an opportunity of expressing myself to that effect. A medical man should be responsible for the quality of the drugs consumed by his patients. That is the *rationale* of the system of charging which has hitherto obtained ; and nothing is more offensive than this ostentation of reform, where there is no real amelioration."

"Ostentation, Hackbutt ? " said Mr. Toller, ironically. " I don't see that. A man can't very well be ostentatious of what nobody believes in. There's no reform in the matter : the question is, whether the profit on the drugs is paid to the medical man by the druggist or by the patient, and whether there shall be extra pay under the name of attendance."

" Ah, to be sure ; one of your damned new versions of old humbug," said Mr. Hawley, passing the decanter to Mr. Wrench.

Mr. Wrench, generally abstemious, often drank wine rather freely at a party, getting the more irritable in consequence.

" As to humbug, Hawley," he said, " that's a word easy to fling about. But what I contend against is the way medical men are fouling their own nest, and setting up a cry about the country as if a general practitioner who dispenses drugs couldn't be a gentleman. I throw back the imputation with scorn. I say, the most ungentlemanly trick a man can be guilty of is to come among the members of his profession with innovations which are a libel on their time-honoured procedure. That is my opinion, and I am ready to maintain it against any one who contradicts me." Mr. Wrench's voice had become exceedingly sharp.

" I can't oblige you there, Wrench," said Mr. Hawley, thrusting his hands into his trouser-pockets.

" My dear fellow," said Mr. Toller, striking in pacifically, and looking at Mr. Wrench, " the physicians have their toes trodden on more than we have. If you come to dignity it is a question for Minchin and Sprague."

" Does medical jurisprudence provide nothing against these infringements ? " said Mr. Hackbutt, with a disinterested desire to offer his lights. " How does the law stand, eh, Hawley ? "

" Nothing to be done there," said Mr. Hawley. " I looked into it for Sprague. You'd only break your nose against a damned judge's decision."

" Pooh ! no need of law," said Mr. Toller. " So far as practice is concerned the attempt is an absurdity. No patient will like it—certainly not Peacock's, who have been used to depletion. Pass the wine."

Mr. Toller's prediction was partly verified. If Mr. and Mrs.

Mawmsey, who had no idea of employing Lydgate, were made uneasy by his supposed declaration against drugs, it was inevitable that those who called him in should watch a little anxiously to see whether he did " use all the means he might use " in the case. Even good Mr. Powderell, who in his constant charity of interpretation was inclined to esteem Lydgate the more for what seemed a conscientious pursuit of a better plan, had his mind disturbed with doubts during his wife's attack of erysipelas, and could not abstain from mentioning to Lydgate that Mr. Peacock on a similar occasion had administered a series of boluses which were not otherwise definable than by their remarkable effect in bringing Mrs. Powderell round before Michaelmas from an illness which had begun in a remarkably hot August. At last, indeed, in the conflict between his desire not to hurt Lydgate and his anxiety that no " means " should be lacking, he induced his wife privately to take Widgeon's Purifying Pills, an esteemed Middlemarch medicine, which arrested every disease at the fountain by setting to work at once upon the blood. This co-operative measure was not to be mentioned to Lydgate, and Mr. Powderell himself had no certain reliance on it, only hoping that it might be attended with a blessing.

But in this doubtful stage of Lydgate's introduction he was helped by what we mortals rashly call good fortune. I suppose no doctor ever came newly to a place without making cures that surprised somebody—cures which may be called fortune's testimonials, and deserve as much credit as the written or printed kind. Various patients got well while Lydgate was attending them, some even of dangerous illnesses ; and it was remarked that the new doctor with his new ways had at least the merit of bringing people back from the brink of death. The trash talked on such occasions was the more vexatious to Lydgate, because it gave precisely the sort of prestige which an incompetent and unscrupulous man would desire, and was sure to be imputed to him by the simmering dislike of the other medical men as an encouragement on his own part of ignorant puffing. But even his proud outspokenness was checked by the discernment that it was as useless to fight against the interpretations of ignorance as to whip the fog ; and " good fortune " insisted on using those interpretations.

Mrs. Larcher having just become charitably concerned about alarming symptoms in her charwoman, when Dr. Minchin called, asked him to see her then and there, and to give her a certificate for the Infirmary ; whereupon after examination he wrote a

statement of the case as one of tumour, and recommended the
bearer Nancy Nash as an out-patient. Nancy, calling at home
on her way to the Infirmary, allowed the staymaker and his
wife, in whose attic she lodged, to read Dr. Minchin's paper,
and by this means became a subject of compassionate conversation in the neighbouring shops of Churchyard Lane as being
afflicted with a tumour at first declared to be as large and
hard as a duck's egg, but later in the day to be about the size
of "your fist." Most hearers agreed that it would have to be
cut out, but one had known of oil and another of "squitchineal"
as adequate to soften and reduce any lump in the body when
taken enough of into the inside—the oil by gradually "soopling,"
the squitchineal by eating away.

Meanwhile when Nancy presented herself at the Infirmary it
happened to be one of Lydgate's days there. After questioning
and examining her, Lydgate said to the house-surgeon in an
undertone, "It's not tumour: it's cramp." He ordered her
a blister and some steel mixture, and told her to go home and
rest, giving her at the same time a note to Mrs. Larcher, who,
she said, was her best employer, to testify that she was in need
of good food.

But by-and-by Nancy, in her attic, became portentously
worse, the supposed tumour having indeed given way to the
blister, but only wandered to another region with angrier pain.
The staymaker's wife went to fetch Lydgate, and he continued
for a fortnight to attend Nancy in her own home, until under his
treatment she got quite well and went to work again. But the
case continued to be described as one of tumour in Churchyard
Lane and other streets—nay, by Mrs. Larcher also; for when
Lydgate's remarkable cure was mentioned to Dr. Minchin, he
naturally did not like to say, "The case was not one of tumour,
and I was mistaken in describing it as such," but answered,
"Indeed! ah! I saw it was a surgical case, not of a fatal kind."
He had been inwardly annoyed, however, when he had asked at
the Infirmary about the woman he had recommended two days
before, to hear from the house-surgeon, a youngster who was not
sorry to vex Minchin with impunity, exactly what had occurred:
he privately pronounced that it was indecent in a general
practitioner to contradict a physician's diagnosis in that open
manner, and afterwards agreed with Wrench that Lydgate was
disagreeably inattentive to etiquette. Lydgate did not make
the affair a ground for valuing himself or (very particularly)
despising Minchin, such rectification of misjudgments often

happening among men of equal qualifications. But report took up this amazing case of tumour, not clearly distinguished from cancer, and considered the more awful for being of the wandering sort ; till much prejudice against Lydgate's method as to drugs was overcome by the proof of his marvellous skill in the speedy restoration of Nancy Nash after she had been rolling and rolling in agonies from the presence of a tumour both hard and obstinate, but nevertheless compelled to yield.

How could Lydgate help himself ? It is offensive to tell a lady when she is expressing her amazement at your skill, that she is altogether mistaken and rather foolish in her amazement. And to have entered into the nature of diseases would only have added to his breaches of medical propriety. Thus he had to wince under a promise of success given by that ignorant praise which misses every valid quality.

In the case of a more conspicuous patient, Mr. Borthrop Trumbull, Lydgate was conscious of having shown himself something better than an everyday doctor, though here too it was an equivocal advantage that he won. The eloquent auctioneer was seized with pneumonia, and having been a patient of Mr. Peacock's, sent for Lydgate, whom he had expressed his intention to patronise. Mr. Trumbull was a robust man, a good subject for trying the expectant theory upon—watching the course of an interesting disease when left as much as possible to itself, so that the stages might be noted for future guidance ; and from the air with which he described his sensations Lydgate surmised that he would like to be taken into his medical man's confidence, and be represented as a partner in his own cure. The auctioneer heard, without much surprise, that his was a constitution which (always with due watching) might be left to itself, so as to offer a beautiful example of a disease with all its phases seen in clear delineation, and that he probably had the rare strength of mind voluntarily to become the test of a rational procedure, and thus make the disorder of his pulmonary functions a general benefit to society.

Mr. Trumbull acquiesced at once, and entered strongly into the view that an illness of his was no ordinary occasion for medical science.

"Never fear, sir ; you are not speaking to one who is altogether ignorant of the *vis medicatrix*," said he, with his usual superiority of expression, made rather pathetic by difficulty of breathing. And he went without shrinking through his abstinence from drugs, much sustained by application of the thermometer which implied the importance of his temperature, by the sense that he furnished objects for the microscope, and by learning many new words which seemed suited to the dignity of his secretions. For Lydgate was acute enough to indulge him with a little technical talk.

It may be imagined that Mr. Trumbull rose from his couch with a disposition to speak of an illness in which he had manifested the strength of his mind as well as constitution ; and he was not backward in awarding credit to the medical man who had discerned the quality of patient he had to deal with. The auctioneer was not an ungenerous man, and liked to give others their due, feeling that he could afford it. He had caught the words " expectant method," and rang chimes on this and other learned phrases to accompany the assurance that Lydgate " knew a thing or two more than the rest of the doctors—was far better versed in the secrets of his profession than the majority of his compeers."

This had happened before the affair of Fred Vincy's illness had given to Mr. Wrench's enmity towards Lydgate more definite personal ground. The new-comer already threatened to be a nuisance in the shape of rivalry, and was certainly a nuisance in the shape of practical criticism or reflections on his hard-driven elders, who had had something else to do than to busy themselves with untried notions. His practice had spread in one or two quarters, and from the first the report of his high family had led to his being pretty generally invited, so that the other medical men had to meet him at dinner in the best houses ; and having to meet a man whom you dislike is not observed always to end in a mutual attachment. There was hardly ever so much unanimity among them as in the opinion that Lydgate was an arrogant young fellow, and yet ready for the sake of ultimately predominating to show a crawling subservience to Bulstrode. That Mr. Farebrother, whose name was a chief flag of the anti-Bulstrode party, always defended Lydgate and made a friend of him, was referred to Farebrother's unaccountable way of fighting on both sides.

Here was plenty of preparation for the outburst of professional disgust at the announcement of the laws Mr. Bulstrode was laying down for the direction of the New Hospital, which were the more exasperating because there was no present possibility of interfering with his will and pleasure, everybody except Lord Medlicote having refused help towards the building, on the ground that they preferred giving to the Old Infirmary. Mr. Bulstrode met all the expenses, and had ceased to be sorry that he was purchasing the right to carry out his notions of improvement without hindrance from prejudiced coadjutors ; but he had had to spend large sums and the building had lingered. Caleb Garth had undertaken it, had failed during its progress, and before the interior fittings were begun had retired from the management of the business ; and when referring to the Hospital he often said that however Bulstrode might ring if you tried him, he liked good solid carpentry and masonry, and had a notion both of drains and chimneys. In fact, the Hospital had become an object of intense interest to Bulstrode, and he would willingly have continued to spare a large yearly sum that he might rule it dictatorially without any Board ; but he had another favourite object which also required money for its accomplishment : he wished to buy some land in the neighbour-hood of Middlemarch, and therefore he wished to get considerable contributions towards maintaining the Hospital. Meanwhile he framed his plan of management. The Hospital was to be reserved for fever in all its forms ; Lydgate was to be chief medical superintendent, that he might have free authority to pursue all comparative investigations which his studies, particu-larly in Paris, had shown him the importance of, the other medical visitors having a consultative influence, but no power to contravene Lydgate's ultimate decisions ; and the general management was to be lodged exclusively in the hands of five directors associated with Mr. Bulstrode, who were to have votes in the ratio of their contributions, the Board itself filling up any vacancy in its numbers, and no mob of small contributors being admitted to a share of government.

There was an immediate refusal on the part of every medical man in the town to become a visitor at the Fever Hospital.

"Very well," said Lydgate to Mr. Bulstrode, "we have a capital house-surgeon and dispenser, a clear-headed, neat-handed fellow ; we'll get Webbe from Crabsley, as good a country practitioner as any of them, to come over twice a-week, and in case of any exceptional operation, Protheroe will come from Brassing. I must work the harder, that's all, and I have given up my post at the Infirmary. The plan will flourish in spite of them, and then they'll be glad to come in. Things can't last as they are : there must be all sorts of reform soon, and then young fellows may be glad to come and study here." Lydgate was in high spirits.

"I shall not flinch, you may depend upon it, Mr. Lydgate," said Mr. Bulstrode. "While I see you carrying out high intentions with vigour, you shall have my unfailing support. And I have humble confidence that the blessing which has hitherto attended my efforts against the spirit of evil in this town will not be withdrawn. Suitable directors to assist me I have no doubt of securing. Mr. Brooke of Tipton has already given me his concurrence, and a pledge to contribute yearly : he has not specified the sum—probably not a great one. But he will be a useful member of the Board."

A useful member was perhaps to be defined as one who would originate nothing, and always vote with Mr. Bulstrode.

The medical aversion to Lydgate was hardly disguised now. Neither Dr. Sprague nor Dr. Minchin said that he disliked Lydgate's knowledge, or his disposition to improve treatment : what they disliked was his arrogance, which nobody felt to be altogether deniable. They implied that he was insolent, pretentious, and given to that reckless innovation for the sake of noise and show which was the essence of the charlatan.

The word charlatan once thrown on the air could not be let drop. In those days the world was agitated about the wondrous doings of Mr. St. John Long, "noblemen and gentlemen" attesting his extraction of a fluid like mercury from the temples of a patient.

Mr. Toller remarked one day, smilingly, to Mrs. Taft, that "Bulstrode had found a man to suit him in Lydgate ; a charlatan in religion is sure to like other sorts of charlatans."

"Yes, indeed, I can imagine," said Mrs. Taft, keeping the number of thirty stitches carefully in her mind all the while ; "there are so many of that sort. I remember Mr. Cheshire, with his irons, trying to make people straight when the Almighty had made them crooked."

"No, no," said Mr. Toller, "Cheshire was all right—all fair and above board. But there's St. John Long—that's the kind of fellow we call a charlatan, advertising cures in ways nobody knows anything about ; a fellow who wants to make a noise by pretending to go deeper than other people. The other day he was pretending to tap a man's brain and get quicksilver out of it."

"Good gracious ! what dreadful trifling with people's constitutions !" said Mrs. Taft.

After this it came to be held in various quarters that Lydgate played even with respectable constitutions for his own purposes, and how much more likely that in his flighty experimenting he should make sixes and sevens of hospital patients. Especially it was to be expected, as the landlady of the Tankard had said, that he would recklessly cut up their dead bodies. For Lydgate having attended Mrs. Goby, who died apparently of a heart-disease not very clearly expressed in the symptoms, too daringly asked leave of her relatives to open the body, and thus gave an offence quickly spreading beyond Parley Street, where that lady had long resided on an income such as made this association of her body with the victims of Burke and Hare a flagrant insult to her memory.

Affairs were in this stage when Lydgate opened the subject of the Hospital to Dorothea. We see that he was bearing enmity and silly misconception with much spirit, aware that they were partly created by his good share of success.

" They will not drive me away," he said, talking confidentially in Mr. Farebrother's study. " I have got a good opportunity here, for the ends I care most about ; and I am pretty sure to get income enough for our wants. By-and-by I shall go on as quietly as possible : I have no seductions now away from home and work. And I am more and more convinced that it will be possible to demonstrate the homogeneous origin of all the tissues. Raspail and others are on the same track, and I have been losing time."

" I have no power of prophecy there," said Mr. Farebrother, who had been puffing at his pipe thoughtfully while Lydgate talked ; " but as to the hostility in the town, you'll weather it if you are prudent."

" How am I to be prudent ? " said Lydgate, " I just do what comes before me to do. I can't help people's ignorance and spite, any more than Vesalius could. It isn't possible to square one's conduct to silly conclusions which nobody can foresee."

" Quite true ; I didn't mean that. I meant only two things. One is, keep yourself as separable from Bulstrode as you can : of course, you can go on doing good work of your own by his help ; but don't get tied. Perhaps it seems like personal feeling in me to say so—and there's a good deal of that, I own—but personal feeling is not always in the wrong if you boil it down to the impressions which make it simply an opinion."

" Bulstrode is nothing to me," said Lydgate, carelessly, " except on public grounds. As to getting very closely united to him, I am not fond enough of him for that. But what was the other thing you meant?" said Lydgate, who was nursing his leg as comfortably as possible, and feeling in no great need of advice.

"Why, this. Take care—*experto crede*—take care not to get hampered about money matters. I know, by a word you let fall one day, that you don't like my playing at cards so much for money. You are right enough there. But try and keep clear of wanting small sums that you haven't got. I am perhaps talking rather superfluously; but a man likes to assume superiority over himself, by holding up his bad example and sermonising on it."

Lydgate took Mr. Farebrother's hints very cordially, though he would hardly have borne them from another man. He could not help remembering that he had lately made some debts, but these had seemed inevitable, and he had no intention now to do more than keep house in a simple way. The furniture for which he owed would not want renewing; nor even the stock of wine for a long while.

Many thoughts cheered him at that time—and justly. A man conscious of enthusiasm for worthy aims is sustained under petty hostilities by the memory of great workers who had to fight their way not without wounds, and who hover in his mind as patron saints, invisibly helping. At home, that same evening when he had been chatting with Mr. Farebrother, he had his long legs stretched on the sofa, his head thrown back, and his hands clasped behind it according to his favourite ruminating attitude, while Rosamond sat at the piano, and played one tune after another, of which her husband only knew (like the emotional elephant he was!) that they fell in with his mood as if they had been melodious sea-breezes.

There was something very fine in Lydgate's look just then, and any one might have been encouraged to bet on his achievement. In his dark eyes and on his mouth and brow there was that placidity which comes from the fulness of contemplative thought—the mind not searching, but beholding, and the glance seeming to be filled with what is behind it.

Presently Rosamond left the piano and seated herself on a chair close to the sofa and opposite her husband's face.

"Is that enough music for you, my lord?" she said, folding her hands before her and putting on a little air of meekness.

"Yes, dear, if you are tired," said Lydgate, gently, turning his eyes and resting them on her, but not otherwise moving. Rosamond's presence at that moment was perhaps no more than a spoonful brought to the lake, and her woman's instinct in this matter was not dull.

"What is absorbing you?" she said, leaning forward and bringing her face nearer to his.

He moved his hands and placed them gently behind her shoulders.

"I am thinking of a great fellow, who was about as old as I am three hundred years ago, and had already begun a new era in anatomy."

"I can't guess," said Rosamond, shaking her head. "We used to play at guessing historical characters at Mrs. Lemon's, but not anatomists."

"I'll tell you. His name was Vesalius. And the only way he could get to know anatomy as he did, was by going to snatch bodies at night, from graveyards and places of execution."

"Oh!" said Rosamond, with a look of disgust on her pretty face, "I am very glad you are not Vesalius. I should have thought he might find some less horrible way than that."

"No, he couldn't," said Lydgate, going on too earnestly to take much notice of her answer. "He could only get a complete skeleton by snatching the whitened bones of a criminal from the gallows, and burying them, and fetching them away by bits secretly, in the dead of night."

"I hope he is not one of your great heroes," said Rosamond, half-playfully, half-anxiously, "else I shall have you getting up in the night to go to St. Peter's churchyard. You know how angry you told me the people were about Mrs. Goby. You have enemies enough already."

"So had Vesalius, Rosy. No wonder the medical fogies in Middlemarch are jealous, when some of the greatest doctors living were fierce upon Vesalius because they had believed in Galen, and he showed that Galen was wrong. They called him a liar and a poisonous monster. But the facts of the human frame were on his side; and so he got the better of them."

"And what happened to him afterwards?" said Rosamond, with some interest.

"Oh, he had a good deal of fighting to the last. And they did exasperate him enough at one time to make him burn a good deal of his work. Then he got shipwrecked just as he was coming from Jerusalem to take a great chair at Padua. He died rather miserably."

There was a moment's pause before Rosamond said. "Do

you know, Tertius, I often wish you had not been a medical man."

"Nay, Rosy, don't say that," said Lydgate, drawing her closer to him. "That is like saying you wish you had married another man."

"Not at all ; you are clever enough for anything : you might easily have been something else. And your cousins at Qualling- ham all think that you have sunk below them in your choice of a profession."

"The cousins at Quallingham may go to the devil ! " said Lydgate, with scorn. "It was like their impudence if they said anything of the sort to you."

"Still," said Rosamond, "I do *not* think it is a nice pro- fession, dear." We know that she had much quiet perseverance in her opinion.

"It is the grandest profession in the world, Rosamond," said Lydgate, gravely. "And to say that you love me without loving the medical man in me, is the same sort of thing as to say that you like eating a peach but don't like its flavour. Don't say that again, dear, it pains me."

"Very well, Doctor Grave-face," said Rosy, dimpling, "I will declare in future that I dote on skeletons, and body-snatchers, and bits of things in phials, and quarrels with everybody, that end in your dying miserably."

"No, no, not so bad as that," said Lydgate, giving up remon- strance and petting her resignedly.

CHAPTER XLVI

"Pues no podemos haber aquello que queremos, queramos aquello que podremos."
"Since we cannot get what we like, let us like what we can get."
—*Spanish Proverb.*

WHILE Lydgate, safely married and with the Hospital under his command, felt himself struggling for Medical Reform against Middlemarch, Middlemarch was becoming more and more conscious of the national struggle for another kind of Reform.

By the time that Lord John Russell's measure was being debated in the House of Commons, there was a new political animation in Middlemarch, and a new definition of parties which might show a decided change of balance if a new election came. And there were some who already predicted this event, declaring that a Reform Bill would never be carried by the actual Parliament. This was what Will Ladislaw dwelt on to Mr. Brooke as a reason for congratulation that he had not yet tried his strength at the hustings.

"Things will grow and ripen as if it were a comet year," said Will. "The public temper will soon get to a cometary heat, now the question of Reform has set in. There is likely to be another election before long, and by that time Middlemarch will have got more ideas into its head. What we have to work at now is the 'Pioneer' and political meetings."

"Quite right, Ladislaw; we shall make a new thing of opinion here," said Mr. Brooke. "Only I want to keep myself independent about Reform, you know: I don't want to go too far. I want to take up Wilberforce's and Romilly's line, you know, and work at Negro Emancipation, Criminal Law—that kind of thing. But of course I should support Grey."

"If you go in for the principle of Reform, you must be prepared to take what the situation offers," said Will. "If everybody pulled for his own bit against everybody else, the whole question would go to tatters."

"Yes, yes, I agree with you—I quite take that point of view. I should put it in that light. I should support Grey, you know. But I don't want to change the balance of the constitution, and I don't think Grey would."

"But that is what the country wants," said Will. "Else there would be no meaning in political unions or any other movement that knows what it's about. It wants to have a House of Commons which is not weighted with nominees of the landed class, but with representatives of the other interests. And as to contending for a reform short of that, it is like asking for a bit of an avalanche which has already begun to thunder."

"That is fine, Ladislaw: that is the way to put it. Write that down, now. We must begin to get documents about the feeling of the country, as well as the machine-breaking and general distress."

"As to documents," said Will, "a two-inch card will hold plenty. A few rows of figures are enough to deduce misery from, and a few more will show the rate at which the political determination of the people is growing."

"Good: draw that out a little more at length, Ladislaw. That is an idea, now: write it out in the 'Pioneer.' Put the

figures and deduce the misery, you know ; and put the other
figures and deduce—and so on. You have a way of putting
things. Burke, now :—when I think of Burke, I can't help
wishing somebody had a pocket-borough to give you, Ladislaw.
You'd never get elected, you know. And we shall always want
talent in the House : reform as we will, we shall always want
talent. That avalanche and the thunder, now, was really a little
like Burke. I want that sort of thing—not ideas, you know,
but a way of putting them."

" Pocket-boroughs would be a fine thing," said Ladislaw, " if
they were always in the right pocket, and there were always a
Burke at hand."

Will was not displeased with that complimentary comparison,
even from Mr. Brooke ; for it is a little too trying to human
flesh to be conscious of expressing one's self better than others
and never to have it noticed, and in the general dearth of
admiration for the right thing, even a chance bray of applause
falling exactly in time is rather fortifying. Will felt that his
literary refinements were usually beyond the limits of Middlemarch perception ; nevertheless, he was beginning thoroughly
to like the work of which when he began he had said to himself
rather languidly, " Why not ? "—and he studied the political
situation with as ardent an interest as he had ever given to
poetic metres or mediævalism. It is undeniable that but for the
desire to be where Dorothea was, and perhaps the want of knowing what else to do, Will would not at this time have been
meditating on the needs of the English people or criticising
English statesmanship : he would probably have been rambling
in Italy sketching plans for several dramas, trying prose and
finding it too jejune, trying verse and finding it too artificial,
beginning to copy " bits " from old pictures, leaving off because
they were " no good," and observing that, after all, self-culture
was the principal point ; while in politics he would have been
sympathising warmly with liberty and progress in general. Our
sense of duty must often wait for some work which shall take
the place of dilettanteism and make us feel that the quality of
our action is not a matter of indifference.

Ladislaw had now accepted his bit of work, though it was not
that indeterminate loftiest thing which he had once dreamed of
as alone worthy of continuous effort. His nature warmed
easily in the presence of subjects which were visibly mixed with
life and action, and the easily-stirred rebellion in him helped the
glow of public spirit. In spite of Mr. Casaubon and the banish-

ment from Lowick, he was rather happy ; getting a great deal of fresh knowledge in a vivid way and for practical purposes, and making the " Pioneer " celebrated as far as Brassing (never mind the smallness of the area ; the writing was not worse than much that reaches the four corners of the earth).

Mr. Brooke was occasionally irritating ; but Will's impatience was relieved by the division of his time between visits to the Grange and retreats to his Middlemarch lodgings, which gave variety to his life.

" Shift the pegs a little," he said to himself, " and Mr. Brooke might be in the Cabinet, while I was Under-Secretary. That is the common order of things : the little waves make the large ones and are of the same pattern. I am better here than in the sort of life Mr. Casaubon would have trained me for, where the doing would be all laid down by a precedent too rigid for me to react upon. I don't care for prestige or high pay."

As Lydgate had said of him, he was a sort of gypsy, rather enjoying the sense of belonging to no class ; he had a feeling of romance in his position, and a pleasant consciousness of creating a little surprise wherever he went. That sort of enjoyment had been disturbed when he had felt some new distance between himself and Dorothea in their accidental meeting at Lydgate's, and his irritation had gone out towards Mr. Casaubon, who had declared beforehand that Will would lose caste. " I never had any caste," he would have said, if that prophecy had been uttered to him, and the quick blood would have come and gone like breath in his transparent skin. But it is one thing to like defiance, and another thing to like its consequences.

Meanwhile, the town opinion about the new editor of the " Pioneer " was tending to confirm Mr. Casaubon's view. Will's relationship in that distinguished quarter did not, like Lydgate's high connections, serve as an advantageous introduction : if it was rumoured that young Ladislaw was Mr. Casaubon's nephew or cousin, it was also rumoured that " Mr. Casaubon would have nothing to do with him."

" Brooke has taken him up," said Mr. Hawley, " because that is what no man in his senses could have expected. Casaubon has devilish good reasons, you may be sure, for turning the cold shoulder on a young fellow whose bringing-up he paid for. Just like Brooke—one of those fellows who would praise a cat to sell a horse."

And some oddities of Will's, more or less poetical, appeared to

support Mr. Keck, the editor of the " Trumpet," in asserting that
Ladislaw, if the truth were known, was not only a Polish
emissary but crack-brained, which accounted for the preternatural quickness and glibness of his speech when he got on to a
platform—as he did whenever he had an opportunity, speaking
with a facility which cast reflections on solid Englishmen
generally.   It was disgusting to Keck to see a strip of a fellow,
with light curls round his head, get up and speechify by the hour
against institutions " which had existed when he was in his
cradle."   And in a leading article of the " Trumpet," Keck
characterised Ladislaw's speech at a Reform meeting as " the
violence of an energumen—a miserable effort to shroud in the
brilliancy of fireworks the daring of irresponsible statements and
the poverty of a knowledge which was of the cheapest and most
recent description."

" That was a rattling article yesterday, Keck," said Dr.
Sprague, with sarcastic intentions.   " But what is an energumen ? "

" Oh, a term that came up in the French Revolution," said
Keck.

This dangerous aspect of Ladislaw was strangely contrasted
with other habits which became matter of remark.   He had a
fondness, half artistic, half affectionate, for little children—the
smaller they were on tolerably active legs, and the funnier
their clothing, the better Will liked to surprise and please them.
We know that in Rome he was given to ramble about
among the poor people, and the taste did not quit him in
Middlemarch.

He had somehow picked up a troop of droll children, little
hatless boys with their galligaskins much worn and scant shirt-
ing to hang out, little girls who tossed their hair out of their eyes
to look at him, and guardian brothers at the mature age of seven.
This troop he had led out on gypsy excursions to Halsell Wood at
nutting-time, and since the cold weather had set in he had taken
them on a clear day to gather sticks for a bonfire in the hollow
of a hillside, where he drew out a small feast of gingerbread for
them, and improvised a Punch-and-Judy drama with some
private home-made puppets.   Here was one oddity.   Another
was, that in houses where he got friendly, he was given to
stretch himself at full length on the rug while he talked, and was
apt to be discovered in this attitude by occasional callers for
whom such an irregularity was likely to confirm the notions of
his dangerously mixed blood and general laxity.

But Will's articles and speeches naturally recommended him in families which the new strictness of party division had marked off on the side of Reform. He was invited to Mr. Bulstrode's; but here he could not lie down on the rug, and Mrs. Bulstrode felt that his mode of talking about Catholic countries, as if there were any truce with Antichrist, illustrated the usual tendency to unsoundness in intellectual men.

At Mr. Farebrother's, however, whom the irony of events had brought on the same side with Bulstrode in the national movement, Will became a favourite with the ladies; especially with little Miss Noble, whom it was one of his oddities to escort when he met her in the street with her little basket, giving her his arm in the eyes of the town, and insisting on going with her to pay some call where she distributed her small filchings from her own share of sweet things.

But the house where he visited oftenest and lay most on the rug was Lydgate's. The two men were not at all alike, but they agreed none the worse. Lydgate was abrupt but not irritable, taking little notice of megrims in healthy people; and Ladislaw did not usually throw away his susceptibilities on those who took no notice of them. With Rosamond, on the other hand, he pouted and was wayward—nay, often uncomplimentary, much to her inward surprise; nevertheless he was gradually becoming necessary to her entertainment by his companionship in her music, his varied talk, and his freedom from the grave preoccupation which, with all her husband's tenderness and indulgence, often made his manners unsatisfactory to her, and confirmed her dislike of the medical profession.

Lydgate, inclined to be sarcastic on the superstitious faith of the people in the efficacy of " the bill," while nobody cared about the low state of pathology, sometimes assailed Will with troublesome questions. One evening in March, Rosamond in her cherry-coloured dress with swansdown trimming about the throat sat at the tea-table; Lydgate, lately come in tired from his outdoor work, was seated sideways on an easy-chair by the fire with one leg over the elbow, his brow looking a little troubled as his eyes rambled over the columns of the " Pioneer," while Rosamond, having noticed that he was perturbed, avoided looking at him, and inwardly thanked heaven that she herself had not a moody disposition. Will Ladislaw was stretched on the rug contemplating the curtain-pole abstractedly, and humming very low the notes of " When first I saw thy face; " while the house spaniel, also stretched out with small choice of room looked from between his paws at the usurper of the rug with silent but strong objection.

Rosamond bringing Lydgate his cup of tea, he threw down the paper, and said to Will, who had started up and gone to the table—

" It's no use your puffing Brooke as a reforming landlord, Ladislaw : they only pick the more holes in his coat in the ' Trumpet.' "

" No matter ; those who read the ' Pioneer ' don't read the ' Trumpet,' " said Will, swallowing his tea and walking about. " Do you suppose the public reads with a view to its own conversion ? We should have a witches' brewing with a vengeance then—' Mingle, mingle, mingle, mingle. You that mingle may ' —and nobody would know which side he was going to take."

" Farebrother says, he doesn't believe Brooke would get elected if the opportunity came : the very men who profess to be for him would bring another member out of the bag at the right moment."

" There's no harm in trying. It's good to have resident members."

" Why ? " said Lydgate, who was much given to use that inconvenient word in a curt tone.

" They represent the local stupidity better," said Will, laughing, and shaking his curls ; " and they are kept on their best behaviour in the neighbourhood. Brooke is not a bad fellow, but he has done some good things on his estate that he never would have done but for this Parliamentary bite."

" He's not fitted to be a public man," said Lydgate, with contemptuous decision. " He would disappoint everybody who counted on him : I can see that at the Hospital. Only, there Bulstrode holds the reins and drives him."

" That depends on how you fix your standard of public men," said Will. " He's good enough for the occasion : when the people have made up their mind as they are making it up now, they don't want a man—they only want a vote."

" That is the way with you political writers, Ladislaw—crying up a measure as if it were a universal cure, and crying up men who are a part of the very disease that wants curing."

" Why not ? Men may help to cure themselves off the face of the land without knowing it," said Will, who could find reasons impromptu, when he had not thought of a question beforehand.

" That is no excuse for encouraging the superstitious exaggeration of hopes about this particular measure, helping the cry to swallow it whole and to send up voting popinjays who are good for nothing but to carry it. You go against rottenness, and there is nothing more thoroughly rotten than making people believe that society can be cured by a political hocus-pocus."

"That's very fine, my dear fellow. But your cure must begin somewhere, and put it that a thousand things which debase a population can never be reformed without this particular reform to begin with. Look what Stanley said the other day— that the House had been tinkering long enough at small questions of bribery, inquiring whether this or that voter has had a guinea when everybody knows that the seats have been sold wholesale. Wait for wisdom and conscience in public agents—fiddlestick ! The only conscience we can trust to is the massive sense of wrong in a class, and the best wisdom that will work is the wisdom of balancing claims. That's my text—which side is injured ? I support the man who supports their claims ; not the virtuous upholder of the wrong."

"That general talk about a particular case is mere question-begging, Ladislaw. When I say, I go in for the dose that cures, it doesn't follow that I go in for opium in a given case of gout."

"I am not begging the question we are upon—whether we are to try for nothing till we find immaculate men to work with. Should you go on that plan ? If there were one man who would carry you a medical reform and another who would oppose it, should you inquire which had the better motives or even the better brains ? "

"Oh, of course," said Lydgate, seeing himself checkmated by a move which he had often used himself, " if one did not work with such men as are at hand, things must come to a dead-lock. Suppose the worst opinion in the town about Bulstrode were a true one, that would not make it less true that he has the sense and the resolution to do what I think ought to be done in the matters I know and care most about ; but that is the only ground on which I go with him," Lydgate added rather proudly, bearing in mind Mr. Farebrother's remarks. " He is nothing to me otherwise ; I would not cry him up on any personal ground— I would keep clear of that."

"Do you mean that I cry up Brooke on any personal ground ? " said Will Ladislaw, nettled, and turning sharp round. For the first time he felt offended with Lydgate ; not the less so, perhaps, because he would have declined any close inquiry into the growth of his relation to Mr. Brooke.

"Not at all," said Lydgate, "I was simply explaining my own action. I meant that a man may work for a special end with others whose motives and general course are equivocal, if he is quite sure of his personal independence, and that he is not working for his private interest—either place or money."

"Then, why don't you extend your liberality to others?" said Will, still nettled. "My personal independence is as important to me as yours is to you. You have no more reason to imagine that I have personal expectations from Brooke, than I have to imagine that you have personal expectations from Bulstrode. Motives are points of honour, I suppose—nobody can prove them. But as to money and place in the world," Will ended, tossing back his head, "I think it is pretty clear that I am not determined by considerations of that sort."

"You quite mistake me, Ladislaw," said Lydgate, surprised. He had been preoccupied with his own vindication, and had been blind to what Ladislaw might infer on his own account. "I beg your pardon for unintentionally annoying you. In fact, I should rather attribute to you a romantic disregard of your own worldly interests. On the political question, I referred simply to intellectual bias."

"How very unpleasant you both are this evening!" said Rosamond. "I cannot conceive why money should have been referred to. Politics and medicine are sufficiently disagreeable to quarrel upon. You can both of you go on quarrelling with all the world and with each other on those two topics."

Rosamond looked mildly neutral as she said this, rising to ring the bell, and then crossing to her work-table.

"Poor Rosy!" said Lydgate, putting out his hand to her as she was passing him. "Disputation is not amusing to cherubs. Have some music. Ask Ladislaw to sing with you."

When Will was gone Rosamond said to her husband, "What put you out of temper this evening, Tertius?"

"Me? It was Ladislaw who was out of temper. He is like a bit of tinder."

"But I mean, before that. Something had vexed you before you came in, you looked cross. And that made you begin to dispute with Mr. Ladislaw. You hurt me very much when you look so, Tertius."

"Do I? Then I am a brute," said Lydgate, caressing her penitently.

"What vexed you?"

"Oh, outdoor things—business."

It was really a letter insisting on the payment of a bill for furniture. But Rosamond was expecting to have a baby, and Lydgate wished to save her from any perturbation.

CHAPTER XLVII

Was never true love loved in vain,
For truest love is highest gain.
No art can make it: it must spring
Where elements are fostering.
  So in heaven's spot and hour
  Springs the little native flower,
  Downward root and upward eye,
  Shapen by the earth and sky.

IT happened to be on a Saturday evening that Will Ladislaw had that little discussion with Lydgate. Its effect when he went to his own rooms was to make him sit up half the night, thinking over again, under a new irritation, all that he had before thought of his having settled in Middlemarch and harnessed himself with Mr. Brooke. Hesitations before he had taken the step had since turned into susceptibility to every hint that he would have been wiser not to take it; and hence came his heat towards Lydgate—a heat which still kept him restless. Was he not making a fool of himself? —and at a time when he was more than ever conscious of being something better than a fool? And for what end?

Well, for no definite end. True, he had dreamy visions of possibilities: there is no human being who having both passions and thoughts does not think in consequence of his passions—does not find images rising in his mind which soothe the passion with hope or sting it with dread. But this, which happens to us all, happens to some with a wide difference; and Will was not one of those whose wit " keeps the roadway : " he had his bypaths where there were little joys of his own choosing, such as gentlemen cantering on the highroad might have thought rather idiotic. The way in which he made a sort of happiness for himself out of his feeling for Dorothea was an example of this. It may seem strange, but it is the fact, that the ordinary vulgar vision of which Mr. Casaubon suspected him—namely, that Dorothea might become a widow, and that the interest he had established in her mind might turn into acceptance of him as a husband—had no tempting, arresting power over him; he did not live in the scenery of such an event, and follow it out, as we all do with that imagined " otherwise " which is our practical heaven. It was not only that he was unwilling to entertain thoughts which could be accused of baseness, and was already uneasy in the sense that he had to justify himself from the charge of ingratitude—the latent consciousness of many other barriers between himself and Dorothea besides the existence of her husband, had helped to turn away his imagination from speculating on what might befall Mr. Casaubon. And there were yet other reasons. Will, we know, could not bear the thought of any flaw appearing in his crystal : he was at once exasperated and delighted by the calm freedom with which Dorothea looked at him and spoke to him, and there was something so exquisite in thinking of her just as she was, that he could not long for a change which must somehow change her. Do we not shun the street version of a fine melody ?—or shrink from the news that the rarity—some bit of chiselling or engraving perhaps—which we have dwelt on even with exultation in the trouble it has cost us to snatch glimpses of it, is really not an uncommon thing, and may be obtained as an everyday possession ? Our good depends on the quality and breadth of our emotion ; and to Will, a creature who cared little for what are called the solid things of life and greatly for its subtler influences, to have within him such a feeling as he had towards Dorothea, was like the inheritance of a fortune. What others might have called the futility of his passion, made an additional delight for his imagination : he was conscious of a generous movement, and of verifying in his own experience that higher love-poetry which had charmed his fancy. Dorothea, he said to himself, was for ever enthroned in his soul : no other woman could sit higher than her footstool ; and if he could have written out in immortal syllables the effect she wrought within him, he might have boasted after the example of old Drayton, that—

> " Queens hereafter might be glad to live
> Upon the alms of her superfluous praise."

But this result was questionable. And what else could he do for Dorothea ? What was his devotion worth to her ? It was impossible to tell. He would not go out of her reach. He saw no creature among her friends to whom he could believe that she spoke with the same simple confidence as to him. She had once said that she would like him to stay ; and stay he would, whatever fire-breathing dragons might hiss around her.

This had always been the conclusion of Will's hesitations. But he was not without contradictoriness and rebellion even towards his own resolve. He had often got irritated, as he was on this particular night, by some outside demonstration that his public exertions with Mr. Brooke as a chief could not seem as heroic as he would like them to be, and this was always associated with the other ground of irritation—that notwithstanding his sacrifice of dignity for Dorothea's sake, he could hardly ever see her. Whereupon, not being able to contradict these unpleasant facts, he contradicted his own strongest bias and said, " I am a fool."

Nevertheless, since the inward debate necessarily turned on Dorothea, he ended, as he had done before, only by getting a livelier sense of what her presence would be to him; and suddenly reflecting that the morrow would be Sunday, he determined to go to Lowick Church and see her. He slept upon that idea, but when he was dressing in the rational morning light, Objection said—

" That will be a virtual defiance of Mr. Casaubon's prohibition to visit Lowick, and Dorothea will be displeased."

" Nonsense ! " argued Inclination, " it would be too monstrous for him to hinder me from going out to a pretty country church on a spring morning. And Dorothea will be glad."

" It will be clear to Mr. Casaubon that you have come either to annoy him or to see Dorothea."

" It is not true that I go to annoy him, and why should I not go to see Dorothea ? Is he to have everything to himself and be always comfortable ? Let him smart a little, as other people are obliged to do. I have always liked the quaintness of the church and congregation ; besides, I know the Tuckers : I shall go into their pew."

Having silenced Objection by force of unreason, Will walked to Lowick as if he had been on the way to Paradise, crossing Halsell Common and skirting the woods, where the sunlight fell broadly under the budding boughs, bringing out the beauties of moss and lichen, and fresh green growths piercing the brown. Everything seemed to know that it was Sunday, and to approve of his going to Lowick Church. Will easily felt happy when nothing crossed his humour, and by this time the thought of vexing Mr. Casaubon had become rather amusing to him, making his face break into its merry smile, pleasant to see as the breaking of sunshine on the water—though the occasion was not exemplary. But most of us are apt to settle within ourselves that the man

who blocks our way is odious, and not to mind causing him a
little of the disgust which his personality excites in ourselves.
Will went along with a small book under his arm and a hand in
each side-pocket, never reading, but chanting a little, as he made
scenes of what would happen in church and coming out.   He was
experimenting in tunes to suit some words of his own, sometimes
trying a ready-made melody, sometimes improvising.   The words
were not exactly a hymn, but they certainly fitted his Sunday
experience :—

> O me, O me, what frugal cheer
>   My love doth feed upon !
> A touch, a ray, that is not here,
>   A shadow that is gone :
>
> A dream of breath that might be near,
>   An inly-echoed tone,
> The thought that one may think me dear,
>   The place where one was known,
>
> The tremor of a banished fear,
>   An ill that was not done—
> O me, O me, what frugal cheer
>   My love doth feed upon !

Sometimes, when he took off his hat, shaking his head backward, and showing his delicate throat as he sang, he looked like
an incarnation of the spring whose spirit filled the air—a bright
creature, abundant in uncertain promises.

The bells were still ringing when he got to Lowick, and he
went into the curate's pew before any one else arrived there.
But he was still left alone in it when the congregation had
assembled.   The curate's pew was opposite the rector's at the
entrance of the small chancel, and Will had time to fear that
Dorothea might not come while he looked round at the group
of rural faces which made the congregation from year to year
within the white-washed walls and dark old pews, hardly with
more change than we see in the boughs of a tree which breaks
here and there with age, but yet has young shoots.   Mr. Rigg's
frog-face was something alien and unaccountable, but notwithstanding this shock to the order of things, there were still the
Waules and the rural stock of the Powderells in their pews side
by side ; brother Samuel's cheek had the same purple round as
ever, and the three generations of decent cottagers came as of
old with a sense of duty to their betters generally—the smaller
children regarding Mr. Casaubon, who wore the black gown and
mounted to the highest box, as probably the chief of all betters,

and the one most awful if offended. Even in 1831 Lowick was at peace, not more agitated by Reform than by the solemn tenor of the Sunday sermon. The congregation had been used to seeing Will at church in former days, and no one took much note of him except the quire, who expected him to make a figure in the singing.

Dorothea did at last appear on this quaint background, walking up the short aisle in her white beaver bonnet and grey cloak—the same she had worn in the Vatican. Her face being, from her entrance, towards the chancel, even her short-sighted eyes soon discerned Will, but there was no outward show of her feeling except a slight paleness and a grave bow as she passed him. To his own surprise Will felt suddenly uncomfortable, and dared not look at her after they had bowed to each other. Two minutes later, when Mr. Casaubon came out of the vestry, and, entering the pew, seated himself in face of Dorothea, Will felt his paralysis more complete. He could look nowhere except at the quire in the little gallery over the vestry-door: Dorothea was perhaps pained, and he had made a wretched blunder. It was no longer amusing to vex Mr. Casaubon, who had the advantage probably of watching him and seeing that he dared not turn his head. Why had he not imagined this beforehand ? —but he could not expect that he should sit in that square pew alone, unrelieved by any Tuckers, who had apparently departed from Lowick altogether, for a new clergyman was in the desk. Still he called himself stupid now for not foreseeing that it would be impossible for him to look towards Dorothea—nay, that she might feel his coming an impertinence. There was no delivering himself from his cage, however ; and Will found his places and looked at his book as if he had been a schoolmistress, feeling that the morning service had never been so immeasurably long before, that he was utterly ridiculous, out of temper, and miserable. This was what a man got by worshipping the sight of a woman ! The clerk observed with surprise that Mr. Ladislaw did not join in the tune of Hanover, and reflected that he might have a cold.

Mr. Casaubon did not preach that morning, and there was no change in Will's situation until the blessing had been pronounced and every one rose. It was the fashion at Lowick for " the betters " to go out first. With a sudden determination to break the spell that was upon him, Will looked straight at Mr. Casaubon. But that gentleman's eyes were on the button of the pew-door, which he opened, allowing Dorothea to pass, and following her immediately without raising his eyelids. Will's glance had caught Dorothea's as she turned out of the pew, and again she bowed, but this time with a look of agitation, as if she were repressing tears. Will walked out after them, but they went on towards the little gate leading out of the churchyard into the shrubbery, never looking round.

It was impossible for him to follow them, and he could only walk back sadly at mid-day along the same road which he had trodden hopefully in the morning. The lights were all changed for him both without and within.

CHAPTER XLVIII

Surely the golden hours are turning grey
And dance no more, and vainly strive to run :
I see their white locks streaming in the wind—
Each face is haggard as it looks at me,
Slow turning in the constant clasping round
Storm-driven.

DOROTHEA'S distress when she was leaving the church came chiefly from the perception that Mr. Casaubon was determined not to speak to his cousin, and that Will's presence at church had served to mark more strongly the alienation between them. Will's coming seemed to her quite excusable, nay, she thought it an amiable movement in him towards a reconciliation which she herself had been constantly wishing for. He had probably imagined, as she had, that if Mr. Casaubon and he could meet easily, they would shake hands and friendly intercourse might return. But now Dorothea felt quite robbed of that hope. Will was banished further than ever, for Mr. Casaubon must have been newly embittered by this thrusting upon him of a presence which he refused to recognise.

He had not been very well that morning, suffering from some difficulty in breathing, and had not preached in consequence ; she was not surprised, therefore, that he was nearly silent at luncheon, still less that he made no allusion to Will Ladislaw. For her own part she felt that she could never again introduce that subject. They usually spent apart the hours between luncheon and dinner on a Sunday ; Mr. Casaubon in the library dozing chiefly, and Dorothea in her boudoir, where she was wont to occupy herself with some of her favourite books. There was a little heap of them on the table in the bow-window—of various sorts, from Herodotus, which she was learning to read with Mr. Casaubon, to her old companion Pascal, and Keble's "Christian Year." But to-day she opened one after another, and could read none of them. Everything seemed dreary : the portents before the birth of Cyrus—Jewish antiquities—oh dear !— devout epigrams—the sacred chime of favourite hymns—all alike were as flat as tunes beaten on wood : even the spring flowers and the grass had a dull shiver in them under the afternoon clouds that hid the sun fitfully : even the sustaining thoughts which had become habits seemed to have in them the weariness of long future days in which she would still live with them for her sole companions. It was another or rather a fuller sort of companionship that poor Dorothea was hungering for, and the hunger had grown from the perpetual effort demanded by her married life. She was always trying to be what her husband wished, and never able to repose on his delight in what she was. The thing that she liked, that she spontaneously cared to have, seemed to be always excluded from her life ; for if it was only granted and not shared by her husband it might as well have been denied. About Will Ladislaw there had been a difference between them from the first, and it had ended, since Mr. Casaubon had so severely repulsed Dorothea's strong feeling about his claims on the family property, by her being convinced that she was in the right and her husband in the wrong, but that she was helpless. This afternoon the helplessness was more wretchedly benumbing than ever : she longed for objects who could be dear to her, and to whom she could be dear. She longed for work which would be directly beneficent like the sunshine and the rain, and now it appeared that she was to live more and more in a virtual tomb, where there was the apparatus of a ghastly labour producing what would never see the light. To-day she had stood at the door of the tomb and seen Will Ladislaw receding into the distant world of warm activity and fellowship—turning his face towards her as he went.

Books were of no use. Thinking was of no use. It was Sunday, and she could not have the carriage to go to Celia, who had lately had a baby. There was no refuge now from spiritual emptiness and discontent, and Dorothea had to bear her bad mood, as she would have borne a headache.

After dinner, at the hour when she usually began to read aloud, Mr. Casaubon proposed that they should go into the library, where, he said, he had ordered a fire and lights. He seemed to have revived and to be thinking intently.

In the library Dorothea observed that he had newly arranged a row of his note-books on a table, and now he took up and put into her hand a well-known volume, which was a table of contents to all the others.

" You will oblige me, my dear," he said, seating himself, " if instead of other reading this evening, you will go through this aloud, pencil in hand, and at each point where I say ' mark,' will make a cross with your pencil. This is the first step in a sifting process which I have long had in view, and as we go on I shall be able to indicate to you certain principles of selection whereby you will, I trust, have an intelligent participation in my purpose."

This proposal was only one more sign added to many since his memorable interview with Lydgate, that Mr. Casaubon's original reluctance to let Dorothea work with him had given place to the contrary disposition, namely, to demand much interest and labour from her.

After she had read and marked for two hours, he said, " We will take the volume up-stairs—and the pencil, if you please— and in case of reading in the night, we can pursue this task. It is not wearisome to you, I trust, Dorothea ? "

" I prefer always reading what you like best to hear," said Dorothea, who told the simple truth ; for what she dreaded was to exert herself in reading or anything else which left him as joyless as ever.

It was a proof of the force with which certain characteristics in Dorothea impressed those around her, that her husband, with all his jealousy and suspicion, had gathered implicit trust in the integrity of her promises, and her power of devoting herself to her idea of the right and best. Of late he had begun to feel that these qualities were a peculiar possession for himself, and he wanted to engross them.

The reading in the night did come. Dorothea in her young weariness had slept soon and fast : she was awakened by a sense of light, which seemed to her at first like a sudden vision of sunset after she had climbed a steep hill : she opened her eyes and saw her husband wrapped in his warm gown seating himself in the arm-chair near the fire-place where the embers were still glowing. He had lit two candles, expecting that Dorothea would awake, but not liking to rouse her by more direct means.

" Are you ill, Edward ? " she said, rising immediately.

" I felt some uneasiness in a reclining posture. I will sit here for a time." She threw wood on the fire, wrapped herself up, and said, " You would like me to read to you ? "

"You would oblige me greatly by doing so, Dorothea," said Mr. Casaubon, with a shade more meekness than usual in his polite manner. "I am wakeful : my mind is remarkably lucid."

"I fear that the excitement may be too great for you," said Dorothea, remembering Lydgate's cautions.

"No, I am not conscious of undue excitement. Thought is easy." Dorothea dared not insist, and she read for an hour or more on the same plan as she had done in the evening, but getting over the pages with more quickness. Mr. Casaubon's mind was more alert, and he seemed to anticipate what was coming after a very slight verbal indication, saying, "That will do—mark that "—or "Pass on to the next head—I omit the second excursus on Crete." Dorothea was amazed to think of the bird-like speed with which his mind was surveying the ground where it had been creeping for years. At last he said—

"Close the book now, my dear. We will resume our work to-morrow. I have deferred it too long, and would gladly see it completed. But you observe that the principle on which my selection is made, is to give adequate, and not disproportionate illustration to each of the theses enumerated in my introduction, as at present sketched. You have perceived that distinctly, Dorothea ? "

"Yes," said Dorothea, rather tremulously. She felt sick at heart.

"And now I think that I can take some repose," said Mr. Casaubon. He lay down again and begged her to put out the lights. When she had lain down too, and there was a darkness only broken by a dull glow on the hearth, he said—

"Before I sleep, I have a request to make, Dorothea."

"What is it ? " said Dorothea, with a dread in her mind.

"It is that you will let me know, deliberately, whether, in case of my death, you will carry out my wishes : whether you will avoid doing what I should deprecate, and apply yourself to do what I should desire."

Dorothea was not taken by surprise : many incidents had been leading her to the conjecture of some intention on her husband's part which might make a new yoke for her. She did not answer immediately.

"You refuse ? " said Mr. Casaubon, with more edge in his tone.

"No, I do not yet refuse," said Dorothea, in a clear voice, the need of freedom asserting itself within her ; "but it is too solemn —I think it is not right—to make a promise when I am ignorant what it will bind me to. Whatever affection prompted I would do without promising."

"But you would use your own judgment : I ask you to obey mine ; you refuse."

"No, dear, no ! " said Dorothea, beseechingly, crushed by opposing fears. " But may I wait and reflect a little while ? I desire with my whole soul to do what will comfort you ; but I cannot give any pledge suddenly—still less a pledge to do I know not what."

"You cannot then confide in the nature of my wishes ? "

"Grant me till to-morrow," said Dorothea, beseechingly.

"Till to-morrow then," said Mr. Casaubon.

Soon she could hear that he was sleeping, but there was no more sleep for her. While she constrained herself to lie still lest she should disturb him, her mind was carrying on a conflict in which imagination ranged its forces first on one side and then on the other. She had no presentiment that the power which her husband wished to establish over her future action had relation to anything else than his work. But it was clear enough to her that he would expect her to devote herself to sifting those mixed heaps of material, which were to be the doubtful illustration of principles still more doubtful. The poor child had become altogether unbelieving as to the trustworthiness of that Key which had made the ambition and the labour of her husband's life. It was not wonderful that, in spite of her small instruction, her judgment in this matter was truer than his : for she looked with unbiassed comparison and healthy sense at probabilities on which he had risked all his egoism. And now she pictured to herself the days, and months, and years which she must spend in sorting what might be called shattered mummies, and fragments of a tradition which was itself a mosaic wrought from crushed ruins—sorting them as food for a theory which was already withered in the birth like an elfin child. Doubtless a vigorous error vigorously pursued has kept the embryos of truth a-breathing : the quest of gold being at the same time a questioning of substances, the body of chemistry is prepared for its soul, and Lavoisier is born. But Mr. Casaubon's theory of the elements which made the seed of all tradition was not likely to bruise itself unawares against discoveries : it floated among flexible conjectures no more solid than those etymologies which seemed strong because of likeness in sound, until it was shown that likeness in sound made them impossible : it was a method of interpretation which was not tested by the necessity of forming anything which had sharper collisions than an elaborate notion of Gog and Magog : it was as free from interruption as a plan for threading the stars together. And Dorothea had so often had to check her weariness and impatience over this questionable riddle-guessing, as it revealed itself to her instead of the fellowship in high knowledge which was to make life worthier ! She could understand well enough now why her husband had come to cling to her, as possibly the only hope left that his labours would ever take a shape in which they could be given to the world. At first it had seemed that he wished to keep even her aloof from any close knowledge of what he was doing ; but gradually the terrible stringency of human need— the prospect of a too speedy death——

And here Dorothea's pity turned from her own future to her husband's past—nay, to his present hard struggle with a lot which had grown out of that past : the lonely labour, the ambition breathing hardly under the pressure of self-distrust ; the goal receding, and the heavier limbs ; and now at last the sword visibly trembling above him ! And had she not wished to marry him that she might help him in his life's labour ?—But she had thought the work was to be something greater, which she could serve in devoutly for its own sake. Was it right, even to soothe his grief—would it be possible, even if she promised—to work as in a treadmill fruitlessly ?

And yet, could she deny him ? Could she say, " I refuse to content this pining hunger ? " It would be refusing to do for him dead, what she was almost sure to do for him living. If he lived, as Lydgate had said he might, for fifteen years or more, her life would certainly be spent in helping him and obeying him.

Still, there was a deep difference between that devotion to the living, and that indefinite promise of devotion to the dead. While he lived, he could claim nothing that she would not still be free to remonstrate against, and even to refuse. But—the thought passed through her mind more than once, though she could not believe in it—might he not mean to demand something more from her than she had been able to imagine, since he wanted her pledge to carry out his wishes without telling her exactly what they were ? No ; his heart was bound up in his work only : that was the end for which his failing life was to be eked out by hers.

And now, if she were to say, " No ! if you die, I will put no finger to your work "—it seemed as if she would be crushing that bruised heart.

For four hours Dorothea lay in this conflict, till she felt ill and bewildered, unable to resolve, praying mutely. Helpless as a child which has sobbed and sought too long, she fell into a late morning sleep, and when she waked Mr. Casaubon was already up. Tantripp told her that he had read prayers, breakfasted, and was in the library.

"I never saw you look so pale, madam," said Tantripp, a solid-figured woman who had been with the sisters at Lausanne.

"Was I ever high-coloured, Tantripp?" said Dorothea, smiling faintly.

"Well, not to say high-coloured, but with a bloom like a Chiny rose. But always smelling those leather books, what can be expected? Do rest a little this morning, madam. Let me say you are ill and not able to go into that close library."

"Oh no, no! let me make haste," said Dorothea. "Mr. Casaubon wants me particularly."

When she went down she felt sure that she should promise to fulfil his wishes; but that would be later in the day—not yet.

As Dorothea entered the library, Mr. Casaubon turned round from the table where he had been placing some books, and said—

"I was waiting for your appearance, my dear. I had hoped to set to work at once this morning, but I find myself under some indisposition, probably from too much excitement yesterday. I am going now to take a turn in the shrubbery, since the air is milder."

"I am glad to hear that," said Dorothea. "Your mind, I feared, was too active last night."

"I would fain have it set at rest on the point I last spoke of, Dorothea. You can now, I hope, give me an answer."

"May I come out to you in the garden presently?" said Dorothea, winning a little breathing space in that way.

"I shall be in the Yew-Tree Walk for the next half-hour," said Mr. Casaubon, and then he left her.

Dorothea, feeling very weary, rang and asked Tantripp to bring her some wraps. She had been sitting still for a few minutes, but not in any renewal of the former conflict: she simply felt that she was going to say "Yes" to her own doom: she was too weak, too full of dread at the thought of inflicting a keen-edged blow on her husband, to do anything but submit completely. She sat still and let Tantripp put on her bonnet and shawl, a passivity which was unusual with her, for she liked to wait on herself.

"God bless you, madam!" said Tantripp, with an irrepressible movement of love towards the beautiful, gentle
creature for whom she felt unable to do anything more, now
that she had finished tying the bonnet.

This was too much for Dorothea's highly-strung feeling, and
she burst into tears, sobbing against Tantripp's arm. But
soon she checked herself, dried her eyes, and went out at the
glass door into the shrubbery.

"I wish every book in that library was built into a caticom
for your master," said Tantripp to Pratt, the butler, finding
him in the breakfast-room. She had been at Rome, and
visited the antiquities, as we know; and she always declined
to call Mr. Casaubon anything but "your master," when
speaking to the other servants.

Pratt laughed. He liked his master very well, but he liked
Tantripp better.

When Dorothea was out on the gravel walks, she lingered
among the nearer clumps of trees, hesitating, as she had done
once before, though from a different cause. Then she had
feared lest her effort at fellowship should be unwelcome; now
she dreaded going to the spot where she foresaw that she must
bind herself to a fellowship from which she shrank. Neither
law nor the world's opinion compelled her to this—only her
husband's nature and her own compassion, only the ideal and
not the real yoke of marriage. She saw clearly enough the
whole situation, yet she was fettered: she could not smite the
stricken soul that entreated hers. If that were weakness,
Dorothea was weak. But the half-hour was passing, and she
must not delay longer. When she entered the Yew-Tree Walk
she could not see her husband; but the walk had bends, and
she went, expecting to catch sight of his figure wrapped in a
blue cloak, which, with a warm velvet cap, was his outer gar-
ment on chill days for the garden. It occurred to her that he
might be resting in the summer-house, towards which the path
diverged a little. Turning the angle, she could see him seated
on the bench, close to a stone table. His arms were resting on
the table, and his brow was bowed down on them, the blue cloak
being dragged forward and screening his face on each side.

"He exhausted himself last night," Dorothea said to herself,
thinking at first that he was asleep, and that the summer-house
was too damp a place to rest in. But then she remembered that
of late she had seen him take that attitude when she was reading
to him, as if he found it easier than any other; and that he

would sometimes speak, as well as listen, with his face down in that way. She went into the summer-house and said, " I am come, Edward ; I am ready."

He took no notice, and she thought that he must be fast asleep. She laid her hand on his shoulder, and repeated, " I am ready ! " Still he was motionless ; and with a sudden confused fear, she leaned down to him, took off his velvet cap, and leaned her cheek close to his head, crying in a distressed tone,

" Wake, dear, wake ! Listen to me. I am come to answer."

But Dorothea never gave her answer.

Later in the day, Lydgate was seated by her bedside, and she was talking deliriously, thinking aloud, and recalling what had gone through her mind the night before. She knew him, and called him by his name, but appeared to think it right that she should explain everything to him ; and again, and again, begged him to explain everything to her husband.

" Tell him I shall go to him soon : I am ready to promise. Only, thinking about it was so dreadful—it has made me ill. Not very ill. I shall soon be better. Go and tell him."

But the silence in her husband's ear was never more to be broken.

CHAPTER XLIX

A task too strong for wizard spells
This squire had brought about ;
'Tis easy dropping stones in wells,
But who shall get them out ?

" I wish to God we could hinder Dorothea from knowing this," said Sir James Chettam, with the little frown on his brow, and an expression of intense disgust about his mouth.

He was standing on the hearth-rug in the library at Lowick Grange, and speaking to Mr. Brooke. It was the day after Mr. Casaubon had been buried, and Dorothea was not yet able to leave her room.

" That would be difficult, you know, Chettam, as she is an executrix, and she likes to go into these things—property, land, that kind of thing. She has her notions, you know," said Mr. Brooke, sticking his eye-glasses on nervously, and exploring the edges of a folded paper which he held in his hand ; " and she would like to act—depend upon it, as an executrix Dorothea would want to act. And she was twenty-one last December, you know. I can hinder nothing."

Sir James looked at the carpet for a minute in silence, and then lifting his eyes suddenly fixed them on Mr. Brooke, saying, " I will tell you what we can do. Until Dorothea is well, all business must be kept from her, and as soon as she is able to be moved she must come to us. Being with Celia and the baby will be the best thing in the world for her, and will pass away the time. And meanwhile you must get rid of Ladislaw : you must send him out of the country." Here Sir James's look of disgust returned in all its intensity.

Mr. Brooke put his hands behind him, walked to the window and straightened his back with a little shake before he replied :

" That is easily said, Chettam, easily said, you know."

" My dear sir," persisted Sir James, restraining his indignation within respectful forms, " it was you who brought him here, and you who keep him here—I mean by the occupation you give him."

" Yes, but I can't dismiss him in an instant without assigning reasons, my dear Chettam. Ladislaw has been invaluable, most satisfactory. I consider that I have done this part of the country a service by bringing him—by bringing him, you know." Mr. Brooke ended with a nod, turning round to give it.

" It's a pity this part of the country didn't do without him, that's all I have to say about it. At any rate, as Dorothea's brother-in-law, I feel warranted in objecting strongly to his being kept here by any action on the part of her friends. You admit, I hope, that I have a right to speak about what concerns the dignity of my wife's sister ? "

Sir James was getting warm.

" Of course, my dear Chettam, of course. But you and I have different ideas—different—— "

" Not about this action of Casaubon's, I should hope," interrupted Sir James. " I say that he has most unfairly compromised Dorothea. I say that there never was a meaner, more ungentlemanly action than this—a codicil of this sort to a will which he made at the time of his marriage with the knowledge and reliance of her family—a positive insult to Dorothea ! "

" Well, you know, Casaubon was a little twisted about Ladislaw. Ladislaw has told me the reason—dislike of the bent he took, you know—Ladislaw didn't think much of Casaubon's notions, Thoth and Dagon—that sort of thing : and I fancy that Casaubon didn't like the independent position Ladislaw had taken up. I saw the letters between them, you know. Poor Casaubon was a little buried in books—he didn't know the world."

" It's all very well for Ladislaw to put that colour on it," said Sir James. " But I believe Casaubon was only jealous of him on Dorothea's account, and the world will suppose that she gave him some reason ; and that is what makes it so abominable —coupling her name with this young fellow's."

" My dear Chettam, it won't lead to anything, you know," said Mr. Brooke, seating himself and sticking on his eye-glass again. " It's all of a piece with Casaubon's oddity. This paper, now, ' Synoptical Tabulation ' and so on, ' for the use of Mrs. Casaubon,' it was locked up in the desk with the will. I suppose he meant Dorothea to publish his researches, eh ? and she'll do it, you know ; she has gone into his studies uncommonly."

" My dear sir," said Sir James, impatiently, " that is neither here nor there. The question is, whether you don't see with me the propriety of sending young Ladislaw away ? "

" Well, no, not the urgency of the thing. By-and-by, perhaps, it may come round. As to gossip, you know, sending him away won't hinder gossip. People say what they like to say, not what they have chapter and verse for," said Mr. Brooke, becoming acute about the truths that lay on the side of his own wishes. " I might get rid of Ladislaw up to a certain point—take away the ' Pioneer ' from him, and that sort of thing ; but I couldn't send him out of the country if he didn't choose to go—didn't choose, you know."

Mr. Brooke, persisting as quietly as if he were only discussing the nature of last year's weather, and nodding at the end with his usual amenity, was an exasperating form of obstinacy.

" Good God ! " said Sir James, with as much passion as he ever showed, " let us get him a post ; let us spend money on him. If he could go in the suite of some Colonial Governor ! Grampus might take him—and I could write to Fulke about it."

" But Ladislaw won't be shipped off like a head of cattle, my dear fellow ; Ladislaw has his ideas. It's my opinion that if he were to part from me to-morrow, you'd only hear the more of him in the country. With his talent for speaking and drawing up documents, there are few men who could come up to him as an agitator—an agitator, you know."

" Agitator ! " said Sir James, with bitter emphasis, feeling that the syllables of this word properly repeated were a sufficient exposure of its hatefulness.

"But be reasonable, Chettam. Dorothea, now. As you say, she had better go to Celia as soon as possible. She can stay under your roof, and in the meantime things may come round quietly. Don't let us be firing off our guns in a hurry, you know. Standish will keep our counsel, and the news will be old before it's known. Twenty things may happen to carry off Ladislaw—without my doing anything, you know."

"Then I am to conclude that you decline to do anything?"

"Decline, Chettam?—no—I didn't say decline. But I really don't see what I could do. Ladislaw is a gentleman."

"I am glad to hear it!" said Sir James, his irritation making him forget himself a little. "I am sure Casaubon was not."

"Well, it would have been worse if he had made the codicil to hinder her from marrying again at all, you know."

"I don't know that," said Sir James. "It would have been less indelicate."

"One of poor Casaubon's freaks! That attack upset his brain a little. It all goes for nothing. She doesn't *want* to marry Ladislaw."

"But this codicil is framed so as to make everybody believe that she did. I don't believe anything of the sort about Dorothea," said Sir James—then frowningly, "but I suspect Ladislaw. I tell you frankly, I suspect Ladislaw."

"I couldn't take any immediate action on that ground, Chettam. In fact, if it were possible to pack him off—send him to Norfolk Island—that sort of thing—it would look all the worse for Dorothea to those who knew about it. It would seem as if we distrusted her—distrusted her, you know."

That Mr. Brooke had hit on an undeniable argument, did not tend to soothe Sir James. He put out his hand to reach his hat, implying that he did not mean to contend further, and said, still with some heat—

"Well, I can only say that I think Dorothea was sacrificed once, because her friends were too careless. I shall do what I can, as her brother, to protect her now."

"You can't do better than get her to Freshitt as soon as possible, Chettam. I approve that plan altogether," said Mr. Brooke, well pleased that he had won the argument. It would have been highly inconvenient to him to part with Ladislaw at that time, when a dissolution might happen any day, and electors were to be convinced of the course by which the interests

of the country would be best served. Mr. Brooke sincerely
believed that this end could be secured by his own return to
Parliament : he offered the forces of his mind honestly to the
nation.

CHAPTER L

" ' This Loller here wol prechen us somewhat.'
  ' Nay by my father's soule ! that schal he nat,'
Sayde the Schipman, ' here schal he not preche,
He schal no gospel glosen here ne teche.
We leven all in the gret God,' quod he.
He wolden sowen some diffcultee."
          —*Canterbury Tales.*

DOROTHEA had been safe at Freshitt Hall nearly a week before
she had asked any dangerous questions. Every morning now
she sat with Celia in the prettiest of up-stairs sitting-rooms,
opening into a small conservatory—Celia all in white and
lavender like a bunch of mixed violets, watching the remarkable
acts of the baby, which were so dubious to her inexperienced
mind that all conversation was interrupted by appeals for their
interpretation made to the oracular nurse. Dorothea sat by
in her widow's dress, with an expression which rather provoked
Celia, as being much too sad ; for not only was baby quite well,
but really when a husband had been so dull and troublesome
while he lived, and besides that had—well, well ! Sir James, of
course, had told Celia everything, with a strong representation
how important it was that Dorothea should not know it sooner
than was inevitable.

But Mr. Brooke had been right in predicting that Dorothea
would not long remain passive where action had been assigned
to her ; she knew the purport of her husband's will made at
the time of their marriage, and her mind, as soon as she was
clearly conscious of her position, was silently occupied with
what she ought to do as the owner of Lowick Manor with the
patronage of the living attached to it.

One morning when her uncle paid his usual visit, though with
an unusual alacrity in his manner which he accounted for by
saying that it was now pretty certain Parliament would be
dissolved forthwith, Dorothea said—

" Uncle, it is right now that I should consider who is to have
the living at Lowick. After Mr. Tucker had been provided for,
I never heard my husband say that he had any clergyman in

his mind as a successor to himself. I think I ought to have the keys now and go to Lowick to examine all my husband's papers. There may be something that would throw light on his wishes."

"No hurry, my dear," said Mr. Brooke, quietly. "By-and-by, you know, you can go, if you like. But I cast my eyes over things in the desks and drawers—there was nothing—nothing but deep subjects, you know—besides the will. Everything can be done by-and-by. As to the living, I have had an application for interest already—I should say rather good. Mr. Tyke has been strongly recommended to me—I had something to do with getting him an appointment before. An apostolic man, I believe—the sort of thing that would suit you, my dear."

"I should like to have fuller knowledge about him, uncle, and judge for myself, if Mr. Casaubon has not left any expression of his wishes. He has perhaps made some addition to his will —there may be some instructions for me," said Dorothea, who had all the while had this conjecture in her mind with relation to her husband's work.

"Nothing about the rectory, my dear—nothing," said Mr. Brooke, rising to go away, and putting out his hand to his nieces: "nor about his researches, you know. Nothing in the will."

Dorothea's lip quivered.

"Come, you must not think of these things yet, my dear. By-and-by, you know."

"I am quite well now, uncle: I wish to exert myself."

"Well, well, we shall see. But I must run away now—I have no end of work now—it's a crisis—a political crisis, you know. And here is Celia and her little man—you are an aunt, you know, now, and I am a sort of grandfather," said Mr. Brooke, with placid hurry, anxious to get away and tell Chettam that it would not be his (Mr. Brooke's) fault if Dorothea insisted on looking into everything.

Dorothea sank back in her chair when her uncle had left the room, and cast her eyes down meditatively on her crossed hands.

"Look, Dodo! look at him! Did you ever see anything like that?" said Celia in her comfortable staccato.

"What, Kitty?" said Dorothea, lifting her eyes rather absently.

"What? why, his upper lip; see how he is drawing it down, as if he meant to make a face. Isn't it wonderful! He may have his little thoughts. I wish nurse were here. Do look at him."

A large tear, which had been for some time gathering, rolled down Dorothea's cheek as she looked up and tried to smile.

"Don't be sad, Dodo ; kiss baby. What are you brooding over so ? I am sure you did everything, and a great deal too much. You should be happy now."

"I wonder if Sir James would drive me to Lowick. I want to look over everything—to see if there were any words written for me."

"You are not to go till Mr. Lydgate says you may go. And he has not said so yet (here you are, nurse ; take baby and walk up and down the gallery). Besides, you have got a wrong notion in your head as usual, Dodo—I can see that : it vexes me."

"Where am I wrong, Kitty ? " said Dorothea, quite meekly. She was almost ready now to think Celia wiser than herself, and was really wondering with some fear what her wrong notion was. Celia felt her advantage, and was determined to use it. None of them knew Dodo as well as she did, or knew how to manage her. Since Celia's baby was born, she had had a new sense of her mental solidity and calm wisdom. It seemed clear that where there was a baby, things were right enough, and that error, in general, was a mere lack of that central poising force.

"I can see what you are thinking of as well as can be, Dodo," said Celia. "You are wanting to find out if there is anything uncomfortable for you to do now, only because Mr. Casaubon wished it. As if you had not been uncomfortable enough before. And he doesn't deserve it, and you will find that out. He has behaved very badly. James is as angry with him as can be. And I had better tell you, to prepare you."

"Celia," said Dorothea, entreatingly, "you distress me. Tell me at once what you mean." It glanced through her mind that Mr. Casaubon had left the property away from her—which would not be so very distressing.

"Why, he has made a codicil to his will, to say the property was all to go away from you if you married—I mean—— "

"That is of no consequence," said Dorothea, breaking in impetuously.

"But if you married Mr. Ladislaw, not anybody else," Celia went on with persevering quietude. "Of course that is of no consequence in one way—you never *would* marry Mr. Ladislaw ; but that only makes it worse of Mr. Casaubon."

The blood rushed to Dorothea's face and neck painfully. But Celia was administering what she thought a sobering dose of fact. It was taking up notions that had done Dodo's health so much harm. So she went on in her neutral tone, as if she had been remarking on baby's robes.

"James says so. He says it is abominable, and not like a gentleman. And there never *was* a better judge than James. It is as if Mr. Casaubon wanted to make people believe that you would wish to marry Mr. Ladislaw—which is ridiculous. Only James says it was to hinder Mr. Ladislaw from wanting to marry you for your money—just as if he ever would think of making you an offer. Mrs. Cadwallader said you might as well marry an Italian with white mice ! But I must just go and look at baby," Celia added, without the least change of tone, throwing a light shawl over her, and tripping away.

Dorothea by this time had turned cold again, and now threw herself back helplessly in her chair. She might have compared her experience at that moment to the vague, alarmed consciousness that her life was taking on a new form, that she was undergoing a metamorphosis in which memory would not adjust itself to the stirring of new organs. Everything was changing its aspect : her husband's conduct, her own duteous feeling towards him, every struggle between them—and yet more, her whole relation to Will Ladislaw. Her world was in a state of convulsive change ; the only thing she could say distinctly to herself was, that she must wait and think anew. One change terrified her as if it had been a sin ; it was a violent shock of repulsion from her departed husband, who had had hidden thoughts, perhaps perverting everything she said and did. Then again she was conscious of another change which also made her tremulous ; it was a sudden strange yearning of heart towards Will Ladislaw. It had never before entered her mind that he could, under any circumstances, be her lover : conceive the effect of the sudden revelation that another had thought of him in that light—that perhaps he himself had been conscious of such a possibility,—and this with the hurrying, crowding vision of unfitting conditions, and questions not soon to be solved.

It seemed a long while—she did not know how long—before she heard Celia saying, "That will do, nurse ; he will be quiet on my lap now. You can go to lunch, and let Garratt stay in the next room." "What I think, Dodo," Celia went on, observing nothing more than that Dorothea was leaning back in her chair, and likely to be passive, " is that Mr. Casaubon was spiteful. I never did like him, and James never did. I think the corners of his mouth were dreadfully spiteful. And now he has behaved in this way, I am sure religion does not require you to make yourself uncomfortable about him. If he has been taken away, that is a mercy, and you ought to be grateful. *We* should not grieve, should we, baby ? " said Celia confidentially to that unconscious centre and poise of the world, who had the most remarkable fists all complete even to the nails, and hair enough, really, when you took his cap off, to make—you didn't know what :—in short, he was Bouddha in a Western form.

At this crisis Lydgate was announced, and one of the first things he said was, " I fear you are not so well as you were, Mrs. Casaubon ; have you been agitated ? allow me to feel your pulse." Dorothea's hand was of a marble coldness.

" She wants to go to Lowick, to look over papers," said Celia. " She ought not, ought she ? "

Lydgate did not speak for a few moments. Then he said, looking at Dorothea, " I hardly know. In my opinion Mrs. Casaubon should do what would give her the most repose of mind. That repose will not always come from being forbidden to act."

" Thank you," said Dorothea, exerting herself, " I am sure that is wise. There are so many things which I ought to attend to. Why should I sit here idle ? " Then, with an effort to recall subjects not connected with her agitation, she added, abruptly, " You know every one in Middlemarch, I think, Mr. Lydgate. I shall ask you to tell me a great deal. I have serious things to do now. I have a living to give away. You know Mr. Tyke and all the—— " But Dorothea's effort was too much for her ; she broke off and burst into sobs.

Lydgate made her drink a dose of sal volatile.

" Let Mrs. Casaubon do as she likes," he said to Sir James whom he asked to see before quitting the house. " She wants perfect freedom, I think, more than any other prescription."

His attendance on Dorothea while her brain was excited, had enabled him to form some true conclusions concerning the trials of her life. He felt sure that she had been suffering from the strain and conflict of self-repression ; and that she was likely now to feel herself only in another sort of pinfold than that from which she had been released.

Lydgate's advice was all the easier for Sir James to follow

when he found that Celia had already told Dorothea the unpleasant fact about the will. There was no help for it now—
no reason for any further delay in the execution of necessary
business. And the next day Sir James complied at once with
her request that he would drive her to Lowick.

"I have no wish to stay there at present," said Dorothea ;
"I could hardly bear it. I am much happier at Freshitt with
Celia. I shall be able to think better about what should be
done at Lowick by looking at it from a distance. And I should
like to be at the Grange a little while with my uncle, and go
about in all the old walks and among the people in the village."

"Not yet, I think. Your uncle is having political company,
and you are better out of the way of such doings," said Sir
James, who at that moment thought of the Grange chiefly as
a haunt of young Ladislaw's. But no word passed between
him and Dorothea about the objectionable part of the will ;
indeed, both of them felt that the mention of it between them
would be impossible. Sir James was shy, even with men, about
disagreeable subjects ; and the one thing that Dorothea would
have chosen to say, if she had spoken on the matter at all, was
forbidden to her at present because it seemed to be a further
exposure of her husband's injustice. Yet she did wish that
Sir James could know what had passed between her and her
husband about Will Ladislaw's moral claim on the property :
it would then, she thought, be apparent to him as it was to her,
that her husband's strange indelicate proviso had been chiefly
urged by his bitter resistance to that idea of claim, and not
merely by personal feelings more difficult to talk about. Also,
it must be admitted, Dorothea wished that this could be known
for Will's sake, since her friends seemed to think of him as
simply an object of Mr. Casaubon's charity. Why should he
be compared with an Italian carrying white mice ? That word
quoted from Mrs. Cadwallader seemed like a mocking travesty
wrought in the dark by an impish finger.

At Lowick Dorothea searched desk and drawer—searched all
her husband's places of deposit for private writing, but found
no paper addressed especially to her, except that " Synoptical
Tabulation " which was probably only the beginning of many
intended directions for her guidance. In carrying out this
bequest of labour to Dorothea, as in all else, Mr. Casaubon had
been slow and hesitating, oppressed in the plan of transmitting
his work, as he had been in executing it, by the sense of moving
heavily in a dim and clogging medium : distrust of Dorothea's

competence to arrange what he had prepared was subdued only by distrust of any other redactor. But he had come at last to create a trust for himself out of Dorothea's nature : she could do what she resolved to do : and he willingly imagined her toiling under the fetters of a promise to erect a tomb with his name upon it. (Not that Mr. Casaubon called the future volumes a tomb ; he called them the Key to all Mythologies.) But the months gained on him and left his plans belated : he had only had time to ask for that promise by which he sought to keep his cold grasp on Dorothea's life.

The grasp had slipped away. Bound by a pledge given from the depths of her pity, she would have been capable of undertaking a toil which her judgment whispered was vain for all uses except that consecration of faithfulness which is a supreme use. But now her judgment, instead of being controlled by duteous devotion, was made active by the imbittering discovery that in her past union there had lurked the hidden alienation of secrecy and suspicion. The living, suffering man was no longer before her to awaken her pity : there remained only the retrospect of painful subjection to a husband whose thoughts had been lower than she had believed, whose exorbitant claims for himself had even blinded his scrupulous care for his own character, and made him defeat his own pride by shocking men of ordinary honour. As for the property which was the sign of that broken tie, she would have been glad to be free from it and have nothing more than her original fortune which had been settled on her, if there had not been duties attached to ownership, which she ought not to flinch from. About this property many troublous questions insisted on rising : had she not been right in thinking that the half of it ought to go to Will Ladislaw —but was it not impossible now for her to do that act of justice ? Mr. Casaubon had taken a cruelly effective means of hindering her : even with indignation against him in her heart, any act that seemed a triumphant eluding of his purpose revolted her.

After collecting papers of business which she wished to examine she locked up again the desks and drawers—all empty of personal words for her—empty of any sign that in her husband's lonely brooding his heart had gone out to her in excuse or explanation ; and she went back to Freshitt with the sense that around his last hard demand and his last injurious assertion of his power, the silence was unbroken.

Dorothea tried now to turn her thoughts towards immediate duties, and one of these was of a kind which others were determined to remind her of. Lydgate's ear had caught eagerly her mention of the living, and as soon as he could, he reopened the subject, seeing here a possibility of making amends for the casting-vote he had once given with an ill-satisfied conscience.

"Instead of telling you anything about Mr. Tyke," he said, "I should like to speak of another man—Mr. Farebrother, the Vicar of St. Botolph's. His living is a poor one, and gives him a stinted provision for himself and his family. His mother, aunt, and sister all live with him, and depend upon him. I believe he has never married because of them. I never heard such good preaching as his—such plain, easy eloquence. He would have done to preach at St. Paul's Cross after old Latimer. His talk is just as good about all subjects: original, simple, clear. I think him a remarkable fellow; he ought to have done more than he has done."

"Why has he not done more?" said Dorothea, interested now in all who had slipped below their own intention.

"That's a hard question," said Lydgate. "I find myself that it's uncommonly difficult to make the right thing work: there are so many strings pulling at once. Farebrother often hints that he has got into the wrong profession; he wants a wider range than that of a poor clergyman, and I suppose he has no interest to help him on. He is very fond of Natural History and various scientific matters, and he is hampered in reconciling these tastes with his position. He has no money to spare—hardly enough to use; and that has led him into card-playing—Middlemarch is a great place for whist. He does play for money, and he wins a good deal. Of course that takes him into company a little beneath him, and makes him slack about some things; and yet, with all that, looking at him as a whole, I think he is one of the most blameless men I ever knew. He has neither venom nor doubleness in him, and those often go with a more correct outside."

"I wonder whether he suffers in his conscience because of that habit," said Dorothea; "I wonder whether he wishes he could leave it off."

"I have no doubt he would leave it off, if he were transplanted into plenty: he would be glad of the time for other things."

"My uncle says that Mr. Tyke is spoken of as an apostolic man," said Dorothea, meditatively. She was wishing it were possible to restore the times of primitive zeal, and yet thinking of Mr. Farebrother with a strong desire to rescue him from his chance-gotten money.

"I don't pretend to say that Farebrother is apostolic," said Lydgate. "His position is not quite like that of the Apostles : he is only a parson among parishioners whose lives he has to try and make better. Practically I find that what is called being apostolic now, is an impatience of everything in which the parson doesn't cut the principal figure. I see something of that in Mr. Tyke at the Hospital : a good deal of his doctrine is a sort of pinching hard to make people uncomfortable aware of him. Besides, an apostolic man at Lowick !—he ought to think, as St. Francis did, that it is needful to preach to the birds."

"True," said Dorothea. "It is hard to imagine what sort of notions our farmers and labourers get from their teaching. I have been looking into a volume of sermons by Mr. Tyke : such sermons would be of no use at Lowick—I mean, about imputed righteousness and the prophecies in the Apocalypse. I have always been thinking of the different ways in which Christianity is taught, and whenever I find one way that makes it a wider blessing than any other, I cling to that as the truest— I mean that which takes in the most good of all kinds, and brings in the most people as sharers in it. It is surely better to pardon too much, than to condemn too much. But I should like to see Mr. Farebrother and hear him preach."

"Do," said Lydgate ; "I trust to the effect of that. He is very much beloved, but he has his enemies too : there are always people who can't forgive an able man for differing from them. And that money-winning business is really a blot. You don't, of course, see many Middlemarch people : but Mr. Ladislaw, who is constantly seeing Mr. Brooke, is a great friend of Mr. Farebrother's old ladies, and would be glad to sing the Vicar's praises. One of the old ladies—Miss Noble, the aunt— is a wonderfully quaint picture of self-forgetful goodness, and Ladislaw gallants her about sometimes. I met them one day in a back street : you know Ladislaw's look—a sort of Daphnis in coat and waistcoat ; and this little old maid reaching up to his arm—they looked like a couple dropped out of a romantic comedy. But the best evidence about Farebrother is to see him and hear him."

Happily Dorothea was in her private sitting-room when this conversation occurred, and there was no one present to make Lydgate's innocent introduction of Ladislaw painful to her. As was usual with him in matters of personal gossip, Lydgate had quite forgotten Rosamond's remark that she thought Will adored Mrs. Casaubon. At that moment he was only caring for what would recommend the Farebrother family; and he had purposely given emphasis to the worst that could be said about the Vicar, in order to forestall objections. In the weeks since Mr. Casaubon's death he had hardly seen Ladislaw, and he had heard no rumour to warn him that Mr. Brooke's confidential secretary was a dangerous subject with Mrs. Casaubon. When he was gone, his picture of Ladislaw lingered in her mind and disputed the ground with that question of the Lowick living. What was Will Ladislaw thinking about her? Would he hear of that fact which made her cheeks burn as they never used to do? And how would he feel when he heard it?—But she could see as well as possible how he smiled down at the little old maid. An Italian with white mice!—on the contrary, he was a creature who entered into every one's feelings, and could take the pressure of their thought instead of urging his own with iron resistance.

CHAPTER LI

Party is Nature too, and you shall see
By force of Logic how they both agree:
The Many in the One, the One in Many;
All is not Some, nor Some the same as Any:
Genus holds species, both are great or small;
One genus highest, one not high at all;
Each species has its differentia too,
This is not That, and He was never You,
Though this and that are AYES, and you and he
Are like as one to one, or three to three.

No gossip about Mr. Casaubon's will had yet reached Ladislaw: the air seemed to be filled with the dissolution of Parliament and the coming election, as the old wakes and fairs were filled with the rival clatter of itinerant shows; and more private noises were taken little notice of. The famous "dry election" was at hand, in which the depths of public feeling might be measured by the low flood-mark of drink. Will Ladislaw was one of the busiest at this time; and though Dorothea's widowhood was continually in his thought, he was so far from wishing to be spoken to on the subject, that when Lydgate sought him out to tell him what had passed about the Lowick living, he answered rather waspishly—

"Why should you bring me into the matter? I never see Mrs. Casaubon, and am not likely to see her, since she is at

Freshitt. I never go there. It is Tory ground, where I and the ' Pioneer ' are no more welcome than a poacher and his gun."

The fact was that Will had been made the more susceptible by observing that Mr. Brooke, instead of wishing him, as before, to come to the Grange oftener than was quite agreeable to himself, seemed now to contrive that he should go there as little as possible. This was a shuffling concession of Mr. Brooke's to Sir James Chettam's indignant remonstrance ; and Will, awake to the slightest hint in this direction, concluded that he was to be kept away from the Grange on Dorothea's account. Her friends, then, regarded him with some suspicion ? Their fears were quite superfluous : they were very much mistaken if they imagined that he would put himself forward as a needy adventurer trying to win the favour of a rich woman.

Until now Will had never fully seen the chasm between himself and Dorothea—until now that he was come to the brink of it, and saw her on the other side. He began, not without some inward rage, to think of going away from the neighbourhood : it would be impossible for him to show any further interest in Dorothea without subjecting himself to disagreeable imputations—perhaps even in her mind, which others might try to poison.

" We are for ever divided," said Will. " I might as well be at Rome ; she would be no farther from me." But what we call our despair is often only the painful eagerness of unfed hope. There were plenty of reasons why he should not go— public reasons why he should not quit his post at this crisis, leaving Mr. Brooke in the lurch when he needed " coaching " for the election, and when there was so much canvassing, direct and indirect, to be carried on. Will could not like to leave his own chessmen in the heat of a game ; and any candidate on the right side, even if his brain and marrow had been as soft as was consistent with a gentlemanly bearing, might help to turn a majority. To coach Mr. Brooke and keep him steadily to the idea that he must pledge himself to vote for the actual Reform Bill, instead of insisting on his independence and power of pulling up in time, was not an easy task. Mr. Farebrother's prophecy of a fourth candidate " in the bag " had not yet been fulfilled, neither the Parliamentary Candidate Society nor any other power on the watch to secure a reforming majority seeing a worthy nodus for interference while there was a second reforming candidate like Mr. Brooke, who might be returned at his own expense; and the fight lay entirely between Pinkerton the old Tory member, Bagster the new Whig member returned at the last election, and Brooke the future independent member, who was to fetter himself for this occasion only. Mr. Hawley and his party would bend all their forces to the return of Pinkerton, and Mr. Brooke's success must depend either on plumpers which would leave Bagster in the rear, or on the new minting of Tory votes into reforming votes. The latter means, of course, would be preferable.

This prospect of converting votes was a dangerous distraction to Mr. Brooke: his impression that waverers were likely to be allured by wavering statements, and also the liability of his mind to stick afresh at opposing arguments as they turned up in his memory, gave Will Ladislaw much trouble.

"You know there are tactics in these things," said Mr. Brooke; "meeting people half-way—tempering your ideas—saying, 'Well now, there's something in that,' and so on. I agree with you that this is a peculiar occasion—the country with a will of its own—political unions—that sort of thing—but we sometimes cut with rather too sharp a knife, Ladislaw. These ten-pound householders, now: why ten? Draw the line somewhere—yes: but why just at ten? That's a difficult question, now, if you go into it."

"Of course it is," said Will, impatiently. "But if you are to wait till we get a logical Bill, you must put yourself forward as a revolutionist, and then Middlemarch would not elect you, I fancy. As for trimming, this is not a time for trimming."

Mr. Brooke always ended by agreeing with Ladislaw, who still appeared to him a sort of Burke with a leaven of Shelley; but after an interval the wisdom of his own methods reasserted itself, and he was again drawn into using them with much hopefulness. At this stage of affairs he was in excellent spirits, which even supported him under large advances of money; for his powers of convincing and persuading had not yet been tested by anything more difficult than a chairman's speech, introducing other orators, or a dialogue with a Middlemarch voter, from which he came away with a sense that he was a tactician by nature, and that it was a pity he had not gone earlier into this kind of thing. He was a little conscious of defeat, however, with Mr. Mawmsey, a chief representative in Middlemarch of that great social power, the retail trader, and naturally one of the most doubtful voters in the borough—willing for his own part to supply an equal quality of teas and

sugars to reformer and anti-reformer, as well as to agree impartially with both, and feeling like the burgesses of old that this
necessity of electing members was a great burthen to a town ;
for even if there were no danger in holding out hopes to all
parties beforehand, there would be the painful necessity at last
of disappointing respectable people whose names were on his
books. He was accustomed to receive large orders from Mr
Brooke of Tipton ; but then, there were many of Pinkerton's
committee whose opinions had a great weight of grocery on
their side. Mr. Mawmsey thinking that Mr. Brooke, as not too
" clever in his intellects," was the more likely to forgive a grocer
who gave a hostile vote under pressure, had become confidential
in his back parlour.

" As to Reform, sir, put it in a family light," he said, rattling
the small silver in his pocket, and smiling affably. " Will it
support Mrs. Mawmsey, and enable her to bring up six children
when I am no more ? I put the question *fictiously*, knowing
what must be the answer. Very well, sir. I ask you what, as
a husband and a father, I am to do when gentlemen come to
me and say, ' Do as you like, Mawmsey ; but if you vote against
us, I shall get my groceries elsewhere ; when I sugar my liquor
I like to feel that I am benefiting the country by maintaining
tradesmen of the right colour.' Those very words have been
spoken to me, sir, in the very chair where you are now sitting.
I don't mean by your honourable self, Mr. Brooke."

" No, no, no—that's narrow, you know. Until my butler
complains to me of your goods, Mr. Mawmsey," said Mr. Brooke,
soothingly, " until I hear that you send bad sugars, spices—that
sort of thing—I shall never order him to go elsewhere."

" Sir, I am your humble servant, and greatly obliged," said
Mr. Mawmsey, feeling that politics were clearing up a little.
" There would be some pleasure in voting for a gentleman who
speaks in that honourable manner."

" Well, you know, Mr. Mawmsey, you would find it the right
thing to put yourself on our side. This Reform will touch
everybody by-and-by—a thoroughly popular measure—a sort
of A, B, C, you know, that must come first before the rest can
follow. I quite agree with you that you've got to look at the
thing in a family light : but public spirit, now. We're all one
family, you know—it's all one cupboard. Such a thing as a
vote, now : why, it may help to make men's fortunes at the
Cape—there's no knowing what may be the effect of a vote,"
Mr. Brooke ended, with a sense of being a little out at sea, though

finding it still enjoyable. But Mr. Mawmsey answered in a tone of decisive check.

"I beg your pardon, sir, but I can't afford that. When I give a vote I must know what I'm doing; I must look to what will be the effects on my till and ledger, speaking respectfully. Prices, I'll admit, are what nobody can know the merits of; and the sudden falls after you've bought in currants, which are a goods that will not keep—I've never myself seen into the ins and outs there; which is a rebuke to human pride. But as to one family, there's debtor and creditor, I hope; they're not going to reform that away; else I should vote for things staying as they are. Few men have less need to cry for change than I have, personally speaking—that is, for self and family. I am not one of those who have nothing to lose; I mean as to respectability both in parish and private business, and noways in respect of your honourable self and custom, which you was good enough to say you would not withdraw from me, vote or no vote, while the article sent in was satisfactory."

After this conversation Mr. Mawmsey went up and boasted to his wife that he had been rather too many for Brooke of Tipton, and that he didn't mind so much now about going to the poll.

Mr. Brooke on this occasion abstained from boasting of his tactics to Ladislaw, who for his part was glad enough to persuade himself that he had no concern with any canvassing except the purely argumentative sort, and that he worked no meaner engine than knowledge. Mr. Brooke, necessarily, had his agents, who understood the nature of the Middlemarch voter and the means of enlisting his ignorance on the side of the Bill— which were remarkably similar to the means of enlisting it on the side against the Bill. Will stopped his ears. Occasionally Parliament, like the rest of our lives, even to our eating and apparel, could hardly go on if our imaginations were too active about processes. There were plenty of dirty-handed men in the world to do dirty business; and Will protested to himself that his share in bringing Mr. Brooke through would be quite innocent.

But whether he should succeed in that mode of contributing to the majority on the right side was very doubtful to him. He had written out various speeches and memoranda for speeches, but he had begun to perceive that Mr. Brooke's mind, if it had the burthen of remembering any train of thought, would let it drop, run away in search of it, and not easily come back again. To collect documents is one mode of serving your country, and to remember the contents of a document is another. No! the only way in which Mr. Brooke could be coerced into thinking of the right arguments at the right time was to be well plied with them till they took up all the room in his brain. But here there was the difficulty of finding room, so many things having been taken in beforehand. Mr. Brooke himself observed that his ideas stood rather in his way when he was speaking.

However, Ladislaw's coaching was forthwith to be put to the test, for before the day of nomination Mr. Brooke was to explain himself to the worthy electors of Middlemarch from the balcony of the White Hart, which looked out advantageously at an angle of the market-place, commanding a large area in front and two converging streets. It was a fine May morning and everything seemed hopeful: there was some prospect of an understanding between Bagster's committee and Brooke's, to which Mr. Bulstrode, Mr. Standish as a Liberal lawyer, and such manufacturers as Mr. Plymdale and Mr. Vincy, gave a solidity which almost counterbalanced Mr. Hawley and his associates who sat for Pinkerton at the Green Dragon. Mr. Brooke, conscious of having weakened the blasts of the "Trumpet" against him, by his reforms as a landlord in the last half year, and hearing himself cheered a little as he drove into the town, felt his heart tolerably light under his buff-coloured waistcoat. But with regard to critical occasions, it often happens that all moments seem comfortably remote until the last.

"This looks well, eh?" said Mr. Brooke as the crowd gathered. "I shall have a good audience, at any rate. I like this, now— this kind of public made up of one's own neighbours, you know."

The weavers and tanners of Middlemarch, unlike Mr. Mawmsey, had never thought of Mr. Brooke as a neighbour, and were not more attached to him than if he had been sent in a box from London. But they listened without much disturbance to the speakers who introduced the candidate, though one of them— a political personage from Brassing, who came to tell Middlemarch its duty—spoke so fully, that it was alarming to think what the candidate could find to say after him. Meanwhile the crowd became denser, and as the political personage neared the end of his speech, Mr. Brooke felt a remarkable change in his sensations while he still handled his eye-glass, trifled with documents before him, and exchanged remarks with his committee, as a man to whom the moment of summons was indifferent.

"I'll take another glass of sherry, Ladislaw," he said, with an easy air, to Will, who was close behind him, and presently handed him the supposed fortifier. It was ill-chosen; for Mr. Brooke was an abstemious man, and to drink a second glass of sherry quickly at no great interval from the first was a surprise to his system which tended to scatter his energies instead of collecting them. Pray pity him: so many English gentlemen make themselves miserable by speechifying on entirely private grounds! whereas Mr. Brooke wished to serve his country by standing for Parliament—which, indeed, may also be done on private grounds, but being once undertaken does absolutely demand some speechifying.

It was not about the beginning of his speech that Mr. Brooke was at all anxious; this, he felt sure, would be all right; he should have it quite pat, cut out as neatly as a set of couplets from Pope. Embarking would be easy, but the vision of open sea that might come after was alarming. "And questions, now," hinted the demon just waking up in his stomach, "somebody may put questions about the schedules—Ladislaw," he continued, aloud, "just hand me the memorandum of the schedules."

When Mr. Brooke presented himself on the balcony, the cheers were quite loud enough to counterbalance the yells, groans, brayings, and other expressions of adverse theory, which were so moderate that Mr. Standish (decidedly an old bird) observed in the ear next to him, "This looks dangerous, by God! Hawley has got some deeper plan than this." Still, the cheers were exhilarating, and no candidate could look more amiable than Mr. Brooke, with the memorandum in his breast-pocket, his left hand on the rail of the balcony, and his right trifling with his eye-glass. The striking points in his appearance were his buff waistcoat, short-clipped blond hair, and neutral physiognomy. He began with some confidence.

"Gentlemen—Electors of Middlemarch!"

This was so much the right thing that a little pause after it seemed natural.

"I'm uncommonly glad to be here—I was never so proud and happy in my life—never so happy, you know."

This was a bold figure of speech, but not exactly the right thing; for, unhappily, the pat opening had slipped away— even couplets from Pope may be but "fallings from us, vanishings," when fear clutches us, and a glass of sherry is hurrying like smoke among our ideas. Ladislaw, who stood at the window behind the speaker, thought, "It's all up now. The only chance is that since the best thing won't always do floundering may answer for once." Mr. Brooke, meanwhile, having lost other clues, fell back on himself and his qualifications—always an appropriate graceful subject for a candidate.

"I am a close neighbour of yours, my good friends—you've known me on the bench a good while—I've always gone a good deal into public questions—machinery, now, and machine-breaking—you're many of you concerned with machinery, and I've been going into that lately. It won't do, you know, break-ing machines: everything must go on—trade, manufactures, commerce, interchange of staples—that kind of thing—since Adam Smith, that must go on. We must look all over the globe :—'Observation with extensive view,' must look every-where, 'from China to Peru,' as somebody says—Johnson, I think, 'The Rambler,' you know. That is what I have done up to a certain point—not as far as Peru ; but I've not always stayed at home—I saw it wouldn't do. I've been in the Levant, where some of your Middlemarch goods go—and then, again, in the Baltic. The Baltic, now."

Plying among his recollections in this way, Mr. Brooke might have got along, easily to himself, and would have come back from the remotest seas without trouble ; but a diabolical procedure had been set up by the enemy. At one and the same moment there had risen above the shoulders of the crowd, nearly opposite Mr. Brooke, and within ten yards of him, the effigy of himself ; buff-coloured waistcoat, eye-glass, and neutral physiognomy, painted on rag ; and there had arisen apparently in the air, like the note of the cuckoo, a parrot-like, Punch-voiced echo of his words. Everybody looked up at the open windows in the houses at the opposite angles of the converging streets ; but they were either blank, or filled by laughing listeners. The most innocent echo has an impish mockery in it when it follows a gravely persistent speaker, and this echo was not at all innocent ; if it did not follow with the precision of a natural echo, it had a wicked choice of the words it overtook. By the time it said, "The Baltic, now," the laugh which had been running through the audience became a general shout, and but for the sobering effects of party and that great public cause which the entanglement of things had identified with "Brooke of Tipton," the laugh might have caught his committee. Mr. Bulstrode asked, reprehensively, what the new police was doing ; but a voice could not well be collared, and an attack on the effigy of the candidate would have been too equivocal since Hawley probably meant it to be pelted.

Mr. Brooke himself was not in a position to be quickly conscious of anything except a general slipping away of ideas within himself : he had even a little singing in the ears, and he was the only person who had not yet taken distinct account of the echo or discerned the image of himself. Few things hold the perceptions more thoroughly captive than anxiety about what we have got to say. Mr. Brooke heard the laughter ; but he had expected some Tory efforts at disturbance, and he was at this moment additionally excited by the tickling, stinging sense that his lost exordium was coming back to fetch him from the Baltic.

" That reminds me," he went on, thrusting a hand into his side-pocket, with an easy air, " if I wanted a precedent, you know—but we never want a precedent for the right thing—but there is Chatham, now ; I can't say I should have supported Chatham, or Pitt, the younger Pitt—he was not a man of ideas, and we want ideas, you know."

" Blast your ideas ! we want the Bill," said a loud rough voice from the crowd below.

Immediately the invisible Punch, who had hitherto followed Mr. Brooke, repeated, " Blast your ideas ! we want the Bill." The laugh was louder than ever, and for the first time Mr. Brooke, being himself silent, heard distinctly the mocking echo. But it seemed to ridicule his interrupter, and in that light was encouraging ; so he replied with amenity—

" There is something in what you say, my good friend, and what do we meet for but to speak our minds—freedom of opinion, freedom of the press, liberty—that kind of thing ? The Bill, now—you shall have the Bill "—here Mr. Brooke paused a moment to fix on his eye-glass and take the paper from his breast-pocket, with a sense of being practical and coming to particulars. The invisible Punch followed :—

" You shall have the Bill, Mr. Brooke, per electioneering contest, and a seat outside Parliament as delivered, five thousand pounds, seven shillings, and fourpence."

Mr. Brooke, amid the roars of laughter, turned red, let his eye-glass fall, and looking about him confusedly, saw the image of himself, which had come nearer. The next moment he saw it dolorously bespattered with eggs. His spirit rose a little, and his voice too.

" Buffoonery, tricks, ridicule the test of truth—all that is very well "—here an unpleasant egg broke on Mr. Brooke's shoulder, as the echo said, " All that is very well ; " then came a hail of eggs, chiefly aimed at the image, but occasionally hitting the original, as if by chance. There was a stream of new men pushing among the crowd; whistles, yells, bellowings, and fifes made all the greater hubbub because there was shouting and struggling to put them down. No voice would have had wing enough to rise above the uproar, and Mr. Brooke, disagreeably anointed, stood his ground no longer. The frustration would have been less exasperating if it had been less gamesome and boyish: a serious assault of which the newspaper reporter "can aver that it endangered the learned gentleman's ribs," or can respectfully bear witness to "the soles of that gentleman's boots having been visible above the railing," has perhaps more consolations attached to it.

Mr. Brooke re-entered the committee-room, saying, as carelessly as he could, "This is a little too bad, you know. I should have got the ear of the people by-and-by—but they didn't give me time. I should have gone into the Bill by-and-by, you know," he added, glancing at Ladislaw. "However, things will come all right at the nomination."

But it was not resolved unanimously that things would come right; on the contrary, the committee looked rather grim, and the political personage from Brassing was writing busily, as if he were brewing new devices.

"It was Bowyer who did it," said Mr. Standish, evasively. "I know it as well as if he had been advertised. He's uncommonly good at ventriloquism, and he did it uncommonly well, by God! Hawley has been having him to dinner lately: there's a fund of talent in Bowyer."

"Well, you know, you never mentioned him to me, Standish, else I would have invited him to dine," said poor Mr. Brooke, who had gone through a great deal of inviting for the good of his country.

"There's not a more paltry fellow in Middlemarch than Bowyer," said Ladislaw, indignantly, "but it seems as if the paltry fellows were always to turn the scale."

Will was thoroughly out of temper with himself as well as with his "principal," and he went to shut himself in his rooms with a half-formed resolve to throw up the "Pioneer" and Mr. Brooke together. Why should he stay? If the impassable gulf between himself and Dorothea were ever to be filled up, it must rather be by his going away and getting into a thoroughly different position than by staying here and slipping into deserved contempt as an understrapper of Brooke's. Then came the young dream of wonders that he might do—in five years, for example : political writing, political speaking, would get a higher value now public life was going to be wider and more national, and they might give him such distinction that he would not seem to be asking Dorothea to step down to him. Five years :—if he could only be sure that she cared for him more than for others ; if he could only make her aware that he stood aloof until he could tell his love without lowering himself —then he could go away easily, and begin a career which at five-and-twenty seemed probable enough in the inward order of things, where talent brings fame, and fame everything else which is delightful. He could speak and he could write ; he could master any subject if he chose, and he meant always to take the side of reason and justice, on which he would carry all his ardour. Why should he not one day be lifted above the shoulders of the crowd, and feel that he had won that eminence well ? Without doubt he would leave Middlemarch, go to town, and make himself fit for celebrity by " eating his dinners."

But not immediately : not until some kind of sign had passed between him and Dorothea. He could not be satisfied until she knew why, even if he were the man she would choose to marry, he would not marry her. Hence he must keep his post and bear with Mr. Brooke a little longer.

But he soon had reason to suspect that Mr. Brooke had anticipated him in the wish to break up their connection. Deputations without and voices within had concurred in inducing that philanthropist to take a stronger measure than usual for the good of mankind ; namely, to withdraw in favour of another candidate, to whom he left the advantages of his canvassing machinery. He himself called this a strong measure, but observed that his health was less capable of sustaining excitement than he had imagined.

" I have felt uneasy about the chest—it won't do to carry that too far," he said to Ladislaw in explaining the affair. " I must pull up. Poor Casaubon was a warning, you know. I've made some heavy advances, but I've dug a channel. It's rather coarse work—this electioneering, eh, Ladislaw ? I daresay you are tired of it. However, we have dug a channel with the ' Pioneer '—put things in a track, and so on. A more ordinary man than you might carry it on now—more ordinary, you know."

" Do you wish me to give it up ? " said Will, the quick colour coming in his face, as he rose from the writing-table, and took a turn of three steps with his hands in his pockets. " I am ready to do so whenever you wish it."

" As to wishing, my dear Ladislaw, I have the highest opinion of your powers, you know. But about the ' Pioneer ' I have been consulting a little with some of the men on our side, and they are inclined to take it into their hands—indemnify me to a certain extent—carry it on, in fact. And under the circumstances, you might like to give up—might find a better field. These people might not take that high view of you which I have always taken, as an *alter ego*, a right hand—though I always looked forward to your doing something else. I think of having a run into France. But I'll write you any letters, you know— to Althorpe and people of that kind. I've met Althorpe."

" I am exceedingly obliged to you," said Ladislaw, proudly. " Since you are going to part with the ' Pioneer,' I need not trouble you about the steps I shall take. I may choose to continue here for the present."

After Mr. Brooke had left him Will said to himself, " The rest of the family have been urging him to get rid of me, and he doesn't care now about my going. I shall stay as long as I like. I shall go of my own movement, and not because they are afraid of me."

CHAPTER LII

" His heart
The lowliest duties on itself did lay."
—WORDSWORTH.

ON that June evening when Mr. Farebrother knew that he was to have the Lowick living, there was joy in the old-fashioned parlour, and even the portraits of the great lawyers seemed to look on with satisfaction. His mother left her tea and toast untouched, but sat with her usual pretty primness, only showing her emotion by that flush in the cheeks and brightness in the eyes which give an old woman a touching momentary identity with her far-off youthful self, and saying decisively—

" The greatest comfort, Camden, is that you have deserved it."

" When a man gets a good berth, mother, half the deserving must come after," said the son, brimful of pleasure, and not trying to conceal it. The gladness in his face was of that active kind which seems to have energy enough not only to flash out—

wardly, but to light up busy vision within : one seemed to see thoughts, as well as delight, in his glances.

"Now, aunt," he went on, rubbing his hands and looking at Miss Noble, who was making tender little beaver-like noises, "there shall be sugar-candy always on the table for you to steal and give to the children, and you shall have a great many new stockings to make presents of, and you shall darn your own more than ever ! "

Miss Noble nodded at her nephew with a subdued half-frightened laugh, conscious of having already dropped an additional lump of sugar into her basket on the strength of the new preferment.

"As for you, Winny "—the Vicar went on—"I shall make no difficulty about your marrying any Lowick bachelor—Mr. Solomon Featherstone, for example, as soon as I find you are in love with him."

Miss Winifred, who had been looking at her brother all the while and crying heartily, which was her way of rejoicing, smiled through her tears and said, "You must set me the example, Cam : *you* must marry now."

"With all my heart. But who is in love with me ? I am a seedy old fellow," said the Vicar, rising, pushing his chair away and looking down at himself. "What do you say, mother ? "

"You are a handsome man, Camden : though not so fine a figure of a man as your father," said the old lady.

"I wish you would marry Miss Garth, brother," said Miss Winifred. "She would make us so lively at Lowick."

"Very fine ! You talk as if young women were tied up to be chosen, like poultry at market ; as if I had only to ask and everybody would have me," said the Vicar, not caring to specify.

"We don't want everybody," said Miss Winifred. "But *you* would like Miss Garth, mother, shouldn't you ? "

"My son's choice shall be mine," said Mrs. Farebrother, with majestic discretion, "and a wife would be most welcome, Camden. You will want your whist at home when we go to Lowick, and Henrietta Noble never was a whist-player." (Mrs. Farebrother always called her tiny old sister by that magnificent name.)

"I shall do without whist now, mother."

"Why so, Camden ? In my time whist was thought an undeniable amusement for a good churchman," said Mrs. Farebrother, innocent of the meaning that whist had for her son, and speaking rather sharply, as at some dangerous countenancing of new doctrine.

"I shall be too busy for whist ; I shall have two parishes," said the Vicar, preferring not to discuss the virtues of that game.

He had already said to Dorothea, "I don't feel bound to give up St. Botolph's. It is protest enough against the pluralism they want to reform if I give somebody else most of the money. The stronger thing is not to give up power, but to use it well."

"I have thought of that," said Dorothea. "So far as self is concerned, I think it would be easier to give up power and money than to keep them. It seems very unfitting that I should have this patronage, yet I felt that I ought not to let it be used by some one else instead of me."

"It is I who am bound to act so that you will not regret your power," said Mr. Farebrother.

His was one of the natures in which conscience gets the more active when the yoke of life ceases to gall them. He made no display of humility on the subject, but in his heart he felt rather ashamed that his conduct had shown laches which others who did not get benefices were free from.

"I used often to wish I had been something else than a clergyman," he said to Lydgate, "but perhaps it will be better to try and make as good a clergyman out of myself as I can. That is the well-beneficed point of view, you perceive, from which difficulties are much simplified," he ended, smiling.

The Vicar did feel then as if his share of duties would be easy. But Duty has a trick of behaving unexpectedly—something like a heavy friend whom we have amiably asked to visit us, and who breaks his leg within our gates.

Hardly a week later, Duty presented itself in his study under the disguise of Fred Vincy, now returned from Omnibus College with his bachelor's degree.

"I am ashamed to trouble you, Mr. Farebrother," said Fred, whose fair open face was propitiating, "but you are the only friend I can consult. I told you everything once before, and you were so good that I can't help coming to you again."

"Sit down, Fred, I'm ready to hear and do anything I can," said the Vicar, who was busy packing some small objects for removal, and went on with his work.

"I wanted to tell you——" Fred hesitated an instant and then went on plungingly, "I might go into the Church now ; and really, look where I may, I can't see anything else to do.

I don't like it, but I know it's uncommonly hard on my father to say so, after he has spent a good deal of money in educating me for it." Fred paused again an instant, and then repeated, " and I can't see anything else to do."

" I did talk to your father about it, Fred, but I made little way with him. He said it was too late. But you have got over one bridge now : what are your other difficulties ? "

" Merely that I don't like it. I don't like divinity, and preaching, and feeling obliged to look serious. I like riding across country, and doing as other men do. I don't mean that I want to be a bad fellow in any way ; but I've no taste for the sort of thing people expect of a clergyman. And yet what else am I to do ? My father can't spare me any capital, else I might go into farming. And he has no room for me in his trade. And of course I can't begin to study for law or physic now, when my father wants me to earn something. It's all very well to say I'm wrong to go into the Church ; but those who say so might as well tell me to go into the backwoods."

Fred's voice had taken a tone of grumbling remonstrance, and Mr. Farebrother might have been inclined to smile if his mind had not been too busy in imagining more than Fred told him.

" Have you any difficulties about doctrines—about the Articles ? " he said, trying hard to think of the question simply for Fred's sake.

" No ; I suppose the Articles are right. I am not prepared with any arguments to disprove them, and much better, cleverer fellows than I am go in for them entirely. I think it would be rather ridiculous in me to urge scruples of that sort, as if I were a judge," said Fred, quite simply.

" I suppose, then, it has occurred to you that you might be a fair parish priest without being much of a divine ? "

" Of course, if I am obliged to be a clergyman, I shall try and do my duty, though I mayn't like it. Do you think anybody ought to blame me ? "

" For going into the Church under the circumstances ? That depends on your conscience, Fred—how far you have counted the cost, and seen what your position will require of you. I can only tell you about myself, that I have always been too lax, and have been uneasy in consequence."

" But there is another hindrance," said Fred, colouring. " I did not tell you before, though perhaps I may have said things that made you guess it. There is somebody I am very fond of : I have loved her ever since we were children."

" Miss Garth, I suppose ? " said the Vicar, examining some labels very closely.

" Yes. I shouldn't mind anything if she would have me. And I know I could be a good fellow then."

" And you think she returns the feeling ? "

" She never will say so ; and a good while ago she made me promise not to speak to her about it again. And she has set her mind especially against my being a clergyman ; I know that. But I can't give her up. I do think she cares about me. I saw Mrs. Garth last night and she said that Mary was staying at Lowick Rectory with Miss Farebrother."

" Yes, she is very kindly helping my sister. Do you wish to go there ? "

" No, I want to ask a great favour of you. I am ashamed to bother you in this way ; but Mary might listen to what you said, if you mentioned the subject to her—I mean about my going into the Church."

" That is rather a delicate task, my dear Fred. I shall have to presuppose your attachment to her ; and to enter on the subject as you wish me to do, will be asking her to tell me whether she returns it."

" That is what I want her to tell you," said Fred, bluntly. " I don't know what to do, unless I can get at her feeling."

" You mean that you would be guided by that as to your going into the Church ? "

" If Mary said she would never have me I might as well go wrong in one way as another."

" That is nonsense, Fred. Men outlive their love, but they don't outlive the consequences of their recklessness."

" Not my sort of love : I have never been without loving Mary. If I had to give her up, it would be like beginning to live on wooden legs."

" Will she not be hurt at my intrusion ? "

" No, I feel sure she will not. She respects you more than any one, and she would not put you off with fun as she does me. Of course I could not have told any one else, or asked any one else to speak to her, but you. There is no one else who could be such a friend to both of us." Fred paused a moment, and then said, rather complainingly, " And she ought to acknowledge that I have worked in order to pass. She ought to believe that I would exert myself for her sake."

There was a moment's silence before Mr. Farebrother laid down his work, and putting out his hand to Fred said—

" Very well, my boy. I will do what you wish."

That very day Mr. Farebrother went to Lowick parsonage on the nag which he had just set up. " Decidedly I am an old stalk," he thought, " the young growths are pushing me aside."

He found Mary in the garden gathering roses and sprinkling the petals on a sheet. The sun was low, and tall trees sent their shadows across the grassy walks where Mary was moving without bonnet or parasol. She did not observe Mr. Farebrother's approach along the grass, and had just stooped down to lecture a small black-and-tan terrier, which would persist in walking on the sheet and smelling at the rose-leaves as Mary sprinkled them. She took his forepaws in one hand, and lifted up the forefinger of the other, while the dog wrinkled his brows and looked embarrassed. " Fly, Fly, I am ashamed of you," Mary was saying in a grave contralto. " This is not becoming in a sensible dog ; anybody would think you were a silly young gentleman."

" You are unmerciful to young gentlemen, Miss Garth," said the Vicar, within two yards of her.

Mary started up and blushed. " It always answers to reason with Fly," she said, laughingly.

" But not with young gentlemen ? "

" Oh, with some, I suppose ; since some of them turn into excellent men."

" I am glad of that admission, because I want at this very moment to interest you in a young gentleman."

" Not a silly one, I hope," said Mary, beginning to pluck the roses again, and feeling her heart beat uncomfortably.

" No ; though perhaps wisdom is not his strong point, but rather affection and sincerity. However, wisdom lies more in those two qualities than people are apt to imagine. I hope you know by those marks what young gentleman I mean."

" Yes, I think I do," said Mary, bravely, her face getting more serious, and her hands cold ; " it must be Fred Vincy."

" He has asked me to consult you about his going into the Church. I hope you will not think that I consented to take a liberty in promising to do so."

" On the contrary, Mr. Farebrother," said Mary, giving up the roses, and folding her arms, but unable to look up, " when-ever you have anything to say to me I feel honoured."

" But before I enter on that question, let me just touch a point on which your father took me into confidence ; by the way, it was that very evening on which I once before fulfilled a mission from

Fred, just after he had gone to college. Mr. Garth told me what happened on the night of Featherstone's death—how you refused to burn the will; and he said that you had some heart-prickings on that subject, because you had been the innocent means of hindering Fred from getting his ten thousand pounds. I have kept that in mind, and I have heard something that may relieve you on that score—may show you that no sin-offering is demanded from you there."

Mr. Farebrother paused a moment and looked at Mary. He meant to give Fred his full advantage, but it would be well, he thought, to clear her mind of any superstitions, such as women sometimes follow when they do a man the wrong of marrying him as an act of atonement. Mary's cheeks had begun to burn a little, and she was mute.

" I mean, that your action made no real difference to Fred's lot. I find that the first will would not have been legally good after the burning of the last; it would not have stood if it had been disputed, and you may be sure it would have been disputed. So, on that score, you may feel your mind free."

"Thank you, Mr. Farebrother," said Mary, earnestly. " I am grateful to you for remembering my feelings."

" Well, now I may go on. Fred, you know, has taken his degree. He has worked his way so far, and now the question is, what is he to do ? That question is so difficult that he is inclined to follow his father's wishes and enter the Church, though you know better than I do that he was quite set against that formerly. I have questioned him on the subject and I confess I see no insuperable objection to his being a clergyman, as things go. He says that he could turn his mind to doing his best in that vocation, on one condition. If that condition were fulfilled I would do my utmost in helping Fred on. After a time—not, of course, at first—he might be with me as my curate, and he would have so much to do that his stipend would be nearly what I used to get as vicar. But I repeat that there is a condition without which all this good cannot come to pass. He has opened his heart to me, Miss Garth, and asked me to plead for him. The condition lies entirely in your feeling."

Mary looked so much moved, that he said after a moment, " Let us walk a little ; " and when they were walking he added, " To speak quite plainly, Fred will not take any course which would lessen the chance that you would consent to be his wife ; but with that prospect, he will try his best at anything you approve."

"I cannot possibly say that I will ever be his wife, Mr. Farebrother : but I certainly never will be his wife if he becomes a clergyman. What you say is most generous and kind ; I don't mean for a moment to correct your judgment. It is only that I have my girlish, mocking way of looking at things," said Mary, with a returning sparkle of playfulness in her answer which only made its modesty more charming.

"He wishes me to report exactly what you think," said Mr. Farebrother.

"I could not love a man who is ridiculous," said Mary, not choosing to go deeper. "Fred has sense and knowledge enough to make him respectable, if he likes, in some good worldly business, but I can never imagine him preaching and exhorting and pronouncing blessings, and praying by the sick, without feeling as if I were looking at a caricature. His being a clergyman would be only for gentility's sake, and I think there is nothing more contemptible than such imbecile gentility. I used to think that of Mr. Crowse, with his empty face and neat umbrella, and mincing little speeches. What right have such men to represent Christianity—as if it were an institution for getting up idiots genteelly—as if——" Mary checked herself. She had been carried along as if she had been speaking to Fred instead of Mr. Farebrother.

"Young women are severe ; they don't feel the stress of action as men do, though perhaps I ought to make you an exception there. But you don't put Fred Vincy on so low a level as that ? "

"No, indeed ; he has plenty of sense, but I think he would not show it as a clergyman. He would be a piece of professional affectation."

"Then the answer is quite decided. As a clergyman he could have no hope ? "

Mary shook her head.

"But if he braved all the difficulties of getting his bread in some other way—will you give him the support of hope ? May he count on winning you ? "

"I think Fred ought not to need telling again what I have already said to him," Mary answered, with a slight resentment in her manner. "I mean that he ought not to put such questions until he has done something worthy, instead of saying that he could do it."

Mr. Farebrother was silent for a minute or more, and then, as they turned and paused under the shadow of a maple at the end of a grassy walk, said, " I understand that you resist any attempt to fetter you, but either your feeling for Fred Vincy excludes your entertaining another attachment, or it does not : either he may count on your remaining single until he shall have earned your hand, or he may in any case be disappointed. Pardon me, Mary—you know I used to catechise you under that name—but when the state of a woman's affections touches the happiness of another life—of more lives than one—I think it would be the nobler course for her to be perfectly direct and open."

Mary in her turn was silent, wondering not at Mr. Farebrother's manner but at his tone, which had a grave restrained emotion in it. When the strange idea flashed across her that his words had reference to himself, she was incredulous and ashamed of entertaining it. She had never thought that any man could love her except Fred, who had espoused her with the umbrella ring, when she wore socks and little strapped shoes ; still less that she could be of any importance to Mr. Farebrother, the cleverest man in her narrow circle. She had only time to feel that all this was hazy and perhaps illusory ; but one thing was clear and determined—her answer.

" Since you think it my duty, Mr. Farebrother, I will tell you that I have too strong a feeling for Fred to give him up for any one else. I should never be quite happy if I thought he was unhappy for the loss of me. It has taken such deep root in me—my gratitude to him for always loving me best, and minding so much if I hurt myself, from the time when we were very little. I cannot imagine any new feeling coming to make that weaker. I should like better than anything to see him worthy of every one's respect. But please tell him I will not promise to marry him till then ; I should shame and grieve my father and mother. He is free to choose some one else."

" Then I have fulfilled my commission thoroughly," said Mr. Farebrother, putting out his hand to Mary, " and I shall ride back to Middlemarch forthwith. With this prospect before him, we shall get Fred into the right niche somehow, and I hope I shall live to join your hands. God bless you ! "

" Oh, please stay, and let me give you some tea," said Mary. Her eyes filled with tears, for something indefinable, something like the resolute suppression of a pain in Mr. Farebrother's manner, made her feel suddenly miserable, as she had once felt when she saw her father's hands trembling in a moment of trouble.

" No, my dear, no. I must get back."

In three minutes the Vicar was on horseback again, having gone magnanimously through a duty much harder than the renunciation of whist, or even than the writing of penitential meditations.

CHAPTER LIII

It is but a shallow haste which concludeth insincerity from what outsiders call inconsistency—putting a dead mechanism of " ifs " and " therefores " for the living myriad of hidden suckers whereby the belief and the conduct are wrought into mutual sustainment.

MR. BULSTRODE, when he was hoping to acquire a new interest in Lowick, had naturally had an especial wish that the new clergyman should be one whom he thoroughly approved ; and he believed it to be a chastisement and admonition directed to his own shortcomings and those of the nation at large, that just about the time when he came in possession of the deeds which made him the proprietor of Stone Court, Mr. Farebrother " read himself " into the quaint little church and preached his first sermon to the congregation of farmers, labourers, and village artisans. It was not that Mr. Bulstrode intended to frequent Lowick Church or to reside at Stone Court for a good while to come : he had bought the excellent farm and fine homestead simply as a retreat which he might gradually enlarge as to the land and beautify as to the dwelling, until it should be conducive to the divine glory that he should enter on it as a residence, partially withdrawing from his present exertions in the administration of business, and throwing more conspicuously on the side of Gospel truth the weight of local landed proprietorship, which Providence might increase by unforeseen occasions of purchase. A strong leading in this direction seemed to have been given in the surprising facility of getting Stone Court, when every one had expected that Mr. Rigg Featherstone would have clung to it as the Garden of Eden. That was what poor old Peter himself had expected ; having often, in imagination, looked up through the sods above him, and, unobstructed by perspective, seen his frog-faced legatee enjoying the fine old place to the perpetual surprise and disappointment of other survivors.

But how little we know what would make paradise for our neighbours ! We judge from our own desires, and our neighbours themselves are not always open enough even to throw out a hint of theirs. The cool and judicious Joshua Rigg had not allowed his parent to perceive that Stone Court was anything less than the chief good in his estimation, and he had certainly wished to call it his own. But as Warren Hastings looked at gold and thought of buying Daylesford, so Joshua Rigg looked at Stone Court and thought of buying gold. He had a very distinct and intense vision of his chief good, the vigorous greed which he had inherited having taken a special form by dint of circumstance : and his chief good was to be a money-changer. From his earliest employment as an errand-boy in a seaport, he had looked through the windows of the money-changers as other boys look through the windows of the pastry-cooks ; the fascination had wrought itself gradually into a deep special passion ; he meant, when he had property, to do many things, one of them being to marry a genteel young person ; but these were all accidents and joys that imagination could dispense with. The one joy after which his soul thirsted was to have a money-changer's shop on a much-frequented quay, to have locks all round him of which he held the keys, and to look sublimely cool as he handled the breeding coins of all nations, while helpless Cupidity looked at him enviously from the other side of an iron lattice. The strength of that passion had been a power enabling him to master all the knowledge necessary to gratify it. And when others were thinking that he had settled at Stone Court for life, Joshua himself was thinking that the moment now was not far off when he should settle on the North Quay with the best appointments in safes and locks.

Enough. We are concerned with looking at Joshua Rigg's sale of his land from Mr. Bulstrode's point of view, and he interpreted it as a cheering dispensation conveying perhaps a sanction to a purpose which he had for some time entertained without external encouragement ; he interpreted it thus, but not too confidently, offering up his thanksgiving in guarded phraseology. His doubts did not arise from the possible relations of the event to Joshua Rigg's destiny, which belonged to the unmapped regions not taken under the providential government, except perhaps in an imperfect colonial way ; but they arose from reflecting that this dispensation too might be a chastisement for himself, as Mr. Farebrother's induction to the living clearly was.

This was not what Mr. Bulstrode said to any man for the sake of deceiving him : it was what he said to himself—it was as genuinely his mode of explaining events as any theory of yours may be, if you happen to disagree with him. For the egoism which enters into our theories does not affect their sincerity; rather, the more our egoism is satisfied, the more robust is our belief.

However, whether for sanction or for chastisement, Mr. Bulstrode, hardly fifteen months after the death of Peter Featherstone, had become the proprietor of Stone Court, and what Peter would say " if he were worthy to know," had become an inexhaustible and consolatory subject of conversation to his disappointed relatives. The tables were now turned on that dear brother departed, and to contemplate the frustration of his cunning by the superior cunning of things in general was a cud of delight to Solomon. Mrs. Waule had a melancholy triumph in the proof that it did not answer to make false Featherstones and cut off the genuine ; and Sister Martha receiving the news in the Chalky Flats said, " Dear, dear ! then the Almighty could have been none so pleased with the alms-houses after all."

Affectionate Mrs. Bulstrode was particularly glad of the advantage which her husband's health was likely to get from the purchase of Stone Court. Few days passed without his riding thither and looking over some part of the farm with the bailiff, and the evenings were delicious in that quiet spot, when the new hay-ricks lately set up were sending forth odours to mingle with the breath of the rich old garden. One evening, while the sun was still above the horizon and burning in golden lamps among the great walnut boughs, Mr. Bulstrode was pausing on horseback outside the front gate waiting for Caleb Garth, who had met him by appointment to give an opinion on a question of stable drainage, and was now advising the bailiff in the rick-yard.

Mr. Bulstrode was conscious of being in a good spiritual frame and more than usually serene, under the influence of his innocent recreation. He was doctrinally convinced that there was a total absence of merit in himself ; but that doctrinal conviction may be held without pain when the sense of demerit does not take a distinct shape in memory and revive the tingling of shame or the pang of remorse. Nay, it may be held with intense satisfaction when the depth of our sinning is but a measure for the depth of forgiveness, and a clenching proof that we are peculiar instruments of the divine intention. The memory has as many moods as the temper, and shifts its scenery like a diorama. At this moment Mr. Bulstrode felt as if the sunshine were all one with that of far-off evenings when he was a very young man and used to go out preaching beyond Highbury. And he would willingly have had that service of exhortation in prospect now. The texts were there still, and so was his own facility in expounding them. His brief reverie was interrupted by the return of Caleb Garth, who also was on horseback, and was just shaking his bridle before starting, when he exclaimed—

" Bless my heart ! what's this fellow in black coming along the lane ? He's like one of those men one sees about after the races." Mr. Bulstrode turned his horse and looked along the lane, but made no reply. The comer was our slight acquaintance Mr. Raffles, whose appearance presented no other change than such as was due to a suit of black and a crape hat-band. He was within three yards of the horsemen now, and they could see the flash of recognition in his face as he whirled his stick upward, looking all the while at Mr. Bulstrode, and at last exclaiming :—

" By Jove, Nick, it's you ! I couldn't be mistaken, though the five-and-twenty years have played old Boguy with us both ! How are you, eh ? you didn't expect to see *me* here. Come, shake us by the hand."

To say that Mr. Raffles' manner was rather excited would be only one mode of saying that it was evening. Caleb Garth could see that there was a moment of struggle and hesitation in Mr. Bulstrode, but it ended in his putting out his hand coldly to Raffles and saying—

" I did not indeed expect to see you in this remote country place."

" Well, it belongs to a stepson of mine," said Raffles, adjusting himself in a swaggering attitude. " I came to see him here before. I'm not so surprised at seeing you, old fellow, because I picked up a letter—what you may call a providential thing. It's uncommonly fortunate I met you, though ; for I don't care about seeing my stepson : he's not affectionate, and his poor mother's gone now. To tell the truth, I came out of love to you, Nick : I came to get your address, for—look here ! " Raffles drew a crumpled paper from his pocket.

Almost any other man than Caleb Garth might have been tempted to linger on the spot for the sake of hearing all he could about a man whose acquaintance with Bulstrode seemed to imply passages in the banker's life so unlike anything that was known of him in Middlemarch that they must have the nature of a secret to pique curiosity. But Caleb was peculiar : certain human tendencies which are commonly strong were almost

absent from his mind ; and one of these was curiosity about
personal affairs. Especially if there was anything discreditable
to be found out concerning another man, Caleb preferred not to
know it ; and if he had to tell anybody under him that his evil
doings were discovered, he was more embarrassed than the
culprit. He now spurred his horse, and saying, " I wish you
good evening, Mr. Bulstrode ; I must be getting home," set off
at a trot.

" You didn't put your full address to this letter," Raffles
continued. " That was not like the first-rate man of business
you used to be. ' The Shrubs,'—they may be anywhere : you
live near at hand, eh ?—have cut the London concern altogether—perhaps turned country squire—have a rural mansion
to invite me to. Lord, how many years it is ago ! The old lady
must have been dead a pretty long while—gone to glory without
the pain of knowing how poor her daughter was, eh ? But, by
Jove ! you're very pale and pasty, Nick. Come, if you're
going home, I'll walk by your side."

Mr. Bulstrode's usual paleness had in fact taken an almost
deathly hue. Five minutes before, the expanse of his life had
been submerged in its evening sunshine which shone backward
to its remembered morning : sin seemed to be a question of
doctrine and inward penitence, humiliation an exercise of the
closet, the bearing of his deeds a matter of private vision
adjusted solely by spiritual relations and conceptions of the
divine purposes. And now, as if by some hideous magic, this
loud red figure had risen before him in unmanageable solidity—
an incorporate past which had not entered into his imagination
of chastisements. But Mr. Bulstrode's thought was busy, and
he was not a man to act or speak rashly.

" I was going home," he said, " but I can defer my ride a little.
And you can, if you please, rest here."

" Thank you," said Raffles, making a grimace. " I don't care
now about seeing my stepson. I'd rather go home with you."

" Your stepson, if Mr. Rigg Featherstone was he, is here no
longer. I am master here now."

Raffles opened wide eyes, and gave a long whistle of surprise,
before he said, " Well, then, I've no objection. I've had enough
walking from the coach-road. I never was much of a walker,
or rider either. What I like is a smart vehicle and a spirited cob.
I was always a little heavy in the saddle. What a pleasant
surprise it must be to you to see me, old fellow ! " he continued,
as they turned towards the house. " You don't say so ; but

you never took your luck heartily—you were always thinking of improving the occasion—you'd such a gift for improving your luck."

Mr. Raffles seemed greatly to enjoy his own wit, and swung his leg in a swaggering manner which was rather too much for his companion's judicious patience.

"If I remember rightly," Mr. Bulstrode observed, with chill anger, "our acquaintance many years ago had not the sort of intimacy which you are now assuming, Mr. Raffles. Any services you desire of me will be the more readily rendered if you will avoid a tone of familiarity which did not lie in our former intercourse, and can hardly be warranted by more than twenty years of separation."

"You don't like being called Nick? Why, I always called you Nick in my heart, and though lost to sight, to memory dear. By Jove! my feelings have ripened for you like fine old cognac. I hope you've got some in the house now. Josh filled my flask well the last time."

Mr. Bulstrode had not yet fully learned that even the desire for cognac was not stronger in Raffles than the desire to torment, and that a hint of annoyance always served him as a fresh cue. But it was at least clear that further objection was useless, and Mr. Bulstrode, in giving orders to the housekeeper for the accommodation to the guest, had a resolute air of quietude.

There was the comfort of thinking that this housekeeper had been in the service of Rigg also, and might accept the idea that Mr. Bulstrode entertained Raffles merely as a friend of her former master. When there was food and drink spread before his visitor in the wainscoted parlour, and no witness in the room, Mr. Bulstrode said—

"Your habits and mine are so different, Mr. Raffles, that we can hardly enjoy each other's society. The wisest plan for both of us will therefore be to part as soon as possible. Since you say that you wished to meet me, you probably considered that you had some business to transact with me. But under the circumstances I will invite you to remain here for the night, and I will myself ride over here early to-morrow morning—before breakfast, in fact, when I can receive any communication you have to make to me."

"With all my heart," said Raffles; "this is a comfortable place—a little dull for a continuance; but I can put up with it for a night, with this good liquor and the prospect of seeing you again in the morning. You're a much better host than my stepson was; but Josh owed me a bit of a grudge for marrying his mother; and between you and me there was never anything but kindness."

Mr. Bulstrode, hoping that the peculiar mixture of joviality and sneering in Raffles' manner was a good deal the effect of drink, had determined to wait till he was quite sober before he spent more words upon him. But he rode home with a terribly lucid vision of the difficulty there would be in arranging any result that could be permanently counted on with this man. It was inevitable that he should wish to get rid of John Raffles, though his reappearance could not be regarded as lying outside the divine plan. The spirit of evil might have sent him to threaten Mr. Bulstrode's subversion as an instrument of good; but the threat must have been permitted, and was a chastisement of a new kind. It was an hour of anguish for him very different from the hours in which his struggle had been securely private, and which had ended with a sense that his secret misdeeds were pardoned and his services accepted. Those misdeeds, even when committed—had they not been half sanctified by the singleness of his desire to devote himself and all he possessed to the furtherance of the divine scheme? And was he after all to become a mere stone of stumbling and a rock of offence? For who would understand the work within him? Who would not, when there was the pretext of casting disgrace upon him, confound his whole life and the truths he had espoused in one heap of obliquy?

In his closest meditations the life-long habit of Mr. Bulstrode's mind clad his most egoistic terrors in doctrinal references to superhuman ends. But even while we are talking and meditating about the earth's orbit and the solar system, what we feel and adjust our movements to is the stable earth and the changing day. And now within all the automatic succession of theoretic phrases—distinct and inmost as the shiver and the ache of oncoming fever when we are discussing abstract pain—was the forecast of disgrace in the presence of his neighbours and of his own wife. For the pain, as well as the public estimate of disgrace, depends on the amount of previous profession. To men who only aim at escaping felony, nothing short of the prisoner's dock is disgrace. But Mr. Bulstrode had aimed at being an eminent Christian.

It was not more than half-past seven in the morning when he again reached Stone Court. The fine old place never looked more like a delightful home than at that moment; the great white lilies were in flower, the nasturtiums, their pretty leaves all silvered with dew, were running away over the low stone wall; the very noises all around had a heart of peace within them. But everything was spoiled for the owner as he walked on the gravel in front and awaited the descent of Mr. Raffles, with whom he was condemned to breakfast.

It was not long before they were seated together in the wains-coated parlour over their tea and toast, which was as much as Raffles cared to take at that early hour. The difference between his morning and evening self was not so great as his companion had imagined that it might be; the delight in tormenting was perhaps even the stronger because his spirits were rather less highly pitched. Certainly his manners seemed more disagreeable by the morning light.

"As I have little time to spare, Mr. Raffles," said the banker, who could hardly do more than sip his tea and break his toast without eating it, "I shall be obliged if you will mention at once the ground on which you wished to meet with me. I presume that you have a home elsewhere and will be glad to return to it."

"Why, if a man has got any heart, doesn't he want to see an old friend, Nick?—I must call you Nick—we always did call you young Nick when we knew you meant to marry the old widow. Some said you had a handsome family likeness to old Nick, but that was your mother's fault, calling you Nicholas. Aren't you glad to see me again? I expected an invite to stay with you at some pretty place. My own establishment is broken up now my wife's dead. I've no particular attachment to any spot; I would as soon settle hereabout as anywhere."

"May I ask why you returned from America? I considered that the strong wish you expressed to go there, when an adequate sum was furnished, was tantamount to an engagement that you would remain there for life."

"Never knew that a wish to go to a place was the same thing as a wish to stay. But I did stay a matter of ten years; it didn't suit me to stay any longer. And I'm not going again, Nick." Here Mr. Raffles winked slowly as he looked as Mr. Bulstrode.

"Do you wish to be settled in any business? What is your calling now?"

"Thank you, my calling is to enjoy myself as much as I can. I don't care about working any more. If I did anything it would be a little travelling in the tobacco line—or something of that sort, which takes a man into agreeable company. But not without an independence to fall back upon. That's what I want : I'm not so strong as I was, Nick, though I've got more colour than you. I want an independence."

" That could be supplied to you, if you would engage to keep at a distance," said Mr. Bulstrode, perhaps with a little too much eagerness in his undertone.

" That must be as it suits my convenience," said Raffles, coolly. " I see no reason why I shouldn't make a few acquaintances hereabout. I'm not ashamed of myself as company for anybody. I dropped my portmanteau at the turnpike when I got down—change of linen—genuine—honour bright !—more than fronts and wristbands ; and with this suit of mourning, straps and everything, I should do you credit among the nobs here." Mr. Raffles had pushed away his chair and looked down at himself, particularly at his straps. His chief intention was to annoy Bulstrode, but he really thought that his appearance now would produce a good effect, and that he was not only handsome and witty, but clad in a mourning style which implied solid connections.

" If you intend to rely on me in any way, Mr. Raffles," said Bulstrode, after a moment's pause, " you will expect to meet my wishes."

" Ah, to be sure," said Raffles, with a mocking cordiality. " Didn't I always do it ? Lord, you made a pretty thing out of me, and I got but little. I've often thought since, I might have done better by telling the old woman that I'd found her daughter and her grandchild : it would have suited my feelings better ; I've got a soft place in my heart. But you've buried the old lady by this time, I suppose—it's all one to her now. And you've got your fortune out of that profitable business which had such a blessing on it. You've taken to being a nob, buying land, being a country bashaw. Still in the Dissenting line, eh ? Still godly ? Or taken to the Church as more genteel ? "

This time Mr. Raffles' slow wink and slight protrusion of his tongue was worse than a nightmare, because it held the certitude that it was not a nightmare, but a waking misery. Mr. Bulstrode felt a shuddering nausea, and did not speak, but was considering diligently whether he should not leave Raffles to do as he would, and simply defy him as a slanderer. The man would soon show himself disreputable enough to make people disbelieve him. " But not when he tells any ugly-looking truth about *you*," said discerning consciousness. And again : it seemed no wrong to keep Raffles at a distance, but Mr. Bulstrode shrank from the

direct falsehood of denying true statements. It was one thing
to look back on forgiven sins, nay, to explain questionable
conformity to lax customs, and another to enter deliberately
on the necessity of falsehood.

But since Bulstrode did not speak, Raffles ran on, by way of
using time to the utmost.

"I've not had such fine luck as you, by Jove! Things went
confoundedly with me in New York; those Yankees are cool
hands, and a man of gentlemanly feelings has no chance with
them. I married when I came back—a nice woman in the
tobacco trade—very fond of me—but the trade was restricted,
as we say. She had been settled there a good many years by
a friend; but there was a son too much in the case. Josh and
I never hit it off. However, I made the most of the position,
and I've always taken my glass in good company. It's been all
on the square with me; I'm as open as the day. You won't take
it ill of me that I didn't look you up before; I've got a
complaint that makes me a little dilatory. I thought you were
trading and praying away in London still, and didn't find you
there. But you see I was sent to you, Nick—perhaps for a
blessing to both of us."

Mr. Raffles ended with a jocose snuffle: no man felt his
intellect more superior to religious cant. And if the cunning
which calculates on the meanest feelings in men could be called
intellect, he had his share, for under the blurting rallying tone
with which he spoke to Bulstrode, there was an evident selection
of statements, as if they had been so many moves at chess.
Meanwhile Bulstrode had determined on his move, and he said,
with gathered resolution—

"You will do well to reflect, Mr. Raffles, that it is possible for
a man to overreach himself in the effort to secure undue
advantage. Although I am not in any way bound to you, I am
willing to supply you with a regular annuity—in quarterly
payments—so long as you fulfil a promise to remain at a distance
from this neighbourhood. It is in your power to choose. If
you insist on remaining here, even for a short time, you will get
nothing from me. I shall decline to know you."

"Ha, ha!" said Raffles, with an affected explosion, "that
reminds me of a droll dog of a thief who declined to know the
constable."

"Your allusions are lost on me, sir," said Bulstrode, with
white heat; "the law has no hold on me either through your
agency or any other."

"You can't understand a joke, my good fellow. I only meant that I should never decline to know you. But let us be serious. Your quarterly payment won't quite suit me. I like my freedom."

Here Raffles rose and stalked once or twice up and down the room, swinging his leg, and assuming an air of masterly meditation. At last he stopped opposite Bulstrode, and said, "I'll tell you what! Give us a couple of hundreds—come, that's modest— and I'll go away—honour bright!—pick up my portmanteau and go away. But I shall not give up my liberty for a dirty annuity. I shall come and go where I like. Perhaps it may suit me to stay away, and correspond with a friend ; perhaps not. Have you the money with you ? "

"No, I have one hundred," said Bulstrode, feeling the immediate riddance too great a relief to be rejected on the ground of future uncertainties. "I will forward you the other if you will mention an address."

"No, I'll wait here till you bring it," said Raffles. "I'll take a stroll, and have a snack, and you'll be back by that time."

Mr. Bulstrode's sickly body, shattered by the agitations he had gone through since the last evening, made him feel abjectly in the power of this loud invulnerable man. At that moment he snatched at a temporary repose to be won on any terms. He was rising to do what Raffles suggested, when the latter said, lifting up his finger as if with a sudden recollection—

"I did have another look after Sarah again, though I didn't tell you ; I'd a tender conscience about that pretty young wo- man. I didn't find her, but I found out her husband's name, and I made a note of it. But hang it, I lost my pocket-book. However, if I heard it, I should know it again. I've got my faculties as if I was in my prime, but names wear out, by Jove ! Sometimes I'm no better than a confounded tax-paper before the names are filled in. However, if I hear of her and her family, you shall know, Nick. You'd like to do something for her, now she's your step-daughter."

"Doubtless," said Mr. Bulstrode, with the usual steady look of his light-grey eyes ; "though that might reduce my power of assisting you."

As he walked out of the room, Raffles winked slowly at his back, and then turned towards the window to watch the banker riding away—virtually at his command. His lips first curled with a smile and then opened with a short triumphant laugh.

"But what the deuce *was* the name ? " he presently said, half aloud, scratching his head, and wrinkling his brows horizontally. He had not really cared or thought about this point of forget-fulness until it occurred to him in his invention of annoyances for Bulstrode.

"It began with L ; it was almost all l's, I fancy," he went on, with a sense that he was getting hold of the slippery name. But the hold was too slight, and he soon got tired of this mental chase ; for few men were more impatient of private occupation or more in need of making themselves continually heard than Mr. Raffles. He preferred using his time in pleasant conversa-tion with the bailiff and the housekeeper, from whom he gathered as much as he wanted to know about Mr. Bulstrode's position in Middlemarch.

After all, however, there was a dull space of time which needed relieving with bread and cheese and ale, and when he was seated alone with these resources in the wainscoted parlour, he suddenly slapped his knee, and exclaimed, "Ladislaw !" That action of memory which he had tried to set going, and had abandoned in despair, had suddenly completed itself without conscious effort—a common experience, agreeable as a completed sneeze, even if the name remembered is of no value. Raffles immediately took out his pocket-book and wrote down the name, not because he expected to use it, but merely for the sake of not being at a loss if he ever did happen to want it. He was not going to tell Bulstrode : there was no actual good in telling, and to a mind like that of Mr. Raffles there is always probable good in a secret.

He was satisfied with his present success, and by three o'clock that day he had taken up his portmanteau at the turn-pike and mounted the coach, relieving Mr. Bulstrode's eyes of an ugly black spot on the landscape at Stone Court, but not relieving him of the dread that the black spot might reappear and become inseparable even from the vision of his hearth.

BOOK VI
THE WIDOW AND THE WIFE

CHAPTER LIV

" Negli occhi porta la mia donna Amore ;
    Per che si fa gentil ciò ch'ella mira :
    Ov'ella passa, ogni uom ver lei si gira,
    E cui saluta fa tremar lo core.
Sicchè, bassando il viso, tutto smore,
    E d'ogni suo difetto allor sospira :
    Fuggon dinanzi a lei Superbia ed Ira :
    Aiutatemi, donne, a farle onore.
Ogni dolcezza, ogni pensiero umile
    Nasce nel core a chi parlar la sente ;
    Ond' è beato chi prima la vide.
Quel ch'ella par quand' un poco sorride,
    Non si può dicer, nè tener a mente,
    Si è nuovo miracolo gentile."
                            —DANTE : *La Vita Nuova.*

By that delightful morning when the hayricks at Stone Court
were scenting the air quite impartially, as if Mr. Raffles had been
a guest worthy of finest incense, Dorothea had again taken up
her abode at Lowick Manor. After three months Freshitt had
become rather oppressive : to sit like a model for Saint Cath-
erine looking rapturously at Celia's baby would not do for many
hours in the day, and to remain in that momentous babe's
presence with persistent disregard was a course that could not
have been tolerated in a childless sister. Dorothea would have
been capable of carrying baby joyfully for a mile if there had
been need, and of loving it the more tenderly for that labour ;
but to an aunt who does not recognise her infant nephew as
Bouddha, and has nothing to do for him but to admire, his
behaviour is apt to appear monotonous, and the interest of
watching him exhaustible.

This possibility was quite hidden from Celia, who felt that
Dorothea's childless widowhood fell in quite prettily with the
birth of little Arthur (baby was named after Mr. Brooke).

" Dodo is just the creature not to mind about having anything
of her own—children or anything ! " said Celia to her husband.

" And if she had had a baby, it never could have been such a dear as Arthur. Could it, James ? "

" Not if it had been like Casaubon," said Sir James, conscious of some indirectness in his answer, and of holding a strictly private opinion as to the perfections of his first-born.

" No ! Just imagine ! Really it was a mercy," said Celia ; " and I think it is very nice for Dodo to be a widow. She can be just as fond of our baby as if it were her own, and she can have as many notions of her own as she likes."

" It is a pity she was not a queen," said the devout Sir James.

" But what should we have been then ? We must have been something else," said Celia, objecting to so laborious a flight of imagination. " I like her better as she is."

Hence, when she found that Dorothea was making arrangements for her final departure to Lowick, Celia raised her eyebrows with disappointment, and in her quiet unemphatic way shot a needle-arrow of sarcasm.

" What will you do at Lowick, Dodo ? You say yourself there is nothing to be done there : everybody is so clean and well off, it makes you quite melancholy. And here you have been so happy going all about Tipton with Mr. Garth into the worst backyards. And now uncle is abroad, you and Mr. Garth can have it all your own way ; and I am sure James does everything you tell him."

" I shall often come here, and I shall see how baby grows all the better," said Dorothea.

" But you will never see him washed," said Celia : " and that is quite the best part of the day." She was almost pouting : it did seem to her very hard in Dodo to go away from the baby when she might stay.

" Dear Kitty, I will come and stay all night on purpose," said Dorothea ; " but I want to be alone now, and in my own home. I wish to know the Farebrothers better, and to talk to Mr. Farebrother about what there is to be done in Middlemarch."

Dorothea's native strength of will was no longer all converted into resolute submission. She had a great yearning to be at Lowick, and was simply determined to go, not feeling bound to tell all her reasons. But every one around her disapproved. Sir James was much pained, and offered that they should all migrate to Cheltenham for a few months with the sacred ark, otherwise called a cradle : at that period a man could hardly know what to propose if Cheltenham were rejected.

The Dowager Lady Chettam, just returned from a visit to her

daughter in town, wished, at least, that Mrs. Vigo should be written to, and invited to accept the office of companion to Mrs. Casaubon : it was not credible that Dorothea as a young widow would think of living alone in the house at Lowick. Mrs. Vigo had been reader and secretary to royal personages, and in point of knowledge and sentiments even Dorothea could have nothing to object to her.

Mrs. Cadwallader said, privately, " You will certainly go mad in that house alone, my dear. You will see visions. We have all got to exert ourselves a little to keep sane, and call things by the same names as other people call them by. To be sure, for younger sons and women who have no money, it is a sort of provision to go mad : they are taken care of then. But you must not run into that. I daresay you are a little bored here with our good dowager ; but think what a bore you might become yourself to your fellow-creatures if you were always playing tragedy queen and taking things sublimely. Sitting alone in that library at Lowick you may fancy yourself ruling the weather ; you must get a few people round you who wouldn't believe you if you told them. That is a good lowering medicine."

" I never called everything by the same name that all the people about me did," said Dorothea, stoutly.

" But I suppose you have found out your mistake, my dear," said Mrs. Cadwallader, " and that is a proof of sanity."

Dorothea was aware of the sting, but it did not hurt her. " No," she said, " I still think that the greater part of the world is mistaken about many things. Surely one may be sane and yet think so, since the greater part of the world has often had to come round from its opinion."

Mrs. Cadwallader said no more on that point to Dorothea, but to her husband she remarked, " It will be well for her to marry again as soon as it is proper, if one could get her among the right people. Of course the Chettams would not wish it. But I see clearly a husband is the best thing to keep her in order. If we were not so poor I would invite Lord Triton. He will be marquis some day, and there is no denying that she would make a good marchioness : she looks handsomer than ever in her mourning."

" My dear Elinor, do let the poor woman alone. Such contrivances are of no use," said the easy Rector.

" No use ? How are matches made, except by bringing men and women together ? And it is a shame that her uncle should have run away and shut up the Grange just now. There ought to be plenty of eligible matches invited to Freshitt and the Grange. Lord Triton is precisely the man : full of plans for making the people happy in a soft-headed sort of way. That would just suit Mrs. Casaubon."

" Let Mrs. Casaubon choose for herself, Elinor."

" That is the nonsense you wise men talk ! How can she choose if she has no variety to choose from ? A woman's choice usually means taking the only man she can get. Mark my words, Humphrey. If her friends don't exert themselves, there will be a worse business than the Casaubon business yet."

" For heaven's sake don't touch on that topic, Elinor ! It is a very sore point with Sir James. He would be deeply offended if you entered on it to him unnecessarily."

" I have never entered on it," said Mrs. Cadwallader, opening her hands. " Celia told me all about the will at the beginning, without any asking of mine."

" Yes, yes ; but they want the thing hushed up, and I understand that the young fellow is going out of the neighbourhood."

Mrs. Cadwallader said nothing, but gave her husband three significant nods, with a very sarcastic expression in her dark eyes.

Dorothea quietly persisted in spite of remonstrance and persuasion. So by the end of June the shutters were all opened at Lowick Manor, and the morning gazed calmly into the library, shining on the rows of note-books as it shines on the weary waste planted with huge stones, the mute memorial of a forgotten faith ; and the evening laden with roses entered silently into the blue-green boudoir where Dorothea chose oftenest to sit. At first she walked into every room, questioning the eighteen months of her married life, and carrying on her thoughts as if they were a speech to be heard by her husband. Then, she lingered in the library and could not be at rest till she had carefully ranged all the note-books as she imagined that he would wish to see them, in orderly sequence. The pity which had been the restraining compelling motive in her life with him still clung about his image, even while she remonstrated with him in indignant thought and told him that he was unjust. One little act of hers may perhaps be smiled at as superstitious. The *Synoptical Tabulation for the use of Mrs. Casaubon*, she carefully enclosed and sealed, writing within the envelope, " *I could not use it. Do you not see now that I could not submit my soul to yours, by working hopelessly at what I have no belief in ?—Dorothea.* Then she deposited the paper in her own desk.

That silent colloquy was perhaps only the more earnest because underneath and through it all there was always the deep longing which had really determined her to come to Lowick. The longing was to see Will Ladislaw. She did not know any good that could come of their meeting : she was helpless ; her hands had been tied from making up to him for any unfairness in his lot. But her soul thirsted to see him. How could it be otherwise ? If a princess in the days of enchantment had seen a four-footed creature from among those which live in herds come to her once and again with a human gaze which rested upon her with choice and beseeching, what would she think of in her journeying, what would she look for when the herds passed her ? Surely for the gaze which had found her, and which she would know again. Life would be no better than candle-light tinsel and daylight rubbish if our spirits were not touched by what has been, to issues of longing and constancy. It was true that Dorothea wanted to know the Farebrothers better, and especially to talk to the new rector, but also true that remembering what Lydgate had told her about Will Ladislaw and little Miss Noble, she counted on Will's coming to Lowick to see the Farebrother family. The very first Sunday, *before* she entered the church, she saw him as she had seen him the last time she was there, alone in the clergyman's pew ; but *when* she entered his figure was gone.

In the week-days when she went to see the ladies at the Rectory, she listened in vain for some word that they might fall about Will ; but it seemed to her that Mrs. Farebrother talked of every one else in the neighbourhood and out of it.

" Probably some of Mr. Farebrother's Middlemarch hearers may follow him to Lowick sometimes. Do you not think so ? " said Dorothea, rather despising herself for having a secret motive in asking the question.

" If they are wise they will, Mrs. Casaubon," said the old lady. " I see that you set a right value on my son's preaching. His grandfather on my side was an excellent clergyman, but his father was in the law :—most exemplary and honest nevertheless, which is a reason for our never being rich. They say Fortune is a woman and capricious. But sometimes she is a good woman and gives to those who merit, which has been the case with you, Mrs. Casaubon, who have given a living to my son."

Mrs. Farebrother recurred to her knitting with a dignified satisfaction in her neat little effort at oratory, but this was not

*D 855

what Dorothea wanted to hear. Poor thing ! she did not even know whether Will Ladislaw was still at Middlemarch, and there was no one whom she dared to ask, unless it were Lydgate. But just now she could not see Lydgate without sending for him or going to seek him. Perhaps Will Ladislaw, having heard of that strange ban against him left by Mr. Casaubon, had felt it better that he and she should not meet again, and perhaps she was wrong to wish for a meeting that others might find many good reasons against. Still " I do wish it " came at the end of those wise reflections as naturally as a sob after holding the breath. And the meeting did happen, but in a formal way quite unexpected by her.

One morning, about eleven, Dorothea was seated in her boudoir with a map of the land attached to the manor and other papers before her, which were to help her in making an exact statement for herself of her income and affairs. She had not yet applied herself to her work, but was seated with her hands folded on her lap, looking out along the avenue of limes to the distant fields. Every leaf was at rest in the sunshine, the familiar scene was changeless, and seemed to represent the prospect of her life, full of motiveless ease—motiveless, if her own energy could not seek out reasons for ardent action. The widow's cap of those times made an oval frame for the face, and had a crown standing up ; the dress was an experiment in the utmost laying on of crape ; but this heavy solemnity of clothing made her face look all the younger, with its recovered bloom, and the sweet, inquiring candour of her eyes.

Her reverie was broken by Tantripp, who came to say that Mr. Ladislaw was below, and begged permission to see Madam if it were not too early.

" I will see him," said Dorothea, rising immediately. " Let him be shown into the drawing-room."

The drawing-room was the most neutral room in the house to her—the one least associated with the trials of her married life : the damask matched the wood-work, which was all white and gold ; there were two tall mirrors and tables with nothing on them—in brief, it was a room where you had no reason for sitting in one place rather than in another. It was below the boudoir, and had also a bow-window looking out on the avenue. But when Pratt showed Will Ladislaw into it the window was open ; and a winged visitor, buzzing in and out now and then without minding the furniture, made the room look less formal and uninhabited.

"Glad to see you here again, sir," said Pratt, lingering to adjust a blind.

"I am only come to say good-bye, Pratt," said Will, who wished even the butler to know that he was too proud to hang about Mrs. Casaubon now she was a rich widow.

"Very sorry to hear it, sir," said Pratt, retiring. Of course, as a servant who was to be told nothing, he knew the fact of which Ladislaw was still ignorant, and had drawn his inferences; indeed, had not differed from his betrothed Tantripp when she said, " *Your* master was as jealous as a fiend—and no reason. Madam would look higher than Mr. Ladislaw, else I don't know her. Mrs. Cadwallader's maid says there's a lord coming who is to marry her when the mourning's over."

There were not many moments for Will to walk about with his hat in his hand before Dorothea entered. The meeting was very different from that first meeting in Rome when Will had been embarrassed and Dorothea calm. This time he felt miserable but determined, while she was in a state of agitation which could not be hidden. Just outside the door she had felt that this longed-for meeting was after all too difficult, and when she saw Will advancing towards her, the deep blush which was rare in her came with painful suddenness. Neither of them knew how it was, but neither of them spoke. She gave her hand for a moment, and then they went to sit down near the window, she on one settee and he on another opposite. Will was peculiarly uneasy : it seemed to him not like Dorothea that the mere fact of her being a widow should cause such a change in her manner of receiving him ; and he knew of no other condition which could have affected their previous relation to each other— except that, as his imagination at once told him, her friends might have been poisoning her mind with their suspicions of him.

"I hope I have not presumed too much in calling," said Will ; "I could not bear to leave the neighbourhood and begin a new life without seeing you to say good-bye."

"Presumed ? Surely not. I should have thought it unkind if you had not wished to see me," said Dorothea, her habit of speaking with perfect genuineness asserting itself through all her uncertainty and agitation. "Are you going away immediately ?"

"Very soon, I think. I intend to go to town and eat my dinners as a barrister, since, they say, that is the preparation for all public business. There will be a great deal of political work to be done by-and-by, and I mean to try and do some of it.

Other men have managed to win an honourable position for themselves without family or money."

"And that will make it all the more honourable," said Dorothea, ardently. "Besides, you have so many talents. I have heard from my uncle how well you speak in public, so that every one is sorry when you leave off, and how clearly you can explain things. And you care that justice should be done to every one. I am so glad. When we were in Rome, I thought you only cared for poetry and art, and the things that adorn life for us who are well off. But now I know you think about the rest of the world."

While she was speaking Dorothea had lost her personal embarrassment and had become like her former self. She looked at Will with a direct glance, full of delighted confidence.

"You approve of my going away for years, then, and never coming here again till I have made myself of some mark in the world?" said Will, trying hard to reconcile the utmost pride with the utmost effort to get an expression of strong feeling from Dorothea.

She was not aware how long it was before she answered. She had turned her head and was looking out of the window on the rosebushes, which seemed to have in them the summers of all the years when Will would be away. This was not judicious behaviour. But Dorothea never thought of studying her manners : she thought only of bowing to a sad necessity which divided her from Will. Those first words of his about his intentions had seemed to make everything clear to her : he knew, she supposed, all about Mr. Casaubon's final conduct in relation to him, and it had come to him with the same sort of shock as to herself. He had never felt more than friendship for her—had never had anything in his mind to justify what she felt to be her husband's outrage on the feelings of both : and that friendship he still felt. Something which may be called an inward silent sob had gone on in Dorothea before she said with a pure voice, just trembling in the last words as if only from its liquid flexibility—

"Yes, it must be right for you to do as you say. I shall be very happy when I hear that you have made your value felt. But you must have patience. It will perhaps be a long while."

Will never quite knew how it was that he saved himself from falling down at her feet, when the "long while" came forth with its gentle tremor. He used to say that the horrible hue and surface of her crape dress was most likely the sufficient controlling force. He sat still, however, and only said—

" I shall never hear from you. And you will forget all about me."

" No," said Dorothea, " I shall never forget you. I have never forgotten any one whom I once knew. My life has never been crowded, and seems not likely to be so. And I have a great deal of space for memory at Lowick, haven't I ? " She smiled.

" Good God ! " Will burst out passionately, rising with his hat still in his hand, and walking to a marble table, where he suddenly turned and leaned his back against it. The blood had mounted to his face and neck, and he looked almost angry. It had seemed to him as if they were like two creatures slowly turning to marble in each other's presence, while their hearts were conscious and their eyes were yearning. But there was no help for it. It should never be true of him that in this meeting to which he had come with bitter resolution he had ended by a confession which might be interpreted into asking for her fortune. Moreover, it was actually true that he was fearful of the effect which such confessions might have on Dorothea herself.

She looked at him from that distance in some trouble, imagining that there might have been an offence in her words. But all the while there was a current of thought in her about his probable want of money, and the impossibility of her helping him. If her uncle had been at home, something might have been done through him ! It was this preoccupation with the hardship of Will's wanting money, while she had what ought to have been his share, which led her to say, seeing that he remained silent and looked away from her—

" I wonder whether you would like to have that miniature which hangs up-stairs—I mean that beautiful miniature of your grandmother. I think it is not right for me to keep it, if you would wish to have it. It is wonderfully like you."

" You are very good," said Will, irritably. " No ; I don't mind about it. It is not very consoling to have one's own likeness. It would be more consoling if others wanted to have it."

" I thought you would like to cherish her memory—I thought ——" Dorothea broke off an instant, her imagination suddenly warning her away from Aunt Julia's history—" you would surely like to have the miniature as a family memorial."

" Why should I have that, when I have nothing else ! A man

with only a portmanteau for his stowage must keep his memorials in his head.''

Will spoke at random : he was merely venting his petulance ; it was a little too exasperating to have his grandmother's portrait offered him at that moment. But to Dorothea's feeling his words had a peculiar sting. She rose and said with a touch of indignation as well as hauteur—

" You are much the happier of us two, Mr. Ladislaw, to have nothing."

Will was startled. Whatever the words might be, the tone seemed like a dismissal ; and quitting his leaning posture, he walked a little way towards her. Their eyes met, but with a strange questioning gravity. Something was keeping their minds aloof, and each was left to conjecture what was in the other. Will had really never thought of himself as having a claim of inheritance on the property which was held by Dorothea, and would have required a narrative to make him understand her present feeling.

" I never felt it a misfortune to have nothing till now," he said. " But poverty may be as bad as leprosy, if it divides us from what we most care for."

The words cut Dorothea to the heart, and made her relent. She answered in a tone of sad fellowship.

" Sorrow comes in so many ways. Two years ago I had no notion of that—I mean of the unexpected way in which trouble comes, and ties our hands, and makes us silent when we long to speak. I used to despise women a little for not shaping their lives more, and doing better things. I was very fond of doing as I liked, but I have almost given it up," she ended, smiling playfully.

" I have not given up doing as I like, but I can very seldom do it," said Will. He was standing two yards from her with his mind full of contradictory desires and resolves—desiring some unmistakable proof that she loved him, and yet dreading the position into which such a proof might bring him. " The thing one most longs for may be surrounded with conditions that would be intolerable."

At this moment Pratt entered and said, " Sir James Chettam is in the library, madam."

" Ask Sir James to come in here," said Dorothea, immediately. It was as if the same electric shock had passed through her and Will. Each of them felt proudly resistant, and neither looked at the other, while they awaited Sir James's entrance.

After shaking hands with Dorothea, he bowed as slightly as possible to Ladislaw, who repaid the slightness exactly, and then going towards Dorothea, said—

"I must say good-bye, Mrs. Casaubon; and probably for a long while."

Dorothea put out her hand and said her good-bye cordially. The sense that Sir James was depreciating Will, and behaving rudely to him, roused her resolution and dignity : there was no touch of confusion in her manner. And when Will had left the room, she looked with such calm self-possession at Sir James, saying, "How is Celia?" that he was obliged to behave as if nothing had annoyed him. And what would be the use of behaving otherwise! Indeed, Sir James shrank with so much dislike from the association even in thought of Dorothea with Ladislaw as her possible lover, that he would himself have wished to avoid an outward show of displeasure which would have recognised the disagreeable possibility. If any one had asked him why he shrank in that way, I am not sure that he would at first have said anything fuller or more precise than "*that* Ladislaw!"—though on reflection he might have urged that Mr. Casaubon's codicil, barring Dorothea's marriage with Will, except under a penalty, was enough to cast unfitness over any relation at all between them. His aversion was all the stronger because he felt himself unable to interfere.

But Sir James was a power in a way unguessed by himself. Entering at that moment, he was an incorporation of the strongest reasons through which Will's pride became a repellent force, keeping him asunder from Dorothea.

CHAPTER LV

Hath she her faults? I would you had them too.
They are the fruity must of soundest wine
Or say, they are regenerating fire
Such as hath turned the dense black element
Into a crystal pathway for the sun.

IF youth is the season of hope, it is often so only in the sense that our elders are hopeful about us ; for no age is so apt as youth to think its emotions, partings, and resolves are the last of their kind. Each crisis seems final, simply because it is new. We are told that the oldest inhabitants in Peru do not cease to be agitated by the earthquakes, but they probably see beyond each shock, and reflect that there are plenty more to come.

To Dorothea, still in that time of youth when the eyes with
their long full lashes look out after their rain of tears unsoiled
and unwearied as a freshly-opened passion-flower, that morning's
parting with Will Ladislaw seemed to be the close of their
personal relations. He was going away into the distance of
unknown years, and if ever he came back he would be another
man. The actual state of his mind—his proud resolve to give
the lie beforehand to any suspicion that he would play the needy
adventurer seeking a rich woman—lay quite out of her imagination, and she had interpreted all his behaviour easily enough by
her supposition that Mr. Casaubon's codicil seemed to him, as
it did to her, a gross and cruel interdict on any active friendship
between them. Their young delight in speaking to each other,
and saying what no one else would care to hear, was for ever
ended, and become a treasure of the past. For this very
reason she dwelt on it without inward check. That unique
happiness too was dead, and in its shadowed silent chamber she
might vent the passionate grief which she herself wondered at.
For the first time she took down the miniature from the wall
and kept it before her, liking to blend the woman who had been
too hardly judged with the grandson whom her own heart and
judgment defended. Can any one who has rejoiced in woman's
tenderness think it a reproach to her that she took the little
oval picture in her palm and made a bed for it there, and leaned
her cheek upon it, as if that would soothe the creature who had
suffered unjust condemnation ? She did not know then that
it was Love who had come to her briefly as in a dream before
awaking, with the hues of morning on his wings—that it was
Love to whom she was sobbing her farewell as his image was
banished by the blameless rigour of irresistible day. She only
felt that there was something irrevocably amiss and lost in her
lot, and her thoughts about the future were the more readily
shapen into resolve. Ardent souls, ready to construct their
coming lives, are apt to commit themselves to the fulfilment
of their own visions.

One day that she went to Freshitt to fulfil her promise of
staying all night and seeing baby washed, Mrs. Cadwallader
came to dine, the Rector being gone on a fishing excursion. It
was a warm evening, and even in the delightful drawing-room,
where the fine old turf sloped from the open window towards
a lilied pool and well-planted mounds, the heat was enough to
make Celia in her white muslin and light curls reflect with pity
on what Dodo must feel in her black dress and close cap. But

this was not until some episodes with baby were over, and had left her mind at leisure. She had seated herself and taken up a fan for some time before she said, in her quiet guttural—

"Dear Dodo, do throw off that cap. I am sure your dress must make you feel ill."

"I am so used to the cap—it has become a sort of shell," said Dorothea, smiling. "I feel rather bare and exposed when it is off."

"I *must* see you without it; it makes us all warm," said Celia, throwing down her fan, and going to Dorothea. It was a pretty picture to see this little lady in white muslin unfastening the widow's cap from her more majestic sister, and tossing it on to a chair. Just as the coils and braids of dark-brown hair had been set free, Sir James entered the room. He looked at the released head, and said, "Ah!" in a tone of satisfaction.

"It was I who did it, James," said Celia. "Dodo need not make such a slavery of her mourning; she need not wear that cap any more among her friends."

"My dear Celia," said Lady Chettam, "a widow must wear her mourning at least a year."

"Not if she marries again before the end of it," said Mrs. Cadwallader, who had some pleasure in startling her good friend the Dowager. Sir James was annoyed, and leaned forward to play with Celia's Maltese dog.

"That is very rare, I hope," said Lady Chettam, in a tone intended to guard against such events. "No friend of ours ever committed herself in that way except Mrs. Beevor, and it was very painful to Lord Grinsell when she did so. Her first husband was objectionable, which made it the greater wonder. And severely she was punished for it. They said Captain Beevor dragged her about by the hair, and held up loaded pistols at her."

"Oh, if she took the wrong man!" said Mrs. Cadwallader, who was in a decidedly wicked mood. "Marriage is always bad then, first or second. Priority is a poor recommendation in a husband if he has got no other. I would rather have a good second husband than an indifferent first."

"My dear, your clever tongue runs away with you," said Lady Chettam. "I am sure you would be the last woman to marry again prematurely, if our dear Rector were taken away."

"Oh, I make no vows; it might be a necessary economy. It is lawful to marry again, I suppose; else we might as well be Hindoos instead of Christians. Of course if a woman accepts the wrong man, she must take the consequences, and one who does it twice over deserves her fate. But if she can marry blood, beauty, and bravery—the sooner the better."

"I think the subject of our conversation is very ill-chosen," said Sir James, with a look of disgust. "Suppose we change it."

"Not on my account, Sir James," said Dorothea, determined not to lose the opportunity of freeing herself from certain oblique references to excellent matches. "If you are speaking on my behalf, I can assure you that no question can be more indifferent and impersonal to me than second marriage. It is no more to me than if you talked of women going fox-hunting : whether it is admirable in them or not, I shall not follow them. Pray let Mrs. Cadwallader amuse herself on that subject as much as on any other."

"My dear Mrs. Casaubon," said Lady Chettam, in her state-liest way, "you do not, I hope, think there was any allusion to you in my mentioning Mrs. Beevor. It was only an instance that occurred to me. She was step-daughter to Lord Grinsell : he married Mrs. Teveroy for his second wife. There could be no possible allusion to you."

"Oh no," said Celia. "Nobody chose the subject ; it all came out of Dodo's cap. Mrs. Cadwallader only said what was quite true. A woman could not be married in a widow's cap, James."

"Hush, my dear !" said Mrs. Cadwallader. "I will not offend again. I will not even refer to Dido or Zenobia. Only what are we to talk about ? I, for my part, object to the discussion of Human Nature, because that is the nature of rectors' wives."

Later in the evening, after Mrs. Cadwallader was gone, Celia said privately to Dorothea, "Really, Dodo, taking your cap off made you like yourself again in more ways than one. You spoke up just as you used to do, when anything was said to displease you. But I could hardly make out whether it was James that you thought wrong, or Mrs. Cadwallader."

"Neither," said Dorothea. "James spoke out of delicacy to me, but he was mistaken in supposing that I minded what Mrs. Cadwallader said. I should only mind if there were a law obliging me to take any piece of blood and beauty that she or anybody else recommended."

"But you know, Dodo, if you ever did marry, it would be all the better to have blood and beauty," said Celia, reflecting that Mr. Casaubon had not been richly endowed with those gifts, and that it would be well to caution Dorothea in time.

"Don't be anxious, Kitty ; I have quite other thoughts about my life. I shall never marry again," said Dorothea, touching her sister's chin, and looking at her with indulgent affection. Celia was nursing her baby, and Dorothea had come to say good-night to her.

"Really—quite?" said Celia. "Not anybody at all— if he were very wonderful indeed?"

Dorothea shook her head slowly. "Not anybody at all. I have delightful plans. I should like to take a great deal of land, and drain it, and make a little colony, where everybody should work, and all the work should be done well. I should know every one of the people and be their friend. I am going to have great consultations with Mr. Garth: he can tell me almost everything I want to know."

"Then you *will* be happy, if you have a plan, Dodo," said Celia. "Perhaps little Arthur will like plans when he grows up, and then he can help you."

Sir James was informed that same night that Dorothea was really quite set against marrying anybody at all, and was going to take to "all sorts of plans," just like what she used to have. Sir James made no remark. To his secret feeling, there was something repulsive in a woman's second marriage, and no match would prevent him from feeling it a sort of desecration for Dorothea. He was aware that the world would regard such a sentiment as preposterous, especially in relation to a woman of one-and-twenty; the practice of "the world" being to treat of a young widow's second marriage as certain and probably near, and to smile with meaning if the widow acts accordingly. But if Dorothea did choose to espouse her solitude, he felt that the resolution would well become her.

CHAPTER LVI

" How happy is he born and taught,
That serveth not another's will?
Whose armour is his honest thought,
And simple truth his utmost skill?

.   .   .   .

This man is freed from servile bands
Of hope to rise, or fear to fall:
Lord of himself, though not of lands,
And having nothing, yet hath all."
—Sir Henry Wotton.

DOROTHEA's confidence in Caleb Garth's knowledge, which had begun on her hearing that he approved of her cottages, had grown fast during her stay at Freshitt, Sir James having induced her to take rides over the two estates in company with himself and Caleb, who quite returned her admiration, and told his wife that Mrs. Casaubon had a head for business most uncommon in a woman. It must be remembered that by "business" Caleb never meant money transactions, but the skilful application of labour.

"Most uncommon!" repeated Caleb. "She said a thing I often used to think myself when I was a lad :—' Mr. Garth, I should like to feel, if I lived to be old, that I had improved a great piece of land and built a great many good cottages, because the work is of a healthy kind while it is being done, and after it is done, men are the better for it.' Those were the very words : she sees into things in that way."

"But womanly, I hope," said Mrs. Garth, half suspecting that Mrs. Casaubon might not hold the true principle of subordination.

"Oh, you can't think!" said Caleb, shaking his head. "You would like to hear her speak, Susan. She speaks in such plain words, and a voice like music. Bless me! it reminds me of bits in the 'Messiah'—' and straightway there appeared a multitude of the heavenly host, praising God and saying;' it has a tone with it that satisfies your ear."

Caleb was very fond of music, and when he could afford it went to hear an oratorio that came within his reach, returning from it with a profound reverence for this mighty structure of tones, which made him sit meditatively, looking on the floor and throwing much unutterable language into his outstretched hands.

With this good understanding between them, it was natural that Dorothea asked Mr. Garth to undertake any business connected with the three farms and the numerous tenements attached to Lowick Manor ; indeed, his expectation of getting work for two was being fast fulfilled. As he said, "Business breeds." And one form of business which was beginning to breed just then was the construction of railways. A projected line was to run through Lowick parish where the cattle had hitherto grazed in a peace unbroken by astonishment ; and thus it happened that the infant struggles of the railway system entered into the affairs of Caleb Garth, and determined the course of this history with regard to two persons who were dear to him.

The submarine railway may have its difficulties ; but the bed of the sea is not divided among various landed proprietors with claims for damages not only measurable but sentimental. In the hundred to which Middlemarch belonged railways were as exciting a topic as the Reform Bill or the imminent horrors of Cholera, and those who held the most decided views on the subject were women and landholders. Women both old and young regarded travelling by steam as presumptuous and dangerous, and argued against it by saying that nothing should induce them to get into a railway carriage; while proprietors, differing from each other in their arguments as much as Mr. Solomon Featherstone differed from Lord Medlicote, were yet unanimous in the opinion that in selling land, whether to the Enemy of mankind or to a company obliged to purchase, these pernicious agencies must be made to pay a very high price to landowners for permission to injure mankind.

But the slower wits, such as Mr. Solomon and Mrs. Waule, who both occupied land of their own, took a long time to arrive at this conclusion, their minds halting at the vivid conception of what it would be to cut the Big Pasture in two, and turn it into three-cornered bits, which would be "nohow;" while accommodation-bridges and high payments were remote and incredible.

"The cows will all cast their calves, brother," said Mrs. Waule, in a tone of deep melancholy, "if the railway comes across the Near Close; and I shouldn't wonder at the mare too, if she was in foal. It's a poor tale if a widow's property is to be spaded away, and the law say nothing to it. What's to hinder 'em from cutting right and left if they begin? It's well known, *I* can't fight."

"The best way would be to say nothing, and set somebody on to send 'em away with a flea in their ear, when they came spying and measuring," said Solomon. "Folks did that about Brassing, by what I can understand. It's all a pretence, if the truth was known, about their being forced to take one way. Let 'em go cutting in another parish. And I don't believe in any pay to make amends for bringing a lot of ruffians to trample your crops. Where's a company's pocket?"

"Brother Peter, God forgive him, got money out of a company," said Mrs. Waule. "But that was for the manganese. That wasn't for railways to blow you to pieces right and left."

"Well, there's this to be said, Jane," Mr. Solomon concluded, lowering his voice in a cautious manner—"the more spokes we put in their wheel, the more they'll pay us to let 'em go on, if they must come whether or not."

This reasoning of Mr. Solomon's was perhaps less thorough than he imagined, his cunning bearing about the same relation to the course of railways as the cunning of a diplomatist bears to the general chill or catarrh or the solar system. But he set about acting on his views in a thoroughly diplomatic manner, by stimulating suspicion. His side of Lowick was the most remote from the village, and the houses of the labouring people were either lone cottages or were collected in a hamlet called Frick, where a water-mill and some stone-pits made a little centre of slow, heavy-shouldered industry.

In the absence of any precise idea as to what railways were, public opinion in Frick was against them; for the human mind in that grassy corner had not the proverbial tendency to admire the unknown, holding rather that it was likely to be against the poor man, and that suspicion was the only wise attitude with regard to it. Even the rumour of Reform had not yet excited any millennial expectations in Frick, there being no definite promise in it, as of gratuitous grains to fatten Hiram Ford's pig, or of a publican at the "Weights and Scales" who would brew beer for nothing, or of an offer on the part of the three neighbouring farmers to raise wages during winter. And without distinct good of this kind in its promises, Reform seemed on a footing with the bragging of pedlars, which was a hint for distrust to every knowing person. The men of Frick were not ill-fed, and were less given to fanaticism than to a strong muscular suspicion; less inclined to believe that they were peculiarly cared for by heaven, than to regard heaven itself as rather disposed to take them in—a disposition observable in the weather.

Thus the mind of Frick was exactly of the sort for Mr. Solomon Featherstone to work upon, he having more plenteous ideas of the same order, with a suspicion of heaven and earth which was better fed and more entirely at leisure. Solomon was overseer of the roads at that time, and on his slow-paced cob often took his rounds by Frick to look at the workmen getting the stones there, pausing with a mysterious deliberation, which might have misled you into supposing that he had some other reason for staying than the mere want of impulse to move. After looking for a long while at any work that was going on, he would raise his eyes a little and look at the horizon; finally he would shake his bridle, touch his horse with the whip, and get it to move slowly onward. The hour-hand of a clock was quick by comparison with Mr. Solomon, who had an agreeable sense that he could afford to be slow. He was in the habit of pausing for a cautious, vaguely-designing chat with every hedger or ditcher on his way, and was especially willing to listen even to news which he had heard before, feeling himself at an advantage over all narrators in partially disbelieving them. One day, however, he got into a dialogue with Hiram Ford, a waggoner, in which he himself contributed information. He wished to know whether Hiram had seen fellows with staves and instruments spying about: they called themselves railroad people, but there was no telling what they were, or what they meant to do. The least they pretended was that they were going to cut Lowick Parish into sixes and sevens.

"Why, there'll be no stirrin' from one pla-ace to another," said Hiram, thinking of his waggon and horses.

"Not a bit," said Mr. Solomon. "And cutting up fine land such as this parish! Let 'em go into Tipton, say I. But there's no knowing what there is at the bottom of it. Traffic is what they put for'ard; but it's to do harm to the land and the poor man in the long-run."

"Why, they're Lunnon chaps, I reckon," said Hiram, who had a dim notion of London as a centre of hostility to the country.

"Ay, to be sure. And in some parts against Brassing, by what I've heard say, the folks fell on 'em when they were spying and broke their peep-holes as they carry, and drove 'em away, so as they knew better than come again."

"It war good foon, I'd be bound," said Hiram, whose fun was much restricted by circumstances.

"Well, I wouldn't meddle with 'em myself," said Solomon. "But some say this country's seen its best days, and the sign is, as it's being overrun with these fellows trampling right and left, and wanting to cut it up into railways; and all for the big traffic to swallow up the little, so as there shan't be a team left on the land, nor a whip to crack."

"I'll crack *my* whip about their ear'n, afore they bring it to that, though," said Hiram, while Mr. Solomon, shaking his bridle, moved onward.

Nettle-seed needs no digging. The ruin of this country-side by railroads was discussed, not only at the "Weights and Scales," but in the hay-field, where the muster of working hands gave opportunities for talk such as were rarely had through the rural year.

One morning, not long after that interview between Mr.

Farebrother and Mary Garth, in which she confessed to him her feeling for Fred Vincy, it happened that her father had some business which took him to Yoddrell's farm in the direction of Frick : it was to measure and value an outlying piece of land belonging to Lowick Manor, which Caleb expected to dispose of advantageously for Dorothea (it must be confessed that his bias was towards getting the best possible terms from railroad companies). He put up his gig at Yoddrell's, and in walking with his assistant and measuring-chain to the scene of his work, he encountered the party of the company's agents, who were adjusting their spirit-level. After a little chat he left them, observing that by-and-by they would reach him again where he was going to measure. It was one of those grey mornings after light rains, which become delicious about twelve o'clock, when the clouds part a little, and the scent of the earth is sweet along the lanes and by the hedgerows.

The scent would have been sweeter to Fred Vincy, who was coming along the lanes on horseback, if his mind had not been worried by unsuccessful efforts to imagine what he was to do, with his father on one side expecting him straightway to enter the Church, with Mary on the other threatening to forsake him if he did enter it, and with the working-day world showing no eager need whatever of a young gentleman without capital and generally unskilled. It was the harder to Fred's disposition because his father, satisfied that he was no longer rebellious, was in good humour with him, and had sent him on this pleasant ride to see after some greyhounds. Even when he had fixed on what he should do, there would be the task of telling his father. But it must be admitted that the fixing, which had to come first, was the more difficult task :—what secular avocation on earth was there for a young man (whose friends could not get him an " appointment ") which was at once gentlemanly, lucrative, and to be followed without special knowledge ? Riding along the lanes by Frick in this mood, and slackening his pace while he reflected whether he should venture to go round by Lowick Parsonage to call on Mary, he could see over the hedges from one field to another. Suddenly a noise roused his attention, and on the far side of a field on his left hand he could see six or seven men in smock-frocks with hay-forks in their hands making an offensive approach towards the four railway agents who were facing them, while Caleb Garth and his assistant were hastening across the field to join the threatened group. Fred, delayed a few moments by having to find the gate, could not gallop up to the spot before the party in smock-frocks, whose work of turning the hay had not been too pressing after swallowing their mid-day beer, were driving the men in coats before them with their hay-forks; while Caleb Garth's assistant, a lad of seventeen, who had snatched up the spirit-level at Caleb's order, had been knocked down and seemed to be lying helpless. The coated men had the advantage as runners, and Fred covered their retreat by getting in front of the smock-frocks and charging them suddenly enough to throw their chase into confusion. "What do you confounded fools mean?" shouted Fred, pursuing the divided group in a zigzag, and cutting right and left with his whip. "I'll swear to every one of you before the magistrate. You've knocked the lad down and killed him, for what I know. You'll every one of you be hanged at the next assizes, if you don't mind," said Fred, who afterwards laughed heartily as he remembered his own phrases.

The labourers had been driven through the gateway into their hayfield, and Fred had checked his horse, when Hiram Ford, observing himself at a safe challenging distance, turned back and shouted a defiance which he did not know to be Homeric.

"Yo're a coward, yo are. Yo git off your horse, young measter, and I'll have a round wi' ye, I wull. Yo daredn't come on wi'out your hoss an' whip. I'd soon knock the breath out on ye, I would."

"Wait a minute, and I'll come back presently, and have a round with you all in turn, if you like," said Fred, who felt confidence in his power of boxing with his dearly-beloved brethren. But just now he wanted to hasten back to Caleb and the prostrate youth.

The lad's ankle was strained, and he was in much pain from it, but he was no further hurt, and Fred placed him on the horse that he might ride to Yoddrell's and be taken care of there.

"Let them put the horse in the stable, and tell the surveyors they can come back for their traps," said Fred. "The ground is clear now."

"No, no," said Caleb, "here's a breakage. They'll have to give up for to-day, and it will be as well. Here, take the things before you on the horse, Tom. They'll see you coming, and they'll turn back."

"I'm glad I happened to be here at the right moment, Mr. Garth," said Fred, as Tom rode away "No knowing what might have happened if the cavalry had not come up in time."

"Ay, ay, it was lucky," said Caleb, speaking rather absently, and looking towards the spot where he had been at work at the moment of interruption. "But—deuce take it—this is what comes of men being fools—I'm hindered of my day's work. I can't get along without somebody to help me with the measuring-chain. However!" He was beginning to move towards the spot with a look of vexation, as if he had forgotten Fred's presence, but suddenly he turned round and said quickly, "What have you got to do to-day, young fellow?"

"Nothing, Mr. Garth. I'll help you with pleasure—can I?" said Fred, with a sense that he should be courting Mary when he was helping her father.

"Well, you mustn't mind stooping and getting hot."

"I don't mind anything. Only I want to go first and have a round with that hulky fellow who turned to challenge me. It would be a good lesson for him. I shall not be five minutes."

"Nonsense!" said Caleb, with his most peremptory intonation. "I shall go and speak to the men myself. It's all ignorance. Somebody has been telling them lies. The poor fools don't know any better."

"I shall go with you, then," said Fred.

"No, no; stay where you are. I don't want your young blood. I can take care of myself."

Caleb was a powerful man and knew little of any fear except the fear of hurting others and the fear of having to speechify. But he felt it his duty at this moment to try and give a little harangue. There was a striking mixture in him—which came from his having always been a hard-working man himself—of rigorous notions about workmen and practical indulgence towards them. To do a good day's work and to do it well, he held to be part of their welfare, as it was the chief part of his own happiness; but he had a strong sense of fellowship with them. When he advanced towards the labourers they had not gone to work again, but were standing in that form of rural grouping which consists in each turning a shoulder towards the other, at a distance of two or three yards. They looked rather sulkily at Caleb, who walked quickly with one hand in his pocket and the other thrust between the buttons of his waistcoat, and had his everyday mild air when he paused among them.

"Why, my lads, how's this?" he began, taking as usual to brief phrases, which seemed pregnant to himself, because he had many thoughts lying under them, like the abundant roots of a plant that just manages to peep above the water. "How came

you to make such a mistake as this! Somebody has been
telling you lies. You thought those men up there wanted to do
mischief."

"Aw!" was the answer, dropped at intervals by each
according to his degree of unreadiness.

"Nonsense! No such thing! They're looking out to see
which way the railroad is to take. Now, my lads, you can't
hinder the railroad: it will be made whether you like it or
not. And if you go fighting against it, you'll get yourselves
into trouble. The law gives those men leave to come here on
the land. The owner has nothing to say against it, and if
you meddle with them you'll have to do with the constable and
Justice Blakesley, and with the handcuffs and Middlemarch
jail. And you might be in for it now, if anybody informed
against you."

Caleb paused here, and perhaps the greatest orator could not
have chosen either his pause or his images better for the occasion.

"But come, you didn't mean any harm. Somebody told
you the railroad was a bad thing. That was a lie. It may do
a bit of harm here and there, to this and to that; and so does
the sun in heaven. But the railway's a good thing."

"Aw! good for the big folks to make money out on," said
old Timothy Cooper, who had stayed behind turning his hay
while the others had been gone on their spree;—" I'n seen
lots o' things turn up sin' I war a young un—the war an' the
peace, and the canells, an' the oald King George, an' the Regen',
an' the new King George, an' the new un as has got a new
ne-ame—an' it's been all aloike to the poor mon. What's the
canells been t' him? They'n brought him neyther me-at nor
be-acon, nor wage to lay by, if he didn't save it wi' clemmin'
his own inside. Times ha' got wusser for him sin' I war a
young un. An' so it'll be wi' the railroads. They'll on'y
leave the poor mon furder behind. But them are fools as
meddle, and so I told the chaps here. This is the big folks's
world, this is. But yo're for the big folks, Muster Garth,
yo are."

Timothy was a wiry old labourer, of a type lingering in those
times—who had his savings in a stocking-foot, lived in a lone
cottage, and was not to be wrought on by any oratory, having
as little of the feudal spirit, and believing as little, as if he had
not been totally unacquainted with the Age of Reason and the
Rights of Man. Caleb was in a difficulty known to any person
attempting in dark times and unassisted by miracle to reason

with rustics who are in possession of an undeniable truth which they know through a hard process of feeling, and can let it fall like a giant's club on your neatly-carved argument for a social benefit which they do *not* feel. Caleb had no cant at command, even if he could have chosen to use it ; and he had been accustomed to meet all such difficulties in no other way than by doing his " business " faithfully. He answered—

" If you don't think well of me, Tim, never mind ; that's neither here nor there now. Things may be bad for the poor man—bad they are ; but I want the lads here not to do what will make things worse for themselves. The cattle may have a heavy load, but it won't help 'em to throw it over into the roadside pit, when it's partly their own fodder."

" We war on'y for a bit o' foon," said Hiram, who was beginning to see consequences. " That war all we war arter."

" Well, promise me not to meddle again, and I'll see that nobody informs against you."

" I'n ne'er meddled, an' I'n no call to promise," said Timothy.

" No, but the rest. Come, I'm as hard at work as any of you to-day, and I can't spare much time. Say you'll be quiet without the constable."

" Aw, we wooant meddle—they may do as they loike for oos "—were the forms in which Caleb got his pledges ; and then he hastened back to Fred, who had followed him, and watched him in the gateway.

They went to work, and Fred helped vigorously. His spirits had risen, and he heartily enjoyed a good slip in the moist earth under the hedgerow, which soiled his perfect summer trousers. Was it his successful onset which had elated him, or the satisfaction of helping Mary's father ? Something more. The accidents of the morning had helped his frustrated imagination to shape an employment for himself which had several attractions. I am not sure that certain fibres in Mr. Garth's mind had not resumed their old vibration towards the very end which now revealed itself to Fred. For the effective accident is but the touch of fire where there is oil and tow ; and it always appeared to Fred that the railway brought the needed touch. But they went on in silence except when their business demanded speech. At last, when they had finished and were walking away, Mr. Garth said—

" A young fellow needn't be a B.A. to do this sort of work, eh, Fred ? "

" I wish I had taken to it before I had thought of being a

B.A.," said Fred. He paused a moment, and then added, more hesitatingly, "Do you think I am too old to learn your business, Mr. Garth?"

"My business is of many sorts, my boy," said Mr. Garth, smiling. "A good deal of what I know can only come from experience: you can't learn it off as you learn things out of a book. But you are young enough to lay a foundation yet." Caleb pronounced the last sentence emphatically, but paused in some uncertainty. He had been under the impression lately that Fred had made up his mind to enter the Church.

"You do think I could do some good at it, if I were to try?" said Fred, more eagerly.

"That depends," said Caleb, turning his head on one side and lowering his voice, with the air of a man who felt himself to be saying something deeply religious. "You must be sure of two things: you must love your work, and not be always looking over the edge of it, wanting your play to begin. And the other is, you must not be ashamed of your work, and think it would be more honourable to you to be doing something else. You must have a pride in your own work and in learning to do it well, and not be always saying, There's this and there's that—if I had this or that to do, I might make something of it. No matter what a man is—I wouldn't give twopence for him"—here Caleb's mouth looked bitter, and he snapped his fingers—"whether he was the prime minister or the rick-thatcher, if he didn't do well what he undertook to do."

"I can never feel that I should do that in being a clergyman," said Fred, meaning to take a step in argument.

"Then let it alone, my boy," said Caleb, abruptly, "else you'll never be easy. Or, if you *are* easy, you'll be a poor stick."

"That is very nearly what Mary thinks about it," said Fred, colouring. "I think you must know what I feel for Mary, Mr. Garth: I hope it does not displease you that I have always loved her better than any one else, and that I shall never love any one as I love her."

The expression of Caleb's face was visibly softening while Fred spoke. But he swung his head with a solemn slowness, and said—

"That makes things more serious, Fred, if you want to take Mary's happiness into your keeping."

"I know that, Mr. Garth," said Fred, eagerly, "and I would do anything for *her*. She says she will never have me if I go into the Church ; and I shall be the most miserable devil in the world if I lose all hope of Mary. Really, if I could get some other profession, business—anything that I am at all fit for, I would work hard, I would deserve your good opinion. I should like to have to do with outdoor things. I know a good deal about land and cattle already. I used to believe, you know—though you will think me rather foolish for it—that I should have land of my own. I am sure knowledge of that sort would come easily to me, especially if I could be under you in any way."

"Softly, my boy," said Caleb, having the image of "Susan" before his eyes. "What have you said to your father about all this ? "

"Nothing, yet ; but I must tell him. I am only waiting to know what I can do instead of entering the Church. I am very sorry to disappoint him, but a man ought to be allowed to judge for himself when he is four-and-twenty. How could I know when I was fifteen, what it would be right for me to do now ? My education was a mistake."

"But hearken to this, Fred," said Caleb. "Are you sure Mary is fond of you, or would ever have you ? "

"I asked Mr. Farebrother to talk to her, because she had forbidden me—I didn't know what else to do," said Fred, apologetically. "And he says that I have every reason to hope, if I can put myself in an honourable position—I mean, out of the Church. I daresay you think it unwarrantable in me, Mr. Garth, to be troubling you and obtruding my own wishes about Mary, before I have done anything at all for myself. Of course I have not the least claim—indeed, I have already a debt to you which will never be discharged, even when I have been able to pay it in the shape of money."

"Yes, my boy, you have a claim," said Caleb, with much feeling in his voice. "The young ones have always a claim on the old to help them forward. I was young myself once and had to do without much help ; but help would have been welcome to me, if it had been only for the fellow-feeling's sake. But I must consider. Come to me to-morrow at the office, at nine o'clock. At the office, mind."

Mr. Garth would take no important step without consulting Susan, but it must be confessed that before he reached home he had taken his resolution. With regard to a large number of matters about which other men are decided or obstinate, he was the most easily manageable man in the world. He never knew what meat he would choose, and if Susan had said that they ought to live in a four-roomed cottage, in order to save, he would have said, " Let us go," without inquiring into details. But where Caleb's feeling and judgment strongly pronounced, he was a ruler ; and in spite of his mildness and timidity in reproving, every one about him knew that on the exceptional occasions when he chose, he was absolute. He never, indeed, chose to be absolute except on some one else's behalf. On ninety-nine points Mrs. Garth decided, but on the hundredth she was often aware that she would have to perform the singularly difficult task of carrying out her own principle, and to make herself subordinate.

" It is come round as I thought, Susan," said Caleb, when they were seated alone in the evening. He had already narrated the adventure which had brought about Fred's sharing in his work, but had kept back the further result. " The children *are* fond of each other—I mean, Fred and Mary."

Mrs. Garth laid her work on her knee, and fixed her penetrating eyes anxiously on her husband.

" After we'd done our work, Fred poured it all out to me. He can't bear to be a clergyman, and Mary says she won't have him if he is one ; and the lad would like to be under me and give his mind to business. And I've determined to take him and make a man of him."

" Caleb ! " said Mrs. Garth, in a deep contralto, expressive of resigned astonishment.

" It's a fine thing to do," said Mr. Garth, settling himself firmly against the back of his chair, and grasping the elbows. " I shall have trouble with him, but I think I shall carry it through. The lad loves Mary, and a true love for a good woman is a great thing, Susan. It shapes many a rough fellow."

" Has Mary spoken to you on the subject ? " said Mrs. Garth, secretly a little hurt that she had to be informed on it herself.

" Not a word. I asked her about Fred once ; I gave her a bit of a warning. But she assured me she would never marry an idle, self-indulgent man—nothing since. But it seems Fred set on Mr. Farebrother to talk to her, because she had forbidden him to speak himself, and Mr. Farebrother has found out that she is fond of Fred, but says he must not be a clergyman. Fred's heart is fixed on Mary, that I can see : it gives me a good opinion of the lad—and we always liked him, Susan."

" It is a pity for Mary, I think," said Mrs. Garth.

" Why—a pity ? "

" Because, Caleb, she might have had a man who is worth twenty Fred Vincys."

" Ah ? " said Caleb, with surprise.

" I firmly believe that Mr. Farebrother is attached to her, and meant to make her an offer ; but of course now that Fred has used him as an envoy, there is an end to that better prospect." There was a severe precision in Mrs. Garth's utterance. She was vexed and disappointed, but she was bent on abstaining from useless words.

Caleb was silent for a few moments under a conflict of feelings. He looked at the floor and moved his head and hands in accompaniment to some inward argumentation. At last he said—

" That would have made me very proud and happy, Susan, and I should have been glad for your sake. I've always felt that your belongings have never been on a level with you. But you took me, though I was a plain man."

" I took the best and cleverest man I had ever known," said Mrs. Garth, convinced that *she* would never have loved any one who came short of that mark.

" Well, perhaps others thought you might have done better. But it would have been worse for me. And that is what touches me close about Fred. The lad is good at bottom, and clever enough to do, if he's put in the right way ; and he loves and honours my daughter beyond anything, and she has given him a sort of promise according to what he turns out. I say, that young man's soul is in my hand ; and I'll do the best I can for him, so help me God ! It's my duty, Susan."

Mrs. Garth was not given to tears, but there was a large one rolling down her face before her husband had finished. It came from the pressure of various feelings, in which there was much affection and some vexation. She wiped it away quickly, saying—

" Few men besides you would think it a duty to add to their anxieties in that way, Caleb."

" That signifies nothing—what other men would think. I've got a clear feeling inside me, and that I shall follow ; and I hope your heart will go with me, Susan, in making everything as light as can be to Mary, poor child."

Caleb, leaning back in his chair, looked with anxious appeal towards his wife. She rose and kissed him, saying, " God bless you, Caleb ! Our children have a good father."

But she went out and had a hearty cry to make up for the

suppression of her words. She felt sure that her husband's conduct would be misunderstood, and about Fred she was rational and unhopeful. Which would turn out to have the more foresight in it—her rationality or Caleb's ardent generosity ?

When Fred went to the office the next morning, there was a test to be gone through which he was not prepared for.

"Now, Fred," said Caleb, "you will have some desk-work. I have always done a good deal of writing myself, but I can't do without help, and as I want you to understand the accounts and get the values into your head, I mean to do without another clerk. So you must buckle to. How are you at writing and arithmetic ? "

Fred felt an awkward movement of the heart ; he had not thought of desk-work ; but he was in a resolute mood, and not going to shrink. " I'm not afraid of arithmetic, Mr. Garth : it always came easily to me. I think you know my writing."

" Let us see," said Calab, taking up a pen, examining it carefully and handing it, well dipped, to Fred with a sheet of ruled paper. " Copy me a line or two of that valuation, with the figures at the end."

At that time the opinion existed that it was beneath a gentleman to write legibly, or with a hand in the least suitable to a clerk. Fred wrote the lines demanded in a hand as gentlemanly as that of any viscount or bishop of the day : the vowels were all alike and the consonants only distinguishable as turning up or down, the strokes had a blotted solidity and the letters disdained to keep the line—in short, it was a manuscript of that venerable kind easy to interpret when you know beforehand what the writer means.

As Caleb looked on, his visage showed a growing depression, but when Fred handed him the paper he gave something like a snarl, and rapped the paper passionately with the back of his hand. Bad work like this dispelled all Caleb's mildness.

" The deuce ! " he exclaimed, snarlingly. " To think that this is a country where a man's education may cost hundreds and hundreds, and it turns you out this ! " Then in a more pathetic tone, pushing up his spectacles and looking at the unfortunate scribe, " The Lord have mercy on us, Fred, I can't put up with this ! "

" What can I do, Mr. Garth ? " said Fred, whose spirits had sunk very low, not only at the estimate of his handwriting, but at the vision of himself as liable to be ranked with office-clerks.

" Do ? Why, you must learn to form your letters and keep the line. What's the use of writing at all if nobody can understand it ?" asked Caleb, energetically, quite preoccupied with the bad quality of the work. " Is there so little business in the world that you must be sending puzzles over the country ? But that's the way people are brought up. I should lose no end of time with the letters some people send me, if Susan did not make them out for me. It's disgusting." Here Caleb tossed the paper from him.

Any stranger peeping into the office at that moment might have wondered what was the drama between the indignant man of business, and the fine-looking young fellow whose blond complexion was getting rather patchy as he bit his lip with mortification. Fred was struggling with many thoughts. Mr. Garth had been so kind and encouraging at the beginning of their interview, that gratitude and hopefulness had been at a high pitch, and the downfall was proportionate. He had not thought of desk-work—in fact, like the majority of young gentlemen, he wanted an occupation which should be free from disagreeables. I cannot tell what might have been the consequences if he had not distinctly promised himself that he would go to Lowick to see Mary and tell her that he was engaged to work under her father. He did not like to disappoint himself there.

" I am very sorry," were all the words that he could muster. But Mr. Garth was already relenting.

" We must make the best of it, Fred," he began, with a return to his usual quiet tone. " Every man can learn to write. I taught myself. Go at it with a will, and sit up at night if the day-time isn't enough. We'll be patient, my boy. Callum shall go on with the books for a bit, while you are learning. But now I must be off," said Caleb, rising. " You must let your father know our agreement. You'll save me Callum's salary, you know, when you can write ; and I can afford to give you eighty pounds for the first year, and more after."

When Fred made the necessary disclosure to his parents, the relative effect on the two was a surprise which entered very deeply into his memory. He went straight from Mr. Garth's office to the warehouse, rightly feeling that the most respectful way in which he could behave to his father, was to make the painful communication as gravely and formally as possible. Moreover, the decision would be more certainly understood to be final, if the interview took place in his father's gravest hours, which were always those spent in his private room at the warehouse.

Fred entered on the subject directly, and declared briefly what he had done and was resolved to do, expressing at the end his regret that he should be the cause of disappointment to his father, and taking the blame on his own deficiencies. The regret was genuine, and inspired Fred with strong, simple words.

Mr. Vincy listened in profound surprise without uttering even an exclamation, a silence which in his impatient temperament was a sign of unusual emotion. He had not been in good spirits about trade that morning, and the slight bitterness in his lips grew intense as he listened. When Fred had ended, there was a pause of nearly a minute, during which Mr. Vincy replaced a book in his desk and turned the key emphatically. Then he looked at his son steadily, and said—

"So you've made up your mind at last, sir?"

"Yes, father."

"Very well; stick to it. I've no more to say. You've thrown away your education, and gone down a step in life, when I had given you the means of rising, that's all."

"I am very sorry that we differ, father. I think I can be quite as much of a gentleman at the work I have undertaken, as if I had been a curate. But I am grateful to you for wishing to do the best for me."

"Very well; I have no more to say. I wash my hands of you. I only hope, when you have a son of your own he will make a better return for the pains you spend on him."

This was very cutting to Fred. His father was using that unfair advantage possessed by us all when we are in a pathetic situation and see our own past as if it were simply part of the pathos. In reality, Mr. Vincy's wishes about his son had had a great deal of pride, inconsiderateness, and egoistic folly in them. But still the disappointed father held a strong lever; and Fred felt as if he were being banished with a malediction.

"I hope you will not object to my remaining at home, sir?" he said, after rising to go; "I shall have a sufficient salary to pay for my board, as of course I should wish to do."

"Board, be hanged!" said Mr. Vincy, recovering himself in his disgust at the notion that Fred's keep would be missed at his table. "Of course your mother will want you to stay. But I shall keep no horse for you, you understand; and you will pay your own tailor. You will do with a suit or two less, I fancy, when you have to pay for 'em."

Fred lingered; there was still something to be said. At last it came.

"I hope you will shake hands with me, father, and forgive me the vexation I have caused you."

Mr. Vincy from his chair threw a quick glance upward at his son, who had advanced near to him, and then gave his hand, saying hurriedly, "Yes, yes, let us say no more."

Fred went through much more narrative and explanation with his mother, but she was inconsolable, having before her eyes what perhaps her husband had never thought of, the certainty that Fred would marry Mary Garth, that her life would hence-forth be spoiled by a perpetual infusion of Garths and their ways, and that her darling boy, with his beautiful face and stylish air "beyond anybody else's son in Middlemarch," would be sure to get like that family in plainness of appearance and carelessness about his clothes. To her it seemed that there was a Garth conspiracy to get possession of the desirable Fred, but she dared not enlarge on this opinion, because a slight hint of it had made him "fly out" at her as he had never done before. Her temper was too sweet for her to show any anger; but she felt that her happiness had received a bruise, and for several days merely to look at Fred made her cry a little as if he were the subject of some baleful prophecy. Perhaps she was the slower to recover her usual cheerfulness because Fred had warned her that she must not reopen the sore question with his father, who had accepted his decision and forgiven him. If her husband had been vehement against Fred, she would have been urged into defence of her darling. It was the end of the fourth day when Mr. Vincy said to her—

"Come, Lucy, my dear, don't be so down-hearted. You always have spoiled the boy, and you must go on spoiling him."

"Nothing ever did cut me so before, Vincy," said the wife, her fair throat and chin beginning to tremble again, "only his illness."

"Pooh, pooh, never mind! We must expect to have trouble with our children. Don't make it worse by letting me see you out of spirits."

"Well, I won't," said Mrs. Vincy, roused by this appeal and adjusting herself with a little shake as of a bird which lays down its ruffled plumage.

"It won't do to begin making a fuss about one," said Mr. Vincy, wishing to combine a little grumbling with domestic cheerfulness. "There's Rosamond as well as Fred."

"Yes, poor thing. I'm sure I felt for her being disappointed of her baby; but she got over it nicely."

" Baby, pooh ! I can see Lydgate is making a mess of his practice, and getting into debt too, by what I hear. I shall have Rosamond coming to me with a pretty tale one of these days. But they'll get no money from me, I know. Let *his* family help him. I never did like that marriage. But it's no use talking. Ring the bell for lemons, and don't look dull any more, Lucy. I'll drive you and Louisa to Riverston to-morrow."

CHAPTER LVII

> They numbered scarce eight summers when a name
>   Rose on their souls and stirred such motions there
> As thrill the buds and shape their hidden frame
>   At penetration of the quickening air :
> His name who told of loyal Evan Dhu,
>   Of quaint Bradwardine, and Vich Ian Vor,
> Making the little world their childhood knew
>   Large with a land of mountain, lake, and scaur,
> And larger yet with wonder, love, belief
>   Toward Walter Scott, who living far away
> Sent them this wealth of joy and noble grief.
>   The book and they must part, but day by day,
>   In lines that thwart like portly spiders ran,
>   They wrote the tale, from Tully Veolan.

THE evening that Fred Vincy walked to Lowick Parsonage (he had begun to see that this was a world in which even a spirited young man must sometimes walk for want of a horse to carry him) he set out at five o'clock and called on Mrs. Garth by the way, wishing to assure himself that she accepted their new relations willingly.

He found the family group, dogs and cats included, under the great apple-tree in the orchard. It was a festival with Mrs. Garth, for her eldest son, Christy, her peculiar joy and pride, had come home for a short holiday—Christy, who held it the most desirable thing in the world to be a tutor, to study all literatures and be a regenerate Porson, and who was an incorporate criticism on poor Fred, a sort of object-lesson given to him by the educational mother. Christy himself, a square-browed, broad-shouldered masculine edition of his mother not much higher than Fred's shoulder—which made it the harder that he should be held superior—was always as simple as possible, and thought no more of Fred's disinclination to scholarship than of a giraffe's, wishing that he himself were more of the same height. He was lying on the ground now by his mother's chair, with his straw-hat laid flat over his eyes, while Jim on the other side was reading aloud from that beloved writer who has made a chief part in the happiness of many young lives. The volume was "Ivanhoe," and Jim was in the great archery scene at the tournament, but suffered much interruption from Ben, who had fetched his own old bow and arrows, and was making himself dreadfully disagreeable, Letty thought, by begging all present to observe his random shots, which no one wished to do except Brownie, the active-minded but probably shallow mongrel, while the grizzled Newfoundland lying in the sun looked on with the dull-eyed neutrality of extreme old age. Letty herself, showing as to her mouth and pinafore some slight signs that she had been assisting at the gathering of the cherries which stood in a coral-heap on the tea-table, was now seated on the grass, listening open-eyed to the reading.

But the centre of interest was changed for all by the arrival of Fred Vincy. When, seating himself on a garden-stool, he said that he was on his way to Lowick Parsonage, Ben, who had thrown down his bow, and snatched up a reluctant half-grown kitten instead, strode across Fred's outstretched leg and said, "Take me!"

"Oh, and me too," said Letty.

"You can't keep up with Fred and me," said Ben.

"Yes, I can. Mother, please say that I am to go," urged Letty, whose life was much checkered by resistance to her depreciation as a girl.

"*I* shall stay with Christy," observed Jim; as much as to say that he had the advantage of those simpletons; whereupon Letty put her hand up to her head and looked with jealous indecision from the one to the other.

"Let us all go and see Mary," said Christy, opening his arms.

"No, my dear child, we must not go in a swarm to the parsonage. And that old Glasgow suit of yours would never do. Besides, your father will come home. We must let Fred go alone. He can tell Mary that you are here, and she will come back to-morrow."

Christy glanced at his own threadbare knees, and then Fred's beautiful white trousers. Certainly Fred's tailoring suggested the advantage of an English university, and he had a graceful way even of looking warm and of pushing his hair back with his handkerchief.

"Children, run away," said Mrs. Garth; "it is too warm to hang about your friends. Take your brother and show him the rabbits."

The eldest understood, and led off the children immediately. Fred felt that Mrs. Garth wished to give him an opportunity of saying anything he had to say, but he could only begin by observing—

" How glad you must be to have Christy here ! "

" Yes ; he has come sooner than I expected. He got down from the coach at nine o'clock, just after his father went out. I am longing for Caleb to come and hear what wonderful progress Christy is making. He has paid his expenses for the last year by giving lessons, carrying on hard study at the same time. He hopes soon to get a private tutorship and go abroad."

" He is a great fellow," said Fred, to whom these cheerful truths had a medicinal taste, " and no trouble to anybody." After a slight pause, he added, " But I fear you will think that I am going to be a great deal of trouble to Mr. Garth."

" Caleb likes taking trouble : he is one of those men who always do more than any one would have thought of asking them to do," answered Mrs. Garth. She was knitting, and could either look at Fred or not, as she chose—always an advantage when one is bent on loading speech with salutary meaning ; and though Mrs. Garth intended to be duly reserved, she did wish to say something that Fred might be the better for.

" I know you think me very undeserving, Mrs. Garth, and with good reason," said Fred, his spirit rising a little at the perception of something like a disposition to lecture him. " I happen to have behaved just the worst to the people I can't help wishing for the most from. But while two men like Mr. Garth and Mr. Farebrother have not given me up, I don't see why I should give myself up." Fred thought it might be well to suggest these masculine examples to Mrs. Garth.

" Assuredly," said she, with gathering emphasis. " A young man for whom two such elders had devoted themselves would indeed be culpable if he threw himself away and made their sacrifices vain."

Fred wondered a little at this strong language, but only said, " I hope it will not be so with me, Mrs. Garth, since I have some encouragement to believe that I may win Mary. Mr. Garth has told you about that ? You were not surprised, I daresay ? " Fred ended, innocently referring only to his own love as probably evident enough.

" Not surprised that Mary has given you encouragement ? " returned Mrs. Garth, who thought it would be well for Fred to be more alive to the fact that Mary's friends could not possibly have wished this beforehand, whatever the Vincys might suppose. "Yes, I confess I *was* surprised."

"She never did give me any—not the least in the world, when I talked to her myself," said Fred, eager to vindicate Mary. "But when I asked Mr. Farebrother to speak for me, she allowed him to tell me there was a hope."

The power of admonition which had begun to stir in Mrs. Garth had not yet discharged itself. It was a little too provoking even for *her* self-control that this blooming youngster should flourish on the disappointments of sadder and wiser people— making a meal of a nightingale and never knowing it—and that all the while his family should suppose that hers was in eager need of this sprig; and her vexation had fermented the more actively because of its total repression towards her husband. Exemplary wives will sometimes find scape-goats in this way. She now said with energetic decision, "You made a great mistake, Fred, in asking Mr. Farebrother to speak for you."

"Did I?" said Fred, reddening instantaneously. He was alarmed, but at a loss to know what Mrs. Garth meant, and added, in an apologetic tone, "Mr. Farebrother has always been such a friend of ours; and Mary, I knew, would listen to him gravely; and he took it on himself quite readily."

"Yes, young people are usually blind to everything but their own wishes, and seldom imagine how much those wishes cost others," said Mrs. Garth. She did not mean to go beyond this salutary general doctrine, and threw her indignation into a needless unwinding of her worsted, knitting her brow at it with a grand air.

"I cannot conceive how it could be any pain to Mr. Farebrother," said Fred, who nevertheless felt that surprising conceptions were beginning to form themselves.

"Precisely; you cannot conceive," said Mrs. Garth, cutting her words as neatly as possible.

For a moment Fred looked at the horizon with a dismayed anxiety, and then turning with a quick movement said almost sharply—

"Do you mean to say, Mrs. Garth, that Mr. Farebrother is in love with Mary?"

"And if it were so, Fred, I think you are the last person who ought to be surprised," returned Mrs. Garth, laying her knitting down beside her and folding her arms. It was an unwonted sign of emotion in her that she should put her work out of her hands. In fact her feelings were divided between the satisfaction of giving Fred his discipline and the sense of having gone a little too far. Fred took his hat and stick and rose quickly.

" Then you think I am standing in his way, and in Mary's too ? " he said, in a tone which seemed to demand an answer.

Mrs. Garth could not speak immediately. She had brought herself into the unpleasant position of being called on to say what she really felt, yet what she knew there were strong reasons for concealing. And to her the consciousness of having exceeded in words was peculiarly mortifying. Besides, Fred had given out unexpected electricity, and he now added, " Mr. Garth seemed pleased that Mary should be attached to me. He could not have known anything of this."

Mrs. Garth felt a severe twinge at this mention of her husband, the fear that Caleb might think her in the wrong not being easily endurable. She answered, wanting to check unintended consequences—

" I spoke from inference only. I am not aware that Mary knows anything of the matter."

But she hesitated to beg that he would keep entire silence on a subject which she had herself unnecessarily mentioned, not being used to stoop in that way ; and while she was hesitating there was already a rush of unintended consequences under the apple-tree where the tea things stood. Ben, bouncing across the grass with Brownie at his heels, and seeing the kitten dragging the knitting by a lengthening line of wool, shouted and clapped his hands ; Brownie barked, the kitten, desperate, jumped on the tea-table and upset the milk, then jumped down again and swept half the cherries with it ; and Ben, snatching up the half-knitted sock-top, fitted it over the kitten's head as a new source of madness, while Letty arriving cried out to her mother against this cruelty—it was a history as full of sensation as " This is the house that Jack built." Mrs. Garth was obliged to interfere, the other young ones came up and the tête-à-tête with Fred was ended. He got away as soon as he could, and Mrs. Garth could only imply some retractation of her severity by saying " God bless you " when she shook hands with him.

She was unpleasantly conscious that she had been on the verge of speaking as " one of the foolish women speaketh "— telling first and entreating silence after. But she had not entreated silence, and to prevent Caleb's blame she determined to blame herself and confess all to him that very night. It was curious what an awful tribunal the mild Caleb's was to her, whenever he set it up. But she meant to point out to him that the revelation might do Fred Vincy a great deal of good.

No doubt it was having a strong effect on him as he walked to Lowick. Fred's light hopeful nature had perhaps never had so much of a bruise as from this suggestion that if he had been out of the way Mary might have made a thoroughly good match. Also he was piqued that he had been what he called such a stupid lout as to ask that intervention from Mr. Farebrother. But it was not in a lover's nature—it was not in Fred's—that the new anxiety raised about Mary's feeling should not surmount every other. Notwithstanding his trust in Mr. Farebrother's generosity, notwithstanding what Mary had said to him, Fred could not help feeling that he had a rival: it was a new consciousness, and he objected to it extremely, not being in the least ready to give up Mary for her good, being ready rather to fight for her with any man whatsoever. But the fighting with Mr. Farebrother must be of a metaphorical kind, which was much more difficult to Fred than the muscular. Certainly this experience was a discipline for Fred hardly less sharp than his disappointment about his uncle's will. The iron had not entered into his soul, but he had begun to imagine what the sharp edge would be. It did not once occur to Fred that Mrs. Garth might be mistaken about Mr. Farebrother, but he suspected that she might be wrong about Mary. Mary had been staying at the parsonage lately, and her mother might know very little of what had been passing in her mind.

He did not feel easier when he found her looking cheerful with the three ladies in the drawing-room. They were in animated discussion on some subject which was dropped when he entered, and Mary was copying the labels from a heap of shallow cabinet drawers, in a minute handwriting which she was skilled in. Mr. Farebrother was somewhere in the village, and the three ladies knew nothing of Fred's peculiar relation to Mary: it was impossible for either of them to propose that they should walk round the garden, and Fred predicted to himself that he should have to go away without saying a word to her in private. He told her first of Christy's arrival and then of his own engagement with her father; and he was comforted by seeing that this latter news touched her keenly. She said hurriedly, "I am so glad," and then bent over her writing to hinder any one from noticing her face. But here was a subject which Mrs. Farebrother could not let pass.

" You don't mean, my dear Miss Garth, that you are glad to hear of a young man giving up the Church for which he was educated : you only mean that things being so, you are glad that he should be under an excellent man like your father."

" No, really, Mrs. Farebrother, I am glad of both, I fear," said Mary, cleverly getting rid of one rebellious tear. " I have a dreadfully secular mind. I never liked any clergyman except the Vicar of Wakefield and Mr. Farebrother."

" Now why, my dear ? " said Mrs. Farebrother, pausing on her large wooden knitting-needles and looking at Mary. " You have always a good reason for your opinions, but this astonishes me. Of course I put out of the question those who preach new doctrine. But why should you dislike clergymen ? "

" Oh dear," said Mary, her face breaking into merriment as she seemed to consider a moment, " I don't like their neck-cloths."

" Why, you don't like Camden's, then," said Miss Winifred, in some anxiety.

" Yes, I do," said Mary. " I don't like the other clergymen's neckcloths, because it is they who wear them."

" How very puzzling ! " said Miss Noble, feeling that her own intellect was probably deficient.

" My dear, you are joking. You would have better reasons than these for slighting so respectable a class of men," said Mrs. Farebrother, majestically.

" Miss Garth has such severe notions of what people should be that it is difficult to satisfy her," said Fred.

" Well, I am glad at least that she makes an exception in favour of my son," said the old lady.

Mary was wondering at Fred's piqued tone, when Mr. Farebrother came in and had to hear the news about the engagement under Mr. Garth. At the end he said with quiet satisfaction, " *That* is right ; " and then bent to look at Mary's labels and praise her handwriting. Fred felt horribly jealous—was glad, of course, that Mr. Farebrother was so estimable, but wished that he had been ugly and fat as men at forty sometimes are. It was clear what the end would be, since Mary openly placed Farebrother above everybody, and these women were all evidently encouraging the affair. He was feeling sure that he should have no chance of speaking to Mary, when Mr. Farebrother said—

" Fred, help me to carry these drawers back into my study— you have never seen my fine new study. Pray come too, Miss

Garth. I want you to see a stupendous spider I found this morning."

Mary at once saw the Vicar's intention. He had never since the memorable evening deviated from his old pastoral kindness towards her, and her momentary wonder and doubt had quite gone to sleep. Mary was accustomed to think rather rigorously of what was probable, and if a belief flattered her vanity she felt warned to dismiss it as ridiculous, having early had much exercise in such dismissals. It was as she had foreseen : when Fred had been asked to admire the fittings of the study, and she had been asked to admire the spider, Mr. Farebrother said—

" Wait here a minute or two. I am going to look out an engraving which Fred is tall enough to hang for me. I shall be back in a few minutes." And then he went out. Nevertheless, the first word Fred said to Mary was—

" It is of no use, whatever I do, Mary. You are sure to marry Farebrother at last." There was some rage in his tone.

" What do you mean, Fred ? " Mary exclaimed indignantly, blushing deeply, and surprised out of all her readiness in reply.

" It is impossible that you should not see it all clearly enough —you who see everything."

" I only see that you are behaving very ill, Fred, in speaking so of Mr. Farebrother after he has pleaded your cause in every way. How can you have taken up such an idea ? "

Fred was rather deep, in spite of his irritation. If Mary had really been unsuspicious, there was no good in telling her what Mrs. Garth had said.

" It follows as a matter of course," he replied. " When you are continually seeing a man who beats me in everything, and whom you set up above everybody, I can have no fair chance."

" You are very ungrateful, Fred," said Mary. " I wish I had never told Mr. Farebrother that I cared for you in the least."

" No, I am not ungrateful ; I should be the happiest fellow in the world if it were not for this. I told your father everything, and he was very kind ; he treated me as if I were his son. I could go at the work with a will, writing and everything, if it were not for this."

" For this ? for what ? " said Mary, imagining now that something specific must have been said or done.

" This dreadful certainty that I shall be bowled out by Farebrother." Mary was appeased by her inclination to laugh.

" Fred," she said, peeping round to catch his eyes, which were sulkily turned away from her, " you are too delightfully ridiculous. If you were not such a charming simpleton, what a temptation this would be to play the wicked coquette, and let you suppose that somebody besides you has made love to me."

" Do you really like me best, Mary ? " said Fred, turning eyes full of affection on her, and trying to take her hand.

" I don't like you at all at this moment," said Mary, retreating, and putting her hands behind her. " I only said that no mortal ever made love to me besides you. And that is no argument that a very wise man ever will," she ended, merrily.

" I wish you would tell me that you could not possibly ever think of him," said Fred.

" Never dare to mention this any more to me, Fred," said Mary, getting serious again. " I don't know whether it is more stupid or ungenerous in you not to see that Mr. Farebrother has left us together on purpose that we might speak freely. I am disappointed that you should be so blind to his delicate feeling."

There was no time to say any more before Mr. Farebrother came back with the engraving ; and Fred had to return to the drawing-room still with a jealous dread in his heart, but yet with comforting arguments from Mary's words and manner. The result of the conversation was on the whole more painful to Mary : inevitably her attention had taken a new attitude, and she saw the possibility of new interpretations. She was in a position in which she seemed to herself to be slighting Mr. Farebrother, and this, in relation to a man who is much honoured, is always dangerous to the firmness of a grateful woman. To have a reason for going home the next day was a relief, for Mary earnestly desired to be always clear that she loved Fred best. When a tender affection has been storing itself in us through many of our years, the idea that we could accept any exchange for it seems to be a cheapening of our lives. And we can set a watch over our affections and our constancy as we can over other treasures.

" Fred has lost all his other expectations ; he must keep this," Mary said to herself, with a smile curling her lips. It was impossible to help fleeting visions of another kind—new dignities and an acknowledged value of which she had often felt the absence. But these things with Fred outside them, Fred forsaken and looking sad for the want of her, could never tempt her deliberate thought.

CHAPTER LVIII

" For there can live no hatred in thine eye,
　Therefore in that I cannot know thy change :
　In many's looks the false heart's history
　Is writ in moods and frowns and wrinkles strange ;
　But Heaven in thy creation did decree
　That in thy face sweet love should ever dwell ;
　Whate'er thy thoughts or thy heart's workings be,
　Thy looks should nothing thence but sweetness tell."
　　　　　　　　—SHAKESPEARE : *Sonnets.*

AT the time when Mr. Vincy uttered that presentiment about Rosamond, she herself had never had the idea that she should be driven to make the sort of appeal which he foresaw. She had not yet had any anxiety about ways and means, although her domestic life had been expensive as well as eventful. Her baby had been born prematurely, and all the embroidered robes and caps had to be laid by in darkness. This misfortune was attributed entirely to her having persisted in going out on horseback one day when her husband had desired her not to do so ; but it must not be supposed that she had shown temper on the occasion, or rudely told him that she would do as she liked. What led her particularly to desire horse-exercise was a visit from Captain Lydgate, the baronet's third son, who, I am sorry to say, was detested by our Tertius of that name as a vapid fop " parting his hair from brow to nape in a despicable fashion " (not followed by Tertius himself), and showing an ignorant security that he knew the proper thing to say on every topic. Lydgate inwardly cursed his own folly that he had drawn down this visit by consenting to go to his uncle's on the wedding-tour, and he made himself rather disagreeable to Rosamond by saying so in private. For to Rosamond this visit was a source of unprecedented but gracefully-concealed exultation. She was so intensely conscious of having a cousin who was a baronet's son staying in the house, that she imagined the knowledge of what was implied by his presence to be diffused through all other minds ; and when she introduced Captain Lydgate to her guests, she had a placid sense that his rank penetrated them as if it had been an odour. The satisfaction was enough for the time to melt away some disappointment in the conditions of marriage with a medical man even of good birth : it seemed now that her marriage was visibly as well as ideally floating her above the Middlemarch level, and the future looked bright with letters and visits to and from Quallingham, and vague advancement in consequence for Tertius. Especially as, probably at the Captain's suggestion, his married sister, Mrs. Mengan, had come with her maid, and stayed two nights on her way from town. Hence it was clearly worth while for Rosamond to take pains with her music and the careful selection of her lace.

As to Captain Lydgate himself, his low brow, his aquiline nose bent on one side, and his rather heavy utterance, might have been disadvantageous in any young gentleman who had not a military bearing and moustache to give him what is doated on by some flower-like blond heads as " style." He had, moreover, that sort of high-breeding which consists in being free from the petty solicitudes of middle-class gentility, and he was a great critic of feminine charms. Rosamond delighted in his admiration now even more than she had done at Quallingham, and he found it easy to spend several hours of the day in flirting with her. The visit altogether was one of the pleasantest larks he had ever had, not the less so perhaps because he suspected that his queer cousin Tertius wished him away : though Lydgate, who would rather (hyperbolically speaking) have died than have failed in polite hospitality, suppressed his dislike, and only pretended generally not to hear what the gallant officer said, consigning the task of answering him to Rosamond. For he was not at all a jealous husband, and preferred leaving a feather-headed young gentleman alone with his wife to bearing him company.

" I wish you would talk more to the Captain at dinner, Tertius," said Rosamond, one evening when the important guest was gone to Loamford to see some brother officers stationed there. " You really look so absent sometimes—you seem to be seeing through his head into something behind it, instead of looking at him."

" My dear Rosy, you don't expect me to talk much to such a conceited ass as that, I hope," said Lydgate, brusquely. " If he got his head broken, I might look at it with interest, not before."

" I cannot conceive why you should speak of your cousin so contemptuously," said Rosamond, her fingers moving at her work while she spoke with a mild gravity which had a touch of disdain in it.

" Ask Ladislaw if he doesn't think your Captain the greatest bore he ever met with. Ladislaw has almost forsaken the house since he came."

Rosamond thought she knew perfectly well why Mr. Ladislaw disliked the Captain: he was jealous, and she liked his being jealous.

"It is impossible to say what will suit eccentric persons," she answered, "but in my opinion Captain Lydgate is a thorough gentleman, and I think you ought not, out of respect to Sir Godwin, to treat him with neglect."

"No, dear; but we have had dinners for him. And he comes in and goes out as he likes. He doesn't want me."

"Still, when he is in the room, you might show him more attention. He may not be a phœnix of cleverness in your sense; his profession is different; but it would be all the better for you to talk a little on his subjects. I think his conversation is quite agreeable. And he is anything but an unprincipled man."

"The fact is, you would wish me to be a little more like him, Rosy," said Lydgate, in a sort of resigned murmur, with a smile which was not exactly tender, and certainly not merry. Rosamond was silent and did not smile again; but the lovely curves of her face looked good-tempered enough without smiling.

Those words of Lydgate's were like a sad milestone marking how far he had travelled from his old dreamland, in which Rosamond Vincy appeared to be that perfect piece of womanhood who would reverence her husband's mind after the fashion of an accomplished mermaid, using her comb and looking-glass and singing her song for the relaxation of his adored wisdom alone. He had begun to distinguish between that imagined adoration and the attraction towards a man's talent because it gives him prestige, and is like an order in his button-hole or an Honourable before his name.

It might have been supposed that Rosamond had travelled too, since she had found the pointless conversation of Mr. Ned Plymdale perfectly wearisome; but to most mortals there is a stupidity which is unendurable and a stupidity which is altogether acceptable—else, indeed, what would become of social bonds? Captain Lydgate's stupidity was delicately scented, carried itself with "style," talked with a good accent, and was closely related to Sir Godwin. Rosamond found it quite agreeable and caught many of its phrases.

Therefore since Rosamond, as we know, was fond of horseback, there were plenty of reasons why she should be tempted to resume her riding when Captain Lydgate, who had ordered his man with two horses to follow him and put up at the "Green

Dragon," begged her to go out on the grey which he warranted to be gentle and trained to carry a lady—indeed he had bought it for his sister, and was taking it to Quallingham. Rosamond went out the first time without telling her husband, and came back before his return ; but the ride had been so thorough a success, and she declared herself so much the better in consequence, that she was informed of it with full reliance on his consent that she should go riding again.

On the contrary Lydgate was more than hurt—he was utterly confounded that she had risked herself on a strange horse without referring the matter to his wish. After the first almost thundering exclamations of astonishment, which sufficiently warned Rosamond of what was coming, he was silent for some moments.

" However, you have come back safely," he said, at last, in a decisive tone. " You will not go again, Rosy ; that is understood. If it were the quietest, most familiar horse in the world, there would always be the chance of accident. And you know very well that I wished you to give up riding the roan on that account."

" But there is the chance of accident indoors, Tertius."

" My darling, don't talk nonsense," said Lydgate, in an imploring tone ; " surely I am the person to judge for you. I think it is enough that I say you are not to go again."

Rosamond was arranging her hair before dinner, and the reflection of her head in the glass showed no change in its loveliness except a little turning aside of the long neck. Lydgate had been moving about with his hands in his pockets, and now paused near her, as if he awaited some assurance.

" I wish you would fasten up my plaits, dear," said Rosamond, letting her arms fall with a little sigh, so as to make a husband ashamed of standing there like a brute. Lydgate had often fastened the plaits before, being among the deftest of men with his large finely-formed fingers. He swept up the soft festoons of plaits and fastened in the tall comb (to such uses do men come !) ; and what could he do then but kiss the exquisite nape which was shown in all its delicate curves ? But when we do what we have done before, it is often with a difference. Lydgate was still angry, and had not forgotten his point.

" I shall tell the Captain that he ought to have known better than offer you his horse," he said, as he moved away.

" I beg you will not do anything of the kind, Tertius," said Rosamond, looking at him with something more marked than usual in her speech. "It will be treating me as if I were a child. Promise that you will leave the subject to me."

There did seem to be some truth in her objection. Lydgate said, "Very well," with a surly obedience, and thus the discussion ended with his promising Rosamond, and not with her promising him.

In fact, she had been determined not to promise. Rosamond had that victorious obstinacy which never wastes its energy in impetuous resistance. What she liked to do was to her the right thing, and all her cleverness was directed to getting the means of doing it. She meant to go out riding again on the grey, and she did go on the next opportunity of her husband's absence, not intending that he should know until it was late enough not to signify to her. The temptation was certainly great : she was very fond of the exercise, and the gratification of riding on a fine horse, with Captain Lydgate, Sir Godwin's son, on another fine horse by her side, and of being met in this position by any one but her husband, was something as good as her dreams before marriage : moreover, she was riveting the connection with the family at Quallingham, which must be a wise thing to do.

But the gentle grey, unprepared for the crash of a tree that was being felled on the edge of Halsell wood, took fright, and caused a worse fright to Rosamond, leading finally to the loss of her baby. Lydgate could not show his anger towards her, but he was rather bearish to the Captain, whose visit naturally soon came to an end.

In all future conversations on the subject, Rosamond was mildly certain that the ride had made no difference, and that if she had stayed at home the same symptoms would have come on and would have ended in the same way, because she had felt something like them before.

Lydgate could only say, "Poor, poor darling!" but he secretly wondered over the terrible tenacity of this mild creature. There was gathering within him an amazed sense of his powerlessness over Rosamond. His superior knowledge and mental force, instead of being, as he had imagined, a shrine to consult on all occasions, was simply set aside on every practical question. He had regarded Rosamond's cleverness as precisely of the receptive kind which became a woman. He was now beginning to find out what that cleverness was—what was the shape into which it had run as into a close network aloof and independent. No one quicker than Rosamond to see causes and effects which lay within the track of her own tastes and interests : she had seen clearly Lydgate's pre-eminence in Middlemarch society, and could go on imaginatively tracing still more agreeable social effects when his talent should have advanced him ; but for her, his professional and scientific ambition had no other relation to these desirable effects than if they had been the fortunate discovery of an ill-smelling oil. And that oil apart, with which she had nothing to do, of course she believed in her own opinion more than she did in his. Lydgate was astounded to find in numberless trifling matters, as well as in this last serious case of the riding, that affection did not make her compliant. He had no doubt that the affection was there, and had no presentiment that he had done anything to repel it. For his own part he said to himself that he loved her as tenderly as ever, and could make up his mind to her negations ; but—well ! Lydgate was much worried, and conscious of new elements in his life as noxious to him as an inlet of mud to a creature that has been used to breathe and bathe and dart after its illuminated prey in the clearest of waters.

Rosamond was soon looking lovelier than ever at her work-table, enjoying drives in her father's phaeton and thinking it likely that she might be invited to Quallingham. She knew that she was a much more exquisite ornament to the drawing-room there than any daughter of the family, and in reflecting that the gentlemen were aware of that, did not perhaps sufficiently consider whether the ladies would be eager to see themselves surpassed.

Lydgate, relieved from anxiety about her, relapsed into what she inwardly called his moodiness—a name which to her covered his thoughtful preoccupation with other subjects than herself, as well as that uneasy look of the brow and distaste for all ordinary things as if they were mixed with bitter herbs, which really made a sort of weatherglass to his vexation and foreboding. These latter states of mind had one cause amongst others, which he had generously but mistakenly avoided mentioning to Rosamond, lest it should affect her health and spirits. Between him and her indeed there was that total missing of each other's mental track, which is too evidently possible even between persons who are continually thinking of each other. To Lydgate it seemed that he had been spending month after month in sacrificing more than half of his best intent and best power to his tenderness for Rosamond ; bearing her little claims and interruptions without impatience, and, above all, bearing without betrayal of bitterness to look through less and less of interfering illusion at the blank unreflecting surface her mind presented to his ardour for the more impersonal ends of his profession and his scientific study, an ardour which he had fancied that the ideal wife must somehow worship as sublime, though not in the least knowing why. But his endurance was mingled with a self-discontent which, if we know how to be candid, we shall confess to make more than half our bitterness under grievances, wife or husband included. It always remains true that if we had been greater, circumstance would have been less strong against us. Lydgate was aware that his concessions to Rosamond were often little more than the lapse of slackening resolution, the creeping paralysis apt to seize an enthusiasm which is out of adjustment to a constant portion of our lives. And on Lydgate's enthusiasm there was constantly pressing not a simple weight of sorrow, but the biting presence of a petty degrading care, such as casts the blight of irony over all higher effort.

This was the care which he had hitherto abstained from mentioning to Rosamond ; and he believed, with some wonder, that it had never entered her mind, though certainly no difficulty could be less mysterious. It was an inference with a conspicuous handle to it, and had been easily drawn by indifferent observers, that Lydgate was in debt ; and he could not succeed in keeping out of his mind for long together that he was every day getting deeper into that swamp, which tempts men towards it with such a pretty covering of flowers and verdure. It is wonderful how soon a man gets up to his chin there—in a condition in which, spite of himself, he is forced to think chiefly of release, though he had a scheme of the universe in his soul.

Eighteen months ago Lydgate was poor, but had never known the eager want of small sums, and felt rather a burning contempt for any one who descended a step in order to gain them. He was now experiencing something worse than a simple deficit ; he was assailed by the vulgar hateful trials of a man who has bought and used a great many things which might have been done without, and which he is unable to pay for, though the demand for payment has become pressing.

How this came about may be easily seen without much arithmetic or knowledge of prices. When a man in setting up a house and preparing for marriage finds that his furniture and other initial expenses come to between four and five hundred pounds more than he has capital to pay for ; when at the end

of a year it appears that his household expenses, horses and
et cæteras, amount to nearly a thousand, while the proceeds
of the practice reckoned from the old books to be worth eight
hundred per annum have sunk like a summer pond and make
hardly five hundred chiefly in unpaid entries, the plain inference
is that, whether he minds it or not, he is in debt. Those were
less expensive times than our own, and provincial life was comparatively modest ; but the ease with which a medical man who
had lately bought a practice, who thought that he was obliged
to keep two horses, whose table was supplied without stint, and
who paid an insurance on his life and a high rent for house and
garden, might find his expenses doubling his receipts, can be
conceived by any one who does not think these details beneath
his consideration. Rosamond, accustomed from her childhood
to an extravagant household, thought that good housekeeping
consisted simply in ordering the best of everything—nothing
else " answered ; " and Lydgate supposed that " if things were
done at all, they must be done properly "—he did not see how
they were to live otherwise. If each head of household expenditure had been mentioned to him beforehand, he would have
probably observed that " it could hardly come to much," and
if any one had suggested a saving on a particular article—for
example, the substitution of cheap fish for dear—it would have
appeared to him simply a penny-wise, mean notion. Rosamond,
even without such an occasion as Captain Lydgate's visit, was
fond of giving invitations, and Lydgate, though he often
thought the guests tiresome, did not interfere. This sociability
seemed a necessary part of professional prudence, and the
entertainment must be suitable. It is true Lydgate was
constantly visiting the homes of the poor and adjusting his
prescriptions of diet to their small means ; but, dear me ! has
it not by this time ceased to be remarkable—is it not rather
what we expect in men, that they should have numerous strands
of experience lying side by side and never compare them with
each other ?   Expenditure—like ugliness and errors—becomes
a totally new thing when we attach our own personality to it,
and measure it by that wide difference which is manifest (in
our own sensations) between ourselves and others. Lydgate
believed himself to be careless about his dress, and he despised
a man who calculated the effects of his costume ; it seemed to
him only a matter of course that he had abundance of fresh
garments—such things were naturally ordered in sheaves. It
must be remembered that he had never hitherto felt the check

of importunate debt, and he walked by habit, not by self-criticism. But the check had come.

Its novelty made it the more irritating. He was amazed, disgusted that conditions so foreign to all his purposes, so hatefully disconnected with the objects he cared to occupy himself with, should have lain in ambush and clutched him when he was unaware. And there was not only the actual debt ; there was the certainty that in his present position he must go on deepening it. Two furnishing tradesmen at Brassing, whose bills had been incurred before his marriage, and whom uncalculated current expenses had ever since prevented him from paying, had repeatedly sent him unpleasant letters which had forced themselves on his attention. This could hardly have been more galling to any disposition than to Lydgate's, with his intense pride—his dislike of asking a favour or being under an obligation to any one. He had scorned even to form conjectures about Mr. Vincy's intentions on money matters, and nothing but extremity could have induced him to apply to his father-in-law, even if he had not been made aware in various indirect ways since his marriage that Mr. Vincy's own affairs were not flourishing, and that the expectation of help from him would be resented. Some men easily trust in the readiness of friends ; it had never in the former part of his life occurred to Lydgate that he should need to do so : he had never thought what borrowing would be to him ; but now that the idea had entered his mind, he felt that he would rather incur any other hardship. In the meantime he had no money or prospects of money ; and his practice was not getting more lucrative.

No wonder that Lydgate had been unable to suppress all signs of inward trouble during the last few months, and now that Rosamond was regaining brilliant health, he meditated taking her entirely into confidence on his difficulties. New conversance with tradesmen's bills had forced his reasoning into a new channel of comparison : he had begun to consider from a new point of view what was necessary and unnecessary in goods ordered, and to see that there must be some change of habits. How could such a change be made without Rosamond's concurrence ? The immediate occasion of opening the disagreeable fact on her was forced upon him.

Having no money, and having privately sought advice as to what security could possibly be given by a man in his position, Lydgate had offered the one good security in his power to the less peremptory creditor, who was a silversmith and jeweller, and who consented to take on himself the upholsterer's credit also, accepting interest for a given term. The security necessary was a bill of sale on the furniture of his house, which might make a creditor easy for a reasonable time about a debt amounting to less than four hundred pounds ; and the silversmith, Mr. Dover, was willing to reduce it by taking back a portion of the plate and any other article which was as good as new. " Any other article " was a phrase delicately implying jewellery, and more particularly some purple amethysts costing thirty pounds, which Lydgate had bought as a bridal present.

Opinions may be divided as to his wisdom in making this present : some may think that it was a graceful attention to be expected from a man like Lydgate, and that the fault of any troublesome consequences lay in the pinched narrowness of provincial life at that time, which offered no conveniences for professional people whose fortune was not proportioned to their tastes ; also, in Lydgate's ridiculous fastidiousness about asking his friends for money.

However, it had seemed a question of no moment to him on that fine morning when he went to give a final order for plate : in the presence of other jewels enormously expensive, and as an addition to orders of which the amount had not been exactly calculated, thirty pounds for ornaments so exquisitely suited to Rosamond's neck and arms could hardly appear excessive when there was no ready cash for it to exceed. But at this crisis Lydgate's imagination could not help dwelling on the possibility of letting the amethysts take their place again among Mr. Dover's stock, though he shrank from the idea of proposing this to Rosamond. Having been roused to discern conse-quences which he had never been in the habit of tracing, he was preparing to act on this discernment with some of the rigour (by no means all) that he would have applied in pursuing an experiment. He was nerving himself to this rigour as he rode from Brassing, and meditated on the representations he must make to Rosamond.

It was evening when he got home. He was intensely miser-able, this strong man of nine-and-twenty and of many gifts. He was not saying angrily within himself that he had made a profound mistake ; but the mistake was at work in him like a recognised chronic disease, mingling its uneasy importunities with every prospect, and enfeebling every thought. As he went along the passage to the drawing-room, he heard the piano and singing. Of course, Ladislaw was there. It was some weeks since Will had parted from Dorothea, yet he was still at the old post in Middlemarch. Lydgate had no objection in general to Ladislaw's coming, but just now he was annoyed that he could not find his hearth free. When he opened the door the two singers went on towards the key-note, raising their eyes and looking at him indeed, but not regarding his entrance as an interruption. To a man galled with his harness as poor Lydgate was, it is not soothing to see two people warbling at him, as he comes in with the sense that the painful day has still pains in store. His face, already paler than usual, took on a scowl as he walked across the room and flung himself into a chair.

The singers, feeling themselves excused by the fact that they had had only three bars to sing, now turned round.

" How are you, Lydgate ? " said Will, coming forward to shake hands.

Lydgate took his hand, but did not think it necessary to speak.

" Have you dined, Tertius ? I expected you much earlier," said Rosamond, who had already seen that her husband was in a " horrible humour." She seated herself in her usual place as she spoke.

" I have dined. I should like some tea, please," said Lydgate, curtly, still scowling and looking markedly at his legs stretched out before him.

Will was too quick to need more. " I shall be off," he said reaching his hat.

" Tea is coming," said Rosamond ;   " pray don't go."

" Yes, Lydgate is bored," said Will, who had more comprehension of Lydgate than Rosamond had, and was not offended by his manner, easily imagining outdoor causes of annoyance.

" There is the more need for you to stay," said Rosamond, playfully, and in her lightest accent ; " he will not speak to me all the evening."

" Yes, Rosamond, I shall," said Lydgate, in his strong baritone. " I have some serious business to speak to you about."

No introduction of the business could have been less like that which Lydgate had intended ; but her indifferent manner had been too provoking.

" There ! you see," said Will. " I'm going to the meeting about the Mechanics' Institute. Good-bye ; " and he went quickly out of the room.

Rosamond did not look at her husband, but presently rose and took her place before the tea-tray. She was thinking that she had never seen him so disagreeable. Lydgate turned his dark eyes on her and watched her as she delicately handled the tea-service with her taper fingers, and looked at the objects immediately before her with no curve in her face disturbed, and yet with an ineffable protest in her air against all people with unpleasant manners. For the moment he lost the sense of his wound in a sudden speculation about this new form of feminine impassibility revealing itself in the sylph-like frame which he had once interpreted as the sign of a ready intelligent sensitiveness. His mind glancing back to Laure while he looked at Rosamond, he said inwardly, " Would *she* kill me because I wearied her ? " and then, " It is the way with all women." But this power of generalising which gives men so much the superiority in mistake over the dumb animals, was immediately thwarted by Lydgate's memory of wandering impressions from the behaviour of another woman—from Dorothea's looks and tones of emotion about her husband when Lydgate began to attend him—from her passionate cry to be taught what would best comfort that man for whose sake it seemed as if she must quell every impulse in her except the yearnings of faithfulness and compassion. These revived impressions succeeded each other quickly and dreamily in Lydgate's mind while the tea was being brewed. He had shut his eyes in the last instant of reverie while he heard Dorothea saying, " Advise me—think what I can do—he has been all his life labouring and looking forward. He minds about nothing else—and I mind about nothing else."

That voice of deep-souled womanhood had remained within him as the enkindling conceptions of dead and sceptred genius had remained within him (is there not a genius for feeling nobly which also reigns over human spirits and their conclusions ?) : the tones were a music from which he was falling away—he had really fallen into a momentary doze, when Rosamond said in her silvery neutral way, " Here is your tea, Tertius," setting it on the small table by his side, and then moved back to her place without looking at him. Lydgate was too hasty in attributing insensibility to her ; after her own fashion, she was sensitive enough, and took lasting impressions. Her impression now was one of offence and repulsion. But then, Rosamond had no scowls and had never raised her voice : she was quite sure that no one could justly find fault with her.

Perhaps Lydgate and she had never felt so far off each other before ; but there were strong reasons for not deferring his revelation, even if he had not already begun it by that abrupt announcement; indeed some of the angry desire to rouse her into more sensibility on his account which had prompted him to speak prematurely, still mingled with his pain in the prospect of her pain. But he waited till the tray was gone, the candles were lit, and the evening quiet might be counted on : the interval had left time for repelled tenderness to return into the old course. He spoke kindly.

"Dear Rosy, lay down your work and come to sit by me," he said, gently, pushing away the table, and stretching out his arm to draw a chair near his own.

Rosamond obeyed. As she came towards him in her drapery of transparent faintly-tinted muslin, her slim yet round figure never looked more graceful ; as she sat down by him and laid one hand on the elbow of his chair, at last looking at him and meeting his eyes, her delicate neck and cheek and purely-cut lips never had more of that untarnished beauty which touches us in spring-time and infancy and all sweet freshness. It touched Lydgate now, and mingled the early moments of his love for her with all the other memories which were stirred in this crisis of deep trouble. He laid his ample hand softly on hers, saying—

"Dear !" with the lingering utterance which affection gives to the word. Rosamond too was still under the power of that same past, and her husband was still in part the Lydgate whose approval had stirred delight. She put his hair lightly away from his forehead, then laid her other hand on his, and was conscious of forgiving him.

"I am obliged to tell you what will hurt you, Rosy. But there are things which husband and wife must think of together. I daresay it has occurred to you already that I am short of money."

Lydgate paused ; but Rosamond turned her neck and looked at a vase on the mantelpiece.

"I was not able to pay for all the things we had to get before we were married, and there have been expenses since which I have been obliged to meet. The consequence is, there is a large debt at Brassing—three hundred and eighty pounds—which has been pressing on me a good while, and in fact we are getting deeper every day, for people don't pay me the faster because others want the money. I took pains to keep it from you while you were not well ; but now we must think together about it, and you must help me."

"What can *I* do, Tertius ?" said Rosamond, turning her

eyes on him again. That little speech of four words, like so many others in all languages, is capable by varied vocal inflexions of expressing all states of mind from helpless dimness to exhaustive argumentative perception, from the completest self-devoting fellowship to the most neutral aloofness. Rosamond's thin utterance threw into the words "What can *I* do!" as much neutrality as they could hold. They fell like a mortal chill on Lydgate's roused tenderness. He did not storm in indignation—he felt too sad a sinking of the heart. And when he spoke again it was more in the tone of a man who forces himself to fulfil a task.

"It is necessary for you to know, because I have to give security for a time, and a man must come to make an inventory of the furniture."

Rosamond coloured deeply. "Have you not asked papa for money?" she said, as soon as she could speak.

"No."

"Then I must ask him!" she said, releasing her hands from Lydgate's, and rising to stand at two yards' distance from him.

"No, Rosy," said Lydgate, decisively. "It is too late to do that. The inventory will be begun to-morrow. Remember it is a mere security : it will make no difference : it is a temporary affair. I insist upon it that your father shall not know, unless I choose to tell him," added Lydgate, with a more peremptory emphasis.

This certainly was unkind, but Rosamond had thrown him back on evil expectation as to what she would do in the way of quiet steady disobedience. The unkindness seemed unpardonable to her : she was not given to weeping and disliked it, but now her chin and lips began to tremble and the tears welled up. Perhaps it was not possible for Lydgate, under the double stress of outward material difficulty and of his own proud resistance to humiliating consequences, to imagine fully what this sudden trial was to a young creature who had known nothing but indulgence, and whose dreams had all been of new indulgence, more exactly to her taste. But he did wish to spare her as much as he could, and her tears cut him to the heart. He could not speak again immediately ; but Rosamond did not go on sobbing : she tried to conquer her agitation and wiped away her tears, continuing to look before her at the mantelpiece.

"Try not to grieve, darling," said Lydgate, turning his eyes up towards her. That she had chosen to move away from him in this moment of her trouble made everything harder to say, but he must absolutely go on. "We must brace ourselves to do what is necessary. It is I who have been in fault : I ought to have seen that I could not afford to live in this way. But many things have told against me in my practice, and it really just now has ebbed to a low point. I may recover it, but in the meantime we must pull up—we must change our way of living. We shall weather it. When I have given this security I shall have time to look about me ; and you are so clever that if you turn your mind to managing you will school me into carefulness. I have been a thoughtless rascal about squaring prices—but come, dear, sit down and forgive me."

Lydgate was bowing his neck under the yoke like a creature who had talons, but who had Reason too, which often reduces us to meekness. When he had spoken the last words in an imploring tone, Rosamond returned to the chair by his side. His self-blame gave her some hope that he would attend to her opinion, and she said—

"Why can you not put off having the inventory made ? You can send the men away to-morrow when they come."

"I shall not send them away," said Lydgate, the peremptoriness rising again. Was it of any use to explain ?

"If we left Middlemarch, there would of course be a sale, and that would do as well."

"But we are not going to leave Middlemarch."

"I am sure, Tertius, it would be much better to do so. Why can we not go to London ? Or near Durham, where your family is known ? "

"We can go nowhere without money, Rosamond."

"Your friends would not wish you to be without money. And surely these odious tradesmen might be made to understand that, and to wait, if you would make proper representations to them."

"This is idle, Rosamond," said Lydgate, angrily. "You must learn to take my judgment on questions you don't understand. I have made necessary arrangements, and they must be carried out. As to friends, I have no expectations whatever from them, and shall not ask them for anything."

Rosamond sat perfectly still. The thought in her mind was that if she had known how Lydgate would behave, she would never have married him.

"We have no time to waste now on unnecessary words, dear," said Lydgate, trying to be gentle again. "There are some details that I want to consider with you. Dover says he will take a good deal of the plate back again, and any of the jewellery we like. He really behaves very well."

" Are we to go without spoons and forks then ? " said Rosamond, whose very lips seemed to get thinner with the thinness of her utterance. She was determined to make no further resistance or suggestions.

" Oh no, dear ! " said Lydgate. " But look here," he continued, drawing a paper from his pocket and opening it ; " here is Dover's account. See, I have marked a number of articles, which if we returned them would reduce the amount by thirty pounds and more. I have not marked any of the jewellery." Lydgate had really felt this point of the jewellery very bitter to himself ; but he had overcome the feeling by severe argument. He could not propose to Rosamond that she should return any particular present of his, but he had told himself that he was bound to put Dover's offer before her, and her inward prompting might make the affair easy.

" It is useless for me to look, Tertius," said Rosamond, calmly ; " you will return what you please." She would not turn her eyes on the paper, and Lydgate, flushing up to the roots of his hair, drew it back and let it fall on his knee. Meanwhile Rosamond quietly went out of the room, leaving Lydgate helpless and wondering. Was she not coming back ? It seemed that she had no more identified herself with him than if they had been creatures of different species and opposing interests. He tossed his head and thrust his hands deep into his pockets with a sort of vengeance. There was still science—there were still good objects to work for. He must give a tug still—all the stronger because other satisfactions were going.

But the door opened and Rosamond re-entered. She carried the leather box containing the amethysts, and a tiny ornamental basket which contained other boxes, and laying them on the chair where she had been sitting, she said, with perfect propriety in her air—

" This is all the jewellery you ever gave me. You can return what you like of it, and of the plate also. You will not, of course, expect me to stay at home to-morrow. I shall go to papa's."

To many women the look Lydgate cast at her would have been more terrible than one of anger : it had in it a despairing acceptance of the distance she was placing between them.

" And when shall you come back again ? " he said, with a bitter edge on his accent.

" Oh, in the evening. Of course I shall not mention the

subject to mamma." Rosamond was convinced that no woman could behave more irreproachably than she was behaving; and she went to sit down at her work-table. Lydgate sat meditating a minute or two, and the result was that he said, with some of the old emotion in his tone—

" Now we have been united, Rosy, you should not leave me to myself in the first trouble that has come."

" Certainly not," said Rosamond; " I shall do everything it becomes me to do."

" It is not right that the thing should be left to servants, or that I should have to speak to them about it. And I shall be obliged to go out—I don't know how early. I understand your shrinking from the humiliation of these money affairs. But, my dear Rosamond, as a question of pride, which I feel just as much as you can, it is surely better to manage the thing our- selves, and let the servants see as little of it as possible ; and since you are my wife, there is no hindering your share in my disgraces—if there were disgraces."

Rosamond did not answer immediately, but at last she said, " Very well, I will stay at home."

" I shall not touch these jewels, Rosy. Take them away again. But I will write out a list of plate that we may return, and that can be packed up and sent at once."

" The servants will know *that*," said Rosamond, with the slightest touch of sarcasm.

" Well, we must meet some disagreeables as necessities. Where is the ink, I wonder ? " said Lydgate, rising, and throw- ing the account on the larger table where he meant to write.

Rosamond went to reach the inkstand, and after setting it on the table was going to turn away, when Lydgate, who was standing close by, put his arm round her and drew her towards him, saying,

" Come, darling, let us make the best of things. It will only be for a time, I hope, that we shall have to be stingy and particular. Kiss me."

His native warm-heartedness took a great deal of quenching, and it is a part of manliness for a husband to feel keenly the fact that an inexperienced girl has got into trouble by marrying him. She received his kiss and returned it faintly, and in this way an appearance of accord was recovered for the time. But Lydgate could not help looking forward with dread to the inevitable future discussions about expenditure and the necessity for a complete change in their way of living.

CHAPTER LIX

They said of old the Soul had human shape,
But smaller, subtler than the fleshly self,
So wandered forth for airing when it pleased.
And see ! beside her cherub-face there floats
A pale-lipped form aerial whispering
Its promptings in that little shell her ear.

NEWS is often dispersed as thoughtlessly and effectively as that
pollen which the bees carry off (having no idea how powdery
they are) when they are buzzing in search of their particular
nectar. This fine comparison has reference to Fred Vincy,
who on that evening at Lowick Parsonage heard a lively discussion among the ladies on the news which their old servant
had got from Tantripp concerning Mr. Casaubon's strange
mention of Mr. Ladislaw in a codicil to his will made not long
before his death. Miss Winifred was astounded to find that
her brother had known the fact before, and observed that
Camden was the most wonderful man for knowing things and
not telling them ; whereupon Mary Garth said that the codicil
had perhaps got mixed up with the habits of spiders, which
Miss Winifred never would listen to. Mrs. Farebrother considered that the news had something to do with their having
only once seen Mr. Ladislaw at Lowick, and Miss Noble made
many small compassionate mewings.

Fred knew little and cared less about Ladislaw and the
Casaubons, and his mind never recurred to that discussion till
one day calling on Rosamond at his mother's request to deliver
a message as he passed, he happened to see Ladislaw going
away. Fred and Rosamond had little to say to each other
now that marriage had removed her from collision with the
unpleasantness of brothers, and especially now that he had
taken what she held the stupid and even reprehensible step of
giving up the Church to take to such a business as Mr. Garth's.
Hence Fred talked by preference of what he considered indifferent
news, and " _a propos_ of that young Ladislaw " mentioned what
he had heard at Lowick Parsonage.

Now Lydgate, like Mr. Farebrother, knew a great deal more
than he told, and when he had once been set thinking about
the relation between Will and Dorothea his conjectures had gone
beyond the fact. He imagined that there was a passionate
attachment on both sides, and this struck him as much too
serious to gossip about. He remembered Will's irritability

when he had mentioned Mrs. Casaubon, and was the more circumspect. On the whole his surmises, in addition to what he knew of the fact, increased his friendliness and tolerance towards Ladislaw, and made him understand the vacillation which kept him at Middlemarch after he had said that he should go away. It was significant of the separateness between Lydgate's mind and Rosamond's that he had no impulse to speak to her on the subject; indeed, he did not quite trust her reticence towards Will. And he was right there; though he had no vision of the way in which her mind would act in urging her to speak.

When she repeated Fred's news to Lydgate, he said, "Take care you don't drop the faintest hint to Ladislaw, Rosy. He is likely to fly out as if you insulted him. Of course it is a painful affair."

Rosamond turned her neck and patted her hair, looking the image of placid indifference. But the next time Will came when Lydgate was away, she spoke archly about his not going to London as he had threatened.

"I know all about it. I have a confidential little bird," said she, showing very pretty airs of her head over the bit of work held high between her active fingers. "There is a powerful magnet in this neighbourhood."

"To be sure there is. Nobody knows that better than you," said Will, with light gallantry, but inwardly prepared to be angry.

"It is really the most charming romance: Mr. Casaubon jealous, and foreseeing that there was no one else whom Mrs. Casaubon would so much like to marry, and no one who would so much like to marry her as a certain gentleman; and then laying a plan to spoil all by making her forfeit her property if she did marry that gentleman—and then—and then—and then—oh, I have no doubt the end will be thoroughly romantic."

"Great God! what do you mean?" said Will, flushing over face and ears, his features seeming to change as if he had had a violent shake. "Don't joke; tell me what you mean."

"You don't really know?" said Rosamond, no longer playful, and desiring nothing better than to tell in order that she might evoke effects.

"No!" he returned, impatiently.

"Don't know that Mr. Casaubon has left it in his will that if Mrs. Casaubon marries you she is to forfeit all her property?"

"How do you know that it is true?" said Will, eagerly.

" My brother Fred heard it from the Farebrothers."

Will started up from his chair and reached his hat.

" I daresay she likes you better than the property," said Rosamond, looking at him from a distance.

" Pray don't say any more about it," said Will, in a hoarse undertone extremely unlike his usual light voice. " It is a foul insult to her and to me." Then he sat down absently, looking before him, but seeing nothing.

" Now you are angry with *me*," said Rosamond. " It is too bad to bear *me* malice. You ought to be obliged to me for telling you."

" So I am," said Will, abruptly, speaking with that kind of double soul which belongs to dreamers who answer questions.

" I expect to hear of the marriage," said Rosamond, playfully.

" Never! You will never hear of the marriage!"

With those words uttered impetuously, Will rose, put out his hand to Rosamond, still with the air of a somnambulist, and went away.

When he was gone, Rosamond left her chair and walked to the other end of the room, leaning when she got there against a *chiffonnière*, and looking out of the window wearily. She was oppressed by ennui, and by that dissatisfaction which in women's minds is continually turning into a trivial jealousy, referring to no real claims, springing from no deeper passion than the vague exactingness of egoism, and yet capable of impelling action as well as speech. " There really is nothing to care for much," said poor Rosamond inwardly, thinking of the family at Quallingham, who did not write to her; and that perhaps Tertius when he came home would tease her about expenses. She had already secretly disobeyed him by asking her father to help them, and he had ended decisively by saying, " I am more likely to want help myself."

CHAPTER LX

" Good phrases are surely, and ever were, very commendable."
— *Justice Shallow.*

A few days afterwards—it was already the end of August— there was an occasion which caused some excitement in Middlemarch: the public, if it chose, was to have the advantage of buying, under the distinguished auspices of Mr. Borthrop Trumbull, the furniture, books, and pictures, which anybody might see by the handbills to be the best in every kind, belonging to Edwin Larcher, Esq. This was not one of the sales indicating the depression of trade ; on the contrary, it was due to Mr. Larcher's great success in the carrying business, which warranted his purchase of a mansion near Riverston already furnished in high style by an illustrious Spa physician—furnished indeed with such large framefuls of expensive flesh-painting in the dining-room, that Mrs. Larcher was nervous until reassured by finding the subjects to be Scriptural. Hence the fine opportunity to purchasers which was well pointed out in the handbills of Mr. Borthrop Trumbull, whose acquaintance with the history of art enabled him to state that the hall furniture, to be sold without reserve, comprised a piece of carving by a contemporary of Gibbons.

At Middlemarch in those times a large sale was regarded as a kind of festival. There was a table spread with the best cold eatables, as at a superior funeral ; and facilities were offered for that generous drinking of cheerful glasses which might lead to generous and cheerful bidding for undesirable articles. Mr. Larcher's sale was the more attractive in the fine weather because the house stood just at the end of the town, with a garden and stables attached, in that pleasant issue from Middlemarch called the London Road, which was also the road to the New Hospital and to Mr. Bulstrode's retired residence, known as the Shrubs. In short, the auction was as good as a fair, and drew all classes with leisure at command : to some, who risked making bids in order simply to raise prices, it was almost equal to betting at the races. The second day, when the best furniture was to be sold, " everybody " was there ; even Mr. Thesiger, the rector of St. Peter's, had looked in for a short time, wishing to buy the carved table, and had rubbed elbows with Mr. Bambridge and Mr. Horrock. There was a wreath of Middlemarch ladies accommodated with seats round the large table in the dining-room, where Mr. Borthrop Trumbull was mounted with desk and hammer ; but the rows chiefly of masculine faces behind were often varied by incomings and outgoings both from the door and the large bow-window opening on to the lawn.

" Everybody " that day did not include Mr. Bulstrode, whose health could not well endure crowds and draughts. But Mrs. Bulstrode had particularly wished to have a certain picture— a Supper at Emmaus, attributed in the catalogue to Guido ;

and at the last moment before the day of the sale Mr. Bulstrode had called at the office of tbe " Pioneer," of which he was now one of the proprietors, to beg of Mr. Ladislaw as a great favour that he would obligingly use his remarkable knowledge of pictures on behalf of Mrs. Bulstrode, and judge of the value of this particular painting—" if," added the scrupulously polite banker, " attendance at the sale would not interfere with the arrangements for your departure, which I know is imminent."

This proviso might have sounded rather satirically in Will's ear if he had been in a mood to care about such satire. It referred to an understanding entered into many weeks before with the proprietors of the paper, that he should be at liberty any day he pleased to hand over the management to the sub-editor whom he had been training ; since he wished finally to quit Middlemarch. But indefinite visions of ambition are weak against the ease of doing what is habitual or beguilingly agree-able ; and we all know the difficulty of carrying out a resolve when we secretly long that it may turn out to be unnecessary. In such states of mind the most incredulous person has a private leaning towards miracle : impossible to conceive how our wish could be fulfilled, still—very wonderful things have happened ! Will did not confess this weakness to himself, but he lingered. What was the use of going to London at that time of the year ? The Rugby men who would remember him were not there ; and so far as political writing was concerned, he would rather for a few weeks go on with the " Pioneer." At the present moment, however, when Mr. Bulstrode was speaking to him, he had both a strengthened resolve to go and an equally strong resolve not to go till he had once more seen Dorothea. Hence he replied that he had reasons for deferring his departure a little, and would be happy to go to the sale.

Will was in a defiant mood, his consciousness being deeply stung with the thought that the people who looked at him probably knew a fact tantamount to an accusation against him as a fellow with low designs which were to be frustrated by a disposal of property. Like most people who assert their freedom with regard to conventional distinction, he was prepared to be sudden and quick at quarrel with any one who might hint that he had personal reasons for that assertion—that there was any-thing in his blood, his bearing, or his character to which he gave the mask of an opinion. When he was under an irritating impression of this kind he would go about for days with a defiant look, the colour changing in his transparent skin as if he were on the *qui vive*, watching for something which he had to dart upon.

This expression was peculiarly noticeable in him at the sale, and those who had only seen him in his moods of gentle oddity or of bright enjoyment would have been struck with a contrast. He was not sorry to have this occasion for appearing in public before the Middlemarch tribes of Toller, Hackbutt, and the rest, who looked down on him as an adventurer, and were in a state of brutal ignorance about Dante—who sneered at his Polish blood, and were themselves of a breed very much in need of crossing. He stood in a conspicuous place not far from the auctioneer, with a fore-finger in each side-pocket and his head thrown backward, not caring to speak to anybody, though he had been cordially welcomed as a connoiss*ure* by Mr. Trumbull, who was enjoying the utmost activity of his great faculties.

And surely among all men whose vocation requires them to exhibit their powers of speech, the happiest is a prosperous provincial auctioneer keenly alive to his own jokes and sensible of his encyclopædic knowledge. Some saturnine, sour-blooded persons might object to be constantly insisting on the merits of all articles from bootjacks to "Berghems;" but Mr. Borthrop Trumbull had a kindly liquid in his veins; he was an admirer by nature, and would have liked to have the universe under his hammer, feeling that it would go at a higher figure for his recommendation.

Meanwhile Mrs. Larcher's drawing-room furniture was enough for him. When Will Ladislaw had come in, a second fender, said to have been forgotten in its right place, suddenly claimed the auctioneer's enthusiasm, which he distributed on the equitable principle of praising those things most which were most in need of praise. The fender was of polished steel, with much lancet-shaped open-work and a sharp edge.

"Now, ladies," said he, "I shall appeal to you. Here is a fender which at any other sale would hardly be offered without reserve, being, as I may say, for quality of steel and quaintness of design, a kind of thing "—here Mr. Trumbull dropped his voice and became slightly nasal, trimming his outlines with his left finger—" that might not fall in with ordinary tastes. Allow me to tell you that by-and-by this style of workmanship will be the only one in vogue—half-a-crown, you said? thank you— going at half-a-crown, this characteristic fender; and I have particular information that the antique style is very much sought after in high quarters. Three shillings—three-and-sixpence

—hold it well up, Joseph ! Look, ladies, at the chastity of the design—I have no doubt myself that it was turned out in the last century ! Four shillings, Mr. Mawmsey ?—four shillings."

" It's not a thing I would put in *my* drawing-room," said Mrs. Mawmsey, audibly, for the warning of the rash husband. " I wonder *at* Mrs. Larcher. Every blessed child's head that fell against it would be cut in two. The edge is like a knife."

" Quite true," rejoined Mr. Trumbull, quickly, " and most uncommonly useful to have a fender at hand that will cut, if you have a leather shoetie or a bit of string that wants cutting and no knife at hand : many a man has been left hanging because there was no knife to cut him down. Gentlemen, here's a fender that if you had the misfortune to hang yourselves would cut you down in no time—with astonishing celerity—four-and-sixpence—five—five-and-sixpence—an appropriate thing fot a spare bedroom where there was a four-poster and a guest a little out of his mind—six shillings—thank you, Mr. Clintup—going at six shillings—going—gone ! " The auctioneer's glance, which had been searching round him with a preternatural susceptibility to all signs of bidding, here dropped on the paper before him, and his voice too dropped into a tone of indifferent despatch as he said, " Mr. Clintup. Be handy, Joseph."

" It was worth six shillings to have a fender you could always tell that joke on," said Mr. Clintup, laughing low and apologetically to his next neighbour. He was a diffident though distinguished nurseryman, and feared that the audience might regard his bid as a foolish one.

Meanwhile Joseph had brought a trayful of small articles. " Now, ladies," said Mr. Trumbull, taking up one of the articles, " this tray contains a very recherchy lot—a collection of trifles for the drawing-room table—and trifles make the sum of human things—nothing more important than trifles—(yes, Mr. Ladislaw, yes, by-and-by)—but pass the tray round, Joseph—these bijoux must be examined, ladies. This I have in my hand is an ingenious contrivance—a sort of practical rebus I may call it : here, you see, it looks like an elegant heart-shaped box, portable —for the pocket ; there, again, it becomes like a splendid double flower—an ornament for the table ; and now "—Mr. Trumbull allowed the flower to fall alarmingly into strings of heart-shaped leaves—" a book of riddles ! No less than five hundred printed in a beautiful red. Gentlemen, if I had less of a conscience, I should not wish you to bid high for this lot— I have a longing for it myself. What can promote innocent mirth, and I may say virtue, more than a good riddle ?—it hinders profane language, and attaches a man to the society of refined females. This ingenious article itself, without the elegant domino-box, card-basket, &c., ought alone to give a high price to the lot. Carried in the pocket it might make an individual welcome in any society. Four shillings, sir ?—four shillings for this remarkable collection of riddles with the et cæteras. Here is a sample : 'How must you spell honey to make it catch lady-birds ? Answer—money.' You hear ?—lady-birds—honey—money. This is an amusement to sharpen the intellect ; it has a sting—it has what we call satire, and wit without indecency. Four-and-sixpence—five shillings."

The bidding ran on with warming rivalry. Mr. Bowyer was a bidder, and this was too exasperating. Bowyer couldn't afford it, and only wanted to hinder every other man from making a figure. The current carried even Mr. Horrock with it, but this committal of himself to an opinion fell from him with so little sacrifice of his neutral expression, that the bid might not have been detected as his but for the friendly oaths of Mr. Bambridge, who wanted to know what Horrock would do with blasted stuff only fit for haberdashers given over to that state of perdition which the horse-dealer so cordially recognised in the majority of earthly existences. The lot was finally knocked down at a guinea to Mr. Spilkins, a young Slender of the neighbourhood, who was reckless with his pocket-money and felt his want of memory for riddles.

" Come, Trumbull, this is too bad—you've been putting some old maid's rubbish into the sale," murmured Mr. Toller, getting close to the auctioneer. " I want to see how the prints go, and I must be off soon."

" *Im*mediately, Mr. Toller. It was only an act of benevolence which your noble heart would approve. Joseph ! quick with the prints—Lot 235. Now, gentlemen, you who are connoiss*ures*, you are going to have a treat. Here is an engraving of the Duke of Wellington surrounded by his staff on the Field of Waterloo ; and notwithstanding recent events which have, as it were, enveloped our great Hero in a cloud, I will be bold to say—for a man in my line must not be blown about by political winds—that a finer subject—of the modern order, belonging to our own time and epoch—the understanding of man could hardly conceive : angels might, perhaps, but not men, sirs, not men."

" Who painted it ? '' said Mr. Powderell, much impressed.

" It is a proof before the letter, Mr. Powderell—the painter is not known," answered Trumbull, with a certain gaspingness in his last words, after which he pursed up his lips and stared round him.

"I'll bid a pound!" said Mr. Powderell, in a tone of resolved emotion, as of a man ready to put himself in the breach. Whether from awe or pity, nobody raised the price on him.

Next came two Dutch prints which Mr. Toller had been eager for, and after he had secured them he went away. Other prints, and afterwards some paintings, were sold to leading Middlemarchers who had come with a special desire for them, and there was a more active movement of the audience in and out ; some, who had bought what they wanted, going away, others coming in either quite newly or from a temporary visit to the refreshments which were spread under the marquee on the lawn. It was this marquee that Mr. Bambridge was bent on buying, and he appeared to like looking inside it frequently, as a foretaste of its possession. On the last occasion of his return from it he was observed to bring with him a new companion, a stranger to Mr. Trumbull and every one else, whose appearance, however, led to the supposition that he might be a relative of the horse-dealer's—also "given to indulgence." His large whiskers, imposing swagger, and swing of the leg, made him a striking figure ; but his suit of black, rather shabby at the edges, caused the prejudicial inference that he was not able to afford himself as much indulgence as he liked.

"Who is it you've picked up, Bam ? " said Mr. Horrock, aside.

"Ask him yourself," returned Mr. Bambridge. "He said he'd just turned in from the road."

Mr. Horrock eyed the stranger, who was leaning back against his stick with one hand, using his toothpick with the other, and looking about him with a certain restlessness apparently under the silence imposed on him by circumstances.

At length the *Supper at Emmaus* was brought forward, to Will's immense relief, for he was getting so tired of the proceedings that he had drawn back a little and leaned his shoulder against the wall just behind the auctioneer. He now came forward again, and his eye caught the conspicuous stranger, who, rather to his surprise, was staring at him markedly. But Will was immediately appealed to by Mr. Trumbull.

"Yes, Mr. Ladislaw, yes ; this interests you as a connoiss*ure*, I think. It is some pleasure," the auctioneer went on with a rising fervour, " to have a picture like this to show to a company of ladies and gentlemen—a picture worth any sum to an individual whose means were on a level with his judgment. It is a painting of the Italian school—by the celebrated *Guydo*, the greatest painter in the world, the chief of the Old Masters, as they are called—I take it, because they were up to a thing or two beyond most of us—in possession of secrets now lost to the bulk of mankind. Let me tell you, gentlemen, I have seen a great many pictures by the Old Masters, and they are not all up to this mark—some of them are darker than you might like, and not family subjects. But here is a *Guydo*—the frame alone is worth pounds—which any lady might be proud to hang up— a suitable thing for what we call a refectory in a charitable institution, if any gentleman of the Corporation wished to show his munifi*cence*. Turn it a little, sir ? yes. Joseph, turn it a little to Mr. Ladislaw—Mr. Ladislaw, having been abroad, understands the merit of these things, you observe."

All eyes were for a moment turned towards Will, who said, coolly, " Five pounds." The auctioneer burst out in deep remonstrance—

" Ah ! Mr. Ladislaw ! the frame alone is worth that. Ladies and gentlemen, for the credit of the town ! Suppose it should be discovered hereafter that a gem of art has been amongst us in this town, and nobody in Middlemarch awake to it. Five guineas—five seven-six—five ten. Still, ladies, still ! It is a gem, and ' Full many a gem,' as the poet says, has been allowed to go at a nominal price because the public knew no better, because it was offered in circles where there was—I was going to say a low feeling, but no !—Six pounds—six guineas—a *Guydo* of the first order going at six guineas—it is an insult to religion, ladies ; it touches us all as Christians, gentlemen, that a subject like this should go at such a low figure—six pounds ten— seven——"

The bidding was brisk, and Will continued to share in it, remembering that Mrs. Bulstrode had a strong wish for the picture, and thinking that he might stretch the price to twelve pounds. But it was knocked down to him at ten guineas, whereupon he pushed his way towards the bow-window and went out. He chose to go under the marquee to get a glass of water, being hot and thirsty : it was empty of other visitors, and he asked the woman in attendance to fetch him some fresh water ; but before she was well gone he was annoyed to see entering the florid stranger who had stared at him. It struck Will at this moment that the man might be one of those political parasitic insects of the bloated kind who had once or twice claimed acquaintance with him as having heard him speak on the Reform question, and who might think of getting a shilling by news. In this light his person, already rather heating to behold on a summer's day, appeared the more disagreeable; and Will, half-seated on the elbow of a garden-chair, turned his eyes carefully away from the comer. But this signified little to our acquaintance Mr. Raffles, who never hesitated to thrust himself on unwilling observation, if it suited his purpose to do so. He moved a step or two till he was in front of Will, and said with full-mouthed haste, " Excuse me, Mr. Ladislaw—was your mother's name Sarah Dunkirk ? "

Will, starting to his feet, moved backward a step, frowning and saying with some fierceness, " Yes, sir, it was. And what is that to you ? "

It was in Will's nature that the first spark it threw out was a direct answer of the question and a challenge of the consequences. To have said, " What is that to you ? " in the first instance, would have seemed like shuffling—as if he minded who knew anything about his origin !

Raffles on his side had not the same eagerness for a collision which was implied in Ladislaw's threatening air. The slim young fellow with his girl's complexion looked like a tiger-cat ready to spring on him. Under such circumstances Mr. Raffles's pleasure in annoying his company was kept in abeyance.

" No offence, my good sir, no offence ! I only remember your mother—knew her when she was a girl. But it is your father that you feature, sir. I had the pleasure of seeing your father too. Parents alive, Mr. Ladislaw ? "

" No ! " thundered Will, in the same attitude as before.

" Should be glad to do you a service, Mr. Ladislaw—by Jove, I should ! Hope to meet again."

Hereupon Raffles, who had lifted his hat with the last words, turned himself round with a swing of his leg and walked away. Will looked after him a moment, and could see that he did not re-enter the auction room, but appeared to be walking towards the road. For an instant he thought that he had been foolish not to let the man go on talking ;—but no ! on the whole he preferred doing without knowledge from that source.

Later in the evening, however, Raffles overtook him in the street, and appearing either to have forgotten the roughness of his former reception or to intend avenging it by a forgiving familiarity, greeted him jovially and walked by his side, remarking at first on the pleasantness of the town and neighbourhood. Will suspected that the man had been drinking and was considering how to shake him off when Raffles said—

"I've been abroad myself, Mr. Ladislaw—I've seen the world—used to parley-vous a little. It was at Boulogne I saw your father—a most uncommon likeness you are of him, by Jove! mouth—nose—eyes—hair turned off your brow just like his—a little in the foreign style. John Bull doesn't do much of that. But your father was very ill when I saw him. Lord, lord! hands you might see through. You were a small youngster then. Did he get well?"

"No," said Will, curtly.

"Ah! Well! I've often wondered what became of your mother. She ran away from her friends when she was a young lass—a proud-spirited lass, and pretty, by Jove! *I* knew the reason why she ran away," said Raffles, winking slowly as he looked sideways at Will.

"You know nothing dishonourable of her, sir," said Will, turning on him rather savagely. But Mr. Raffles just now was not sensitive to shades of manner.

"Not a bit!" said he, tossing his head decisively. "She was a little too honourable to like her friends—that was it!" Here Raffles again winked slowly. "Lord bless you, I knew all about 'em—a little in what you may call the respectable thieving line—the high style of receiving-house—none of your holes and corners—first-rate. Slap-up shop, high profits and no mistake. But Lord! Sarah would have known nothing about it—a dashing young lady she was—fine boarding-school—fit for a lord's wife—only Archie Duncan threw it at her out of spite, because she would have nothing to do with him. And so she ran away from the whole concern. I travelled for 'em, sir, in a gentlemanly way—at a high salary. They didn't mind her running away at first—godly folk, sir, very godly—and she was for the stage. The son was alive then, and the daughter was at a discount. Hallo! here we are at the Blue Bull. What do you say, Mr. Ladislaw? shall we turn in and have a glass?"

"No, I must say good evening," said Will, dashing up a passage which led into Lowick Gate, and almost running to get out of Raffles's reach.

He walked a long while on the Lowick Road away from the town, glad of the starlit darkness when it came. He felt as if he had had dirt cast on him amidst shouts of scorn. There was this to confirm the fellow's statement—that his mother never would tell him the reason why she had run away from her family.

Well! what was he, Will Ladislaw, the worse, supposing the truth about that family to be the ugliest? His mother had braved hardship in order to separate herself from it. But if Dorothea's friends had known this story—if the Chettams had known it—they would have had a fine colour to give their suspicions, a welcome ground for thinking him unfit to come near her. However, let them suspect what they pleased, they would find themselves in the wrong. They would find out that the blood in his veins was as free from the taint of meanness as theirs.

CHAPTER LXI

"'Inconsistencies,' answered Imlac, 'cannot both be right, but imputed to man they may both be true.'"—*Rasselas*.

THE same night, when Mr. Bulstrode returned from a journey to Brassing on business, his good wife met him in the entrance-hall and drew him into his private sitting-room.

"Nicholas," she said, fixing her honest eyes upon him anxiously, "there has been such a disagreeable man here asking for you—it has made me quite uncomfortable."

"What kind of man, my dear?" said Mr. Bulstrode, dreadfully certain of the answer.

"A red-faced man with large whiskers, and most impudent in his manner. He declared he was an old friend of yours, and said you would be sorry not to see him. He wanted to wait for you here, but I told him he could see you at the Bank to-morrow morning. Most impudent he was!—stared at me, and said his friend Nick had luck in wives. I don't believe he would have gone away if Blücher had not happened to break his chain and come running round on the gravel—for I was in the garden; so I said, 'You'd better go away—the dog is very fierce, and I can't hold him.' Do you really know anything of such a man?"

"I believe I know who he is, my dear," said Mr. Bulstrode, in his usual subdued voice, "an unfortunate, dissolute wretch, whom I helped too much in days gone by. However, I presume you will not be troubled by him again. He will probably come to the Bank—to beg, doubtless."

No more was said on the subject until the next day, when

Mr. Bulstrode had returned from the town and was dressing for dinner. His wife, not sure that he was come home, looked into his dressing-room and saw him with his coat and cravat off, leaning one arm on a chest of drawers and staring absently at the ground. He started nervously and looked up as she entered.

"You look very ill, Nicholas. Is there anything the matter?"

"I have a good deal of pain in my head," said Mr. Bulstrode, who was so frequently ailing that his wife was always ready to believe in this cause of depression.

"Sit down and let me sponge it with vinegar."

Physically Mr. Bulstrode did not want the vinegar, but morally the affectionate attention soothed him. Though always polite, it was his habit to receive such services with marital coolness, as his wife's duty. But to-day, while she was bending over him, he said, "You are very good, Harriet," in a tone which had something new in it to her ear; she did not know exactly what the novelty was, but her woman's solicitude shaped itself into a darting thought that he might be going to have an illness.

"Has anything worried you?" she said. "Did that man come to you at the Bank?"

"Yes; it was as I had supposed. He is a man who at one time might have done better. But he has sunk into a drunken debauched creature."

"Is he quite gone away?" said Mrs. Bulstrode, anxiously; but for certain reasons she refrained from adding, "it was very disagreeable to hear him calling himself a friend of yours." At that moment she would not have liked to say anything which implied her habitual consciousness that her husband's earlier connections were not quite on a level with her own. Not that she knew much about them. That her husband had at first been employed in a bank, that he had afterwards entered into what he called city business and gained a fortune before he was three-and-thirty, that he had married a widow who was much older than himself—a Dissenter, and in other ways probably of that disadvantageous quality usually perceptible in a first wife if inquired into with the dispassionate judgment of a second—was almost as much as she had cared to learn beyond the glimpses which Mr. Bulstrode's narrative occasionally gave of his early bent towards religion, his inclination to be a preacher, and his association with missionary and philanthropic efforts. She believed in him as an excellent man whose piety carried a peculiar eminence in belonging to a layman, whose influence had turned her own mind towards seriousness, and whose share of perishable good had been the means of raising her own position. But she also liked to think that it was well in every sense for Mr. Bulstrode to have won the hand of Harriet Vincy ; whose family was undeniable in a Middlemarch light—a better light surely than any thrown in London thoroughfares or dissenting chapel-yards. The unreformed provincial mind distrusted London ; and while true religion was everywhere saving, honest Mrs. Bulstrode was convinced that to be saved in the Church was more respectable. She so much wished to ignore towards others that her husband had ever been a London Dissenter, that she liked to keep it out of sight even in talking to him. He was quite aware of this ; indeed in some respects he was rather afraid of this ingenuous wife, whose imitative piety and native worldliness were equally sincere, who had nothing to be ashamed of, and whom he had married out of a thorough inclination still subsisting. But his fears were such as belong to a man who cares to maintain his recognised supremacy : the loss of high consideration from his wife, as from every one else who did not clearly hate him out of enmity to the truth, would be as the beginning of death to him. When she said—

"Is he quite gone away ? "

"Oh, I trust so," he answered, with an effort to throw as much sober unconcern into his tone as possible.

But in truth Mr. Bulstrode was very far from a state of quiet trust. In the interview at the Bank, Raffles had made it evident that his eagerness to torment was almost as strong in him as any other greed. He had frankly said that he had turned out of the way to come to Middlemarch, just to look about him and see whether the neighbourhood would suit him to live in. He had certainly had a few debts to pay more than he expected, but the two hundred pounds were not gone yet : a cool five-and-twenty would suffice him to go away with for the present. What he had wanted chiefly was to see his friend Nick and family, and know all about the prosperity of a man to whom he was so much attached. By-and-by he might come back for a longer stay. This time Raffles declined to be " seen off the premises," as he expressed it—declined to quit Middlemarch under Bulstrode's eyes. He meant to go by coach the next day—if he chose.

Bulstrode felt himself helpless. Neither threats nor coaxing could avail : he could not count on any persistent fear nor on any promise. On the contrary, he felt a cold certainty at his heart that Raffles—unless providence sent death to hinder him—

would come back to Middlemarch before long. And that certainty was a terror.

It was not that he was in danger of legal punishment or of beggary : he was in danger only of seeing disclosed to the judgment of his neighbours and the mournful perception of his wife certain facts of his past life which would render him an object of scorn and an opprobrium of the religion with which he had diligently associated himself. The terror of being judged sharpens the memory : it sends an inevitable glare over that long-unvisited past which has been habitually recalled only in general phrases. Even without memory, the life is bound into one by a zone of dependence in growth and decay ; but intense memory forces a man to own his blameworthy past. With memory set smarting like a reopened wound, a man's past is not simply a dead history, an outworn preparation of the present : it is not a repented error shaken loose from the life : it is a still quivering part of himself, bringing shudders and bitter flavours and the tinglings of a merited shame.

Into this second life Bulstrode's past had now risen, only the pleasures of it seeming to have lost their quality. Night and day, without interruption save of brief sleep which only wove retrospect and fear into a fantastic present, he felt the scenes of his earlier life coming between him and everything else, as obstinately as when we look through the window from a lighted room, the objects we turn our backs on are still before us, instead of the grass and the trees. The successive events inward and outward were there in one view : though each might be dwelt on in turn, the rest still kept their hold in the consciousness.

Once more he saw himself the young banker's clerk, with an agreeable person, as clever in figures as he was fluent in speech and fond of theological definition : an eminent though young member of a Calvinistic dissenting church at Highbury, having had striking experience in conviction of sin and sense of pardon. Again he heard himself called for as Brother Bulstrode in prayer meetings, speaking on religious platforms, preaching in private houses. Again he felt himself thinking of the ministry as possibly his vocation, and inclined towards missionary labour. That was the happiest time of his life : that was the spot he would have chosen now to awake in and find the rest a dream. The people among whom Brother Bulstrode was distinguished were very few, but they were very near to him, and stirred his satisfaction the more ; his power stretched through a narrow space, but he felt its effect the more intensely   He believed without effort in the peculiar work of grace within him, and in the signs that God intended him for special instrumentality.

Then came the moment of transition ; it was with the sense of promotion he had when he, an orphan educated at a commercial charity-school, was invited to a fine villa belonging to Mr. Dunkirk, the richest man in the congregation. Soon he became an intimate there, honoured for his piety by the wife, marked out for his ability by the husband, whose wealth was due to a flourishing city and west-end trade. That was the setting-in of a new current for his ambition, directing his prospects of "instrumentality" towards the uniting of distinguished religious gifts with successful business.

By-and-by came a decided external leading : a confidential subordinate partner died, and nobody seemed to the principal so well fitted to fill the severely-felt vacancy as his young friend Bulstrode, if he would become confidential accountant. The offer was accepted. The business was a pawnbroker's, of the most magnificent sort both in extent and profits ; and on a short acquaintance with it Bulstrode became aware that one source of magnificent profit was the easy reception of any goods offered without strict inquiry as to where they came from, But there was a branch house at the west end, and no pettiness or dinginess to give suggestions of shame.

He remembered his first moments of shrinking. They were private, and were filled with arguments ; some of these taking the form of prayer. The business was established and had old roots ; is it not one thing to set up a new gin-palace and another to accept an investment in an old one ? The profits made out of lost souls—where can the line be drawn at which they begin in human transactions ? Was it not even God's way of saving His chosen ? "Thou knowest,"—the young Bulstrode had said then, as the older Bulstrode was saying now—"Thou knowest how loose my soul sits from these things—how I view them all as implements for tilling Thy garden rescued here and there from the wilderness."

Metaphors and precedents were not wanting ; peculiar spiritual experiences were not wanting which at last made the retention of his position seem a service demanded of him : the vista of a fortune had already opened itself, and Bulstrode's shrinking remained private. Mr. Dunkirk had never expected that there would be any shrinking at all : he had never conceived that trade had anything to do with the scheme of

salvation. And it was true that Bulstrode found himself
carrying on two distinct lives ; his religious activity could not
be incompatible with his business as soon as he had argued
himself into not feeling it incompatible.

Mentally surrounded with that past again, Bulstrode had the
same pleas—indeed, the years had been perpetually spinning
them into intricate thickness, like masses of spider-web, padding
the moral sensibility ; nay, as age made egoism more eager
but less enjoying, his soul had become more saturated with the
belief that he did everything for God's sake, being indifferent
to it for his own. And yet—if he could be back in that far-off
spot with his youthful poverty—why, then he would choose to
be a missionary.

But the train of causes in which he had locked himself went
on. There was trouble in the fine villa at Highbury. Years
before, the only daughter had run away, defied her parents,
and gone on the stage ; and now the only boy died, and after a
short time Mr. Dunkirk died also. The wife, a simple pious
woman, left with all the wealth in and out of the magnificent
trade, of which she never knew the precise nature, had come to
believe in Bulstrode, and innocently adore him as women often
adore their priest or " man-made " minister. It was natural
that after a time marriage should have been thought of between
them. But Mrs. Dunkirk had qualms and yearnings about her
daughter, who had long been regarded as lost both to God and
her parents. It was known that the daughter had married,
but she was utterly gone out of sight. The mother, having lost
her boy, imagined a grandson, and wished in a double sense to
reclaim her daughter. If she were found, there would be a
channel for property—perhaps a wide one, in the provision for
several grandchildren. Efforts to find her must be made before
Mrs. Dunkirk would marry again. Bulstrode concurred ; but
after advertisement as well as other modes of inquiry had
been tried, the mother believed that her daughter was not to
be found, and consented to marry without reservation of
property.

The daughter had been found ; but only one man besides
Bulstrode knew it, and he was paid for keeping silence and carrying himself away.

That was the bare fact which Bulstrode was now forced to see
in the rigid outline with which acts present themselves to on-
lookers. But for himself at that distant time, and even now in
burning memory, the fact was broken into little sequences, each

justified as it came by reasonings which seemed to prove it righteous. Bulstrode's course up to that time had, he thought, been sanctioned by remarkable providences, appearing to point the way for him to be the agent in making the best use of a large property and withdrawing it from perversion. Death and other striking dispositions, such as feminine trustfulness, had come, and Bulstrode would have adopted Cromwell's words—"Do you call these bare events? The Lord pity you!" The events were comparatively small, but the essential condition was there—namely, that they were in favour of his own ends. It was easy for him to settle what was due from him to others by inquiring what were God's intentions with regard to himself. Could it be for God's service that this fortune should in any considerable proportion go to a young woman and her husband who were given up to the lightest pursuits, and might scatter it abroad in triviality—people who seemed to lie outside the path of remarkable providences? Bulstrode had never said to himself beforehand, "The daughter shall not be found"—nevertheless when the moment came he kept her existence hidden; and when other moments followed, he soothed the mother with consolation in the probability that the unhappy young woman might be no more.

There were hours in which Bulstrode felt that his action was unrighteous; but how could he go back? He had mental exercises, called himself nought, laid hold on redemption, and went on in his course of instrumentality. And after five years Death again came to widen his path, by taking away his wife. He did gradually withdraw his capital, but he did not make the sacrifices requisite to put an end to the business, which was carried on for thirteen years afterwards before it finally collapsed. Meanwhile Nicholas Bulstrode had used his hundred thousand discreetly, and was becoming provincially, solidly important—a banker, a Churchman, a public benefactor; also a sleeping partner in trading concerns, in which his ability was directed to economy in the raw material, as in the case of the dyes which rotted Mr. Vincy's silk. And now, when this respectability had lasted undisturbed for nearly thirty years—when all that preceded it had long lain benumbed in the consciousness—that past had risen and immersed his thought as if with the terrible irruption of a new sense overburthening the feeble being.

Meanwhile, in his conversation with Raffles, he had learned something momentous, something which entered actively into the struggle of his longings and terrors. There, he thought, lay an opening towards spiritual, perhaps towards material rescue.

The spiritual kind of rescue was a genuine need with him. There may be coarse hypocrites, who consciously affect beliefs and emotions for the sake of gulling the world, but Bulstrode was not one of them. He was simply a man whose desires had been stronger than his theoretic beliefs, and who had gradually explained the gratification of his desires into satisfactory agreement with those beliefs. If this be hypocrisy, it is a process which shows itself occasionally in us all, to whatever confession we belong, and whether we believe in the future perfection of our race or in the nearest date fixed for the end of the world ; whether we regard the earth as a putrefying nidus for a saved remnant, including ourselves, or have a passionate belief in the solidarity of mankind.

The service he could do to the cause of religion had been through life the ground he alleged to himself for his choice of action : it had been the motive which he had poured out in his prayers. Who would use money and position better than he meant to use them ? Who could surpass him in self-abhorrence and exaltation of God's cause ? And to Mr. Bulstrode God's cause was something distinct from his own rectitude of conduct : it enforced a discrimination of God's enemies, who were to be used merely as instruments, and whom it would be as well if possible to keep out of money and consequent influence. Also, profitable investments in trades where the power of the prince of this world showed its most active devices, became sanctified by a right application of the profits in the hands of God's servant.

This implicit reasoning is essentially no more peculiar to evangelical belief than the use of wide phrases for narrow motives is peculiar to Englishmen. There is no general doctrine which is not capable of eating out our morality if unchecked by the deep-seated habit of direct fellow-feeling with individual fellow-men.

But a man who believes in something else than his own greed, has necessarily a conscience or standard to which he more or less adapts himself. Bulstrode's standard had been his serviceableness to God's cause : " I am sinful and nought—a vessel to be consecrated by use—but use me ! "—had been the mould into which he had constrained his immense need of being something important and predominating. And now had come a moment in which that mould seemed in danger of being broken and utterly cast away.

What if the acts he had reconciled himself to, because they made him a stronger instrument of the divine glory, were to become the pretext of the scoffer, and a darkening of that glory ? If this were to be the ruling of Providence, he was cast out from the temple as one who had brought unclean offerings.

He had long poured out utterances of repentance. But to-day a repentance had come which was of a bitterer flavour, and a threatening Providence urged him to a kind of propitiation which was not simply a doctrinal transaction. The divine tribunal had changed its aspect for him ; self-prostration was no longer enough, and he must bring restitution in his hand. It was really before his God that Bulstrode was about to attempt such restitution as seemed possible : a great dread had seized his susceptible frame, and the scorching approach of shame wrought in him a new spiritual need. Night and day, while the resurgent threatening past was making a conscience within him, he was thinking by what means he could recover peace and trust—by what sacrifice he could stay the rod. His belief in these moments of dread was, that if he spontaneously did something right, God would save him from the consequences of wrong-doing. For religion can only change when the emotions which fill it are changed ; and the religion of personal fear remains nearly at the level of the savage.

He had seen Raffles actually going away on the Brassing coach, and this was a temporary relief ; it removed the pressure of an immediate dread, but did not put an end to the spiritual conflict and the need to win protection. At last he came to a difficult resolve, and wrote a letter to Will Ladislaw, begging him to be at the Shrubs that evening for a private interview at nine o'clock. Will had felt no particular surprise at the request, and connected it with some new notions about the " Pioneer " ; but when he was shown into Mr. Bulstrode's private room, he was struck with the painfully worn look on the banker's face, and was going to say, " Are you ill ? " when, checking himself in that abruptness, he only inquired after Mrs. Bulstrode, and her satisfaction with the picture bought for her.

" Thank you, she is quite satisfied ; she has gone out with her daughters this evening. I begged you to come, Mr. Ladislaw, because I have a communication of a very private—indeed, I will say, of a sacredly confidential nature, which I desire to make to you. Nothing, I daresay, has been farther from your thoughts than that there had been important ties in the past which could connect your history with mine."

Will felt something like an electric shock. He was already in a state of keen sensitiveness and hardly allayed agitation on the subject of ties in the past, and his presentiments were not agreeable. It seemed like the fluctuations of a dream—as if the action begun by that loud bloated stranger were being carried on by this pale-eyed sickly-looking piece of respectability, whose subdued tone and glib formality of speech were at this moment almost as repulsive to him as their remembered contrast. He answered, with a marked change of colour—

"No, indeed, nothing."

"You see before you, Mr. Ladislaw, a man who is deeply stricken. But for the urgency of conscience and the knowledge that I am before the bar of One who seeth not as man seeth, I should be under no compulsion to make the disclosure which has been my object in asking you to come here to-night. So far as human laws go, you have no claim on me whatever."

Will was even more uncomfortable than wondering. Mr. Bulstrode had paused, leaning his head on his hand, and looking at the floor. But he now fixed his examining glance on Will and said—

"I am told that your mother's name was Sarah Dunkirk, and that she ran away from her friends to go on the stage. Also, that your father was at one time much emaciated by illness. May I ask if you can confirm these statements ? "

"Yes, they are all true," said Will, struck with the order in which an inquiry had come, that might have been expected to be preliminary to the banker's previous hints. But Mr. Bulstrode had to-night followed the order of his emotions ; he entertained no doubt that the opportunity for restitution had come, and he had an overpowering impulse towards the penitential expression by which he was deprecating chastisement.

"Do you know any particulars of your mother's family ? " he continued.

"No ; she never liked to speak of them. She was a very generous, honourable woman," said Will, almost angrily.

"I do not wish to allege anything against her. Did she never mention her mother to you at all ? "

"I have heard her say that she thought her mother did not know the reason of her running away. She said ' poor mother ' in a pitying tone."

"That mother became my wife," said Bulstrode, and then paused a moment before he added, "you have a claim on me, Mr. Ladislaw : as I said before, not a legal claim, but one which

my conscience recognises. I was enriched by that marriage—
a result which would probably not have taken place—certainly
not to the same extent—if your grandmother could have discovered her daughter. That daughter, I gather, is no longer
living ! "

" No," said Will, feeling suspicion and repugnance rising so
strongly within him, that without quite knowing what he did,
he took his hat from the floor and stood up. The impulse
within him was to reject the disclosed connection.

" Pray be seated, Mr. Ladislaw," said Bulstrode, anxiously.
" Doubtless you are startled by the suddenness of this discovery.
But I entreat your patience with one who is already bowed down
by inward trial."

Will reseated himself, feeling some pity which was half
contempt for this voluntary self-abasement of an elderly
man.

" It is my wish, Mr. Ladislaw, to make amends for the depriva-
tion which befell your mother. I know that you are without
fortune, and I wish to supply you adequately from a store which
would have probably already been yours had your grandmother
been certain of your mother's existence and been able to find
her."

Mr. Bulstrode paused. He felt that he was performing a
striking piece of scrupulosity in the judgment of his auditor,
and a penitential act in the eyes of God. He had no clue to the
state of Will Ladislaw's mind, smarting as it was from the clear
hints of Raffles, and with its natural quickness in construction
stimulated by the expectation of discoveries which he would
have been glad to conjure back into darkness. Will made no
answer for several moments, till Mr. Bulstrode, who at the end
of his speech had cast his eyes on the floor, now raised them with
an examining glance, which Will met fully, saying—

" I suppose you did know of my mother's existence, and knew
where she might have been found."

Bulstrode shrank—there was a visible quivering in his face
and hands. He was totally unprepared to have his advances met
in this way, or to find himself urged into more revelation than he
had beforehand set down as needful. But at that moment he
dared not tell a lie, and he felt suddenly uncertain of his ground
which he had trodden with some confidence before.

" I will not deny that you conjecture rightly," he answered,
with a faltering in his tone. " And I wish to make atonement
to you as the one still remaining who has suffered a loss through

me. You enter, I trust, into my purpose, Mr. Ladislaw, which has a reference to higher than merely human claims, and as I have already said, is entirely independent of any legal compulsion. I am ready to narrow my own resources and the prospects of my family by binding myself to allow you five hundred pounds yearly during my life, and to leave you a proportional capital at my death—nay, to do still more, if more should be definitely necessary to any laudable project on your part." Mr. Bulstrode had gone on to particulars in the expectation that these would work strongly on Ladislaw, and merge other feelings in grateful acceptance.

But Will was looking as stubborn as possible, with his lip pouting and his fingers in his side-pockets. He was not in the least touched, and said firmly—

"Before I make any reply to your proposition, Mr. Bulstrode, I must beg you to answer a question or two. Were you connected with the business by which that fortune you speak of was originally made?"

Mr. Bulstrode's thought was, "Raffles has told him." How could he refuse to answer when he had volunteered what drew forth the question? He answered, "Yes."

"And was that business—or was it not—a thoroughly dishonourable one—nay, one that, if its nature had been made public, might have ranked those concerned in it with thieves and convicts?"

Will's tone had a cutting bitterness: he was moved to put his question as nakedly as he could.

Bulstrode reddened with irrepressible anger. He had been prepared for a scene of self-abasement, but his intense pride and his habit of supremacy overpowered penitence, and even dread, when this young man, whom he had meant to benefit, turned on him with the air of a judge.

"The business was established before I became connected with it, sir; nor is it for you to institute an inquiry of that kind," he answered, not raising his voice, but speaking with quick defiantness.

"Yes, it is," said Will, starting up again with his hat in his hand. "It is eminently mine to ask such questions, when I have to decide whether I will have transactions with you and accept your money. My unblemished honour is important to me. It is important to me to have no stain on my birth and connections. And now I find there is a stain which I can't help. My mother felt it, and tried to keep as clear of it as she could, and so will I. You shall keep your ill-gotten money. If I had any fortune of my own, I would willingly pay it to any one who could disprove what you have told me. What I have to thank you for is that you kept the money till now, when I can refuse it. It ought to lie with a man's self that he is a gentleman. Goodnight, sir."

Bulstrode was going to speak, but Will with determined quickness was out of the room in an instant, and in another the halldoor had closed behind him. He was too strongly possessed with passionate rebellion against this inherited blot which had been thrust on his knowledge to reflect at present whether he had not been too hard on Bulstrode—too arrogantly merciless towards a man of sixty, who was making efforts at retrieval when time had rendered them vain.

No third person listening could have thoroughly understood the impetuosity of Will's repulse or the bitterness of his words. No one but himself then knew how everything connected with the sentiment of his own dignity had an immediate bearing for him on his relation to Dorothea and to Mr. Casaubon's treatment of him. And in the rush of impulses by which he flung back that offer of Bulstrode's, there was mingled the sense that it would have been impossible for him ever to tell Dorothea that he had accepted it

As for Bulstrode—when Will was gone he suffered a violent reaction, and wept like a woman. It was the first time he had encountered an open expression of scorn from any man higher than Raffles ; and with that scorn hurrying like venom through his system, there was no sensibility left to consolations. But the relief of weeping had to be checked. His wife and daughters soon came home from hearing the address of an Oriental missionary, and were full of regret that papa had not heard, in the first instance, the interesting things which they tried to repeat to him.

Perhaps, through all other hidden thoughts, the one that breathed most comfort, was that Will Ladislaw at least was not likely to publish what had taken place that evening.

CHAPTER LXII

" He was a squyer of lowe degre,
  That loved the king's daughter of Hungrie."
                    —*Old Romance.*

WILL LADISLAW's mind was now wholly bent on seeing Dorothea
again, and forthwith quitting Middlemarch. The morning after
his agitating scene with Bulstrode he wrote a brief letter to her,
saying that various causes had detained him in the neighbourhood longer than he had expected, and asking her permission to
call again at Lowick at some hour which she would mention on
the earliest possible day, he being anxious to depart, but unwilling to do so until she had granted him an interview. He left
the letter at the office, ordering the messenger to carry it to
Lowick Manor, and wait for an answer.

Ladislaw felt the awkwardness of asking for more last words.
His former farewell had been made in the hearing of Sir James
Chettam, and had been announced as final even to the butler.
It is certainly trying to a man's dignity to reappear when he is
not expected to do so : a first farewell has pathos in it, but to
come back for a second lends an opening to comedy, and it was
possible even that there might be bitter sneers afloat about
Will's motives for lingering. Still it was on the whole more
satisfactory to his feeling to take the directest means of seeing
Dorothea, than to use any device which might give an air of
chance to a meeting of which he wished her to understand that
it was what he earnestly sought. When he had parted from
her before, he had been in ignorance of facts which gave a new
aspect to the relation between them, and made a more absolute
severance than he had then believed in. He knew nothing of
Dorothea's private fortune, and being little used to reflect on
such matters, took it for granted that according to Mr. Casaubon's
arrangement marriage to him, Will Ladislaw, would mean that
she consented to be penniless. That was not what he could
wish for even in his secret heart, or even if she had been ready
to meet such hard contrast for his sake. And then, too, there
was the fresh smart of that disclosure about his mother's family,
which if known would be an added reason why Dorothea's
friends should look down upon him as utterly below her. The
secret hope that after some years he might come back with the
sense that he had at least a personal value equal to her wealth,

seemed now the dreamy continuation of a dream. This change would surely justify him in asking Dorothea to receive him once more.

But Dorothea on that morning was not at home to receive Will's note. In consequence of a letter from her uncle announcing his intention to be at home in a week, she had driven first to Freshitt to carry the news, meaning to go on to the Grange to deliver some orders with which her uncle had intrusted her—thinking, as he said, "a little mental occupation of this sort good for a widow."

If Will Ladislaw could have overheard some of the talk at Freshitt that morning, he would have felt all his suppositions confirmed as to the readiness of certain people to sneer at his lingering in the neighbourhood. Sir James, indeed, though much relieved concerning Dorothea, had been on the watch to learn Ladislaw's movements, and had an instructed informant in Mr. Standish, who was necessarily in his confidence on this matter. That Ladislaw had stayed in Middlemarch nearly two months after he had declared that he was going immediately, was a fact to embitter Sir James's suspicions, or at least to justify his aversion to a "young fellow" whom he represented to himself as slight, volatile, and likely enough to show such recklessness as naturally went along with a position unriveted by family ties or a strict profession. But he had just heard something from Standish which, while it justified these surmises about Will, offered a means of nullifying all danger with regard to Dorothea.

Unwonted circumstances may make us all rather unlike ourselves : there are conditions under which the most majestic person is obliged to sneeze, and our emotions are liable to be acted on in the same incongruous manner. Good Sir James was this morning so far unlike himself that he was irritably anxious to say something to Dorothea on a subject which he usually avoided as if it had been a matter of shame to them both. He could not use Celia as a medium, because he did not choose that she should know the kind of gossip he had in his mind ; and before Dorothea happened to arrive he had been trying to imagine how, with his shyness and unready tongue, he could ever manage to introduce his communication. Her unexpected presence brought him to utter hopelessness in his own power of saying anything unpleasant ; but desperation suggested a resource ; he sent the groom on an unsaddled horse across the park with a pencilled note to Mrs. Cadwallader, who already knew the gossip, and would think it no compromise of herself to repeat it as often as required.

Dorothea was detained on the good pretext that Mr. Garth, whom she wanted to see, was expected at the hall within the hour, and she was still talking to Caleb on the gravel when Sir James, on the watch for the rector's wife, saw her coming and met her with the needful hints.

"Enough! I understand," said Mrs. Cadwallader. "You shall be innocent. I am such a blackamoor that I cannot smirch myself."

"I don't mean that it's of any consequence," said Sir James, disliking that Mrs. Cadwallader should understand too much. "Only it is desirable that Dorothea should know there are reasons why she should not receive him again; and I really can't say so to her. It will come lightly from you."

It came very lightly indeed. When Dorothea quitted Caleb and turned to meet them, it appeared that Mrs. Cadwallader had stepped across the park by the merest chance in the world, just to chat with Celia in a matronly way about the baby. And so Mr. Brooke was coming back? Delightful!—coming back, it was to be hoped, quite cured of Parliamentary fever and pioneering. *Apropos* of the 'Pioneer'—somebody had prophesied that it would soon be like a dying dolphin, and turn all colours for want of knowing how to help itself, because Mr. Brooke's *protégé*, the brilliant young Ladislaw, was gone or going. Had Sir James heard that?

The three were walking along the gravel slowly, and Sir James, turning aside to whip a shrub, said he had heard something of that sort.

"All false!" said Mrs. Cadwallader. "He is not gone, or going, apparently; the 'Pioneer' keeps its colour, and Mr. Orlando Ladislaw is making a sad dark-blue scandal by warbling continually with your Mr. Lydgate's wife, who they tell me is as pretty as pretty can be. It seems nobody ever goes into the house without finding this young gentleman lying on the rug or warbling at the piano. But the people in manufacturing towns are always disreputable."

"You began by saying that one report was false, Mrs. Cadwallader, and I believe this is false too," said Dorothea, with indignant energy; "at least, I feel sure it is a misrepresentation. I will not hear any evil spoken of Mr. Ladislaw; he has already suffered too much injustice."

Dorothea when thoroughly moved cared little what any one

thought of her feelings ; and even if she had been able to reflect, she would have held it petty to keep silence at injurious words about Will from fear of being herself misunderstood. Her face was flushed and her lip trembled.

Sir James, glancing at her, repented of his stratagem ; but Mrs. Cadwallader, equal to all occasions, spread the palms of her hands outward and said, " Heaven grant it, my dear !— I mean that all bad tales about anybody may be false. But it is a pity that young Lydgate should have married one of these Middlemarch girls. Considering he's a son of somebody, he might have got a woman with good blood in her veins, and not too young, who would have put up with his profession. There's Clara Harfager, for instance, whose friends don't know what to do with her ; and she has a portion. Then we might have had her among us. However !—it's no use being wise for other people. Where is Celia ? Pray let us go in."

" I am going on immediately to Tipton," said Dorothea, rather haughtily. " Good-bye."

Sir James could say nothing as he accompanied her to the carriage. He was altogether discontented with the result of a contrivance which had cost him some secret humiliation beforehand.

Dorothea drove along between the berried hedge-rows and the shorn corn-fields, not seeing or hearing anything around. The tears came and rolled down her cheeks, but she did not know it. The world, it seemed, was turning ugly and hateful, and there was no place for her trustfulness. " It is not true— it is not true ! " was the voice within her that she listened to ; but all the while a remembrance to which there had always clung a vague uneasiness would thrust itself on her attention— the remembrance of that day when she had found Will Ladislaw with Mrs. Lydgate, and had heard his voice accompanied by the piano.

" He said he would never do anything that I disapproved—I wish I could have told him that I disapproved of that," said poor Dorothea, inwardly, feeling a strange alternation between anger with Will and the passionate defence of him. " They all try to blacken him before me ; but I will care for no pain, if he is not to blame. I always believed he was good."—These were her last thoughts before she felt that the carriage was passing under the archway of the lodge-gate at the Grange, when she hurriedly pressed her handkerchief to her face and began to think of her errands. The coachman begged leave to take out the horses for half an hour as there was something wrong with a shoe; and Dorothea, having the sense that she was going to rest, took off her gloves and bonnet, while she was leaning against a statue in the entrance-hall, and talking to the house-keeper. At last she said—

"I must stay here a little, Mrs. Kell. I will go into the library and write you some memoranda from my uncle's letter, if you will open the shutters for me."

"The shutters are open, madam," said Mrs. Kell, following Dorothea, who had walked along as she spoke. "Mr. Ladislaw is there, looking for something."

(Will had come to fetch a portfolio of his own sketches which he had missed in the act of packing his movables, and did not choose to leave behind.)

Dorothea's heart seemed to turn over as if it had had a blow, but she was not perceptibly checked: in truth, the sense that Will was there was for the moment all-satisfying to her, like the sight of something precious that one has lost. When she reached the door she said to Mrs. Kell—

"Go in first, and tell him that I am here."

Will had found his portfolio, and had laid it on the table at the far end of the room, to turn over the sketches and please himself by looking at the memorable piece of art which had a relation to nature too mysterious for Dorothea. He was smiling at it still, and shaking the sketches into order with the thought that he might find a letter from her awaiting him at Middle-march, when Mrs. Kell close to his elbow said—

"Mrs. Casaubon is coming in, sir."

Will turned round quickly, and the next moment Dorothea was entering. As Mrs. Kell closed the door behind her they met: each was looking at the other, and consciousness was overflowed by something that suppressed utterance. It was not confusion that kept them silent, for they both felt that parting was near, and there is no shamefacedness in a sad parting.

She moved automatically towards her uncle's chair against the writing-table, and Will, after drawing it out a little for her, went a few paces off and stood opposite to her.

"Pray sit down," said Dorothea, crossing her hands on her lap; "I am very glad you were here." Will thought that her face looked just as it did when she first shook hands with him in Rome; for her widow's cap, fixed in her bonnet, had gone off with it, and he could see that she had lately been shedding tears. But the mixture of anger in her agitation had vanished at the sight of him; she had been used, when they were face to face, always to feel confidence and the happy freedom which comes with mutual understanding, and how could other people's words hinder that effect on a sudden? Let the music which can take possession of our frame and fill the air with joy for us, sound once more—what does it signify that we heard it found fault with in its absence?

"I have sent a letter to Lowick Manor to-day, asking leave to see you," said Will, seating himself opposite to her. "I am going away immediately, and I could not go without speaking to you again."

"I thought we had parted when you came to Lowick many weeks ago—you thought you were going then," said Dorothea, her voice trembling a little.

"Yes; but I was in ignorance then of things which I know now—things which have altered my feelings about the future. When I saw you before, I was dreaming that I might come back some day. I don't think I ever shall—now." Will paused here.

"You wished me to know the reasons?" said Dorothea, timidly.

"Yes," said Will, impetuously, shaking his head backward, and looking away from her with irritation in his face. "Of course I must wish it. I have been grossly insulted in your eyes and in the eyes of others. There has been a mean impli cation against my character. I wish you to know that under no circumstances would I have lowered myself by—under no circumstances would I have given men the chance of saying that I sought money under the pretext of seeking—something else. There was no need of other safeguard against me—the safeguard of wealth was enough."

Will rose from his chair with the last word and went—he hardly knew where; but it was to the projecting window nearest him, which had been open as now about the same season a year ago, when he and Dorothea had stood within it and talked together. Her whole heart was going out at this moment in sympathy with Will's indignation: she only wanted to convince him that she had never done him injustice, and he seemed to have turned away from her as if she too had been part of the unfriendly world.

"It would be very unkind of you to suppose that I ever attributed any meanness to you," she began. Then in her

ardent way, wanting to plead with him, she moved from her
chair and went in front of him to her old place in the window,
saying, "Do you suppose that I ever disbelieved in you ? "

When Will saw her there, he gave a start and moved backward out of the window, without meeting her glance. Dorothea
was hurt by this movement following up the previous anger of
his tone. She was ready to say that it was as hard on her as
on him, and that she was helpless ; but those strange particulars
of their relation which neither of them could explicitly mention
kept her always in dread of saying too much. At this moment
she had no belief that Will would in any case have wanted to
marry her, and she feared using words which might imply such
a belief. She only said earnestly, recurring to his last word—

" I am sure no safeguard was ever needed against you."

Will did not answer. In the stormy fluctuation of his feelings
these words of hers seemed to him cruelly neutral, and he looked
pale and miserable after his angry outburst. He went to the
table and fastened up his portfolio, while Dorothea looked at
him from the distance. They were wasting these last moments
together in wretched silence. What could he say, since what
had got obstinately uppermost in his mind was the passionate
love for her which he forbade himself to utter ? What could
she say, since she might offer him no help—since she was forced
to keep the money that ought to have been his ?—since to-day
he seemed not to respond as he used to do to her thorough trust
and liking ?

But Will at last turned away from his portfolio and approached the window again.

" I must go," he said, with that peculiar look of the eyes which
sometimes accompanies bitter feeling, as if they had been tired
and burned with gazing too close at a light.

" What shall you do in life ? " said Dorothea, timidly.
" Have your intentions remained just the same as when we
said good-bye before ? "

" Yes," said Will, in a tone that seemed to waive the subject
as uninteresting. " I shall work away at the first thing that
offers. I suppose one gets a habit of doing without happiness
or hope."

" Oh, what sad words ! " said Dorothea, with a dangerous
tendency to sob. Then trying to smile, she added, " We used
to agree that we were alike in speaking too strongly."

" I have not spoken too strongly now," said Will, leaning
back against the angle of the wall. " There are certain things

which a man can only go through once in his life ; and he must know some time or other that the best is over with him. This experience has happened to me while I am very young—that is all. What I care more for than I can ever care for anything else is absolutely forbidden to me—I don't mean merely by being out of my reach, but forbidden me, even if it were within my reach, by my own pride and honour—by everything I respect myself for. Of course I shall go on living as a man might do who had seen heaven in a trance."

Will paused, imagining that it would be impossible for Dorothea to misunderstand this ; indeed he felt that he was contradicting himself and offending against his self-approval in speaking to her so plainly ; but still—it could not be fairly called wooing a woman to tell her that he would never woo her. It must be admitted to be a ghostly kind of wooing.

But Dorothea's mind was rapidly going over the past with quite another vision than his. The thought that she herself might be what Will most cared for did throb through her an instant, but then came doubt : the memory of the little they had lived through together turned pale and shrank before the memory which suggested how much fuller might have been the intercourse between Will and some one else with whom he had had constant companionship. Everything he had said might refer to that other relation, and whatever had passed between him and herself was thoroughly explained by what she had always regarded as their simple friendship and the cruel obstruction thrust upon it by her husband's injurious act. Dorothea stood silent, with her eyes cast down dreamily, while images crowded upon her which left the sickening certainty that Will was referring to Mrs. Lydgate. But why sickening ? He wanted her to know that here too his conduct should be above suspicion.

Will was not surprised at her silence. His mind also was tumultuously busy while he watched her, and he was feeling rather wildly that something must happen to hinder their parting—some miracle, clearly nothing in their own deliberate speech. Yet, after all, had she any love for him ?—he could not pretend to himself that he would rather believe her to be without that pain. He could not deny that a secret longing for the assurance that she loved him was at the root of all his words.

Neither of them knew how long they stood in that way. Dorothea was raising her eyes, and was about to speak, when the door opened and her footman came to say—

" The horses are ready, madam, whenever you like to start."

" Presently," said Dorothea. Then turning to Will, she said, " I have some memoranda to write for the housekeeper."

" I must go," said Will, when the door had closed again— advancing towards her. " The day after to-morrow I shall leave Middlemarch."

" You have acted in every way rightly," said Dorothea, in a low tone, feeling a pressure at her heart which made it difficult to speak.

She put out her hand, and Will took it for an instant without speaking, for her words had seemed to him cruelly cold and unlike herself. Their eyes met, but there was discontent in his, and in hers there was only sadness. He turned away and took his portfolio under his arm.

" I have never done you injustice. Please remember me," said Dorothea, repressing a rising sob.

" Why should you say that ? " said Will, with irritation. " As if I were not in danger of forgetting everything else."

He had really a movement of anger against her at that moment, and it impelled him to go away without pause. It was all one flash to Dorothea—his last words—his distant bow to her as he reached the door—the sense that he was no longer there. She sank into the chair, and for a few moments sat like a statue, while images and emotions were hurrying upon her. Joy came first, in spite of the threatening train behind it—joy in the impression that it was really herself whom Will loved and was renouncing, that there was really no other love less permissible, more blameworthy, which honour was hurrying him away from. They were parted all the same, but—Dorothea drew a deep breath and felt her strength return—she could think of him unrestrainedly. At that moment the parting was easy to bear : the first sense of loving and being loved excluded sorrow. It was as if some hard icy pressure had melted, and her conscious-ness had room to expand ; her past was come back to her with larger interpretation. The joy was not the less—perhaps it was the more complete just then—because of the irrevocable parting ; for there was no reproach, no contemptuous wonder to imagine in any eye or from any lips. He had acted so as to defy reproach, and make wonder respectful.

Any one watching her might have seen that there was a fortifying thought within her. Just as when inventive power is working with glad ease some small claim on the attention is fully met as if it were only a cranny opened to the sunlight, it was easy now for Dorothea to write her memoranda. She spoke her last words to the housekeeper in cheerful tones, and when she seated herself in the carriage her eyes were bright and her cheeks blooming under the dismal bonnet. She threw back the heavy " weepers," and looked before her, wondering which road Will had taken. It was in her nature to be proud that he was blameless, and through all her feelings there ran this vein— " I was right to defend him."

The coachman was used to drive his greys at a good pace, Mr. Casaubon being unenjoying and impatient in everything away from his desk, and wanting to get to the end of all journeys; and Dorothea was now bowled along quickly. Driving was pleasant, for rain in the night had laid the dust, and the blue sky looked far off, away from the region of the great clouds that sailed in masses. The earth looked like a happy place under the vast heavens, and Dorothea was wishing that she might overtake Will and see him once more.

After a turn of the road, there he was with the portfolio under his arm ; but the next moment she was passing him while he raised his hat, and she felt a pang at being seated there in a sort of exaltation, leaving him behind. She could not look back at him. It was as if a crowd of indifferent objects had thrust them asunder, and forced them along different paths, taking them farther and farther away from each other, and making it useless to look back. She could no more make any sign that would seem to say, " Need we part ? " than she could stop the carriage to wait for him. Nay, what a world of reasons crowded upon her against any movement of her thought towards a future that might reverse the decision of this day !

" I only wish I had known before—I wish he knew—then we could be quite happy in thinking of each other, though we are for ever parted. And if I could but have given him the money, and made things easier for him ! "—were the longings that came back the most persistently. And yet, so heavily did the world weigh on her in spite of her independent energy, that with this idea of Will as in need of such help and at a disadvantage with the world, there came always the vision of that unfittingness of any closer relation between them which lay in the opinion of every one connected with her. She felt to the full all the imperativeness of the motives which urged Will's conduct. How could he dream of her defying the barrier that her husband had placed between them ?—how could she ever say to herself that she would defy it ?

Will's certainty, as the carriage grew smaller in the distance, had much more bitterness in it. Very slight matters were enough to gall him in his sensitive mood, and the sight of Dorothea driving past him while he felt himself plodding along as a poor devil seeking a position in a world which in his present temper offered him little that he coveted, made his conduct seem a mere matter of necessity, and took away the sustainment of resolve. After all, he had no assurance that she loved him : could any man pretend that he was simply glad in such a case to have the suffering all on his own side ?

That evening Will spent with the Lydgates ; the next evening he was gone.

BOOK VII
TWO TEMPTATIONS

CHAPTER LXIII

"These little things are great to little man."—GOLDSMITH.

"HAVE you seen much of your scientific phœnix, Lydgate, lately?" said Mr. Toller at one of his Christmas dinner-parties, speaking to Mr. Farebrother on his right hand.

"Not much, I am sorry to say," answered the Vicar, accustomed to parry Mr. Toller's banter about his belief in the new medical light. "I am out of the way, and he is too busy."

"Is he? I am glad to hear it," said Dr. Minchin, with mingled suavity and surprise.

"He gives a great deal of time to the New Hospital," said Mr. Farebrother, who had his reasons for continuing the subject : "I hear of that from my neighbour, Mrs. Casaubon, who goes there often. She says Lydgate is indefatigable, and is making a fine thing of Bulstrode's institution. He is preparing a new ward in case of the cholera coming to us."

"And preparing theories of treatment to try on the patients, I suppose," said Mr. Toller.

"Come, Toller, be candid," said Mr. Farebrother. "You are too clever not to see the good of a bold fresh mind in medicine, as well as in everything else ; and as to cholera, I fancy, none of you are very sure what you ought to do. If a man goes a little too far along a new road, it is usually himself that he harms more than any one else."

"I am sure you and Wrench ought to be obliged to him," said Dr. Minchin, looking towards Toller, "for he has sent you the cream of Peacock's patients."

"Lydgate has been living at a great rate for a young beginner," said Mr. Harry Toller, the brewer. "I suppose his relations in the North back him up."

"I hope so," said Mr. Chichely, "else he ought not to have married that nice girl we were all so fond of. Hang it, one has a grudge against a man who carries off the prettiest girl in the town."

"Ay, by God! and the best too," said Mr. Standish.

"My friend Vincy didn't half like the marriage, I know that," said Mr. Chichely. "*He* wouldn't do much. How the relations on the other side may have come down I can't say." There was an emphatic kind of reticence in Mr. Chichely's manner of speaking.

"Oh, I shouldn't think Lydgate ever looked to practice for a living," said Mr. Toller, with a slight touch of sarcasm; and there the subject was dropped.

This was not the first time that Mr. Farebrother had heard hints of Lydgate's expenses being obviously too great to be met by his practice, but he thought it not unlikely that there were resources of expectations which excused the large outlay at the time of Lydgate's marriage, and which might hinder any bad consequences from the disappointment in his practice. One evening, when he took the pains to go to Middlemarch on purpose to have a chat with Lydgate as of old, he noticed in him an air of excited effort quite unlike his usual easy way of keeping silence or breaking it with abrupt energy whenever he had anything to say. Lydgate talked persistently when they were in his work-room, putting arguments for and against the probability of certain biological views; but he had none of those definite things to say or to show which give the way-marks of a patient uninterrupted pursuit, such as he used himself to insist on, saying that "there must be a systole and diastole in all inquiry," and that "a man's mind must be continually expanding and shrinking between the whole human horizon and the horizon of an object-glass." That evening he seemed to be talking widely for the sake of resisting any personal bearing; and before long they went into the drawing-room, where Lydgate, having asked Rosamond to give them music, sank back in his chair in silence, but with a strange light in his eyes. "He may have been taking an opiate," was a thought that crossed Mr. Farebrother's mind—"tic-douloureux perhaps—or medical worries."

It did not occur to him that Lydgate's marriage was not delightful: he believed, as the rest did, that Rosamond was an amiable, docile creature, though he had always thought her rather uninteresting—a little too much the pattern-card of the finishing-school; and his mother could not forgive Rosamond because she never seemed to see that Henrietta Noble was in the room. " However, Lydgate fell in love with her," said the Vicar to himself, " and she must be to his taste."

Mr. Farebrother was aware that Lydgate was a proud man, but having very little corresponding fibre in himself, and perhaps too little care about personal dignity, except the dignity of not being mean or foolish, he could hardly allow enough for the way in which Lydgate shrank, as from a burn, from the utterance of any word about his private affairs. And soon after that conversation at Mr. Toller's, the Vicar learned something which made him watch the more eagerly for an opportunity of indirectly letting Lydgate know that if he wanted to open himself about any difficulty there was a friendly ear ready.

The opportunity came at Mr. Vincy's, where, on New Year's Day, there was a party, to which Mr. Farebrother was irresistibly invited, on the plea that he must not forsake his old friends on the first new year of his being a greater man, and Rector as well as Vicar. And this party was thoroughly friendly : all the ladies of the Farebrother family were present ; the Vincy children all dined at the table, and Fred had persuaded his mother that if she did not invite Mary Garth, the Farebrothers would regard it as a slight to themselves, Mary being their particular friend. Mary came, and Fred was in high spirits, though his enjoyment was of a checkered kind—triumph that his mother should see Mary's importance with the chief personages in the party being much streaked with jealousy when Mr. Farebrother sat down by her. Fred used to be much more easy about his own accomplishments in the days when he had not begun to dread being " bowled out by Farebrother," and this terror was still before him. Mrs. Vincy, in her fullest matronly bloom, looked at Mary's little figure, rough wavy hair, and visage quite without lilies and roses, and wondered ; trying unsuccessfully to fancy herself caring about Mary's appearance in wedding clothes, or feeling complacency in grandchildren who would " feature " the Garths. However, the party was a merry one, and Mary was particularly bright ; being glad, for Fred's sake, that his friends were getting kinder to her, and being also quite willing that they should see how much she was valued by others whom they must admit to be judges.

Mr. Farebrother noticed that Lydgate seemed bored, and that Mr. Vincy spoke as little as possible to his son-in-law. Rosamond was perfectly graceful and calm, and only a subtle observation such as the Vicar had not been roused to bestow on her would have perceived the total absence of that interest in her husband's presence which a loving wife is sure to betray, even if etiquette keeps her aloof from him. When Lydgate was taking part in the conversation, she never looked towards him any more than if she had been a sculptured Psyche modelled to look another way : and when, after being called out for an hour or two, he re-entered the room, she seemed unconscious of the fact, which eighteen months before would have had the effect of a numeral before cyphers. In reality, however, she was intensely aware of Lydgate's voice and movements ; and her pretty good-tempered air of unconsciousness was a studied negation by which she satisfied her inward opposition to him without compromise of propriety. When the ladies were in the drawing-room after Lydgate had been called away from the dessert, Mrs. Farebrother, when Rosamond happened to be near her, said—" You have to give up a great deal of your husband's society, Mrs. Lydgate."

" Yes, the life of a medical man is very arduous ; especially when he is so devoted to his profession as Mr. Lydgate is," said Rosamond, who was standing, and moved easily away at the end of this correct little speech.

" It is dreadfully dull for her when there is no company," said Mrs. Vincy, who was seated at the old lady's side. " I am sure I thought so when Rosamond was ill, and I was staying with her. You know, Mrs. Farebrother, ours is a cheerful house. I am of a cheerful disposition myself, and Mr. Vincy always likes something to be going on. That is what Rosamond has been used to. Very different from a husband out at odd hours, and never knowing when he will come home, and of a close, proud disposition, *I* think "—indiscreet Mrs. Vincy did lower her tone slightly with this parenthesis. " But Rosamond always had an angel of a temper ; her brothers used very often not to please her, but she was never the girl to show temper ; from a baby she was always as good as good, and with a complexion beyond anything. But my children are all good-tempered, thank God."

This was easily credible to any one looking at Mrs. Vincy as she threw back her broad cap-strings, and smiled towards her three little girls, aged from seven to eleven. But in that smiling glance she was obliged to include Mary Garth, whom the three girls had got into a corner to make her tell them stories. Mary was just finishing the delicious tale of Rumpel-stiltskin which she had well by heart, because Letty was never tired of communicating it to her ignorant elders from a favourite red volume. Louisa, Mrs. Vincy's darling, now ran to her with wide-eyed serious excitement, crying, "O mamma, mamma, the little man stamped so hard on the floor he couldn't get his leg out again!"

"Bless you, my cherub!" said mamma; "you shall tell me all about it to-morrow. Go and listen!" and then, as her eyes followed Louisa back towards the attractive corner, she thought that if Fred wished her to invite Mary again she would make no objection, the children being so pleased with her.

But presently the corner became still more animated, for Mr. Farebrother came in, and seating himself behind Louisa, took her on his lap; whereupon the girls all insisted that he must hear Rumpelstiltskin, and Mary must tell it over again. He insisted too, and Mary, without fuss, began again in her neat fashion, with precisely the same words as before. Fred, who had also seated himself near, would have felt unmixed triumph in Mary's effectiveness if Mr. Farebrother had not been looking at her with evident admiration, while he dramatised an intense interest in the tale to please the children.

"You will never care any more about my one-eyed giant, Loo," said Fred at the end.

"Yes, I shall. Tell about him now," said Louisa.

"Oh, I daresay; I am quite cut out. Ask Mr. Farebrother."

"Yes," added Mary; "ask Mr. Farebrother to tell you about the ants whose beautiful house was knocked down by a giant named Tom, and he thought they didn't mind because he couldn't hear them cry, or see them use their pocket-handkerchiefs."

"Please," said Louisa, looking up at the Vicar.

"No, no, I am a grave old parson. If I try to draw a story out of my bag a sermon comes instead. Shall I preach you a sermon?" said he, putting on his short-sighted glasses, and pursing up his lips.

"Yes," said Louisa, falteringly.

"Let me see, then. Against cakes: how cakes are bad things, especially if they are sweet and have plums in them."

Louisa took the affair rather seriously, and got down from the Vicar's knee to go to Fred.

"Ah, I see it will not do to preach on New Year's Day," said Mr. Farebrother, rising and walking away. He had discovered of late that Fred had become jealous of him, and also that he himself was not losing his preference for Mary above all other women.

"A delightful young person is Miss Garth," said Mrs. Fare-brother, who had been watching her son's movements.

"Yes," said Mrs. Vincy, obliged to reply, as the old lady turned to her expectantly. "It is a pity she is not better-looking."

"I cannot say that," said Mrs. Farebrother, decisively. "I like her countenance. We must not always ask for beauty, when a good God has seen fit to make an excellent young woman without it. I put good manners first, and Miss Garth will know how to conduct herself in any station."

The old lady was a little sharp in her tone, having a prospective reference to Mary's becoming her daughter-in-law; for there was this inconvenience in Mary's position with regard to Fred, that it was not suitable to be made public, and hence the three ladies at Lowick Parsonage were still hoping that Camden would choose Miss Garth.

New visitors entered, and the drawing-room was given up to music and games, while whist-tables were prepared in the quiet room on the other side of the hall. Mr. Farebrother played a rubber to satisfy his mother, who regarded her occasional whist as a protest against scandal and novelty of opinion, in which light even a revoke had its dignity. But at the end he got Mr. Chichely to take his place, and left the room. As he crossed the hall, Lydgate had just come in and was taking off his greatcoat.

"You are the man I was going to look for," said the Vicar; and instead of entering the drawing-room, they walked along the hall and stood against the fireplace, where the frosty air helped to make a glowing bank. "You see, I can leave the whist-table easily enough," he went on, smiling at Lydgate, "now I don't play for money. I owe that to you, Mrs. Casaubon says."

"How?" said Lydgate, coldly.

"Ah, you didn't mean me to know it; I call that ungenerous reticence. You should let a man have the pleasure of feeling that you have done him a good turn. I don't enter into some people's dislike of being under an obligation; upon my word, I prefer being under an obligation to everybody for behaving well to me."

"I can't tell what you mean," said Lydgate, "unless it is that I once spoke of you to Mrs. Casaubon. But I did not think that she would break her promise not to mention that I had done so," said Lydgate, leaning his back against the corner of the mantelpiece, and showing no radiance in his face.

" It was Brooke who let it out, only the other day. He paid me the compliment of saying that he was very glad I had the living, though you had come across his tactics, and had praised me up as a Ken and a Tillotson, and that sort of thing, till Mrs. Casaubon would hear of no one else."

" Oh, Brooke is such a leaky-minded fool," said Lydgate contemptuously.

" Well, I was glad of the leakiness then. I don't see why you shouldn't like me to know that you wished to do me a service, my dear fellow. And you certainly have done me one. It's rather a strong check to one's self-complacency to find how much of one's right doing depends on not being in want of money. A man will not be tempted to say the Lord's Prayer backward to please the devil, if he doesn't want the devil's services. I have no need to hang on the smiles of chance now."

" I don't see that there's any money-getting without chance," said Lydgate ; " if a man gets it in a profession, it's pretty sure to come by chance."

Mr. Farebrother thought he could account for this speech, in striking contrast with Lydgate's former way of talking, as the perversity which will often spring from the moodiness of a man ill at ease in his affairs. He answered in a tone of good-humoured admission—

" Ah, there's enormous patience wanted with the way of the world. But it is easier for a man to wait patiently when he has friends who love him, and ask for nothing better than to help him through, so far as it lies in their power."

" Oh yes," said Lydgate, in a careless tone, changing his attitude and looking at his watch. " People make much more of their difficulties than they need to do."

He knew as distinctly as possible that this was an offer of help to himself from Mr. Farebrother, and he could not bear it. So strangely determined are we mortals, that, after having been long gratified with the sense that he had privately done the Vicar a service, the suggestion that the Vicar discerned his need of a service in return made him shrink into unconquerable reticence. Besides, behind all making of such offers what else must come ? —that he should " mention his case," imply that he wanted specific things. At that moment, suicide seemed easier.

Mr. Farebrother was too keen a man not to know the meaning of that reply, and there was a certain massiveness in Lydgate's manner and tone, corresponding with his physique, which if he repelled your advances in the first instance seemed to put persuasive devices out of question.

"What time are you?" said the Vicar, devouring his wounded feeling.

"After eleven," said Lydgate. And they went into the drawing-room.

CHAPTER LXIV

> 1st Gent. Where lies the power, there let the blame lie too.
> 2nd Gent. Nay, power is relative ; you cannot fright
> The coming pest with border fortresses,
> Or catch your carp with subtle argument.
> All force is twain in one : cause is not cause
> Unless effect be there ; and action's self
> Must needs contain a passive. So command
> Exists but with obedience.

EVEN if Lydgate had been inclined to be quite open about his affairs, he knew that it would have hardly been in Mr. Farebrother's power to give him the help he immediately wanted. With the year's bills coming in from his tradesmen, with Dover's threatening hold on his furniture, and with nothing to depend on but slow dribbling payments from patients who must not be offended—for the handsome fees he had had from Freshitt Hall and Lowick Manor had been easily absorbed—nothing less than a thousand pounds would have freed him from actual embarrassment, and left a residue which, according to the favourite phrase of hopefulness in such circumstances, would have given him "time to look about him."

Naturally, the merry Christmas bringing the happy New Year, when fellow-citizens expect to be paid for the trouble and goods they have smilingly bestowed on their neighbours, had so tightened the pressure of sordid cares on Lydgate's mind that it was hardly possible for him to think unbrokenly of any other subject, even the most habitual and soliciting. He was not an ill-tempered man ; his intellectual activity, the ardent kindness of his heart, as well as his strong frame, would always, under tolerably easy conditions, have kept him above the petty uncontrolled susceptibilities which make bad temper. But he was now a prey to that worst irritation which arises not simply from annoyance, but from the second consciousness underlying those annoyances, of wasted energy and a degrading preoccupation, which was the reverse of all his former purposes.

' *This* is what I am thinking of ; and *that* is what I might have been thinking of," was the bitter incessant murmur within him, making every difficulty a double goad to impatience.

Some gentlemen have made an amazing figure in literature by general discontent with the universe as a trap of dulness into which their great souls have fallen by mistake ; but the sense of a stupendous self and an insignificant world may have its consolations. Lydgate's discontent was much harder to bear ; it was the sense that there was a grand existence in thought and effective action lying around him, while his self was being narrowed into the miserable isolation of egoistic fears, and vulgar anxieties for events that might allay such fears. His troubles will perhaps appear miserably sordid, and beneath the attention of lofty persons who can know nothing of debt except on a magnificent scale. Doubtless they were sordid ; and for the majority, who are not lofty, there is no escape from sordidness but by being free from money-craving, with all its base hopes and temptations, its watching for death, its hinted requests, its horse-dealer's desire to make bad work pass for good, its seeking for function which ought to be another's, its compulsion often to long for Luck in the shape of a wide calamity.

It was because Lydgate writhed under the idea of getting his neck beneath this vile yoke that he had fallen into a bitter moody state which was continually widening Rosamond's alienation from him. After the first disclosure about the bill of sale, he had made many efforts to draw her into sympathy with him about possible measures for narrowing their expenses, and with the threatening approach of Christmas his propositions grew more and more definite. " We two can do with only one servant, and live on very little," he said, " and I shall manage with one horse." For Lydgate, as we have seen, had begun to reason, with a more distinct vision, about the expenses of living, and any share of pride he had given to appearances of that sort was meagre compared with the pride which made him revolt from exposure as a debtor, or from asking men to help him with their money.

" Of course you can dismiss the other two servants, if you like," said Rosamond ; " but I should have thought it would be very injurious to your position for us to live in a poor way. You must expect your practice to be lowered."

" My dear Rosamond, it is not a question of choice. We have begun too expensively. Peacock, you know, lived in a much smaller house than this. It is my fault : I ought to have known better, and I deserve a thrashing—if there were anybody who had a right to give it me—for bringing you into the necessity of living in a poorer way than you have been used to. But we married because we loved each other, I suppose. And that may help us to pull along till things get better. Come, dear, put down that work and come to me."

He was really in chill gloom about her at that moment, but he dreaded a future without affection, and was determined to resist the oncoming of division between them. Rosamond obeyed him, and he took her on his knee, but in her secret soul she was utterly aloof from him. The poor thing saw only that the world was not ordered to her liking, and Lydgate was part of that world. But he held her waist with one hand and laid the other gently on both of hers ; for this rather abrupt man had much tenderness in his manners towards women, seeming to have always present in his imagination the weakness of their frames and the delicate poise of their health both in body and mind. And he began again to speak persuasively.

" I find, now I look into things a little, Rosy, that it is wonderful what an amount of money slips away in our house-keeping. I suppose the servants are careless, and we have had a great many people coming. But there must be many in our rank who manage with much less : they must do with commoner things, I suppose, and look after the scraps. It seems, money goes but a little way in these matters, for Wrench has every-thing as plain as possible, and he has a very large practice."

" Oh, if you think of living as the Wrenches do ! " said Rosamond, with a little turn of her neck. " But I have heard you express your disgust at that way of living."

" Yes, they have bad taste in everything—they make economy look ugly. We needn't do that. I only meant that they avoid expenses, although Wrench has a capital practice."

" Why should not you have a good practice, Tertius ? Mr. Peacock had. You should be more careful not to offend people, and you should send out medicines as the others do. I am sure you began well, and you got several good houses. It cannot answer to be eccentric ; you should think what will be generally liked," said Rosamond, in a decided little tone of admonition.

Lydgate's anger rose ; he was prepared to be indulgent towards feminine weakness, but not towards feminine dictation. The shallowness of a waternixie's soul may have a charm until she becomes didactic. But he controlled himself, and only said, with a touch of despotic firmness—

" What I am to do in my practice, Rosy, it is for me to judge. That is not the question between us. It is enough for you to know that our income is likely to be a very narrow one—hardly four hundred, perhaps less, for a long time to come, and we must try to rearrange our lives in accordance with that fact."

Rosamond was silent for a moment or two, looking before her, and then said, " My uncle Bulstrode ought to allow you a salary for the time you give to the Hospital : it is not right that you should work for nothing."

" It was understood from the beginning that my services would be gratuitous. That, again, need not enter into our discussion. I have pointed out what is the only probability," said Lydgate, impatiently. Then checking himself, he went on more quietly—

" I think I see one resource which would free us from a good deal of the present difficulty. I hear that young Ned Plymdale is going to be married to Miss Sophy Toller. They are rich, and it is not often that a good house is vacant in Middlemarch. I feel sure that they would be glad to take this house from us with most of our furniture, and they would be willing to pay handsomely for the lease. I can employ Trumbull to speak to Plymdale about it."

Rosamond left her husband's knee and walked slowly to the other end of the room ; when she turned round and walked towards him it was evident that the tears had come, and that she was biting her under-lip and clasping her hands to keep herself from crying. Lydgate was wretched—shaken with anger and yet feeling that it would be unmanly to vent the anger just now.

" I am very sorry, Rosamond ; I know this is painful."

" I thought, at least, when I had borne to send the plate back and have that man taking an inventory of the furniture—I should have thought *that* would suffice."

" I explained it to you at the time, dear. That was only a security and behind that security there is a debt. And that debt must be paid within the next few months, else we shall have our furniture sold. If young Plymdale will take our house and most of our furniture, we shall be able to pay that debt, and some others too, and we shall be quit of a place too expensive for us. We might take a smaller house : Trumbull, I know, has a very decent one to let at thirty pounds a year, and this is ninety." Lydgate uttered this speech in the curt hammering

way with which we usually try to nail down a vague mind to
imperative facts. Tears rolled silently down Rosamond's
cheeks; she just pressed her handkerchief against them, and
stood looking at the large vase on the mantelpiece. It was a
moment of more intense bitterness than she had ever felt before.
At last, she said, without hurry and with careful emphasis—

"I never could have believed that you would like to act in
that way."

"Like it?" burst out Lydgate, rising from his chair, thrusting his hands in his pockets and stalking away from the hearth;
"it's not a question of liking. Of course, I don't like it; it's
the only thing I can do." He wheeled round there, and turned
towards her.

"I should have thought there were many other means than
that," said Rosamond. "Let us have a sale and leave Middlemarch altogether."

"To do what? What is the use of my leaving my work in
Middlemarch to go where I have none? We should be just as
penniless elsewhere as we are here," said Lydgate still more
angrily.

"If we are to be in that position it will be entirely your own
doing, Tertius," said Rosamond, turning round to speak with
the fullest conviction. "You will not behave as you ought to
do to your own family. You offended Captain Lydgate. Sir
Godwin was very kind to me when we were at Quallingham, and
I am sure if you showed proper regard to him and told him your
affairs, he would do anything for you. But rather than that,
you like giving up our house and furniture to Mr. Ned Plymdale."

There was something like fierceness in Lydgate's eyes, as he
answered with new violence, "Well then, if you will have it so,
I do like it. I admit that I like it better than making a fool of
myself by going to beg where it's of no use. Understand then,
that it is what *I like to do*."

There was a tone in the last sentence which was equivalent
to the clutch of his strong hand on Rosamond's delicate arm.
But for all that, his will was not a whit stronger than hers. She
immediately walked out of the room in silence, but with an
intense determination to hinder what Lydgate liked to do.

He went out of the house, but as his blood cooled he felt that
the chief result of the discussion was a deposit of dread within
him at the idea of opening with his wife in future subjects
which might again urge him to violent speech. It was as if a
fracture in delicate crystal had begun, and he was afraid of any

movement that might make it fatal. His marriage would be a mere piece of bitter irony if they could not go on loving each other. He had long ago made up his mind to what he thought was her negative character—her want of sensibility, which showed itself in disregard both of his specific wishes and of his general aims. The first great disappointment had been borne : the tender devotedness and docile adoration of the ideal wife must be renounced, and life must be taken up on a lower stage of expectation, as it is by men who have lost their limbs. But the real wife had not only her claims, she had still a hold on his heart, and it was his intense desire that the hold should remain strong. In marriage, the certainty, " She will never love me much," is easier to bear than the fear, " I shall love her no more." Hence, after that outburst, his inward effort was entirely to excuse her, and to blame the hard circumstances which were partly his fault. He tried that evening, by petting her, to heal the wound he had made in the morning, and it was not in Rosamond's nature to be repellent or sulky ; indeed, she welcomed the signs that her husband loved her and was under control. But this was something quite distinct from loving *him*.

Lydgate would not have chosen soon to recur to the plan of parting with the house ; he was resolved to carry it out, and say as little more about it as possible. But Rosamond herself touched on it at breakfast by saying, mildly—

" Have you spoken to Trumbull yet ? "

" No," said Lydgate, " but I shall call on him as I go by this morning. No time must be lost." He took Rosamond's question as a sign that she withdrew her inward opposition, and kissed her head caressingly when he got up to go away.

As soon as it was late enough to make a call, Rosamond went to Mrs. Plymdale, Mr. Ned's mother, and entered with pretty congratulations into the subject of the coming marriage. Mrs. Plymdale's maternal view was, that Rosamond might possibly now have retrospective glimpses of her own folly ; and feeling the advantages to be at present all on the side of her son, was too kind a woman not to behave graciously.

" Yes, Ned is most happy, I must say. And Sophy Toller is all I could desire in a daughter-in-law. Of course her father is able to do something handsome for her—that is only what would be expected with a brewery like his. And the connection is everything we should desire. But that is not what I look at. She is such a very nice girl—no airs, no pretensions, though on a level with the first. I don't mean with the titled aristocracy.

I see very little good in people aiming out of their own sphere.
I mean that Sophy is equal to the best in the town, and she is
contented with that."

" I have always thought her very agreeable," said Rosamond.

" I look upon it as a reward for Ned, who never held his head
too high, that he should have got into the very best connection,"
continued Mrs. Plymdale, her native sharpness softened by a
fervid sense that she was taking a correct view.   " And such
particular people as the Tollers are, they might have objected
because some of our friends are not theirs.   It is well known
that your aunt Bulstrode and I have been intimate from our
youth, and Mr. Plymdale has been always on Mr. Bulstrode's
side.   And I myself prefer serious opinions.   But the Tollers
have welcomed Ned all the same."

" I am sure he is a very deserving, well-principled young man,"
said Rosamond, with a neat air of patronage, in return for Mrs.
Plymdale's wholesome corrections.

" Oh, he has not the style of a captain in the army, or that
sort of carriage as if everybody was beneath him, or that showy
kind of talking, and singing, and intellectual talent.   But I am
thankful he has not.   It is a poor preparation both for here and
Hereafter."

" Oh dear, yes ; appearances have very little to do with
happiness," said Rosamond.   " I think there is every prospect of
their being a happy couple.   What house will they take ? "

" Oh, as for that, they must put up with what they can get.
They have been looking at the house in St. Peter's Place, next to
Mr. Hackbutt's ; it belongs to him, and he is putting it nicely in
repair.   I suppose they are not likely to hear of a better.
Indeed, I think Ned will decide the matter to-day."

" I should think it is a nice house ; I like St. Peter's Place."

" Well, it is near the Church, and a genteel situation.   But the
windows are narrow, and it is all ups and downs.   You don't
happen to know of any other that would be at liberty ? " said
Mrs. Plymdale, fixing her round black eyes on Rosamond with
the animation of a sudden thought in them.

" Oh no ; I hear so little of those things."

Rosamond had not foreseen that question and answer in setting
out to pay her visit ; she had simply meant to gather any
information which would help her to avert the parting with her
own house under circumstances thoroughly disagreeable to her.
As to the untruth in her reply, she no more reflected on it than
she did on the untruth there was in her saying that appearances

had very little to do with happiness. Her object, she was convinced, was thoroughly justifiable : it was Lydgate whose intention was inexcusable ; and there was a plan in her mind which, when she had carried it out fully, would prove how very false a step it would have been for him to have descended from his position.

She returned home by Mr. Borthrop Trumbull's office, meaning to call there. It was the first time in her life that Rosamond had thought of doing anything in the form of business, but she felt equal to the occasion. That she should be obliged to do what she intensely disliked, was an idea which turned her quiet tenacity into active invention. Here was a case in which it could not be enough simply to disobey and be serenely, placidly obstinate : she must act according to her judgment, and she said to herself that her judgment was right—" indeed, if it had not been, she would not have wished to act on it."

Mr. Trumbull was in the back-room of his office, and received Rosamond with his finest manners, not only because he had much sensibility to her charms, but because the good-natured fibre in him was stirred by his certainty that Lydgate was in difficulties, and that this uncommonly pretty woman—this young lady with the highest personal attractions—was likely to feel the pinch of trouble—to find herself involved in circumstances beyond her control. He begged her to do him the honour to take a seat, and stood before her trimming and comporting himself with an eager solicitude, which was chiefly benevolent. Rosamond's first question was, whether her husband had called on Mr. Trumbull that morning, to speak about disposing of their house.

" Yes, ma'am, yes, he did ; he did so," said the good auctioneer, trying to throw something soothing into his iteration. " I was about to fulfil his order, if possible, this afternoon. He wished me not to procrastinate."

" I called to tell you not to go any further, Mr. Trumbull ; and I beg of you not to mention what has been said on the subject. Will you oblige me ? "

" Certainly I will, Mrs. Lydgate, certainly. Confidence is sacred with me on business or any other topic. I am then to consider the commission withdrawn ? " said Mr. Trumbull, adjusting the long ends of his blue cravat with both hands, and looking at Rosamond deferentially.

" Yes, if you please. I find that Mr. Ned Plymdale has taken a house—the one in St. Peter's Place next to Mr. Hackbutt's.

Mr. Lydgate would be annoyed that his orders should be fulfilled
uselessly.   And besides that, there are other circumstances
which render the proposal unnecessary."

"Very good, Mrs. Lydgate, very good.   I am at your com-
mands, whenever you require any service of me," said Mr.
Trumbull, who felt pleasure in conjecturing that some new
resources had been opened.   "Rely on me, I beg.   The affair
shall go no further."

That evening Lydgate was a little comforted by observing
that Rosamond was more lively than she had usually been of
late, and even seemed interested in doing what would please him
without being asked.   He thought, "If she will be happy and
I can rub through, what does it all signify ?   It is only a narrow
swamp that we have to pass in a long journey.   If I can get my
mind clear again, I shall do."

He was so much cheered that he began to search for an
account of experiments which he had long ago meant to look up,
and had neglected out of that creeping self-despair which comes
in the train of petty anxieties.   He felt again some of the old
delightful absorption in a far-reaching inquiry, while Rosamond
played the quiet music which was as helpful to his meditation
as the plash of an oar on the evening lake.   It was rather late ;
he had pushed away all the books, and was looking at the fire
with his hands clasped behind his head in forgetfulness of
everything except the construction of a new controlling experiment, when Rosamond, who had left the piano and was leaning
back in her chair watching him, said—

"Mr. Ned Plymdale has taken a house already."

Lydgate, startled and jarred, looked up in silence for a
moment, like a man who has been disturbed in his sleep.   Then
flushing with an unpleasant consciousness, he asked—

"How do you know ? "

"I called at Mrs. Plymdale's this morning, and she told me
that he had taken the house in St. Peter's Place next to Mr.
Hackbutt's."

Lydgate was silent.   He drew his hands from behind his
head and pressed them against the hair which was hanging,
as it was apt to do, in a mass on his forehead, while he rested his
elbows on his knees.   He was feeling bitter disappointment, as
if he had opened a door out of a suffocating place and had found
it walled up ; but he also felt sure that Rosamond was pleased
with the cause of his disappointment.   He preferred not looking
at her and not speaking, until he had got over the first spasm

of vexation.   After all, he said in his bitterness, what can a
woman care about so much as house and furniture ? a husband
without them is an absurdity.   When he looked up and pushed
his hair aside, his dark eyes had a miserable blank non-expect-
ance of sympathy in them, but he only said, coolly—

"Perhaps some one else may turn up.   I told Trumbull to be
on the look-out if he failed with Plymdale."

Rosamond made no remark.   She trusted to the chance that
nothing more would pass between her husband and the auctioneer
until some issue should have justified her interference ; at any
rate, she had hindered the event which she immediately dreaded.
After a pause, she said—

"How much money is it that those disagreeable people
want ? "

"What disagreeable people ? "

"Those who took the list—and the others.   I mean, how
much money would satisfy them so that you need not be
troubled any more ? "

Lydgate surveyed her for a moment, as if he were looking for
symptoms, and then said, "Oh, if I could have got six hundred
from Plymdale for furniture and as premium, I might have
managed.   I could have paid off Dover, and given enough on
account to the others to make them wait patiently, if we con-
tracted our expenses."

"But I mean how much should you want if we stayed in this
house ? "

"More than I am likely to get anywhere," said Lydgate, with
rather a grating sarcasm in his tone.   It angered him to
perceive that Rosamond's mind was wandering over impractic-
able wishes instead of facing possible efforts.

"Why should you not mention the sum ? " said Rosamond,
with a mild indication that she did not like his manners.

"Well," said Lydgate, in a guessing tone, "it would take at
least a thousand to set me at ease.   But," he added incisively,
"I have to consider what I shall do without it, not with it."

Rosamond said no more.

But the next day she carried out her plan of writing to Sir
Godwin Lydgate.   Since the Captain's visit, she had received a
letter from him, and also one from Mrs. Mengan, his married
sister, condoling with her on the loss of her baby, and expressing
vaguely the hope that they should see her again at Quallingham.
Lydgate had told her that this politeness meant nothing ; but
she was secretly convinced that any backwardness in Lydgate's

family towards him was due to his cold and contemptuous behaviour, and she had answered the letters in her most charming manner, feeling some confidence that a specific invitation would follow. But there had been total silence. The Captain evidently was not a great penman, and Rosamond reflected that the sisters might have been abroad. However, the season was come for thinking of friends at home, and at any rate Sir Godwin, who had chucked her under the chin, and pronounced her to be like the celebrated beauty, Mrs. Croly, who had made a conquest of him in 1790, would be touched by any appeal from her, and would find it pleasant for her sake to behave as he ought to do towards his nephew. Rosamond was naïvely convinced of what an old gentleman ought to do to prevent her from suffering annoyance. And she wrote what she considered the most judicious letter possible—one which would strike Sir Godwin as a proof of her excellent sense—pointing out how desirable it was that Tertius should quit such a place as Middlemarch for one more fitted to his talents, how the unpleasant character of the inhabitants had hindered his professional success, and how in consequence he was in money difficulties, from which it would require a thousand pounds thoroughly to extricate him. She did not say that Tertius was unaware of her intention to write ; for she had the idea that his supposed sanction of her letter would be in accordance with what she did say of his great regard for his uncle Godwin as the relative who had always been his best friend. Such was the force of poor Rosamond's tactics now she applied them to affairs.

This had happened before the party on New Year's Day, and no answer had yet come from Sir Godwin. But on the morning of that day Lydgate had to learn that Rosamond had revoked his order to Borthrop Trumbull. Feeling it necessary that she should be gradually accustomed to the idea of their quitting the house in Lowick Gate, he overcame his reluctance to speak to her again on the subject, and when they were breakfasting, said—

" I shall try to see Trumbull this morning, and tell him to advertise the house in the ' Pioneer ' and the ' Trumpet.' If the thing were advertised, some one might be inclined to take it who would not otherwise have thought of a change. In these country places many people go on in their old houses when their families are too large for them, for want of knowing where they can find another. And Trumbull seems to have got no bite at all."

Rosamond knew that the inevitable moment was come. " I ordered Trumbull not to inquire further," she said, with a careful calmness which was evidently defensive.

Lydgate stared at her in mute amazement. Only half an hour before he had been fastening up her plaits for her, and talking the " little language " of affection, which Rosamond, though not returning it, accepted as if she had been a serene and lovely image, now and then miraculously dimpling towards her votary. With such fibres still astir in him, the shock he received could not at once be distinctly anger ; it was confused pain. He laid down the knife and fork with which he was carving, and throwing himself back in his chair, said at last, with a cool irony in his tone—

" May I ask when and why you did so ? "

" When I knew that the Plymdales had taken a house, I called to tell him not to mention ours to them ; and at the same time I told him not to let the affair go on any further. I knew that it would be very injurious to you if it were known that you wished to part with your house and furniture, and I had a very strong objection to it. I think that was reason enough."

" It was of no consequence then that I had told you imperative reasons of another kind ; of no consequence that I had come to a different conclusion, and given an order accordingly ? " said Lydgate, bitingly, the thunder and lightning gathering about his brow and eyes.

The effect of any one's anger on Rosamond had always been to make her shrink in cold dislike, and to become all the more calmly correct, in the conviction that she was not the person to misbehave, whatever others might do. She replied—

" I think I had a perfect right to speak on a subject which concerns me at least as much as you."

" Clearly—you had a right to speak, but only to me. You had no right to contradict my orders secretly, and treat me as if I were a fool," said Lydgate, in the same tone as before. Then with some added scorn, " Is it possible to make you understand what the consequences will be ? Is it of any use for me to tell you again why we *must* try to part with the house ? "

" It is not necessary for you to tell me again," said Rosamond, in a voice that fell and trickled like cold water-drops. " I remembered what you said. You spoke just as violently as you do now. But that does not alter my opinion that you ought to try every other means rather than take a step which is so painful to me. And as to advertising the house, I think it would be perfectly degrading to you."

" And suppose I disregard your opinion as you disregard mine ? "

" You can do so, of course. But I think you ought to have told me before we were married that you would place me in the worst position, rather than give up your own will."

Lydgate did not speak, but tossed his head on one side, and twitched the corners of his mouth in despair. Rosamond, seeing that he was not looking at her, rose and set his cup of coffee before him ; but he took no notice of it, and went on with an inward drama and argument, occasionally moving in his seat, resting one arm on the table, and rubbing his hand against his hair. There was a conflux of emotions and thoughts in him that would not let him either give thorough way to his anger or persevere with simple rigidity of resolve. Rosamond took advantage of his silence.

" When we were married every one felt that your position was very high. I could not have imagined then that you would want to sell our furniture, and take a house in Bride Street, where the rooms are like cages. If we are to live in that way let us at least leave Middlemarch."

" These would be very strong considerations," said Lydgate, half ironically—still there was a withered paleness about his lips as he looked at his coffee, and did not drink—" these would be very strong considerations if I did not happen to be in debt."

" Many persons must have been in debt in the same way, but if they are respectable, people trust them. I am sure I have heard papa say that the Torbits were in debt, and they went on very well. It cannot be good to act rashly," said Rosamond, with serene wisdom.

Lydgate sat paralysed by opposing impulses : since no reasoning he could apply to Rosamond seemed likely to conquer her assent, he wanted to smash and grind some object on which he could at least produce an impression, or else to tell her brutally that he was master, and she must obey. But he not only dreaded the effect of such extremities on their mutual life— he had a growing dread of Rosamond's quiet elusive obstinacy, which would not allow any assertion of power to be final ; and again, she had touched him in a spot of keenest feeling by implying that she had been deluded with a false vision of happiness in marrying him. As to saying that he was master, it was not the fact. The very resolution to which he had wrought himself by dint of logic and honourable pride was beginning to relax under her torpedo contact. He swallowed half his cup of coffee, and then rose to go.

" I may at least request that you will not go to Trumbull at present—until it has been seen that there are no other means," said Rosamond. Although she was not subject to much fear, she felt it safer not to betray that she had written to Sir Godwin. " Promise me that you will not go to him for a few weeks, or without telling me."

Lydgate gave a short laugh. " I think it is I who should exact a promise that you will do nothing without telling me," he said, turning his eyes sharply upon her, and then moving to the door.

" You remember that we are going to dine at papa's," said Rosamond, wishing that he should turn and make a more thorough concession to her. But he only said, " Oh yes," impatiently, and went away. She held it to be very odious in him that he did not think the painful propositions he had had to make to her were enough, without showing so unpleasant a temper. And when she put the moderate request that he would defer going to Trumbull again, it was cruel in him not to assure her of what he meant to do. She was convinced of her having acted in every way for the best ; and each grating or angry speech of Lydgate's served only as an addition to the register of offences in her mind. Poor Rosamond for months had begun to associate her husband with feelings of disappointment, and the terribly inflexible relation of marriage had lost its charm of encouraging delightful dreams. It had freed her from the disagreeables of her father's house, but it had not given her everything that she had wished and hoped. The Lydgate with whom she had been in love had been a group of airy conditions for her, most of which had disappeared, while their place had been taken by everyday details which must be lived through slowly from hour to hour, not floated through with a rapid selection of favourable aspects. The habits of Lydgate's profession, his home preoccupation with scientific subjects, which seemed to her almost like a morbid vampire's taste, his peculiar views of things which had never entered into the dialogue of courtship—all these continually-alienating influences, even without the fact of his having placed himself at a disadvantage in the town, and without that first shock of revelation about Dover's debt, would have made his presence dull to her. There was another presence which ever since the early days of

her marriage, until four months ago, had been an agreeable
excitement, but that was gone : Rosamond would not confess
to herself how much the consequent blank had to do with her
utter *ennui ;* and it seemed to her (perhaps she was right)
that an invitation to Quallingham, and an opening for Lydgate
to settle elsewhere than in Middlemarch—in London, or somewhere likely to be free from unpleasantness—would satisfy her
quite well, and make her indifferent to the absence of Will
Ladislaw, towards whom she felt some resentment for his
exaltation of Mrs. Casaubon.

That was the state of things with Lydgate and Rosamond on
the New Year's Day when they dined at her father's, she looking
mildly neutral towards him in remembrance of his ill-tempered
behaviour at breakfast, and he carrying a much deeper effect
from the inward conflict in which that morning scene was only
one of many epochs. His flushed effort while talking to Mr.
Farebrother—his effort after the cynical pretence that all ways
of getting money are essentially the same, and that chance has
an empire which reduces choice to a fool's illusion—was but the
symptom of a wavering resolve, a benumbed response to the old
stimuli of enthusiasm.

What was he to do? He saw even more keenly than Rosamond
did the dreariness of taking her into the small house in Bride
Street, where she would have scanty furniture around her and
discontent within : a life of privation and life with Rosamond
were two images which had become more and more irreconci-
lable ever since the threat of privation had disclosed itself.
But even if his resolves had forced the two images into combination, the useful preliminaries to that hard change were not
visibly within reach. And though he had not given the promise
which his wife had asked for, he did not go again to Trumbull.
He even began to think of taking a rapid journey to the North
and seeing Sir Godwin. He had once believed that nothing
would urge him into making an application for money to his
uncle, but he had not then known the full pressure of alterna-
tives yet more disagreeable. He could not depend on the effect
of a letter ; it was only in an interview, however disagreeable
this might be to himself, that he could give a thorough explanation and could test the effectiveness of kinship. No sooner
had Lydgate begun to represent this step to himself as the
easiest than there was a reaction of anger that he—he who had
long ago determined to live aloof from such abject calculations,
such self-interested anxiety about the inclinations and the

pockets of men with whom he had been proud to have no aims in common—should have fallen not simply to their level, but to the level of soliciting them.

CHAPTER LXV

" One of us two must bowen douteless,
And, sith a man is more reasonable
Than woman is, ye [men] moste be suffrable."
—CHAUCER : *Canterbury Tales.*

THE bias of human nature to be slow in correspondence triumphs even over the present quickening in the general pace of things : what wonder then that in 1832 old Sir Godwin Lydgate was slow to write a letter which was of consequence to others rather than to himself ? Nearly three weeks of the new year were gone, and Rosamond, awaiting an answer to her winning appeal, was every day disappointed. Lydgate, in total ignorance of her expectations, was seeing the bills come in, and feeling that Dover's use of his advantage over other creditors was imminent. He had never mentioned to Rosamond his brooding purpose of going to Quallingham : he did not want to admit what would appear to her a concession to her wishes after indignant refusal, until the last moment ; but he was really expecting to set off soon. A slice of the railway would enable him to manage the whole journey and back in four days.

But one morning after Lydgate had gone out, a letter came addressed to him, which Rosamond saw clearly to be from Sir Godwin. She was full of hope. Perhaps there might be a particular note to her enclosed ; but Lydgate was naturally addressed on the question of money or other aid, and the fact that he was written to, nay, the very delay in writing at all, seemed to certify that the answer was thoroughly compliant. She was too much excited by these thoughts to do anything but light stitching in a warm corner of the dining-room, with the outside of this momentous letter lying on the table before her. About twelve she heard her husband's step in the passage, and tripping to open the door, she said in her lightest tones, " Tertius, come in here—here is a letter for you."

" Ah ? " he said, not taking off his hat, but just turning her round within his arm to walk towards the spot where the letter lay. " My uncle Godwin ! " he exclaimed, while Rosamond

reseated herself, and watched him as he opened the letter.
She had expected him to be surprised.

While Lydgate's eyes glanced rapidly over the brief letter,
she saw his face, usually of a pale brown, taking on a dry
whiteness ; with nostrils and lips quivering he tossed down the
letter before her, and said violently—

"It will be impossible to endure life with you, if you will
always be acting secretly—acting in opposition to me and
hiding your actions."

He checked his speech and turned his back on her—then
wheeled round and walked about, sat down, and got up again
restlessly, grasping hard objects deep down in his pockets. He
was afraid of saying something irremediably cruel.

Rosamond too had changed colour as she read. The letter
ran in this way :—

"DEAR TERTIUS,—Don't set your wife to write to me when
you have anything to ask. It is a roundabout wheedling sort of
thing which I should not have credited you with. I never
choose to write to a woman on matters of business. As to my
supplying you with a thousand pounds, or only half that sum,
I can do nothing of the sort. My own family drains me to the
last penny. With two younger sons and three daughters, I
am not likely to have cash to spare. You seem to have got
through your own money pretty quickly, and to have made a
mess where you are ; the sooner you go somewhere else the
better. But I have nothing to do with men of your profession,
and can't help you there. I did the best I could for you as
guardian, and let you have your own way in taking to medicine.
You might have gone into the army or the Church. Your
money would have held out for that, and there would have been
a surer ladder before you. Your uncle Charles has had a
grudge against you for not going into his profession, but not I.
I have always wished you well, but you must consider yourself
on your own legs entirely now.—Your affectionate uncle,
                                    "GODWIN LYDGATE."

When Rosamond had finished reading the letter she sat quite
still, with her hands folded before her, restraining any show of her
keen disappointment, and intrenching herself in quiet passivity
under her husband's wrath. Lydgate paused in his movements,
looked at her again, and said, with biting severity—

"Will this be enough to convince you of the harm you may do

by secret meddling ? Have you sense enough to recognise now your incompetence to judge and act for me—to interfere with your ignorance in affairs which it belongs to me to decide on ? "

The words were hard ; but this was not the first time that Lydgate had been frustrated by her. She did not look at him, and made no reply.

" I had nearly resolved on going to Quallingham. It would have cost me pain enough to do it, yet it might have been of some use. But it has been of no use for me to think of anything. You have always been counteracting me secretly. You delude me with a false assent, and then I am at the mercy of your devices. If you mean to resist every wish I express, say so and defy me. I shall at least know what I am doing then."

It is a terrible moment in young lives when the closeness of love's bond has turned to this power of galling. In spite of Rosamond's self-control a tear fell silently and rolled over her lips. She still said nothing ; but under that quietude was hidden an intense effect : she was in such entire disgust with her husband that she wished she had never seen him. Sir Godwin's rudeness towards her and utter want of feeling ranged him with Dover and all other creditors—disagreeable people who only thought of themselves, and did not mind how annoying they were to her. Even her father was unkind, and might have done more for them. In fact there was but one person in Rosamond's world whom she did not regard as blameworthy, and that was the graceful creature with blond plaits and with little hands crossed before her, who had never expressed herself unbecomingly, and had always acted for the best—the best naturally being what she best liked.

Lydgate pausing and looking at her began to feel that half-maddening sense of helplessness which comes over passionate people when their passion is met by an innocent-looking silence whose meek victimised air seems to put them in the wrong, and at last infects even the justest indignation with a doubt of its justice. He needed to recover the full sense that he was in the right by moderating his words.

" Can you not see, Rosamond," he began again, trying to be simply grave and not bitter, " that nothing can be so fatal as a want of openness and confidence between us ? It has happened again and again that I have expressed a decided wish, and you have seemed to assent, yet after that you have secretly disobeyed my wish. In that way I can never know what I have to trust to. There would be some hope for us if you would admit this. Am I such an unreasonable, furious brute? Why should you not be open with me?"

Still silence.

"Will you only say that you have been mistaken, and that I may depend on your not acting secretly in future?" said Lydgate, urgently, but with something of request in his tone which Rosamond was quick to perceive. She spoke with coolness.

"I cannot possibly make admissions or promises in answer to such words as you have used towards me. I have not been accustomed to language of that kind. You have spoken of my 'secret meddling,' and my 'interfering ignorance,' and my 'false assent.' I have never expressed myself in that way to you, and I think that you ought to apologise. You spoke of its being impossible to live with me. Certainly you have not made my life pleasant to me of late. I think it was to be expected that I should try to avert some of the hardships which our marriage has brought on me." Another tear fell as Rosamond ceased speaking, and she pressed it away as quietly as the first.

Lydgate flung himself into a chair, feeling checkmated. What place was there in her mind for a remonstrance to lodge in? He laid down his hat, flung an arm over the back of his chair, and looked down for some moments without speaking. Rosamond had the double purchase over him of insensibility to the point of justice in his reproach, and of sensibility to the undeniable hardships now present in her married life. Although her duplicity in the affair of the house had exceeded what he knew, and had really hindered the Plymdales from knowing of it, she had no consciousness that her action could rightly be called false. We are not obliged to identify our own acts according to a strict classification, any more than the materials of our grocery and clothes. Rosamond felt that she was aggrieved, and that this was what Lydgate had to recognise.

As for him, the need of accommodating himself to her nature, which was inflexible in proportion to its negations, held him as with pincers. He had begun to have an alarmed foresight of her irrevocable loss of love for him, and the consequent dreariness of their life. The ready fulness of his emotions made this dread alternate quickly with the first violent movements of his anger. It would assuredly have been a vain boast in him to say that he was her master.

"You have not made my life pleasant to me of late"—"the

hardships which our marriage has brought on me "—these words were stinging his imagination as a pain makes an exaggerated dream. If he were not only to sink from his highest resolve, but to sink into the hideous fettering of domestic hate?

" Rosamond," he said, turning his eyes on her with a melancholy look, " you should allow for a man's words when he is disappointed and provoked. You and I cannot have opposite interests. I cannot part my happiness from yours. If I am angry with you, it is that you seem not to see how any concealment divides us. How could I wish to make anything hard to you either by my words or conduct? When I hurt you, I hurt part of my own life. I should never be angry with you if you would be quite open with me."

" I have only wished to prevent you from hurrying us into wretchedness without any necessity," said Rosamond, the tears coming again from a softened feeling now that her husband had softened. " It is so very hard to be disgraced here among all the people we know, and to live in such a miserable way. I wish I had died with the baby."

She spoke and wept with that gentleness which makes such words and tears omnipotent over a loving-hearted man. Lydgate drew his chair near to hers and pressed her delicate head against his cheek with his powerful tender hand. He only caressed her; he did not say anything; for what was there to say? He could not promise to shield her from the dreaded wretchedness, for he could see no sure means of doing so. When he left her to go out again, he told himself that it was ten times harder for her than for him: he had a life away from home, and constant appeals to his activity on behalf of others. He wished to excuse everything in her if he could—but it was inevitable that in that excusing mood he should think of her as if she were an animal of another and feebler species. Nevertheless she had mastered him.

CHAPTER LXVI

" 'Tis one thing to be tempted, Escalus,
  Another thing to fall."
          —*Measure for Measure.*

LYDGATE certainly had good reason to reflect on the service his practice did him in counteracting his personal cares. He had no longer free energy enough for spontaneous research and speculative thinking, but by the bedside of patients the direct external calls on his judgment and sympathies brought the added impulse needed to draw him out of himself. It was not simply that beneficent harness of routine which enables silly men to live respectably and unhappy men to live calmly—it was a perpetual claim on the immediate fresh application of thought, and on the consideration of another's need and trial. Many of us looking back through life would say that the kindest man we have ever known has been a medical man, or perhaps that surgeon whose fine tact, directed by deeply-informed perception, has come to us in our need with a more sublime beneficence than that of miracle-workers. Some of that twice-blessed mercy was always with Lydgate in his work at the Hospital or in private houses, serving better than any opiate to quiet and sustain him under his anxieties and his sense of mental degeneracy.

Mr. Farebrother's suspicion as to the opiate was true, however. Under the first galling pressure of foreseen difficulties, and the first perception that his marriage, if it were not to be a yoked loneliness, must be a state of effort to go on loving without too much care about being loved, he had once or twice tried a dose of opium. But he had no hereditary constitutional craving after such transient escapes from the hauntings of misery. He was strong, could drink a great deal of wine, but did not care about it ; and when the men round him were drinking spirits, he took sugar and water, having a contemptuous pity even for the earliest stages of excitement from drink. It was the same with gambling. He had looked on at a great deal of gambling in Paris, watching it as if it had been a disease. He was no more tempted by such winning than he was by drink. He had said to himself that the only winning he cared for must be attained by a conscious process of high, difficult combination tending towards a beneficent result. The power he longed for could not be represented by agitated fingers, clutching a heap of coin, or by the half-barbarous, half-idiotic triumph in the eyes of a man who sweeps within his arms the ventures of twenty chapfallen companions.

But just as he had tried opium, so his thought now began to turn upon gambling—not with appetite for its excitement, but with a sort of wistful inward gaze after that easy way of getting money, which implied no asking and brought no responsibility. If he had been in London or Paris at that time, it is probable that such thoughts, seconded by opportunity, would have taken him into a gambling-house, no longer to watch the gamblers, but to watch them in kindred eagerness. Repugnance would have been surmounted by the immense need to win, if chance would be kind enough to let him. An incident which happened not very long after that airy notion of getting aid from his uncle had been excluded, was a strong sign of the effect that might have followed any extant opportunity of gambling.

The billiard-room at the Green Dragon was the constant resort of a certain set, most of whom, like our acquaintance Mr. Bambridge, were regarded as men of pleasure. It was here that poor Fred Vincy had made part of his memorable debt, having lost money in betting, and been obliged to borrow of that gay companion. It was generally known in Middlemarch that a good deal of money was lost and won in this way ; and the consequent repute of the Green Dragon as a place of dissipation naturally heightened in some quarters the temptation to go there. Probably its regular visitants, like the initiates of freemasonry, wished that there were something a little more tremendous to keep to themselves concerning it ; but they were not a closed community, and many decent seniors as well as juniors occasionally turned into the billiard-room to see what was going on. Lydgate, who had the muscular aptitude for billiards, and was fond of the game, had once or twice in the early days after his arrival in Middlemarch taken his turn with the cue at the Green Dragon ; but afterwards he had no leisure for the game, and no inclination for the socialities there. One evening, however, he had occasion to seek Mr. Bambridge at that resort. The horsedealer had engaged to get him a customer for his remaining good horse, for which Lydgate had determined to substitute a cheap hack, hoping by this reduction of style to get perhaps twenty pounds ; and he cared now for every small sum, as a help towards feeding the patience of his tradesmen. To run up to the billiard-room, as he was passing, would save time.

Mr. Bambridge was not yet come, but would be sure to arrive by-and-by, said his friend Mr. Horrock ; and Lydgate stayed, playing a game for the sake of passing the time. That evening he had the peculiar light in the eyes and the unusual vivacity which had been once noticed in him by Mr. Farebrother. The exceptional fact of his presence was much noticed in the room, where there was a good deal of Middlemarch company ; and several lookers-on, as well as some of the players, were betting with animation. Lydgate was playing well, and felt confident ;

the bets were dropping round him, and with a swift glancing thought of the probable gain which might double the sum he was saving from his horse, he began to bet on his own play, and won again and again. Mr. Bambridge had come in, but Lydgate did not notice him. He was not only excited with his play, but visions were gleaming on him of going the next day to Brassing, where there was gambling on a grander scale to be had, and where, by one powerful snatch at the devil's bait, he might carry it off without the hook, and buy his rescue from his daily solicitings.

He was still winning when two new visitors entered. One of them was a young Hawley, just come from his law studies in town, and the other was Fred Vincy, who had spent several evenings of late at this old haunt of his. Young Hawley, an accomplished billiard-player, brought a cool fresh hand to the cue. But Fred Vincy, startled at seeing Lydgate, and astonished to see him betting with an excited air, stood aside, and kept out of the circle round the table.

Fred had been rewarding resolution by a little laxity of late. He had been working heartily for six months at all outdoor occupations under Mr. Garth, and by dint of severe practice had nearly mastered the defects of his handwriting, this practice being, perhaps, a little the less severe that it was often carried on in the evening at Mr. Garth's under the eyes of Mary. But the last fortnight Mary had been staying at Lowick Parsonage with the ladies there, during Mr. Farebrother's residence in Middlemarch, where he was carrying out some parochial plans ; and Fred, not seeing anything more agreeable to do, had turned into the Green Dragon, partly to play at billiards, partly to taste the old flavour of discourse about horses, sport, and things in general, considered from a point of view which was not strenuously correct. He had not been out hunting once this season, had had no horse of his own to ride, and had gone from place to place chiefly with Mr. Garth in his gig, or on the sober cob which Mr. Garth could lend him. It was a little too bad, Fred began to think, that he should be kept in the traces with more severity than if he had been a clergyman. " I will tell you what, Mistress Mary—it will be rather harder work to learn surveying and drawing plans than it would have been to write sermons," he had said, wishing her to appreciate what he went through for her sake ; " and as to Hercules and Theseus, they were nothing to me. They had sport, and never learned to write a book-keeping hand." And now, Mary being out of the way for a little while, Fred, like any other strong dog who cannot slip his collar, had pulled up the staple of his chain and made a small escape, not of course meaning to go fast or far. There could be no reason why he should not play at billiards, but he was determined not to bet. As to money just now, Fred had in his mind the heroic project of saving almost all of the eighty pounds that Mr. Garth offered him, and returning it, which he could easily do by giving up all futile money-spending, since he had a superfluous stock of clothes, and no expense in his board. In that way he could, in one year, go a good way towards repaying the ninety pounds of which he had deprived Mrs. Garth, unhappily at a time when she needed that sum more than she did now. Nevertheless, it must be acknowledged that on this evening, which was the fifth of his recent visits to the billiard-room, Fred had, not in his pocket, but in his mind, the ten pounds which he meant to reserve for himself from his half-year's salary (having before him the pleasure of carrying thirty to Mrs. Garth when Mary was likely to be come home again)—he had those ten pounds in his mind as a fund from which he might risk something, if there were a chance of a good bet. Why? Well, when sovereigns were flying about, why shouldn't he catch a few? He would never go far along that road again; but a man likes to assure himself, and men of pleasure generally, what he could do in the way of mischief if he chose, and that if he abstains from making himself ill, or beggaring himself, or talking with the utmost looseness which the narrow limits of human capacity will allow, it is not because he is a spooney. Fred did not enter into formal reasons, which are a very artificial, inexact way of representing the tingling returns of old habit, and the caprices of young blood: but there was lurking in him a prophetic sense that evening, that when he began to play he should also begin to bet—that he should enjoy some punch-drinking, and in general prepare himself for feeling " rather seedy " in the morning. It is in such indefinable movements that action often begins.

But the last thing likely to have entered Fred's expectation was that he should see his brother-in-law Lydgate—of whom he had never quite dropped the old opinion that he was a prig, and tremendously conscious of his superiority—looking excited and betting, just as he himself might have done. Fred felt a shock greater than he could quite account for by the vague knowledge that Lydgate was in debt, and that his father had refused to help him; and his own inclination to enter into the play was suddenly checked. It was a strange reversal of attitudes:

Fred's blond face and blue eyes, usually bright and careless, ready to give attention to anything that held out a promise of amusement, looking involuntarily grave and almost embarrassed as if by the sight of something unfitting ; while Lydgate, who had habitually an air of self-possessed strength, and a certain meditativeness that seemed to lie behind his most observant attention, was acting, watching, speaking with that excited narrow consciousness which reminds one of an animal with fierce eyes and retractile claws.

Lydgate, by betting on his own strokes, had won sixteen pounds ; but young Hawley's arrival had changed the poise of things. He made first-rate strokes himself, and began to bet against Lydgate's strokes, the strain of whose nerves was thus changed from simple confidence in his own movements to defying another person's doubt in them. The defiance was more exciting than the confidence, but it was less sure. He continued to bet on his own play, but began often to fail. Still he went on, for his mind was as utterly narrowed into that precipitous crevice of play as if he had been the most ignorant lounger there. Fred observed that Lydgate was losing fast, and found himself in the new situation of puzzling his brains to think of some device by which, without being offensive, he could withdraw Lydgate's attention, and perhaps suggest to him a reason for quitting the room. He saw that others were observing Lydgate's strange unlikeness to himself, and it occurred to him that merely to touch his elbow and call him aside for a moment might rouse him from his absorption. He could think of nothing cleverer than the daring improbability of saying that he wanted to see Rosy, and wished to know if she were at home this evening ; and he was going desperately to carry out this weak device, when a waiter came up to him with a message, saying that Mr. Farebrother was below, and begged to speak with him.

Fred was surprised, not quite comfortably, but sending word that he would be down immediately, he went with a new impulse up to Lydgate, said, " Can I speak to you a moment ? " and drew him aside.

" Farebrother has just sent up a message to say he wants to speak to me. He is below. I thought you might like to know he was there, if you had anything to say to him."

Fred had simply snatched up this pretext for speaking, because he could not say, " You are losing confoundedly, and are making everybody stare at you ; you had better come away." But inspiration could hardly have served him better. Lydgate had not before seen that Fred was present, and his sudden appearance with an announcement of Mr. Farebrother had the effect of a sharp concussion.

"No, no," said Lydgate; "I have nothing particular to say to him. But—the game is up—I must be going—I came in just to see Bambridge."

"Bambridge is over there, but he is making a row—I don't think he's ready for business. Come down with me to Farebrother. I expect he is going to blow me up, and you will shield me," said Fred, with some adroitness.

Lydgate felt shame, but could not bear to act as if he felt it, by refusing to see Mr. Farebrother; and he went down. They merely shook hands, however, and spoke of the frost; and when all three had turned into the street, the Vicar seemed quite willing to say good-bye to Lydgate. His present purpose was clearly to talk with Fred alone, and he said, kindly, "I disturbed you, young gentleman, because I have some pressing business with you. Walk with me to St. Botolph's, will you?"

It was a fine night, the sky thick with stars, and Mr. Farebrother proposed that they should make a circuit to the old church by the London road. The next thing he said was—

"I thought Lydgate never went to the Green Dragon?"

"So did I," said Fred. "But he said that he went to see Bambridge."

"He was not playing, then?"

Fred had not meant to tell this, but he was obliged now to say, "Yes, he was. But I suppose it was an accidental thing. I have never seen him there before."

"You have been going often yourself, then, lately?"

"Oh, about five or six times."

"I think you had some good reason for giving up the habit of going there?"

"Yes. You know all about it," said Fred, not liking to be catechised in this way. "I made a clean breast to you."

"I suppose that gives me a warrant to speak about the matter now. It is understood between us—is it not?—that we are on a footing of open friendship: I have listened to you, and you will be willing to listen to me. I may take my turn in talking a little about myself?"

"I am under the deepest obligation to you, Mr. Farebrother," said Fred, in a state of uncomfortable surmise.

"I will not affect to deny that you are under some obligation to me. But I am going to confess to you, Fred, that I have been tempted to reverse all that by keeping silence with you just now. When somebody said to me, ' Young Vincy has taken to being at the billiard-table every night again—he won't bear the curb long ; ' I was tempted to do the opposite of what I am doing—to hold my tongue and wait while you went down the ladder again, betting first and then——"

" I have not made any bets," said Fred, hastily.

" Glad to hear it. But I say, my prompting was to look on and see you take the wrong turning, wear out Garth's patience, and lose the best opportunity of your life—the opportunity which you made some rather difficult effort to secure. You can guess the feeling which raised that temptation in me—I am sure you know it. I am sure you know that the satisfaction of your affections stands in the way of mine."

There was a pause. Mr. Farebrother seemed to wait for a recognition of the fact ; and the emotion perceptible in the tones of his fine voice gave solemnity to his words. But no feeling could quell Fred's alarm.

" I could not be expected to give her up," he said, after a moment's hesitation : it was not a case for any pretence of generosity.

" Clearly not, when her affection met yours. But relations of this sort, even when they are of long standing, are always liable to change. I can easily conceive that you might act in a way to loosen the tie she feels towards you—it must be remembered that she is only conditionally bound to you—and that in that case, another man, who may flatter himself that he has a hold on her regard, might succeed in winning that firm place in her love as well as respect which you had let slip. I can easily conceive such a result," repeated Mr. Farebrother, emphatically. " There is a companionship of ready sympathy, which might get the advantage even over the longest associations."

It seemed to Fred that if Mr. Farebrother had had a beak and talons instead of his very capable tongue, his mode of attack could hardly be more cruel. He had a horrible conviction that behind all this hypothetic statement there was a knowledge of some actual change in Mary's feeling.

" Of course I know it might easily be all up with me," he said, in a troubled voice. " If she is beginning to compare——" He broke off, not liking to betray all he felt, and then said, by the help of a little bitterness, " But I thought you were friendly to me."

" So I am ; that is why we are here. But I have had a strong disposition to be otherwise. I have said to myself, ' If there is a likelihood of that youngster doing himself harm, why should you interfere ? Aren't you worth as much as he is, and don't your sixteen years over and above his, in which you have gone rather hungry, give you more right to satisfaction than he has ? If there's a chance of his going to the dogs, let him— perhaps you could nohow hinder it—and do you take the benefit."

There was a pause, in which Fred was seized by a most un- comfortable chill. What was coming next ? He dreaded to hear that something had been said to Mary—he felt as if he were listening to a threat rather than a warning. When the Vicar began again there was a change in his tone like the encouraging transition to a major key.

" But I had once meant better than that, and I am come back to my old intention. I thought that I could hardly *secure myself* in it better, Fred, than by telling you just what had gone on in me. And now, do you understand me ? I want you to make the happiness of her life and your own, and if there is any chance that a word of warning from me may turn aside any risk to the contrary—well, I have uttered it."

There was a drop in the Vicar's voice when he spoke the last words. He paused—they were standing on a patch of green where the road diverged towards St. Botolph's, and he put out his hand, as if to imply that the conversation was closed. Fred was moved quite newly. Some one highly susceptible to the contemplation of a fine act has said, that it produces a sort of regenerating shudder through the frame, and makes one feel ready to begin a new life. A good degree of that effect was just then present in Fred Vincy.

" I will try to be worthy," he said, breaking off before he could say " of you as well as of her." And meanwhile Mr. Farebrother had gathered the impulse to say something more.

" You must not imagine that I believe there is at present any decline in her preference of you, Fred. Set your heart at rest, that if you keep right, other things will keep right."

" I shall never forget what you have done," Fred answered. " I can't say anything that seems worth saying—only I will try that your goodness shall not be thrown away."

" That's enough. Good-bye, and God bless you."

In that way they parted. But both of them walked about a long while before they went out of the starlight. Much of Fred's rumination might be summed up in the words, " It certainly would have been a fine thing for her to marry Farebrother— but if she loves me best and I am a good husband ? "

Perhaps Mr. Farebrother's might be concentrated into a single shrug and one little speech. " To think of the part one little woman can play in the life of a man, so that to renounce her may be a very good imitation of heroism, and to win her may be a discipline ! "

CHAPTER LXVII

Now is there civil war within the soul ;
Resolve is thrust from off the sacred throne
By clamorous Needs, and Pride the grand-vizier
Makes humble compact, plays the supple part
Of envoy and deft-tongued apologist
For hungry rebels.

HAPPILY Lydgate had ended by losing in the billiard-room, and brought away no encouragement to make a raid on luck. On the contrary, he felt unmixed disgust with himself the next day when he had to pay four or five pounds over and above his gains, and he carried about with him a most unpleasant vision of the figure he had made, not only rubbing elbows with the men at the Green Dragon but behaving just as they did. A philosopher fallen to betting is hardly distinguishable from a Philistine under the same circumstances : the difference will chiefly be found in his subsequent reflections, and Lydgate chewed a very disagreeable cud in that way. His reason told him how the affair might have been magnified into ruin by a slight change of scenery— if it had been a gambling-house that he had turned into, where chance could be clutched with both hands instead of being picked up with thumb and forefinger. Nevertheless, though reason strangled the desire to gamble, there remained the feeling that, with an assurance of luck to the needful amount, he would have liked to gamble, rather than take the alternative which was beginning to urge itself as inevitable.

That alternative was to apply to Mr. Bulstrode. Lydgate had so many times boasted both to himself and others that he was totally independent of Bulstrode, to whose plans he had lent himself solely because they enabled him to carry out his own ideas of professional work and public benefit—he had so constantly in their personal intercourse had his pride sustained by the sense that he was making a good social use of this predominating banker, whose opinions he thought contemptible and whose motives often seemed to him an absurd mixture of contradictory impressions—that he had been creating for himself strong ideal obstacles to the proffering of any considerable request to him on his own account.

Still, early in March his affairs were at that pass in which men begin to say that their oaths were delivered in ignorance, and to perceive that the act which they had called impossible to them is becoming manifestly possible. With Dover's ugly security soon to be put in force, with the proceeds of his practice immediately absorbed in paying back-debts, and with the chance, if the worst were known, of daily supplies being refused on credit, above all with the vision of Rosamond's hopeless discontent continually haunting him, Lydgate had begun to see that he should inevitably bend himself to ask help from somebody or other. At first he had considered whether he should write to Mr. Vincy ; but on questioning Rosamond he found that, as he had suspected, she had already applied twice to her father, the last time being since the disappointment from Sir Godwin ; and papa had said that Lydgate must look out for himself. "Papa said he had come, with one bad year after another, to trade more and more on borrowed capital, and had had to give up many indulgences : he could not spare a single hundred from the charges of his family. He said, let Lydgate ask Bulstrode : they have always been hand in glove."

Indeed, Lydgate himself had come to the conclusion that if he must end by asking for a free loan, his relations with Bulstrode, more at least than with any other man, might take the shape of a claim which was not purely personal. Bulstrode had indirectly helped to cause the failure of his practice, and had also been highly gratified by getting a medical partner in his plans :—but who among us ever reduced himself to the sort of dependence in which Lydgate now stood, without trying to believe that he had claims which diminished the humiliation of asking ? It was true that of late there had seemed to be a new languor of interest in Bulstrode about the Hospital ; but his health had got worse, and showed signs of a deep-seated nervous affection. In other respects he did not appear to be changed : he had always been highly polite, but Lydgate had observed in him from the first a marked coldness about his marriage and other private circumstances, a coldness which he had hitherto preferred to any warmth of familiarity between them. He deferred the intention from day to day, his habit of acting on his conclusions being made infirm by his repugnance to every possible conclusion and its consequent act. He saw Mr. Bulstrode often, but he did not try to use any occasion for his private purpose. At one moment he thought, "I will write a letter: I prefer that to any circuitous talk;" at another he thought, "No; if I were talking to him, I could make a retreat before any signs of disinclination."

Still the days passed and no letter was written, no special interview sought. In his shrinking from the humiliation of a dependent attitude towards Bulstrode, he began to familiarise his imagination with another step even more unlike his remembered self. He began spontaneously to consider whether it would be possible to carry out that puerile notion of Rosamond's which had often made him angry, namely, that they should quit Middlemarch without seeing anything beyond that preface. The question came—"Would any man buy the practice of me even now, for as little as it is worth? Then the sale might happen as a necessary preparation for going away."

But against his taking this step, which he still felt to be a contemptible relinquishment of present work, a guilty turning aside from what was a real and might be a widening channel for worthy activity, to start again without any justified destination, there was this obstacle, that the purchaser, if procurable at all, might not be quickly forthcoming. And afterwards? Rosamond in a poor lodging, though in the largest city or most distant town, would not find the life that could save her from gloom, and save him from the reproach of having plunged her into it. For when a man is at the foot of the hill in his fortunes, he may stay a long while there in spite of professional accomplishment. In the British climate there is no incompatibility between scientific insight and furnished lodgings: the incompatibility is chiefly between scientific ambition and a wife who objects to that kind of residence.

But in the midst of his hesitation, opportunity came to decide him. A note from Mr. Bulstrode requested Lydgate to call on him at the Bank. A hypochondriacal tendency had shown itself in the banker's constitution of late; and a lack of sleep, which was really only a slight exaggeration of an habitual dyspeptic symptom, had been dwelt on by him as a sign of threatening insanity. He wanted to consult Lydgate without delay on that particular morning, although he had nothing to tell beyond what he had told before. He listened eagerly to what Lydgate had to say in dissipation of his fears, though this

too was only repetition ; and this moment, in which Bulstrode
was receiving a medical opinion with a sense of comfort, seemed
to make the communication of a personal need to him easier
than it had been in Lydgate's contemplation beforehand. He
had been insisting that it would be well for Mr. Bulstrode to
relax his attention to business.

" One sees how any mental strain, however slight, may affect
a delicate frame," said Lydgate at that stage of the consultation
when the remarks tend to pass from the personal to the general,
" by the deep stamp which anxiety will make for a time even on
the young and vigorous. I am naturally very strong ; yet I
have been thoroughly shaken lately by an accumulation of
trouble."

" I presume that a constitution in the susceptible state in which
mine at present is, would be especially liable to fall a victim to
cholera, if it visited our district. And since its appearance near
London, we may well besiege the Mercy-seat for our protection,"
said Mr. Bulstrode, not intending to evade Lydgate's allusion,
but really preoccupied with alarms about himself.

" You have at all events taken your share in using good
practical precautions for the town, and that is the best mode of
asking for protection," said Lydgate, with a strong distaste for
the broken metaphor and bad logic of the banker's religion,
somewhat increased by the apparent deafness of his sympathy.
But his mind had taken up its long-prepared movement towards
getting help, and was not yet arrested. He added, " The town
has done well in the way of cleansing, and finding appliances ;
and I think that if the cholera should come, even our enemies
will admit that the arrangements in the Hospital are a public
good."

" Truly," said Mr. Bulstrode, with some coldness. " With
regard to what you say, Mr. Lydgate, about the relaxation of my
mental labour, I have for some time been entertaining a purpose
to that effect—a purpose of a very decided character. I contemplate at least a temporary withdrawal from the management
of much business, whether benevolent or commercial. Also I
think of changing my residence for a time : probably I shall
close or let ' The Shrubs,' and take some place near the coast—
under advice, of course, as to salubrity. That would be a
measure which you would recommend ? "

" Oh yes," said Lydgate, falling backward in his chair, with
ill-repressed impatience under the banker's pale earnest eyes and
intense preoccupation with himself.

" I have for some time felt that I should open this subject with you in relation to our Hospital," continued Bulstrode.   " Under the circumstances I have indicated, of course I must cease to have any personal share in the management, and it is contrary to my views of responsibility to continue a large application of means to an institution which I cannot watch over and to some extent regulate.   I shall therefore, in case of my ultimate decision to leave Middlemarch, consider that I withdraw other support to the New Hospital than that which will subsist in the fact that I chiefly supplied the expenses of building it, and have contributed further large sums to its successful working."

Lydgate's thought, when Bulstrode paused according to his wont, was, " He has perhaps been losing a good deal of money." This was the most plausible explanation of a speech which had caused rather a startling change in his expectations.   He said in reply—

" The loss to the Hospital can hardly be made up, I fear."

" Hardly," returned Bulstrode, in the same deliberate, silvery tone ; " except by some changes of plan.   The only person who may be certainly counted on as willing to increase her contributions is Mrs. Casaubon.   I have had an interview with her on the subject, and I have pointed out to her, as I am about to do to you, that it will be desirable to win a more general support to the New Hospital by a change of system."

Another pause, but Lydgate did not speak.

" The change I mean is an amalgamation with the Infirmary, so that the New Hospital shall be regarded as a special addition to the elder institution, having the same directing board.   It will be necessary, also, that the medical management of the two shall be combined.   In this way any difficulty as to the adequate maintenance of our new establishment will be removed ; the benevolent interests of the town will cease to be divided."

Mr. Bulstrode had lowered his eyes from Lydgate's face to the buttons of his coat as he again paused.

" No doubt that is a good device as to ways and means," said Lydgate, with an edge of irony in his tone.   " But I can't be expected to rejoice in it at once, since one of the first results will be that the other medical men will upset or interrupt my methods, if it were only because they are mine."

" I myself, as you know, Mr. Lydgate, highly value the opportunity of new and independent procedure which you have diligently employed : the original plan, I confess, was one which I had much at heart, under submission to the Divine Will. But since providential indications demand a renunciation from me, I renounce."

Bulstrode showed a rather exasperating ability in this conversation. The broken metaphor and bad logic of motive which had stirred his hearer's contempt were quite consistent with a mode of putting the facts which made it difficult for Lydgate to vent his own indignation and disappointment. After some rapid reflection, he only asked,

" What did Mrs. Casaubon say ? "

" That was the further statement which I wished to make to you," said Bulstrode, who had thoroughly prepared his ministerial explanation. " She is, you are aware, a woman of most munificent disposition, and happily in possession—not I presume of great wealth, but of funds which she can well spare. She has informed me that though she had destined the chief part of those funds to another purpose, she is willing to consider whether she cannot fully take my place in relation to the Hospital. But she wishes for ample time to mature her thoughts on the subject, and I have told her that there is no need for haste—that, in fact, my own plans are not yet absolute."

Lydgate was ready to say, " If Mrs. Casaubon would take your place, there would be gain, instead of loss." But there was still a weight on his mind which arrested this cheerful candour. He replied, " I suppose, then, that I may enter into the subject with Mrs. Casaubon."

" Precisely ; that is what she expressly desires. Her decision, she says, will much depend on what you can tell her. But not at present : she is, I believe, just setting out on a journey. I have her letter here," said Mr. Bulstrode, drawing it out, and reading from it. " ' I am immediately otherwise engaged,' she says. ' I am going into Yorkshire with Sir James and Lady Chettam ; and the conclusions I come to about some land which I am to see there may affect my power of contributing to the Hospital.' Thus, Mr. Lydgate, there is no haste necessary in this matter ; but I wished to apprise you beforehand of what may possibly occur."

Mr. Bulstrode returned the letter to his side-pocket, and changed his attitude as if his business were closed. Lydgate, whose renewed hope about the Hospital only made him more conscious of the facts which poisoned his hope, felt that his effort after help, if made at all, must be made now and vigorously.

" I am much obliged to you for giving me full notice," he said, with a firm intention in his tone, yet with an interruptedness in his delivery which showed that he spoke unwillingly. " The highest object to me is my profession, and I had identified the Hospital with the best use I can at present make of my profession. But the best use is not always the same with monetary success. Everything which has made the Hospital unpopular has helped with other causes—I think they are all connected with my professional zeal—to make me unpopular as a practitioner. I get chiefly patients who can't pay me. I should like them best, if I had nobody to pay on my own side." Lydgate waited a little, but Bulstrode only bowed, looking at him fixedly, and he went on with the same interrupted enunciation—as if he were biting an objectionable leek.

" I have slipped into money difficulties which I can see no way out of, unless some one who trusts me and my future will advance me a sum without other security. I had very little fortune left when I came here. I have no prospects of money from my own family. My expenses, in consequence of my marriage, have been very much greater than I had expected. The result at this moment is that it would take a thousand pounds to clear me. I mean, to free me from the risk of having all my goods sold in security of my largest debt—as well as to pay my other debts—and leave anything to keep us a little beforehand with our small income. I find that it is out of the question that my wife's father should make such an advance. That is why I mention my position to—to the only other man who may be held to have some personal connection with my prosperity or ruin."

Lydgate hated to hear himself. But he had spoken now, and had spoken with unmistakable directness. Mr. Bulstrode replied without haste, but also without hesitation.

" I am grieved, though, I confess, not surprised by this information, Mr. Lydgate. For my own part, I regretted your alliance with my brother-in-law's family, which has always been of prodigal habits, and which has already been much indebted to me for sustainment in its present position. My advice to you, Mr. Lydgate, would be, that instead of involving yourself in further obligations, and continuing a doubtful struggle, you should simply become a bankrupt."

" That would not improve my prospect," said Lydgate, rising, and speaking bitterly, " even if it were a more agreeable thing in itself."

" It is always a trial," said Mr. Bulstrode; " but trial, my dear sir, is our portion here, and is a needed corrective. I recommend you to weigh the advice I have given."

"Thank you," said Lydgate, not quite knowing what he said. "I have occupied you too long. Good-day."

CHAPTER LXVIII

> " What suit of grace hath Virtue to put on
> If Vice shall wear as good, and do as well ?
> If Wrong, if Craft, if Indiscretion
> Act as fair parts with ends as laudable ?
> Which all this mighty volume of events
> The world, the universal map of deeds,
> Strongly controls, and proves from all descents,
> That the directest course still best succeeds.
> For should not grave and learn'd Experience
> That looks with the eyes of all the world beside,
> And with all ages holds intelligence,
> Go safer than Deceit without a guide ? "
> —DANIEL : *Musophilus.*

THAT change of plan and shifting of interest which Bulstrode stated or betrayed in his conversation with Lydgate, had been determined in him by some severe experience which he had gone through since the epoch of Mr. Larcher's sale, when Raffles had recognised Will Ladislaw, and when the banker had in vain attempted an act of restitution which might move Divine Providence to arrest painful consequences.

His certainty that Raffles, unless he were dead, would return to Middlemarch before long, had been justified. On Christmas Eve he had reappeared at The Shrubs. Bulstrode was at home to receive him, and hinder his communication with the rest of the family, but he could not altogether hinder the circumstances of the visit from compromising himself and alarming his wife. Raffles proved more unmanageable than he had shown himself to be in his former appearances, his chronic state of mental restlessness, the growing effect of habitual intemperance, quickly shaking off every impression from what was said to him. He insisted on staying in the house, and Bulstrode, weighing two sets of evils, felt that this was at least not a worse alternative than his going into the town. He kept him in his own room for the evening and saw him to bed, Raffles all the while amusing himself with the annoyance he was causing this decent and highly prosperous fellow-sinner, an amusement which he facetiously expressed as sympathy with his friend's pleasure in entertaining a man who had been serviceable to him, and who had not had all his earnings. There was a cunning calculation under this noisy joking—a cool resolve to extract something the handsomer from Bulstrode as payment for release from this new application of torture. But his cunning had a little overcast its mark.

Bulstrode was indeed more tortured than the coarse fibre of Raffles could enable him to imagine. He had told his wife that he was simply taking care of this wretched creature, the victim of vice, who might otherwise injure himself; he implied, without the direct form of falsehood, that there was a family tie which bound him to this care, and that there were signs of mental alienation in Raffles which urged caution. He would himself drive the unfortunate being away the next morning. In these hints he felt that he was supplying Mrs. Bulstrode with precautionary information for his daughters and servants, and accounting for his allowing no one but himself to enter the room even with food and drink. But he sat in an agony of fear lest Raffles should be overheard in his loud and plain references to past facts—lest Mrs. Bulstrode should be even tempted to listen at the door. How could he hinder her, how betray his terror by opening the door to detect her? She was a woman of honest direct habits, and little likely to take so low a course in order to arrive at painful knowledge; but fear was stronger than the calculation of probabilities.

In this way Raffles had pushed the torture too far, and produced an effect which had not been in his plan. By showing himself hopelessly unmanageable he had made Bulstrode feel that a strong defiance was the only resource left. After taking Raffles to bed that night the banker ordered his closed carriage to be ready at half-past seven the next morning. At six o'clock he had already been long dressed, and had spent some of his wretchedness in prayer, pleading his motives for averting the worst evil if in anything he had used falsity and spoken what was not true before God. For Bulstrode shrank from a direct lie with an intensity disproportionate to the number of his more indirect misdeeds. But many of these misdeeds were like the subtle muscular movements which are not taken account of in the consciousness, though they bring about the end that we fix our mind on and desire. And it is only what we are vividly conscious of that we can vividly imagine to be seen by Omniscience.

Bulstrode carried his candle to the bedside of Raffles, who was apparently in a painful dream. He stood silent, hoping that the

presence of the light would serve to waken the sleeper gradually
and gently, for he feared some noise as the consequence of a too
sudden awakening. He had watched for a couple of minutes or
more the shudderings and pantings which seemed likely to end
in waking, when Raffles, with a long half-stifled moan, started up
and stared round him in terror, trembling and gasping. But he
made no further noise, and Bulstrode, setting down the candle,
awaited his recovery.

It was a quarter of an hour later before Bulstrode, with a cold
peremptoriness of manner which he had not before shown, said,
"I came to call you thus early, Mr. Raffles, because I have
ordered the carriage to be ready at half-past seven, and intend
myself to conduct you as far as Ilsely, where you can either
take the railway or await a coach."

Raffles was about to speak, but Bulstrode anticipated him
imperiously, with the words, "Be silent, sir, and hear what I
have to say. I shall supply you with money now, and I will
furnish you with a reasonable sum from time to time, on your
application to me by letter ; but if you choose to present yourself here again, if you return to Middlemarch, if you use your
tongue in a manner injurious to me, you will have to live on
such fruits as your malice can bring you, without help from me.
Nobody will pay you well for blasting my name : I know the
worst you can do against me, and I shall brave it if you dare to
thrust yourself upon me again. Get up, sir, and do as I order
you, without noise, or I will send for a policeman to take you off
my premises, and you may carry your stories into every pothouse
in the town, but you shall have no sixpence from me to pay your
expenses there."

Bulstrode had rarely in his life spoken with such nervous
energy : he had been deliberating on this speech and its probable
effects through a large part of the night ; and though he did not
trust to its ultimately saving him from any return of Raffles, he
had concluded that it was the best throw he could make. It
succeeded in enforcing submission from the jaded man this
morning : his empoisoned system at this moment quailed before
Bulstrode's cold, resolute bearing, and he was taken off quietly
in the carriage before the family breakfast-time. The servants
imagined him to be a poor relation, and were not surprised that
a strict man like their master, who held his head high in the
world, should be ashamed of such a cousin and want to get rid
of him. The banker's drive of ten miles with his hated companion was a dreary beginning of the Christmas day ; but at the

end of the drive, Raffles had recovered his spirits, and parted in a contentment for which there was the good reason that the banker had given him a hundred pounds. Various motives urged Bulstrode to this open-handedness, but he did not himself inquire closely into all of them. As he had stood watching Raffles in his uneasy sleep, it had certainly entered his mind that the man had been much shattered since the first gift of two hundred pounds.

He had taken care to repeat the incisive statement of his resolve not to be played on any more ; and had tried to penetrate Raffles with the fact that he had shown the risks of bribing him to be quite equal to the risks of defying him. But when, freed from his repulsive presence, Bulstrode returned to his quiet home, he brought with him no confidence that he had secured more than a respite. It was as if he had had a loathsome dream, and could not shake off its images with their hateful kindred of sensations—as if on all the pleasant surroundings of his life a dangerous reptile had left his slimy traces.

Who can know how much of his most inward life is made up of the thoughts he believes other men to have about him, until that fabric of opinion is threatened with ruin ?

Bulstrode was only the more conscious that there was a deposit of uneasy presentiment in his wife's mind, because she carefully avoided any allusion to it. He had been used every day to taste the flavour of supremacy and the tribute of complete deference ; and the certainty that he was watched or measured with a hidden suspicion of his having some discreditable secret, made his voice totter when he was speaking to edification. Foreseeing, to men of Bulstrode's anxious temperament, is often worse than seeing ; and his imagination continually heightened the anguish of an imminent disgrace. Yes, imminent ; for if his defiance of Raffles did not keep the man away—and though he prayed for this result he hardly hoped for it—the disgrace was certain. In vain he said to himself that, if permitted, it would be a divine visitation, a chastisement, a preparation ; he recoiled from the imagined burning ; and he judged that it must be more for the Divine glory that he should escape dishonour. That recoil had at last urged him to make preparations for quitting Middlemarch. If evil truth must be reported of him, he would then be at a less scorching distance from the contempt of his old neighbours ; and in a new scene, where his life would not have gathered the same wide sensibility, the tormentor, if he pursued him, would be less formidable. To leave the place finally would, he knew, be extremely painful to his wife, and on other grounds he would have preferred to stay where he had struck root. Hence he made his preparations at first in a conditional way, wishing to leave on all sides an opening for his return after brief absence, if any favourable intervention of Providence should dissipate his fears. He was preparing to transfer his management of the Bank, and to give up any active control of other commercial affairs in the neighbourhood, on the ground of his failing health, but without excluding his future resumption of such work. The measure would cause him some added expense and some diminution of income beyond what he had already undergone from the general depression of trade ; and the Hospital presented itself as a principal object of outlay on which he could fairly economise.

This was the experience which had determined his conversation with Lydgate. But at this time his arrangements had most of them gone no farther than a stage at which he could recall them if they proved to be unnecessary. He continually deferred the final steps ; in the midst of his fears, like many a man who is in danger of shipwreck or of being dashed from his carriage by runaway horses, he had a clinging impression that something would happen to hinder the worst, and that to spoil his life by a late transplantation might be over-hasty—especially since it was difficult to account satisfactorily to his wife for the project of their indefinite exile from the only place where she would like to live.

Among the affairs Bulstrode had to care for, was the management of the farm at Stone Court in case of his absence ; and on this as well as on all other matters connected with any houses and land he possessed in or about Middlemarch, he had consulted Caleb Garth. Like every one else who had business of that sort, he wanted to get the agent who was more anxious for his employer's interests than his own. With regard to Stone Court, since Bulstrode wished to retain his hold on the stock, and to have an arrangement by which he himself could, if he chose, resume his favourite recreation of superintendence, Caleb had advised him not to trust to a mere bailiff, but to let the land, stock, and implements yearly, and take a proportionate share of the proceeds.

"May I trust to you to find me a tenant on these terms, Mr. Garth ? " said Bulstrode. " And will you mention to me the yearly sum which would repay you for managing these affairs which we have discussed together ? "

" I'll think about it," said Caleb, in his blunt away. " I'll see how I can make it out."

If it had not been that he had to consider Fred Vincy's future, Mr. Garth would not probably have been glad of any addition to his work, of which his wife was always fearing an excess for him as he grew older. But on quitting Bulstrode after that conversation, a very alluring idea occurred to him about this said letting of Stone Court. What if Bulstrode would agree to his placing Fred Vincy there on the understanding that he, Caleb Garth, should be responsible for the management? It would be an excellent schooling for Fred; he might make a modest income there, and still have time left to get knowledge by helping in other business. He mentioned his notion to Mrs. Garth with such evident delight that she could not bear to chill his pleasure by expressing her constant fear of his undertaking too much.

" The lad would be as happy as two," he said, throwing himself back in his chair, and looking radiant, " if I could tell him it was all settled. Think, Susan! His mind had been running on that place for years before old Featherstone died. And it would be as pretty a turn of things as could be that he should hold the place in a good industrious way after all—by his taking to business. For it's likely enough Bulstrode might let him go on, and gradually buy the stock. He hasn't made up his mind, I can see, whether or not he shall settle somewhere else as a lasting thing. I never was better pleased with a notion in my life. And then the children might be married by-and-by, Susan."

" You will not give any hint of the plan to Fred, until you are sure that Bulstrode would agree to the plan?" said Mrs. Garth, in a tone of gentle caution. " And as to marriage, Caleb, we old people need not help to hasten it."

" Oh, I don't know," said Caleb, swinging his head aside. " Marriage is a taming thing. Fred would want less of my bit and bridle. However, I shall say nothing till I know the ground I'm treading on. I shall speak to Bulstrode again."

He took his earliest opportunity of doing so. Bulstrode had anything but a warm interest in his nephew Fred Vincy, but he had a strong wish to secure Mr. Garth's services on many scattered points of business at which he was sure to be a considerable loser, if they were under less conscientious management. On that ground he made no objection to Mr. Garth's proposal; and there was also another reason why he was not sorry to give a consent which was to benefit one of the Vincy family. It was that Mrs. Bulstrode, having heard of Lydgate's debts, had been anxious to know whether her husband could not do something for poor Rosamond, and had been much troubled on learning from him that Lydgate's affairs were not easily remediable, and that the wisest plan was to let them " take their course." Mrs. Bulstrode had then said for the first time, " I think you are always a little hard towards my family, Nicholas. And I am sure I have no reason to deny any of my relatives. Too worldly they may be, but no one ever had to say that they were not respectable."

" My dear Harriet," said Mr. Bulstrode, wincing under his wife's eyes, which were filling with tears, " I have supplied your brother with a great deal of capital. I cannot be expected to take care of his married children."

That seemed to be true, and Mrs. Bulstrode's remonstrance subsided into pity for poor Rosamond, whose extravagant education she had always foreseen the fruits of.

But remembering that dialogue, Mr. Bulstrode felt that when he had to talk to his wife fully about his plan of quitting Middlemarch, he should be glad to tell her that he had made an arrangement which might be for the good of her nephew Fred. At present he had merely mentioned to her that he thought of shutting up The Shrubs for a few months, and taking a house on the Southern Coast.

Hence Mr. Garth got the assurance he desired, namely, that in case of Bulstrode's departure from Middlemarch for an indefinite time, Fred Vincy should be allowed to have the tenancy of Stone Court on the terms proposed.

Caleb was so elated with his hope of this " neat turn " being given to things, that if his self-control had not been braced by a little affectionate wifely scolding, he would have betrayed everything to Mary, wanting " to give the child comfort." However, he restrained himself, and kept in strict privacy from Fred certain visits which he was making to Stone Court, in order to look more thoroughly into the state of the land and stock, and take a preliminary estimate. He was certainly more eager in these visits than the probable speed of events required him to be ; but he was stimulated by a fatherly delight in occupying his mind with this bit of probable happiness which he held in store like a hidden birthday gift for Fred and Mary.

" But suppose the whole scheme should turn out to be a castle in the air ? " said Mrs. Garth.

"Well, well," replied Caleb; "the castle will tumble about nobody's head."

CHAPTER LXIX

"If thou hast heard a word, let it die with thee."
—*Ecclesiasticus.*

MR. BULSTRODE was still seated in his manager's room at the Bank, about three o'clock of the same day on which he had received Lydgate there, when the clerk entered to say that his horse was waiting, and also that Mr. Garth was outside and begged to speak with him.

"By all means," said Bulstrode; and Caleb entered. "Pray sit down, Mr. Garth," continued the banker, in his suavest tone. "I am glad that you arrived just in time to find me here. I know you count your minutes."

"Oh," said Caleb, gently, with a slow swing of his head on one side, as he seated himself and laid his hat on the floor. He looked at the ground, leaning forward and letting his long fingers droop between his legs, while each finger moved in succession, as if it were sharing some thought which filled his large quiet brow.

Mr. Bulstrode, like every one else who knew Caleb, was used to his slowness in beginning to speak on any topic which he felt to be important, and rather expected that he was about to recur to the buying of some houses in Blindman's Court, for the sake of pulling them down, as a sacrifice of property which would be well repaid by the influx of air and light on that spot. It was by propositions of this kind that Caleb was sometimes troublesome to his employers; but he had usually found Bulstrode ready to meet him in projects of improvement, and they had got on well together. When he spoke again, however, it was to say, in rather a subdued voice—

"I have just come away from Stone Court, Mr. Bulstrode."

"You found nothing wrong there, I hope," said the banker; "I was there myself yesterday. Abel has done well with the lambs this year."

"Why, yes," said Caleb, looking up gravely, "there *is* something wrong—a stranger, who is very ill, I think. He wants a doctor, and I came to tell you of that. His name is Raffles."

He saw the shock of his words passing through Bulstrode's frame. On this subject the banker had thought that his fears were too constantly on the watch to be taken by surprise; but he had been mistaken.

"Poor wretch!" he said in a compassionate tone, though his lips trembled a little. "Do you know how he came there?"

"I took him myself," said Caleb, quietly—"took him up in my gig. He had got down from the coach, and was walking a little beyond the turning from the toll-house, and I overtook him. He remembered seeing me with you once before, at Stone Court, and he asked me to take him on. I saw he was ill: it seemed to me the right thing to do, to carry him under shelter. And now I think you should lose no time in getting advice for him." Caleb took up his hat from the floor as he ended, and rose slowly from his seat.

"Certainly," said Bulstrode, whose mind was very active at this moment. "Perhaps you will yourself oblige me, Mr. Garth, by calling at Mr. Lydgate's as you pass—or stay! he may at this hour probably be at the Hospital. I will first send my man on the horse there with a note this instant, and then I will myself ride to Stone Court."

Bulstrode quickly wrote a note, and went out himself to give the commission to his man. When he returned, Caleb was standing as before with one hand on the back of the chair, holding his hat with the other. In Bulstrode's mind the dominant thought was, "Perhaps Raffles only spoke to Garth of his illness. Garth may wonder, as he must have done before, at this disreputable fellow's claiming intimacy with me; but he will know nothing. And he is friendly to me—I can be of use to him."

He longed for some confirmation of this hopeful conjecture, but to have asked any question as to what Raffles had said or done would have been to betray fear.

"I am exceedingly obliged to you, Mr. Garth," he said, in his usual tone of politeness. "My servant will be back in a few minutes, and I shall then go myself to see what can be done for this unfortunate man. Perhaps you had some other business with me? If so, pray be seated."

"Thank you," said Caleb, making a slight gesture with his right hand to waive the invitation. "I wish to say, Mr. Bulstrode, that I must request you to put your business into some other hands than mine. I am obliged to you for your handsome way of meeting me—about the letting of Stone Court, and all other business. But I must give it up."

A sharp certainty entered like a stab into Bulstrode's soul.

"This is sudden, Mr. Garth," was all he could say at first.

"It is," said Caleb; "but it is quite fixed. I must give it up."

He spoke with a firmness which was very gentle, and yet he could see that Bulstrode seemed to cower under that gentleness, his face looking dried and his eyes swerving away from the glance which rested on him. Caleb felt a deep pity for him, but he could have used no pretexts to account for his resolve, even if they would have been of any use.

"You have been led to this, I apprehend, by some slanders concerning me uttered by that unhappy creature," said Bulstrode, anxious now to know the utmost.

"That is true. I can't deny that I act upon what I heard from him."

"You are a conscientious man, Mr. Garth—a man, I trust, who feels himself accountable to God. You would not wish to injure me by being too ready to believe a slander," said Bulstrode, casting about for pleas that might be adapted to his hearer's mind. "That is a poor reason for giving up a connection which I think I may say will be mutually beneficial."

"I would injure no man if I could help it," said Caleb; "even if I thought God winked at it. I hope I should have a feeling for my fellow-creature. But, sir—I am obliged to believe that this Raffles has told me the truth. And I can't be happy in working with you, or profiting by you. It hurts my mind. I must beg you to seek another agent."

"Very well, Mr. Garth. But I must at least claim to know the worst that he has told you. I must know what is the foul speech that I am liable to be the victim of," said Bulstrode, a certain amount of anger beginning to mingle with his humiliation before this quiet man who renounced his benefits.

"That's needless," said Caleb, waving his hand, bowing his head slightly, and not swerving from the tone which had in it the merciful intention to spare this pitiable man. "What he has said to me will never pass from my lips, unless something now unknown forces it from me. If you led a harmful life for gain, and kept others out of their rights by deceit, to get the more for yourself, I daresay you repent—you would like to go back, and can't: that must be a bitter thing"—Caleb paused a moment and shook his head—"it is not for me to make your life harder to you."

"But you do—you do make it harder to me," said Bulstrode,

constrained into a genuine, pleading cry. "You make it harder to me by turning your back on me."

"That I'm forced to do," said Caleb, still more gently, lifting up his hand. "I am sorry. I don't judge you and say, he is wicked, and I am righteous. God forbid. I don't know everything. A man may do wrong, and his will may rise clear out of it, though he can't get his life clear. That's a bad punishment. If it is so with you,—well, I'm very sorry for you. But I have that feeling inside me, that I can't go on working with you. That's all, Mr. Bulstrode. Everything else is buried, so far as my will goes. And I wish you good-day."

"One moment, Mr. Garth!" said Bulstrode, hurriedly. "I may trust then to your solemn assurance that you will not repeat either to man or woman what—even if it have any degree of truth in it—is yet a malicious representation?"

Caleb's wrath was stirred, and he said, indignantly—

"Why should I have said it if I didn't mean it? I am in no fear of you. Such tales as that will never tempt my tongue."

"Excuse me—I am agitated—I am the victim of this abandoned man."

"Stop a bit! you have got to consider whether you didn't help to make him worse, when you profited by his vices."

"You are wronging me by too readily believing him," said Bulstrode, oppressed, as by a nightmare, with the inability to deny flatly what Raffles might have said; and yet feeling it an escape that Caleb had not so stated it to him as to ask for that flat denial.

"No," said Caleb, lifting his hand deprecatingly; "I am ready to believe better, when better is proved. I rob you of no good chance. As to speaking, I hold it a crime to expose a man's sin unless I'm clear it must be done to save the innocent. That is my way of thinking, Mr. Bulstrode, and what I say, I've no need to swear. I wish you good-day."

Some hours later, when he was at home, Caleb said to his wife, incidentally, that he had had some little differences with Bulstrode, and that in consequence, he had given up all notion of taking Stone Court, and indeed had resigned doing further business for him.

"He was disposed to interfere too much, was he?" said Mrs. Garth, imagining that her husband had been touched on his sensitive point, and not been allowed to do what he thought right as to materials and modes of work.

"Oh," said Caleb, bowing his head and waving his hand

gravely. And Mrs. Garth knew that this was a sign of his not intending to speak further on the subject.

As for Bulstrode, he had almost immediately mounted his horse and set off for Stone Court, being anxious to arrive there before Lydgate.

His mind was crowded with images and conjectures, which were a language to his hopes and fears, just as we hear tones from the vibrations which shake our whole system. The deep humiliation with which he had winced under Caleb Garth's knowledge of his past and rejection of his patronage, alternated with and almost gave way to the sense of safety in the fact that Garth, and no other, had been the man to whom Raffles had spoken. It seemed to him a sort of earnest that Providence intended his rescue from worse consequences ; the way being thus left open for the hope of secrecy. That Raffles should be afflicted with illness, that he should have been led to Stone Court rather than elsewhere—Bulstrode's heart fluttered at the vision of probabilities which these events conjured up. If it should turn out that he was freed from all danger of disgrace —if he could breathe in perfect liberty—his life should be more consecrated than it had ever been before. He mentally lifted up this vow as if it would urge the result he longed for—he tried to believe in the potency of that prayerful resolution—its potency to determine death. He knew that he ought to say, " Thy will be done ; " and he said it often. But the intense desire remained that the will of God might be the death of that hated man.

Yet when he arrived at Stone Court he could not see the change in Raffles without a shock. But for his pallor and feebleness, Bulstrode would have called the change in him entirely mental. Instead of his loud tormenting mood, he showed an intense, vague terror, and seemed to deprecate Bulstrode's anger, because the money was all gone—he had been robbed—it had half of it been taken from him. He had only come here because he was ill and somebody was hunting him—somebody was after him : he had told nobody anything, he had kept his mouth shut. Bulstrode, not knowing the significance of these symptoms, interpreted this new nervous susceptibility into a means of alarming Raffles into true confessions, and taxed him with falsehood in saying that he had not told anything, since he had just told the man who took him up in his gig and brought him to Stone Court. Raffles denied this with solemn adjurations ; the fact being that the links of consciousness were interrupted in him, and that his minute terror-stricken narrative to Caleb Garth had been delivered under a set of visionary impulses which had dropped back into darkness.

Bulstrode's heart sank again at this sign that he could get no grasp over the wretched man's mind, and that no word of Raffles could be trusted as to the fact which he most wanted to know, namely, whether or not he had really kept silence to every one in the neighbourhood except Caleb Garth. The housekeeper had told him without the least constraint of manner that since Mr. Garth left, Raffles had asked her for beer, and after that had not spoken, seeming very ill. On that side it might be concluded that there had been no betrayal. Mrs. Abel thought, like the servants at The Shrubs, that the strange man belonged to the unpleasant " kin " who are among the troubles of the rich ; she had at first referred the kinship to Mr. Rigg, and where there was property left, the buzzing presence of such large blue-bottles seemed natural enough. How he could be " kin " to Bulstrode as well was not so clear, but Mrs. Abel agreed with her husband that there was " no knowing," a proposition which had a great deal of mental food for her, so that she shook her head over it without further speculation.

In less than an hour Lydgate arrived. Bulstrode met him outside the wainscoted parlour, where Raffles was, and said—

" I have called you in, Mr. Lydgate, to an unfortunate man who was once in my employment, many years ago. Afterwards he went to America, and returned I fear to an idle dissolute life. Being destitute, he has a claim on me. He was slightly connected with Rigg, the former owner of this place, and in consequence found his way here. I believe he is seriously ill : apparently his mind is affected, I feel bound to do the utmost for him."

Lydgate, who had the remembrance of his last conversation with Bulstrode strongly upon him, was not disposed to say an unnecessary word to him, and bowed slightly in answer to this account ; but just before entering the room he turned automatically and said, " What is his name ? "—to know names being as much a part of the medical man's accomplishment as of the practical politician's.

" Raffles, John Raffles," said Bulstrode, who hoped that whatever became of Raffles, Lydgate would never know any more of him.

When he had thoroughly examined and considered the patient, Lydgate ordered that he should go to bed, and be kept there in as complete quiet as possible, and then went with Bulstrode into another room.

"It is a serious case, I apprehend," said the banker, before Lydgate began to speak.

"No—and yes," said Lydgate, half dubiously. "It is difficult to decide as to the possible effect of long-standing complications; but the man had a robust constitution to begin with. I should not expect this attack to be fatal, though of course the system is in a ticklish state. He should be well watched and attended to."

"I will remain here myself," said Bulstrode. "Mrs. Abel and her husband are inexperienced. I can easily remain here for the night, if you will oblige me by taking a note for Mrs. Bulstrode."

"I should think that is hardly necessary," said Lydgate. "He seems tame and terrified enough. He might become more unmanageable. But there is a man here—is there not?"

"I have more than once stayed here a few nights for the sake of seclusion," said Bulstrode, indifferently; "I am quite disposed to do so now. Mrs. Abel and her husband can relieve or aid me, if necessary."

"Very well. Then I need give my directions only to you," said Lydgate, not feeling surprised at a little peculiarity in Bulstrode.

"You think, then, that the case is hopeful?" said Bulstrode, when Lydgate had ended giving his orders.

"Unless there turn out to be further complications, such as I have not at present detected—yes," said Lydgate. "He may pass on to a worse stage; but I should not wonder if he got better in a few days, by adhering to the treatment I have prescribed. There must be firmness. Remember, if he calls for liquors of any sort, not to give them to him. In my opinion, men in his condition are oftener killed by treatment than by the disease. Still, new symptoms may arise. I shall come again to-morrow morning."

After waiting for the note to be carried to Mrs. Bulstrode, Lydgate rode away, forming no conjectures, in the first instance, about the history of Raffles, but rehearsing the whole argument, which had lately been much stirred by the publication of Dr. Ware's abundant experience in America, as to the right way of treating cases of alcoholic poisoning such as this. Lydgate, when abroad, had already been interested in this question : he was strongly convinced against the prevalent practice of allowing alcohol and persistently administering large doses of opium ; and he had repeatedly acted on this conviction with a favourable result.

"The man is in a diseased state," he thought, "but there's a good deal of wear in him still. I suppose he is an object of charity to Bulstrode. It is curious what patches of hardness and tenderness lie side by side in men's dispositions. Bulstrode seems the most unsympathetic fellow I ever saw about some people, and yet he has taken no end of trouble, and spent a great deal of money, on benevolent objects. I suppose he has some test by which he finds out whom Heaven cares for—he has made up his mind that it doesn't care for me."

This streak of bitterness came from a plenteous source, and kept widening in the current of his thought as he neared Lowick Gate. He had not been there since his first interview with Bulstrode in the morning, having been found at the Hospital by the banker's messenger ; and for the first time he was returning to his home without the vision of any expedient in the background which left him a hope of raising money enough to deliver him from the coming destitution of everything which made his married life tolerable—everything which saved him and Rosamond from that bare isolation in which they would be forced to recognise how little of a comfort they could be to each other. It was more bearable to do without tenderness for himself than to see that his own tenderness could make no amends for the lack of other things to her. The sufferings of his own pride from humiliations past and to come were keen enough, yet they were hardly distinguishable to himself from that more acute pain which dominated them—the pain of foreseeing that Rosamond would come to regard him chiefly as the cause of disappointment and unhappiness to her. He had never liked the makeshifts of poverty, and they had never before entered into his prospects for himself ; but he was beginning now to imagine how two creatures who loved each other, and had a stock of thoughts in common, might laugh over their shabby furniture, and their calculations how far they could afford butter and eggs. But the glimpse of that poetry seemed as far off from him as the carelessness of the golden age ; in poor Rosamond's mind there was not room enough for luxuries to look small in. He got down from his horse in a very sad mood, and went into the house, not expecting to be cheered except by his dinner, and reflecting that before the evening closed it would be wise to tell Rosamond of his application to Bulstrode and its failure. It would be well not to lose time in preparing her for the worst.

But his dinner waited long for him before he was able to eat it. For on entering he found that Dover's agent had already put a man in the house, and when he asked where Mrs. Lydgate was, he was told that she was in her bedroom. He went up and found her stretched on the bed pale and silent, without an answer even in her face to any word or look of his. He sat down by the bed and leaning over her said with almost a cry of prayer—

"Forgive me for this misery, my poor Rosamond! Let us only love one another."

She looked at him silently, still with the blank despair on her face; but then the tears began to fill her blue eyes, and her lip trembled. The strong man had had too much to bear that day. He let his head fall beside hers and sobbed.

He did not hinder her from going to her father early in the morning—it seemed now that he ought not to hinder her from doing as she pleased. In half an hour she came back, and said that papa and mamma wished her to go and stay with them while things were in this miserable state. Papa said he could do nothing about the debt—if he paid this, there would be half-a-dozen more. She had better come back home again till Lydgate had got a comfortable home for her. "Do you object, Tertius?"

"Do as you like," said Lydgate. "But things are not coming to a crisis immediately. There is no hurry."

"I should not go till to-morrow," said Rosamond; "I shall want to pack my clothes."

"Oh, I would wait a little longer than to-morrow—there is no knowing what may happen," said Lydgate, with bitter irony. "I may get my neck broken, and that may make things easier to you."

It was Lydgate's misfortune and Rosamond's too, that his tenderness towards her, which was both an emotional prompting and a well-considered resolve, was inevitably interrupted by these outbursts of indignation either ironical or remonstrant. She thought them totally unwarranted, and the repulsion which this exceptional severity excited in her was in danger of making the more persistent tenderness unacceptable.

"I see you do not wish me to go," she said, with chill mildness; "why can you not say so, without that kind of violence? I shall stay until you request me to do otherwise."

Lydgate said no more, but went out on his rounds. He felt bruised and shattered, and there was a dark line under his eyes which Rosamond had not seen before. She could not bear to look at him. Tertius had a way of taking things which made them a great deal worse for her.

CHAPTER LXX

Our deeds still travel with us from afar,
And what we have been makes us what we are.

BULSTRODE'S first object after Lydgate had left Stone Court was to examine Raffles's pockets, which he imagined were sure to carry signs in the shape of hotel-bills of the places he had stopped in, if he had not told the truth in saying that he had come straight from Liverpool because he was ill and had no money. There were various bills crammed into his pocket-book, but none of a later date than Christmas at any other place, except one, which bore date that morning. This was crumpled up with a handbill about a horse-fair in one of his tail-pockets, and represented the cost of three days' stay at an inn at Bilkley, where the fair was held—a town at least forty miles from Middlemarch. The bill was heavy, and since Raffles had no luggage with him, it seemed probable that he had left his portmanteau behind in payment, in order to save money for his travelling fare; for his purse was empty, and he had only a couple of sixpences and some loose pence in his pockets.

Bulstrode gathered a sense of safety from these indications that Raffles had really kept at a distance from Middlemarch since his memorable visit at Christmas. At a distance and among people who were strangers to Bulstrode, what satisfaction could there be to Raffles's tormenting, self-magnifying vein in telling old scandalous stories about a Middlemarch banker? And what harm if he did talk? The chief point now was to keep watch over him as long as there was any danger of that intelligible raving, that unaccountable impulse to tell, which seemed to have acted towards Caleb Garth; and Bulstrode felt much anxiety lest some such impulse should come over him at the sight of Lydgate. He sat up alone with him through the night, only ordering the housekeeper to lie down in her clothes, so as to be ready when he called her, alleging his own indisposition to sleep, and his anxiety to carry out the doctor's orders. He did carry them out faithfully, although Raffles was incessantly asking for brandy, and declaring that he was sinking away—that the earth was sinking away from under him. He was restless and sleepless, but still quailing and manageable. On the offer of the food ordered by Lydgate, which he refused, and the denial of other things which he demanded, he seemed to concentrate all his terror on Bulstrode, imploringly deprecating his anger, his revenge on him by starvation, and declaring with strong oaths that he had never told any mortal a word against him. Even this Bulstrode felt that he would not have liked Lydgate to hear ; but a more alarming sign of fitful alternation in his delirium was, that in the morning twilight Raffles suddenly seemed to imagine a doctor present, addressing him and declaring that Bulstrode wanted to starve him to death out of revenge for telling, when he never had told.

Bulstrode's native imperiousness and strength of determination served him well. This delicate-looking man, himself nervously perturbed, found the needed stimulus in his strenuous circumstances, and through that difficult night and morning, while he had the air of an animated corpse returned to movement without warmth, holding the mastery by its chill impassibility, his mind was intensely at work thinking of what he had to guard against and what would win him security. Whatever prayers he might lift up, whatever statements he might inwardly make of this man's wretched spiritual condition, and the duty he himself was under to submit to the punishment divinely appointed for him rather than to wish for evil to another— through all this effort to condense words into a solid mental state, there pierced and spread with irresistible vividness the images of the events he desired. And in the train of those images came their apology. He could not but see the death of Raffles, and see in it his own deliverance. What was the removal of this wretched creature ? He was impenitent—but were not public criminals impenitent ?—yet the law decided on their fate. Should Providence in this case award death, there was no sin in contemplating death as the desirable issue—if he kept his hands from hastening it—if he scrupulously did what was prescribed. Even here there might be a mistake : human prescriptions were fallible things : Lydgate had said that treatment had hastened death,—why not his own method of treatment? But of course intention was everything in the question of right and wrong.

And Bulstrode set himself to keep his intention separate from his desire. He inwardly declared that he intended to obey orders. Why should he have got into any argument about the validity of these orders? It was only the common trick of desire—which avails itself of any irrelevant scepticism, finding larger room for itself in all uncertainty about effects, in every obscurity that looks like the absence of law. Still, he did obey the orders.

His anxieties continually glanced towards Lydgate, and his remembrance of what had taken place between them the morning before was accompanied with sensibilities which had not been roused at all during the actual scene. He had then cared but little about Lydgate's painful impressions with regard to the suggested change in the Hospital, or about the disposition towards himself which what he held to be his justifiable refusal of a rather exorbitant request might call forth. He recurred to the scene now with a perception that he had probably made Lydgate his enemy, and with an awakened desire to propitiate him, or rather to create in him a strong sense of personal obligation. He regretted that he had not at once made even an unreasonable money-sacrifice. For in case of unpleasant suspicions or even knowledge gathered from the raving of Raffles, Bulstrode would have felt that he had a defence in Lydgate's mind by having conferred a momentous benefit on him. But the regret had perhaps come too late.

Strange, piteous conflict in the soul of this unhappy man, who had longed for years to be better than he was—who had taken his selfish passions into discipline and clad them in severe robes, so that he had walked with them as a devout quire, till now that a terror had risen among them, and they could chant no longer, but threw out their common cries for safety.

It was nearly the middle of the day before Lydgate arrived: he had meant to come earlier, but had been detained, he said; and his shattered looks were noticed by Bulstrode. But he immediately threw himself into the consideration of the patient, and inquired strictly into all that had occurred. Raffles was worse, would take hardly any food, was persistently wakeful and restlessly raving; but still not violent. Contrary to Bulstrode's alarmed expectation, he took little notice of Lydgate's presence, and continued to talk or murmur incoherently.

"What do you think of him?" said Bulstrode, in private.

"The symptoms are worse."

"You are less hopeful?"

"No; I still think he may come round. Are you going to stay here yourself?" said Lydgate, looking at Bulstrode with an abrupt question, which made him uneasy, though in reality it was not due to any suspicious conjecture.

"Yes, I think so," said Bulstrode, governing himself and speaking with deliberation. "Mrs. Bulstrode is advised of the reasons which detain me. Mrs. Abel and her husband are not experienced enough to be left quite alone, and this kind of responsibility is scarcely included in their service of me. You have some fresh instructions, I presume."

The chief new instruction that Lydgate had to give was on the administration of extremely moderate doses of opium, in case of the sleeplessness continuing after several hours. He had taken the precaution of bringing opium in his pocket, and he gave minute directions to Bulstrode as to the doses, and the point at which they should cease. He insisted on the risk of not ceasing; and repeated his order that no alcohol should be given.

"From what I see of the case," he ended, "narcotism is the only thing I should be much afraid of. He may wear through even without much food. There's a good deal of strength in him."

"You look ill yourself, Mr. Lydgate—a most unusual, I may say unprecedented thing in my knowledge of you," said Bulstrode, showing a solicitude as unlike his indifference the day before, as his present recklessness about his own fatigue was unlike his habitual self-cherishing anxiety. "I fear you are harassed."

"Yes, I am," said Lydgate, brusquely, holding his hat, and ready to go.

"Something new, I fear," said Bulstrode, inquiringly. "Pray be seated."

"No, thank you," said Lydgate, with some *hauteur*. "I mentioned to you yesterday what was the state of my affairs. There is nothing to add, except that the execution has since then been actually put into my house. One can tell a good deal of trouble in a short sentence. I will say good-morning."

"Stay, Mr. Lydgate, stay," said Bulstrode; "I have been reconsidering this subject. I was yesterday taken by surprise and saw it superficially. Mrs. Bulstrode is anxious for her niece, and I myself should grieve at a calamitous change in your position. Claims on me are numerous, but on reconsideration, I esteem it right that I should incur a small sacrifice rather than leave you unaided. You said, I think, that a thousand pounds would suffice entirely to free you from your burthens, and enable you to recover a firm stand?"

"Yes," said Lydgate, a great leap of joy within him surmounting every other feeling; "that would pay all my debts, and leave me a little on hand. I could set about economising in our way of living. And by-and-by my practice might look up."

"If you will wait a moment, Mr. Lydgate, I will draw a cheque to that amount. I am aware that help, to be effectual in these cases, should be thorough."

While Bulstrode wrote, Lydgate turned to the window thinking of his home—thinking of his life with its good start saved from frustration, its good purposes still unbroken.

"You can give me a note of hand for this, Mr. Lydgate," said the banker, advancing towards him with the cheque. "And by-and-by, I hope, you may be in circumstances gradually to repay me. Meanwhile, I have pleasure in thinking that you will be released from further difficulty."

"I am deeply obliged to you," said Lydgate. "You have restored to me the prospect of working with some happiness and some chance of good."

It appeared to him a very natural movement in Bulstrode that he should have reconsidered his refusal: it corresponded with the more munificent side of his character. But as he put his hack into a canter, that he might get the sooner home, and tell the good news to Rosamond, and get cash at the bank to pay over to Dover's agent, there crossed his mind, with an unpleasant impression, as from a dark-winged flight of evil augury across his vision, the thought of that contrast in himself which a few months had brought—that he should be overjoyed at being under a strong personal obligation—that he should be overjoyed at getting money for himself from Bulstrode.

The banker felt that he had done something to nullify one cause of uneasiness, and yet he was scarcely the easier. He did not measure the quantity of diseased motive which had made him wish for Lydgate's goodwill, but the quantity was none the less actively there, like an irritating agent in his blood. A man vows, and yet will not cast away the means of breaking his vow. Is it that he distinctly means to break it? Not at all; but the desires which tend to break it are at work in him dimly, and make their way into his imagination, and relax his muscles in the very moments when he is telling himself over again the reasons for his vow. Raffles, recovering quickly, returning to the free use of his odious powers—how could Bulstrode wish for that? Raffles dead was the image that brought release, and indirectly he prayed for that way of release, beseeching that, if it were possible, the rest of his days here below might be freed from the threat of an ignominy which would break him utterly as an instrument of God's service. Lydgate's opinion was not on the side of promise that this prayer would be fulfilled; and as the day advanced, Bulstrode felt himself getting irritated at the persistent life in this man, whom he would fain have seen sinking into the silence of death: imperious will stirred murderous impulses towards this brute life, over which will, by itself, had no power. He said inwardly that he was getting too much worn; he would not sit up with the patient to-night, but leave him to Mrs. Abel, who, if necessary, could call her husband.

At six o'clock, Raffles, having had only fitful perturbed snatches of sleep, from which he waked with fresh restlessness and perpetual cries that he was sinking away, Bulstrode began to administer the opium according to Lydgate's directions. At the end of half an hour or more he called Mrs. Abel and told her that he found himself unfit for further watching. He must now consign the patient to her care; and he proceeded to repeat to her Lydgate's directions as to the quantity of each dose. Mrs. Abel had not before known anything of Lydgate's prescriptions; she had simply prepared and brought whatever Bulstrode ordered, and had done what he pointed out to her. She began now to ask what else she should do besides administering the opium.

"Nothing at present, except the offer of the soup or the soda-water: you can come to me for further directions. Unless there is any important change, I shall not come into the room again to-night. You will ask your husband for help, if necessary. I must go to bed early."

"You've much need, sir, I'm sure," said Mrs. Abel, "and to take something more strengthening than what you've done."

Bulstrode went away now without anxiety as to what Raffles might say in his raving, which had taken on a muttering incoherence not likely to create any dangerous belief. At any rate he must risk this. He went down into the wainscoted parlour first, and began to consider whether he would not have his horse saddled and go home by the moonlight, and give up caring for earthly consequences. Then, he wished that he had begged Lydgate to come again that evening. Perhaps he might deliver a different opinion, and think that Raffles was getting into a less hopeful state. Should he send for Lydgate? If Raffles were really getting worse, and slowly dying, Bulstrode felt that he could go to bed and sleep in gratitude to Providence. But was he worse? Lydgate might come and simply say that he was going on as he expected, and predict that he would by-and-by fall into a good sleep, and get well. What was the use of sending for him? Bulstrode shrank from that result. No ideas or opinions could hinder him from seeing the one probability to be, that Raffles recovered would be just the same man as before, with his strength as a tormentor renewed, obliging him to drag away his wife to spend her years apart from her friends and native place, carrying an alienating suspicion against him in her heart.

He had sat an hour and a half in this conflict by the firelight only, when a sudden thought made him rise and light the bed-candle, which he had brought down with him. The thought was, that he had not told Mrs. Abel when the doses of opium must cease.

He took hold of the candlestick, but stood motionless for a long while. She might already have given him more than Lydgate had prescribed. But it was excusable in him, that he should forget part of an order, in his present wearied condition. He walked up-stairs, candle in hand, not knowing whether he should straightway enter his own room and go to bed, or turn to the patient's room and rectify his omission. He paused in the passage, with his face turned towards Raffles's room, and he could hear him moaning and murmuring. He was not asleep, then. Who could know that Lydgate's prescription would not be better disobeyed than followed, since there was still no sleep?

He turned into his own room. Before he had quite undressed, Mrs. Abel rapped at the door; he opened it an inch, so that he could hear her speak low.

" If you please, sir, should I have no brandy nor nothing to give the poor creetur? He feels sinking away, and nothing else will he swaller—and but little strength in it, if he did—only the opium. And he says more and more he's sinking down through the earth."

To her surprise, Mr. Bulstrode did not answer. A struggle was going on within him.

"I think he must die for want o' support, if he goes on in that way. When I nursed my poor master, Mr. Robisson, I had to give him port-wine and brandy constant, and a big glass at a time," added Mrs. Abel, with a touch of remonstrance in her tone.

But again Mr. Bulstrode did not answer immediately, and she continued, "It's not a time to spare when people are at death's door, nor would you wish it, sir, I'm sure. Else I should give him our own bottle o' rum as we keep by us. But a sitter-up so as you've been, and doing everything as laid in your power——"

Here a key was thrust through the inch of doorway, and Mr. Bulstrode said huskily, "That is the key of the wine-cooler. You will find plenty of brandy there."

Early in the morning—about six—Mr. Bulstrode rose and spent some time in prayer. Does any one suppose that private prayer is necessarily candid—necessarily goes to the roots of action? Private prayer is inaudible speech, and speech is representative : who can represent himself just as he is, even in his own reflections? Bulstrode had not yet unravelled in his thought the confused promptings of the last four-and-twenty hours.

He listened in the passage, and could hear hard stertorous breathing. Then he walked out in the garden, and looked at the early rime on the grass and fresh spring leaves. When he re-entered the house, he felt startled at the sight of Mrs. Abel.

"How is your patient—asleep, I think?" he said, with an attempt at cheerfulness in his tone.

"He's gone very deep, sir," said Mrs. Abel. "He went off gradual between three and four o'clock. Would you please to go and look at him? I thought it no harm to leave him. My man's gone afield, and the little girl's seeing to the kettles."

Bulstrode went up. At a glance he knew that Raffles was not in the sleep which brings revival, but in the sleep which streams deeper and deeper into the gulf of death.

He looked round the room and saw a bottle with some brandy in it, and the almost empty opium phial. He put the phial out of sight, and carried the brandy-bottle down-stairs with him, locking it again in the wine-cooler.

While breakfasting he considered whether he should ride to Middlemarch at once, or wait for Lydgate's arrival. He decided to wait, and told Mrs. Abel that she might go about her work—he could watch in the bed-chamber.

As he sat there and beheld the enemy of his peace going irrevocably into silence, he felt more at rest than he had done for many months. His conscience was soothed by the enfolding wing of secrecy, which seemed just then like an angel sent down for his relief. He drew out his pocket-book to review various memoranda there as to the arrangements he had projected and partly carried out in the prospect of quitting Middlemarch, and considered how far he would let them stand or recall them, now that his absence would be brief. Some economies which he felt desirable might still find a suitable occasion in his temporary withdrawal from management, and he hoped still that Mrs. Casaubon would take a large share in the expenses of the Hospital. In that way the moments passed, until a change in the stertorous breathing was marked enough to draw his attention wholly to the bed, and forced him to think of the departing life, which had once been subservient to his own—which he had once been glad to find base enough for him to act as he would. It was his gladness then which impelled him now to be glad that the life was at an end.

And who could say that the death of Raffles had been hastened? Who knew what would have saved him?

Lydgate arrived at half-past ten, in time to witness the final pause of the breath. When he entered the room Bulstrode observed a sudden expression in his face, which was not so much surprise as a recognition that he had not judged correctly. He stood by the bed in silence for some time, with his eyes turned on the dying man, but with that subdued activity of expression which showed that he was carrying on an inward debate.

" When did this change begin ? " said he, looking at Bulstrode.

" I did not watch by him last night," said Bulstrode. " I was overworn, and left him under Mrs. Abel's care. She said that he sank into sleep between three and four o'clock. When I came in before eight he was nearly in this condition."

Lydgate did not ask another question, but watched in silence until he said, " It's all over."

This morning Lydgate was in a state of recovered hope and freedom. He had set out on his work with all his old animation, and felt strong enough to bear all the deficiencies of his married life. And he was conscious that Bulstrode had been a benefactor to him. But he was uneasy about this case. He had not expected it to terminate as it had done. Yet he hardly

knew how to put a question on the subject to Bulstrode without
appearing to insult him ; and if he examined the housekeeper—
why, the man was dead.   There seemed to be no use in implying
that somebody's ignorance or imprudence had killed him.   And
after all, he himself might be wrong.

He and Bulstrode rode back to Middlemarch together, talking
of many things—chiefly cholera and the chances of the Reform
Bill in the House of Lords, and the firm resolve of the Political
Unions.   Nothing was said about Raffles, except that Bulstrode mentioned the necessity of having a grave for him in
Lowick churchyard and observed that, so far as he knew, the
poor man had no connections, except Rigg, whom he had stated
to be unfriendly towards him.

On returning home Lydgate had a visit from Mr. Farebrother.
The Vicar had not been in the town the day before, but the news
that there was an execution in Lydgate's house had got to
Lowick by the evening, having been carried by Mr. Spicer,
shoemaker and parish-clerk, who had it from his brother, the
respectable bell-hanger in Lowick Gate.   Since that evening
when Lydgate had come down from the billiard-room with
Fred Vincy, Mr. Farebrother's thoughts about him had been
rather gloomy.   Playing at the Green Dragon once or oftener
might have been a trifle in another man ; but in Lydgate it was
one of several signs that he was getting unlike his former self.
He was beginning to do things for which he had formerly even
an excessive scorn.   Whatever certain dissatisfactions in
marriage, which some silly tinklings of gossip had given him
hints of, might have to do with this change, Mr. Farebrother
felt that it was chiefly connected with the debts which were
being more and more distinctly reported, and he began to fear
that any notion of Lydgate's having resources or friends in the
background must be quite illusory.   The rebuff he had met with
in his first attempt to win Lydgate's confidence, disinclined him
to a second ; but this news of the execution being actually in
the house, determined the Vicar to overcome his reluctance.

Lydgate had just dismissed a poor patient, in whom he was
much interested, and he came forward to put out his hand with
an open cheerfulness which surprised Mr. Farebrother.   Could
this too be a proud rejection of sympathy and help ?   Never
mind ; the sympathy and help should be offered.

" How are you, Lydgate ?   I came to see you because I had
heard something which made me anxious about you," said the
Vicar, in the tone of a good brother, only that there was no

reproach in it. They were both seated by this time, and Lydgate answered immediately—

"I think I know what you mean. You had heard that there was an execution in the house?"

"Yes; is it true?"

"It was true," said Lydgate, with an air of freedom, as if he did not mind talking about the affair now. "But the danger is over; the debt is paid. I am out of my difficulties now: I shall be freed from debts, and able, I hope, to start afresh on a better plan."

"I am very thankful to hear it," said the Vicar, falling back in his chair, and speaking with that low-toned quickness which often follows the removal of a load. "I like that better than all the news in the 'Times.' I confess I came to you with a heavy heart."

"Thank you for coming," said Lydgate, cordially. "I can enjoy the kindness all the more because I am happier. I have certainly been a good deal crushed. I'm afraid I shall find the bruises still painful by-and-by," he added, smiling rather sadly; "but just now I can only feel that the torture-screw is off."

Mr. Farebrother was silent for a moment, and then said earnestly, "My dear fellow, let me ask you one question. Forgive me if I take a liberty."

"I don't believe you will ask anything that ought to offend me."

"Then—this is necessary to set my heart quite at rest—you have not—have you?—in order to pay your debts, incurred another debt which may harass you worse hereafter?"

"No," said Lydgate, colouring slightly. "There is no reason why I should not tell you—since the fact is so—that the person to whom I am indebted is Bulstrode. He has made me a very handsome advance—a thousand pounds—and he can afford to wait for repayment"

"Well, that is generous," said Mr. Farebrother, compelling himself to approve of the man whom he disliked. His delicate feeling shrank from dwelling even in his thought on the fact that he had always urged Lydgate to avoid any personal entanglement with Bulstrode. He added immediately, "And Bulstrode must naturally feel an interest in your welfare, after you have worked with him in a way which has probably reduced your income instead of adding to it. I am glad to think that he has acted accordingly."

Lydgate felt uncomfortable under these kindly suppositions. They made more distinct within him the uneasy consciousness which had shown its first dim stirrings only a few hours before, that Bulstrode's motives for his sudden beneficence following close upon the chillest indifference might be merely selfish. He let the kindly suppositions pass. He could not tell the history of the loan, but it was more vividly present with him than ever, as well as the fact which the Vicar delicately ignored—that this relation of personal indebtedness to Bulstrode was what he had once been most resolved to avoid.

He began, instead of answering, to speak of his projected economies, and of his having come to look at his life from a different point of view.

" I shall set up a surgery," he said. " I really think I made a mistaken effort in that respect. And if Rosamond will not mind, I shall take an apprentice. I don't like these things, but if one carries them out faithfully they are not really lowering. I have had a severe galling to begin with : that will make the small rubs seem easy."

Poor Lydgate ! the " if Rosamond will not mind," which had fallen from him involuntarily as part of his thought, was a significant mark of the yoke he bore. But Mr. Farebrother, whose hopes entered strongly into the same current with Lydgate's, and who knew nothing about him that could now raise a melancholy presentiment, left him with affectionate congratulation.

CHAPTER LXXI

Clown. . . . 'Twas in the Bunch of Grapes, where, indeed, you have a delight to sit, have you not ?
Froth. I have so ; because it is an open room, and good for winter.
Clo. Why, very well then : I hope here be truths.
                                        —*Measure for Measure.*

FIVE days after the death of Raffles, Mr. Bambridge was standing at his leisure under the large archway leading into the yard of the Green Dragon. He was not fond of solitary contemplation, but he had only just come out of the house, and any human figure standing at ease under the archway in the early afternoon was as certain to attract companionship as a pigeon which has found something worth pecking at. In this case there was no material object to feed upon, but the eye of reason saw a probability of mental sustenance in the shape of gossip.

Mr. Hopkins, the meek-mannered draper opposite, was the first to act on this inward vision, being the more ambitious of a little masculine talk because his customers were chiefly women. Mr. Bambridge was rather curt to the draper, feeling that Hopkins was of course glad to talk to *him*, but that he was not going to waste much of his talk on Hopkins. Soon, however, there was a small cluster of more important listeners, who were either deposited from the passers-by, or had sauntered to the spot expressly to see if there were anything going on at the Green Dragon; and Mr. Bambridge was finding it worth his while to say many impressive things about the fine studs he had been seeing and the purchases he had made on a journey in the north from which he had just returned. Gentlemen present were assured that when they could show him anything to cut out a blood mare, a bay, rising four, which was to be seen at Doncaster if they chose to go and look at it, Mr. Bambridge would gratify them by being shot " from here to Hereford." Also, a pair of blacks which he was going to put into the break recalled vividly to his mind a pair which he had sold to Faulkner in '19, for a hundred guineas, and which Faulkner had sold for a hundred and sixty two months later—any gent who could disprove this statement being offered the privilege of calling Mr. Bambridge by a very ugly name until the exercise made his throat dry.

When the discourse was at this point of animation, came up Mr. Frank Hawley. He was not a man to compromise his dignity by lounging at the Green Dragon, but happening to pass along the High Street and seeing Bambridge on the other side, he took some of his long strides across to ask the horse-dealer whether he had found the first-rate gig-horse which he had engaged to look for. Mr. Hawley was requested to wait until he had seen a grey selected at Bilkley: if that did not meet his wishes to a hair, Bambridge did not know a horse when he saw it, which seemed to be the highest conceivable unlikelihood. Mr. Hawley, standing with his back to the street, was fixing a time for looking at the grey and seeing it tried, when a horseman passed slowly by.

" Bulstrode ! " said two or three voices at once in a low tone, one of them, which was the draper's, respectfully prefixing the " Mr. ; " but nobody having more intention in this interjectional naming than if they had said " the Riverston coach " when that vehicle appeared in the distance. Mr. Hawley gave a careless glance round at Bulstrode's back, but as Bambridge's eyes followed it he made a sarcastic grimace.

"By jingo! that reminds me," he began, lowering his voice a little, "I picked up something else at Bilkley besides your gig-horse, Mr. Hawley. I picked up a fine story about Bulstrode. Do you know how he came by his fortune? Any gentleman wanting a bit of curious information, I can give it him free of expense. If everybody got their deserts, Bulstrode might have had to say his prayers at Botany Bay."

"What do you mean?" said Mr. Hawley, thrusting his hands into his pockets, and pushing a little forward under the archway. If Bulstrode should turn out to be a rascal, Frank Hawley had a prophetic soul.

"I had it from a party who was an old chum of Bulstrode's. I'll tell you where I first picked him up," said Bambridge, with a sudden gesture of his forefinger. "He was at Larcher's sale, but I knew nothing of him then—he slipped through my fingers —was after Bulstrode, no doubt. He tells me he can tap Bulstrode to any amount, knows all his secrets. However, he blabbed to me at Bilkley: he takes a stiff glass. Damme if I think he meant to turn king's evidence; but he's that sort of bragging fellow, the bragging runs over hedge and ditch with him, till he'd brag of a spavin as if it 'ud fetch money. A man should know when to pull up." Mr. Bambridge made this remark with an air of disgust, satisfied that his own bragging showed a fine sense of the marketable.

"What's the man's name? Where can he be found?" said Mr. Hawley.

"As to where he is to be found, I left him to it at the Saracen's Head; but his name is Raffles."

"Raffles!" exclaimed Mr. Hopkins. "I furnished his funeral yesterday. He was buried at Lowick. Mr. Bulstrode followed him. A very decent funeral."

There was a strong sensation among the listeners. Mr. Bambridge gave an ejaculation in which "brimstone" was the mildest word, and Mr. Hawley, knitting his brows and bending his head forward, exclaimed, "What?—where did the man die?"

"At Stone Court," said the draper. "The housekeeper said he was a relation of the master's. He came there ill on Friday."

"Why, it was on Wednesday I took a glass with him," interposed Bambridge.

"Did any doctor attend him?" said Mr. Hawley.

" Yes, Mr. Lydgate. Mr. Bulstrode sat up with him one night. He died the third morning."

" Go on, Bambridge," said Mr. Hawley, insistently. " What did this fellow say about Bulstrode ? "

The group had already become larger, the town-clerk's presence being a guarantee that something worth listening to was going on there ; and Mr. Bambridge delivered his narrative in the hearing of seven. It was mainly what we know, including the fact about Will Ladislaw, with some local colour and circumstance added : it was what Bulstrode had dreaded the betrayal of—and hoped to have buried for ever with the corpse of Raffles—it was that haunting ghost of his earlier life which as he rode past the archway of the Green Dragon he was trusting that Providence had delivered him from. Yes, Providence. He had not confessed to himself yet that he had done anything in the way of contrivance to this end ; he had accepted what seemed to have been offered. It was impossible to prove that he had done anything which hastened the departure of that man's soul.

But this gossip about Bulstrode spread through Middlemarch like the smell of fire. Mr. Frank Hawley followed up his information by sending a clerk whom he could trust to Stone Court on a pretext of inquiring about hay, but really to gather all that could be learned about Raffles and his illness from Mrs. Abel. In this way it came to his knowledge that Mr. Garth had carried the man to Stone Court in his gig ; and Mr. Hawley in consequence took an opportunity of seeing Caleb, calling at his office to ask whether he had time to undertake an arbitration if it were required, and then asking him incidentally about Raffles. Caleb was betrayed into no word injurious to Bulstrode beyond the fact which he was forced to admit, that he had given up acting for him within the last week. Mr. Hawley drew his inferences, and feeling convinced that Raffles had told his story to Garth, and that Garth had given up Bulstrode's affairs in consequence, said so a few hours later to Mr. Toller. The statement was passed on until it had quite lost the stamp of an inference, and was taken as information coming straight from Garth, so that even a diligent historian might have concluded Caleb to be the chief publisher of Bulstrode's misdemeanours.

Mr. Hawley was not slow to perceive that there was no handle for the law either in the revelations made by Raffles or in the circumstances of his death. He had himself ridden to Lowick village that he might look at the register and talk over the whole

matter with Mr. Farebrother, who was not more surprised than
the lawyer that an ugly secret should have come to light about
Bulstrode, though he had always had justice enough in him to
hinder his antipathy from turning into conclusions. But while
they were talking another combination was silently going forward in Mr. Farebrother's mind, which foreshadowed what was
soon to be loudly spoken of in Middlemarch as a necessary
" putting of two and two together." With the reasons which
kept Bulstrode in dread of Raffles there flashed the thought that
the dread might have something to do with his munificence
towards his medical man ; and though he resisted the suggestion
that it had been consciously accepted in any way as a bribe, he
had a foreboding that this complication of things might be of
malignant effect on Lydgate's reputation. He perceived that
Mr. Hawley knew nothing at present of the sudden relief from
debt, and he himself was careful to glide away from all ap-
proaches towards the subject.

" Well," he said, with a deep breath, wanting to wind up the
illimitable discussion of what might have been, though nothing
could be legally proven, " it is a strange story. So our mercurial
Ladislaw has a queer genealogy ! A high-spirited young lady and
a musical Polish patriot made a likely enough stock for him to
spring from, but I should never have suspected a grafting of the
Jew pawnbroker. However, there's no knowing what a mixture
will turn out beforehand. Some sorts of dirt serve to clarify."

" It's just what I should have expected," said Mr. Hawley,
mounting his horse. " Any cursed alien blood, Jew, Corsican,
or Gypsy."

" I know he's one of your black sheep, Hawley. But he is
really a disinterested, unworldly fellow," said Mr. Farebrother,
smiling.

" Ay, ay, that is your Whiggish twist," said Mr. Hawley, who
had been in the habit of saying apologetically that Farebrother
was such a damned pleasant good-hearted fellow you would
mistake him for a Tory.

Mr. Hawley rode home without thinking of Lydgate's attendance on Raffles in any other light than as a piece of evidence on
the side of Bulstrode. But the news that Lydgate had all at
once become able not only to get rid of the execution in his house
but to pay all his debts in Middlemarch was spreading fast,
gathering round it conjectures and comments which gave it new
body and impetus, and soon filling the ears of other persons
besides Mr. Hawley, who were not slow to see a significant

relation between this sudden command of money and Bulstrode's desire to stifle the scandal of Raffles. That the money came from Bulstrode would infallibly have been guessed even if there had been no direct evidence of it; for it had beforehand entered into the gossip about Lydgate's affairs, that neither his father-in-law nor his own family would do anything for him, and direct evidence was furnished not only by a clerk at the Bank, but by innocent Mrs. Bulstrode herself, who mentioned the loan to Mrs. Plymdale, who mentioned it to her daughter-in-law of the house of Toller, who mentioned it generally. The business was felt to be so public and important that it required dinners to feed it, and many invitations were just then issued and accepted on the strength of this scandal concerning Bulstrode and Lydgate; wives, widows, and single ladies took their work and went out to tea oftener than usual; and all public conviviality, from the Green Dragon to Dollop's, gathered a zest which could not be won from the question whether the Lords would throw out the Reform Bill.

For hardly anybody doubted that some scandalous reason or other was at the bottom of Bulstrode's liberality to Lydgate. Mr. Hawley, indeed, in the first instance, invited a select party, including the two physicians, with Mr. Toller and Mr. Wrench, expressly to hold a close discussion as to the probabilities of Raffles's illness, reciting to them all the particulars which had been gathered from Mrs. Abel in connection with Lydgate's certificate, that the death was due to *delirium tremens ;* and the medical gentlemen, who all stood undisturbedly on the old paths in relation to this disease, declared that they could see nothing in these particulars which could be transformed into a positive ground of suspicion. But the moral grounds of suspicion remained; the strong motives Bulstrode clearly had for wishing to be rid of Raffles, and the fact that at this critical moment he had given Lydgate the help which he must for some time have known the need for; the disposition, moreover, to believe that Bulstrode would be unscrupulous, and the absence of any indisposition to believe that Lydgate might be as easily bribed as other haughty-minded men when they have found themselves in want of money. Even if the money had been given merely to make him hold his tongue about the scandal of Bulstrode's earlier life, the fact threw an odious light on Lydgate, who had long been sneered at as making himself subservient to the banker for the sake of working himself into predominance, and discrediting the older members of his profession. Hence,

in spite of the negative as to any direct sign of guilt in relation
to the death at Stone Court, Mr. Hawley's select party broke up
with the sense that the affair had " an ugly look."

But this vague conviction of indeterminable guilt, which was
enough to keep up much head-shaking and biting innuendo even
among substantial professional seniors, had for the general mind
all the superior power of mystery over fact.　Everybody liked
better to conjecture how the thing was, than simply to know it ;
for conjecture soon became more confident than knowledge, and
had a more liberal allowance for the incompatible.　Even the
more definite scandal concerning Bulstrode's earlier life was, for
some minds, melted into the mass of mystery, as so much lively
metal to be poured out in dialogue, and to take such fantastic
shapes as heaven pleased.

This was the tone of thought chiefly sanctioned by Mrs. Dollop, the spirited landlady of the Tankard in Slaughter Lane,
who had often to resist the shallow pragmatism of customers
disposed to think that their reports from the outer world were of
equal force with what had " come up " in her mind.　How it
had been brought to her she didn't know, but it was there before
her as if it had been scored with the chalk on the chimney-
board—" as Bulstrode should say, his inside was *that black* as
if the hairs of his head knowed the thoughts of his heart, he'd
tear 'em up by the roots."

" That's odd," said Mr. Limp, a meditative shoemaker, with
weak eyes and a piping voice.　" Why, I read in the ' Trumpet '
that was what the Duke of Wellington said when he turned his
coat and went over to the Romans."

" Very like," said Mrs. Dollop.　" If one raskill said it, it's
more reason why another should.　But hypo*crite* as he's been,
and holding things with that high hand, as there was no parson
i' the country good enough for him, he was forced to take Old
Harry into his counsel, and Old Harry's been too many for him."

" Ay, ay, he's a 'complice you can't sent out o' the country,"
said Mr. Crabbe the glazier, who gathered much news and groped
among it dimly.　" But by what I can make out, there's them
says Bulstrode was for running away, for fear o' being found out,
before now."

" He'll be drove away, whether or no," said Mr. Dill, the
barber, who had just dropped in.　" I shaved Fletcher, Hawley's
clerk, this morning—he's got a bad finger—and he says they're
all of one mind to get rid of Bulstrode.　Mr. Thesiger is turned
against him, and wants him out o' the parish.　And there's

gentlemen in this town says they'd as soon dine with a fellow from the hulks. ' And a deal sooner I would,' says Fletcher ; ' for what's more against one's stomach than a man coming and making himself bad company with his religion, and giving out as the Ten Commandments are not enough for him, and all the while he's worse than half the men at the tread-mill ? ' Fletcher said so himself."

" It'll be a bad thing for the town though, if Bulstrode's money goes out of it," said Mr. Limp, quaveringly.

" Ah, there's better folk spend their money worse," said a firm-voiced dyer, whose crimson hands looked out of keeping with his good-natured face.

" But he won't keep his money, by what I can make out," said the glazier. " Don't they say as there's somebody can strip it off him ? By what I can understan', they could take every penny off him, if they went to lawing."

" No such thing ! " said the barber, who felt himself a little above his company at Dollop's, but liked it none the worse. " Fletcher says it's no such thing. He says they might prove over and over again whose child this young Ladislaw was, and they'd do no more than if they proved I came out of the Fens—he couldn't touch a penny."

" Look you there now ! " said Mrs. Dollop, indignantly. " I thank the Lord he took my children to Himself, if that's all the law can do for the motherless. Then by that, it's o' no use who your father and mother is. But as to listening to what one lawyer says without asking another—I wonder at a man o' your cleverness, Mr. Dill. It's well known there's always two sides, if no more ; else who'd go to law, I should like to know ? It's a poor tale, with all the law as there is up and down, if it's no use proving whose child you are. Fletcher may say that if he likes, but I say, don't Fletcher *me* ! "

Mr. Dill affected to laugh in a complimentary way at Mrs. Dollop, as a woman who was more than a match for the lawyers ; being disposed to submit to much twitting from a landlady who had a long score against him.

" If they come to lawing, and it's all true as folks say, there's more to be looked to nor money," said the glazier. " There's this poor creetur as is dead and gone : by what I can make out, he'd seen the day when he was a deal finer gentleman nor Bulstrode."

" Finer gentleman ! I'll warrant him," said Mrs. Dollop ; " and a far personable man, by what I can hear. As I said when

Mr. Baldwin, the tax-gatherer, comes in, a-standing where you sit, and says, ' Bulstrode got all his money as he brought into this town by thieving and swindling,'—I said, ' You don't make me no wiser, Mr. Baldwin : it's set my blood a-creeping to look at him ever sin' here he came into Slaughter Lane a-wanting to buy the house over my head : folks don't look the colour o' the dough-tub and stare at you as if they wanted to see into your backbone for nothingk.' That was what I said, and Mr. Baldwin can bear me witness."

" And in the rights of it too," said Mr. Crabbe. " For by what I can make out, this Raffles, as they call him, was a lusty, fresh-coloured man as you'd wish to see, and the best o' company —though dead he lies in Lowick churchyard sure enough ; and by what I can understan', there's them knows more than they *should* know about how he got there."

" I'll believe you ! " said Mrs. Dollop, with a touch of scorn at Mr. Crabbe's apparent dimness. " When a man's been 'ticed to a lone house, and there's them can pay for hospitals and nurses for half the country-side choose to be sitters-up night and day, and nobody to come near but a doctor as is known to stick at nothingk, and as poor as he can hang together, and after that so flushed o' money as he can pay off Mr. Byles the butcher as his bill has been running on for the best o' joints since last Michael-mas was a twelvemonth—I don't want anybody to come and tell me as there's been more going on nor the Prayer-book's got a service for—I don't want to stand winking and blinking and thinking."

Mrs. Dollop looked round with the air of a landlady accustomed to dominate her company. There was a chorus of adhesion from the more courageous; but Mr. Limp, after taking a draught, placed his flat hands together and pressed them hard between his knees, looking down at them with blear-eyed contemplation, as if the scorching power of Mrs. Dollop's speech had quite dried up and nullified his wits until they could be brought round again by further moisture.

" Why shouldn't they dig the man up and have the Crowner ?" said the dyer. " It's been done many and many's the time. If there's been foul play they might find it out."

" Not they, Mr. Jonas ! " said Mrs. Dollop, emphatically. " I know what doctors are. They're a deal too cunning to be found out. And this Dr. Lydgate that's been for cutting up everybody before the breath was well out o' their body—it's plain enough what use he wanted to make o' looking into respectable people's insides. He knows drugs, you may be sure, as you can neither smell nor see, neither before they're swallowed nor after. Why, I've seen drops myself ordered by Doctor Gambit, as is our club doctor and a good charikter, and has brought more live children into the world nor ever another i' Middlemarch—I say I've seen drops myself as made no difference whether they was in the glass or out, and yet have griped you the next day. So I'll leave your own sense to judge. Don't tell me ! All I say is, it's a mercy they didn't take this Doctor Lydgate on to our club. There's many a mother's child might ha' rued it."

The heads of this discussion at " Dollop's " had been the common theme among all classes in the town, had been carried to Lowick Parsonage on one side and to Tipton Grange on the other, had come fully to the ears of the Vincy family, and had been discussed with sad reference to " poor Harriet " by all Mrs. Bulstrode's friends, before Lydgate knew distinctly why people were looking strangely at him, and before Bulstrode himself suspected the betrayal of his secrets. He had not been accustomed to very cordial relations with his neighbours, and hence he could not miss the signs of cordiality ; moreover, he had been taking journeys on business of various kinds, having now made up his mind that he need not quit Middlemarch, and feeling able consequently to determine on matters which he had before left in suspense.

" We will make a journey to Cheltenham in the course of a month or two," he had said to his wife. " There are great spiritual advantages to be had in that town along with the air and the waters, and six weeks there will be eminently refreshing to us."

He really believed in the spiritual advantages, and meant that his life henceforth should be the more devoted because of those later sins which he represented to himself as hypothetic, praying hypothetically for their pardon :—" if I have herein transgressed."

As to the Hospital, he avoided saying anything further to Lydgate, fearing to manifest a too sudden change of plans immediately on the death of Raffles. In his secret soul he believed that Lydgate suspected his orders to have been intentionally disobeyed, and suspecting this he must also suspect a motive. But nothing had been betrayed to him as to the history of Raffles, and Bulstrode was anxious not to do anything which would give emphasis to his undefined suspicions. As to any certainty that a particular method of treatment would either save or kill, Lydgate himself was constantly arguing against such dogmatism; he had no right to speak, and he had every motive for being silent. Hence Bulstrode felt himself providentially secured. The only incident he had strongly winced under had been an occasional encounter with Caleb Garth, who, however, had raised his hat with mild gravity.

Meanwhile, on the part of the principal townsmen a strong determination was growing against him.

A meeting was to be held in the Town Hall on a sanitary question which had risen into pressing importance by the occurrence of a cholera case in the town. Since the Act of Parliament, which had been hurriedly passed, authorising assessments for sanitary measures, there had been a Board for the superintendence of such measures appointed in Middlemarch, and much cleansing and preparation had been concurred in by Whigs and Tories. The question now was, whether a piece of ground outside the town should be secured as a burial-ground by means of assessment or by private subscription. The meeting was to be open, and almost everybody of importance in the town was expected to be there.

Mr. Bulstrode was a member of the Board, and just before twelve o'clock he started from the Bank with the intention of urging the plan of private subscription. Under the hesitation of his projects, he had for some time kept himself in the background, and he felt that he should this morning resume his old position as a man of action and influence in the public affairs of the town where he expected to end his days. Among the various persons going in the same direction, he saw Lydgate; they joined, talked over the object of the meeting, and entered it together.

It seemed that everybody of mark had been earlier than they. But there were still spaces left near the head of the large central table, and they made their way thither. Mr. Farebrother sate opposite, not far from Mr. Hawley; all the medical men were there; Mr. Thesiger was in the chair, and Mr. Brooke of Tipton was on his right hand.

Lydgate noticed a peculiar interchange of glances when he and Bulstrode took their seats.

After the business had been fully opened by the chairman, who pointed out the advantages of purchasing by subscription a piece of ground large enough to be ultimately used as a general cemetery, Mr. Bulstrode, whose rather high-pitched but sub-dued and fluent voice the town was used to at meetings of this sort, rose and asked leave to deliver his opinion. Lydgate could see again the peculiar interchange of glances before Mr. Hawley started up, and said in his firm resonant voice, "Mr. Chairman, I request that before any one delivers his opinion on this point I may be permitted to speak on a question of public feeling, which not only by myself, but by many gentlemen present, is regarded as preliminary."

Mr. Hawley's mode of speech, even when public decorums repressed his "awful language," was formidable in its curtness and self-possession. Mr. Thesiger sanctioned the request, Mr. Bulstrode sat down, and Mr. Hawley continued.

"In what I have to say, Mr. Chairman, I am not speaking simply on my own behalf : I am speaking with the concurrence and at the express request of no fewer than eight of my fellow-townsmen, who are immediately around us. It is our united sentiment that Mr. Bulstrode should be called upon—and I do now call upon him—to resign public positions which he holds not simply as a tax-payer, but as a gentleman among gentlemen. There are practices and there are acts which, owing to circumstances, the law cannot visit, though they may be worse than many things which are legally punishable. Honest men and gentlemen, if they don't want the company of people who perpetrate such acts, have got to defend themselves as they best can, and that is what I and the friends whom I may call my clients in this affair are determined to do. I don't say that Mr. Bulstrode has been guilty of shameful acts, but I call upon him either publicly to deny and confute the scandalous statements made against him by a man now dead, and who died in his house —the statement that he was for many years engaged in nefarious practices, and that he won his fortune by dishonest procedures— or else to withdraw from positions which could only have been allowed him as a gentleman among gentlemen."

All eyes in the room were turned on Mr. Bulstrode, who, since the first mention of his name, had been going through a crisis of feeling almost too violent for his delicate frame to support. Lydgate, who himself was undergoing a shock as from the terrible practical interpretation of some faint augury, felt, nevertheless, that his own movement of resentful hatred was checked by that instinct of the Healer which thinks first of bringing rescue or relief to the sufferer, when he looked at the shrunken misery of Bulstrode's livid face.

The quick vision that his life was after all a failure, that he was a dishonoured man, and must quail before the glance of those towards whom he had habitually assumed the attitude of a

reprover—that God had disowned him before men and left him
unscreened to the triumphant scorn of those who were glad to
have their hatred justified—the sense of utter futility in that
equivocation with his conscience in dealing with the life of his
accomplice, an equivocation which now turned venomously upon
him with the full-grown fang of a discovered lie :—all this rushed
through him like the agony of terror which fails to kill, and
leaves the ears still open to the returning wave of execration.
The sudden sense of exposure after the re-established sense of
safety came—not to the coarse organisation of a criminal but—
to the susceptible nerve of a man whose intensest being lay in
such mastery and predominance as the conditions of his life had
shaped for him.

But in that intense being lay the strength of reaction. Through
all his bodily infirmity there ran a tenacious nerve of ambitious
self-preserving will, which had continually leaped out like a
flame, scattering all doctrinal fears, and which, even while he
sat an object of compassion for the merciful, was beginning to
stir and glow under his ashy paleness. Before the last words
were out of Mr. Hawley's mouth, Bulstrode felt that he should
answer, and that his answer would be a retort. He dared not
get up and say, " I am not guilty, the whole story is false "—
even if he had dared this, it would have seemed to him, under
his present keen sense of betrayal, as vain as to pull, for covering
to his nakedness, a frail rag which would rend at every little
strain.

For a few moments there was total silence, while every man
in the room was looking at Bulstrode. He sat perfectly still,
leaning hard against the back of his chair ; he could not venture
to rise, and when he began to speak he pressed his hands upon
the seat on each side of him. But his voice was perfectly
audible, though hoarser than usual, and his words were distinctly
pronounced, though he paused between each sentence as if
short of breath. He said, turning first towards Mr. Thesiger,
and then looking at Mr. Hawley—

" I protest before you, sir, as a Christian minister, against
the sanction of proceedings towards me which are dictated by
virulent hatred. Those who are hostile to me are glad to
believe any libel uttered by a loose tongue against me. And
their consciences become strict against me. Say that the evil-
speaking of which I am to be made the victim accuses me of
malpractices——" here Bulstrode's voice rose and took on a
more biting accent till it seemed a low cry—" who shall be my

accuser ? Not men whose own lives are unchristian, nay, scandalous—not men who themselves use low instruments to carry out their ends—whose profession is a tissue of chicanery— who have been spending their income on their own sensual enjoyments, while I have been devoting mine to advance the best objects with regard to this life and the next."

After the word chicanery there was a growing noise, half of murmurs and half of hisses, while four persons started up at once—Mr. Hawley, Mr. Toller, Mr. Chichely, and Mr. Hackbutt; but Mr. Hawley's outburst was instantaneous, and left the others behind in silence.

"If you mean me, sir, I call you and every one else to the inspection of my professional life. As to Christian or unchristian, I repudiate your canting palavering Christianity ; and as to the way in which I spend my income, it is not my principle to main- tain thieves and cheat offspring of their due inheritance in order to support religion and set myself up as a saintly Kill-joy. I affect no niceness of conscience—I have not found any nice standards necessary yet to measure your actions by, sir. And I again call upon you to enter into satisfactory explanations con- cerning the scandals against you, or else to withdraw from posts in which we at any rate decline you as a colleague. I say, sir, we decline to co-operate with a man whose character is not cleared from infamous lights cast upon it, not only by reports but by recent actions."

"Allow me, Mr. Hawley," said the chairman ; and Mr. Haw- ley, still fuming, bowed half impatiently, and sat down with his hands thrust deep in his pockets.

"Mr. Bulstrode, it is not desirable, I think, to prolong the present discussion," said Mr. Thesiger, turning to the pallid trembling man ; "I must so far concur with what has fallen from Mr. Hawley in expression of a general feeling, as to think it due to your Christian profession that you should clear your- self, if possible, from unhappy aspersions. I for my part should be willing to give you full opportunity and hearing. But I must say that your present attitude is painfully inconsistent with those principles which you have sought to identify yourself with, and for the honour of which I am bound to care. I recommend you at present as your clergyman, and one who hopes for your reinstatement in respect, to quit the room, and avoid further hindrance to business."

Bulstrode, after a moment's hesitation, took his hat from the floor and slowly rose, but he grasped the corner of the chair so

totteringly that Lydgate felt sure there was not strength enough
in him to walk away without support. What could he do?
He could not see a man sink close to him for want of help. He
rose and gave his arm to Bulstrode, and in that way led him out
of the room; yet this act, which might have been one of gentle
duty and pure compassion, was at this moment unspeakably
bitter to him. It seemed as if he were putting his sign-manual
to that association of himself with Bulstrode, of which he now
saw the full meaning as it must have presented itself to other
minds. He now felt the conviction that this man who was
leaning tremblingly on his arm, had given him the thousand
pounds as a bribe, and that somehow the treatment of Raffles
had been tampered with from an evil motive. The inferences
were closely linked enough: the town knew of the loan, believed
it to be a bribe, and believed that he took it as a bribe.

Poor Lydgate, his mind struggling under the terrible clutch of
this revelation, was all the while morally forced to take Mr.
Bulstrode to the Bank, send a man off for his carriage, and wait
to accompany him home.

Meanwhile the business of the meeting was despatched, and
fringed off into eager discussion among various groups concerning this affair of Bulstrode—and Lydgate.

Mr. Brooke, who had before heard only imperfect hints of it,
and was very uneasy that he had " gone a little too far " in
countenancing Bulstrode, now got himself fully informed, and
felt some benevolent sadness in talking to Mr. Farebrother about
the ugly light in which Lydgate had come to be regarded. Mr.
Farebrother was going to walk back to Lowick.

" Step into my carriage," said Mr. Brooke. " I am going
round to see Mrs. Casaubon. She was to come back from
Yorkshire last night. She will like to see me, you know."

So they drove along, Mr. Brooke chatting with good-natured
hope that there had not really been anything black in Lydgate's
behaviour—a young fellow whom he had seen to be quite
above the common mark, when he brought a letter from his
uncle, Sir Godwin. Mr. Farebrother said little: he was deeply
mournful: with a keen perception of human weakness, he could
not be confident that under the pressure of humiliating needs
Lydgate had not fallen below himself.

When the carriage drove up to the gate of the manor, Dorothea
was out on the gravel, and came to greet them.

" Well, my dear," said Mr. Brooke, " we have just come from a
meeting—a sanitary meeting, you know."

" Was Mr. Lydgate there ? " said Dorothea, who looked full of health and animation, and stood with her head bare under the gleaming April lights. " I want to see him and have a great consultation with him about the Hospital. I have engaged with Mr. Bulstrode to do so."

" Oh, my dear," said Mr. Brooke, " we have been hearing bad news—bad news, you know."

They walked through the garden towards the churchyard gate, Mr. Farebrother wanting to go on to the parsonage ; and Dorothea heard the whole sad story.

She listened with deep interest, and begged to hear twice over the facts and impressions concerning Lydgate. After a short silence, pausing at the churchyard gate, and addressing Mr. Farebrother, she said energetically—

" You don't believe that Mr. Lydgate is guilty of anything base ? I will not believe it. Let us find out the truth and clear him ! "

BOOK VIII
SUNSET AND SUNRISE

CHAPTER LXXII

Full souls are double mirrors, making still
An endless vista of fair things before,
Repeating things behind.

DOROTHEA'S impetuous generosity, which would have leaped at
once to the vindication of Lydgate from the suspicion of having
accepted money as a bribe, underwent a melancholy check when
she came to consider all the circumstances of the case by the
light of Mr. Farebrother's experience.

"It is a delicate matter to touch," he said. "How can we
begin to inquire into it ? It must be either publicly by setting
the magistrate and coroner to work, or privately by questioning
Lydgate. As to the first proceeding there is no solid ground
to go upon, else Hawley would have adopted it ; and as to
opening the subject with Lydgate, I confess I should shrink
from it. He would probably take it as a deadly insult. I have
more than once experienced the difficulty of speaking to him
on personal matters. And—one should know the truth about
his conduct beforehand, to feel very confident of a good result."

"I feel convinced that his conduct has not been guilty : I
believe that people are almost always better then their neighbours think they are," said Dorothea. Some of her intensest
experience in the last two years had set her mind strongly in
opposition to any unfavourable construction of others ; and
for the first time she felt rather discontented with Mr. Farebrother. She disliked this cautious weighing of consequences,
instead of an ardent faith in efforts of justice and mercy, which
would conquer by their emotional force. Two days afterwards,
he was dining at the Manor with her uncle and the Chettams,
and when the dessert was standing uneaten, the servants were
out of the room, and Mr. Brooke was nodding in a nap, she
returned to the subject with renewed vivacity.

"Mr. Lydgate would understand that if his friends hear a calumny about him their first wish must be to justify. What do we live for, if it is not to make life less difficult to each other? I cannot be indifferent to the troubles of a man who advised me in *my* trouble, and attended me in my illness."

Dorothea's tone and manner were not more energetic than they had been when she was at the head of her uncle's table nearly three years before, and her experience since had given her more right to express a decided opinion. But Sir James Chettam was no longer the diffident and acquiescent suitor: he was the anxious brother-in-law, with a devout admiration for his sister, but with a constant alarm lest she should fall under some new illusion almost as bad as marrying Casaubon. He smiled much less; when he said "Exactly" it was more often an introduction to a dissentient opinion than in those submissive bachelor days; and Dorothea found to her surprise that she had to resolve not to be afraid of him—all the more because he was really her best friend. He disagreed with her now.

"But, Dorothea," he said, remonstrantly, "you can't undertake to manage a man's life for him in that way. Lydgate must know—at least he will soon come to know how he stands. If he can clear himself, he will. He must act for himself."

"I think his friends must wait till they find an opportunity," added Mr. Farebrother. "It is possible—I have often felt so much weakness in myself that I can conceive even a man of honourable disposition, such as I have always believed Lydgate to be, succumbing to such a temptation as that of accepting money which was offered more or less indirectly as a bribe to insure his silence about scandalous facts long gone by. I say, I can conceive this, if he were under the pressure of hard circumstances—if he had been harassed as I feel sure Lydgate has been. I would not believe anything worse of him except under stringent proof. But there is the terrible Nemesis following on some errors, that it is always possible for those who like it to interpret them into a crime: there is no proof in favour of the man outside his own consciousness and assertion."

"Oh, how cruel!" said Dorothea, clasping her hands. "And would you not like to be the one person who believed in that man's innocence, if the rest of the world belied him? Besides, there is a man's character beforehand to speak for him."

"But, my dear Mrs. Casaubon," said Mr. Farebrother, smiling gently at her ardour, "character is not cut in marble—

it is not something solid and unalterable. It is something living and changing, and may become diseased as our bodies do."

"Then it may be rescued and healed," said Dorothea. "I should not be afraid of asking Mr. Lydgate to tell me the truth, that I might help him. Why should I be afraid? Now that I am not to have the land, James, I might do as Mr. Bulstrode proposed, and take his place in providing for the hospital; and I have to consult Mr. Lydgate, to know thoroughly what are the prospects of doing good by keeping up the present plans. There is the best opportunity in the world for me to ask for his confidence; and he would be able to tell me things which might make all the circumstances clear. Then we would all stand by him and bring him out of his trouble. People glorify all sorts of bravery except the bravery they might show on behalf of their nearest neighbours." Dorothea's eyes had a moist brightness in them, and the changed tones of her voice roused her uncle, who began to listen.

"It is true that a woman may venture on some efforts of sympathy which would hardly succeed if we men undertook them," said Mr. Farebrother, almost converted by Dorothea's ardour.

"Surely, a woman is bound to be cautious and listen to those who know the world better than she does," said Sir James, with his little frown. "Whatever you do in the end, Dorothea, you should really keep back at present, and not volunteer any meddling with this Bulstrode business. We don't know yet what may turn up. You must agree with me?" he ended, looking at Mr. Farebrother.

"I do think it would be better to wait," said the latter.

"Yes, yes, my dear," said Mr. Brooke, not quite knowing at what point the discussion had arrived, but coming up to it with a contribution which was generally appropriate. "It is easy to go too far, you know. You must not let your ideas run away with you. And as to being in a hurry to put money into schemes—it won't do, you know. Garth has drawn me in uncommonly with repairs, draining, that sort of thing: I'm uncommonly out of pocket with one thing or another. I must pull up. As for you, Chettam, you are spending a fortune on those oak fences round your demesne."

Dorothea, submitting uneasily to this discouragement, went with Celia into the library, which was her usual drawing-room.

"Now, Dodo, do listen to what James says," said Celia, "else you will be getting into a scrape. You always did, and you always will, when you set about doing as you please. And I think it is a mercy now after all that you have got James to think for you. He lets you have your plans, only he hinders you from being taken in. And that is the good of having a brother instead of a husband. A husband would not let you have your plans."

"As if I wanted a husband!" said Dorothea. "I only want not to have my feelings checked at every turn." Mrs. Casaubon was still undisciplined enough to burst into angry tears.

"Now, really, Dodo," said Celia, with rather a deeper guttural than usual, "you *are* contradictory: first one thing and then another. You used to submit to Mr. Casaubon quite shamefully: I think you would have given up ever coming to see me if he had asked you."

"Of course I submitted to him, because it was my duty; it was my feeling for him," said Dorothea, looking through the prism of her tears.

"Then why can't you think it your duty to submit a little to what James wishes?" said Celia, with a sense of stringency in her argument. "Because he only wishes what is for your own good. And, of course men know best about everything, except what women know better."

Dorothea laughed and forgot her tears.

"Well, I mean about babies and those things," explained Celia. "I should not give up to James when I knew he was wrong, as you used to do to Mr. Casaubon."

CHAPTER LXXIII

Pity the laden one; this wandering woe
May visit you and me.

WHEN Lydgate had allayed Mrs. Bulstrode's anxiety by telling her that her husband had been seized with faintness at the meeting, but that he trusted soon to see him better and would call again the next day, unless she sent for him earlier, he went directly home, got on his horse, and rode three miles out of the town for the sake of being out of reach.

He felt himself becoming violent and unreasonable as if raging under the pain of stings: he was ready to curse the day on which he had come to Middlemarch. Everything that had happened to him there seemed a mere preparation for this hateful fatality, which had come as a blight on his honourable ambition, and must make even people who had only vulgar standards regard his reputation as irrevocably damaged. In such moments a man can hardly escape being unloving. Lydgate thought of himself as the sufferer, and of others as the agents who had injured his lot. He had meant everything to turn out differently; and others had thrust themselves into his life and thwarted his purposes. His marriage seemed an unmitigated calamity; and he was afraid of going to Rosamond before he had vented himself in this solitary rage, lest the mere sight of her should exasperate him and make him behave unwarrantably. There are episodes in most men's lives in which their highest qualities can only cast a deterring shadow over the objects that fill their inward vision: Lydgate's tender-heartedness was present just then only as a dread lest he should offend against it, not as an emotion that swayed him to tenderness. For he was very miserable. Only those who know the supremacy of the intellectual life—the life which has a seed of ennobling thought and purpose within it—can understand the grief of one who falls from that serene activity into the absorbing soul-wasting struggle with worldly annoyances.

How was he to live on without vindicating himself among people who suspected him of baseness? How could he go silently away from Middlemarch as if he were retreating before a just condemnation? And yet how was he to set about vindicating himself?

For that scene at the meeting, which he had just witnessed, although it had told him no particulars, had been enough to make his own situation thoroughly clear to him. Bulstrode had been in dread of scandalous disclosures on the part of Raffles. Lydgate could now construct all the probabilities of the case. "He was afraid of some betrayal in my hearing: all he wanted was to bind me to him by a strong obligation: that was why he passed on a sudden from hardness to liberality. And he may have tampered with the patient—he may have disobeyed my orders. I fear he did. But whether he did or not, the world believes that he somehow or other poisoned the man and that I winked at the crime, if I didn't help in it. And yet—and yet he may not be guilty of the last offence; and it is just possible that the change towards me may have been a genuine relenting—the effect of second thoughts such as he alleged. What we call the 'just possible' is sometimes true and the thing we find it easier to believe is grossly false. In his last dealings with this man Bulstrode may have kept his hands pure, in spite of my suspicion to the contrary."

There was a benumbing cruelty in his position. Even if he renounced every other consideration than that of justifying himself—if he met shrugs, cold glances, and avoidance as an accusation, and made a public statement of all the facts as he knew them, who would be convinced ? It would be playing the part of a fool to offer his own testimony on behalf of himself, and say, " I did not take the money as a bribe." The circumstances would always be stronger than his assertion. And besides, to come forward and tell everything about himself must include declarations about Bulstrode which would darken the suspicions of others against him. He must tell that he had not known of Raffles's existence when he first mentioned his pressing need of money to Bulstrode, and that he took the money innocently as a result of that communication, not knowing that a new motive for the loan might have arisen on his being called in to this man. And after all, the suspicion of Bulstrode's motives might be unjust.

But then came the question whether he should have acted in precisely the same way if he had not taken the money ? Certainly, if Raffles had continued alive and susceptible of further treatment when he arrived, and he had then imagined any disobedience to his orders on the part of Bulstrode, he would have made a strict inquiry, and if his conjecture had been verified he would have thrown up the case, in spite of his recent heavy obligation. But if he had not received any money—if Bulstrode had never revoked his cold recommendation of bankruptcy—would he, Lydgate, have abstained from all inquiry even on finding the man dead ?—would the shrinking from an insult to Bulstrode—would the dubiousness of all medical treatment and the argument that his own treatment would pass for the wrong with most members of his profession —have had just the same force or significance with him ?

That was the uneasy corner of Lydgate's consciousness while he was reviewing the facts and resisting all reproach. If he had been independent, this matter of a patient's treatment and the distinct rule that he must do or see done that which he believed best for the life committed to him, would have been the point on which he would have been the sturdiest. As it was, he had rested in the consideration that disobedience to his orders, however it might have arisen, could not be considered a crime, that in the dominant opinion obedience to his orders was just as likely to be fatal, and that the affair was simply one of etiquette. Whereas, again and again, in his time of freedom, he had denounced the perversion of pathological doubt into moral doubt and had said—" the purest experiment in treatment may still be conscientious : my business is to take care of life, and to do the best I can think of for it. Science is properly more scrupulous than dogma. Dogma gives a charter to mistake, but the very breath of science is a contest with mistake, and must keep the conscience alive." Alas ! the scientific conscience had got into the debasing company of money obligation and selfish respects.

" Is there a medical man of them all in Middlemarch who would question himself as I do ? " said poor Lydgate, with a renewed outburst of rebellion against the oppression of his lot. " And yet they will all feel warranted in making a wide space between me and them, as if I were a leper ! My practice and my reputation are utterly damned—I can see that. Even if I could be cleared by valid evidence, it would make little difference to the blessed world here. I have been set down as tainted and should be cheapened to them all the same."

Already there had been abundant signs which had hitherto puzzled him, that just when he had been paying off his debts and getting cheerfully on his feet, the townsmen were avoiding him or looking strangely at him, and in two instances it came to his knowledge that patients of his had called in another practitioner. The reasons were too plain now. The general black-balling had begun.

No wonder that in Lydgate's energetic nature the sense of a hopeless misconstruction easily turned into a dogged resistance. The scowl which occasionally showed itself on his square brow was not a meaningless accident. Already when he was re-entering the town after that ride taken in the first hours of stinging pain, he was setting his mind on remaining in Middlemarch in spite of the worst that could be done against him. He would not retreat before calumny, as if he submitted to it. He would face it to the utmost, and no act of his should show that he was afraid. It belonged to the generosity as well as defiant force of his nature that he resolved not to shrink from showing to the full his sense of obligation to Bulstrode. It was true that the association with this man had been fatal to him— true that if he had had the thousand pounds still in his hands with all his debts unpaid he would have returned the money to Bulstrode, and taken beggary rather than the rescue which had been sullied with the suspicion of a bribe (for, remember, he was one of the proudest among the sons of men)—nevertheless, he would not turn away from this crushed fellow-mortal whose aid he had used, and make a pitiful effort to get acquittal for himself by howling against another. " I shall do as I think right, and explain to nobody. They will try to starve me out, but—— " he was going on with an obstinate resolve, but he was getting near home, and the thought of Rosamond urged itself again into that chief place from which it had been thrust by the agonised struggles of wounded honour and pride.

How would Rosamond take it all? Here was another weight of chain to drag, and poor Lydgate was in a bad mood for bearing her dumb mastery. He had no impulse to tell her the trouble which must soon be common to them both. He preferred waiting for the incidental disclosure which events must soon bring about.

CHAPTER LXXIV

" Mercifully grant that we may grow aged together."
—BOOK OF TOBIT : *Marriage Prayer*.

IN Middlemarch a wife could not long remain ignorant that the town held a bad opinion of her husband. No feminine intimate might carry her friendship so far as to make a plain statement to the wife of the unpleasant fact known or believed about her husband ; but when a woman with her thoughts much at leisure got them suddenly employed on something grievously dis-advantageous to her neighbours, various moral impulses were called into play which tended to stimulate utterance. Candour was one. To be candid, in Middlemarch phraseology, meant, to use an early opportunity of letting your friends know that you did not take a cheerful view of their capacity, their conduct, or their position ; and a robust candour never waited to be asked for its opinion. Then, again, there was the love of truth—a wide phrase, but meaning in this relation, a lively objection to seeing a wife look happier than her husband's character warranted, or manifest too much satisfaction in her lot : the poor thing should have some hint given her that if she knew the truth she would have less complacency in her bonnet, and in light dishes for a supper-party. Stronger than all, there was the regard for a friend's moral improvement, sometimes called her soul, which was likely to be benefited by remarks tending to gloom, uttered with the accompaniment of pensive staring at the furniture and a manner implying that the speaker would not tell what was on her mind, from regard to the feelings of her hearer. On the whole, one might say that an ardent charity was at work setting the virtuous mind to make a neighbour unhappy for her good.

There were hardly any wives in Middlemarch whose matrimonial misfortunes would in different ways be likely to call forth more of this moral activity than Rosamond and her aunt Bulstrode. Mrs. Bulstrode was not an object of dislike, and had never consciously injured any human being. Men had always thought her a handsome comfortable woman, and had reckoned it among the signs of Bulstrode's hypocrisy that he had chosen a red-blooded Vincy, instead of a ghastly and melancholy person suited to his low esteem for earthly pleasure. When the scandal about her husband was disclosed they remarked of her—" Ah, poor woman ! She's as honest as the day— *she* never suspected anything wrong in him, you may depend on it." Women, who were intimate with her, talked together much of " poor Harriet," imagined what her feelings must be when she came to know everything, and conjectured how much she had already come to know. There was no spiteful disposition towards her ; rather, there was a busy benevolence anxious to ascertain what it would be well for her to feel and do under the circumstances, which of course kept the imagination occupied with her character and history from the time when she was Harriet Vincy till now. With the review of Mrs. Bulstrode and her position it was inevitable to associate Rosamond, whose prospects were under the same blight with her aunt's. Rosamond was more severely criticised and less pitied, though she too, as one of the good old Vincy family who had always been known in Middlemarch, was regarded as a victim to marriage with an interloper. The Vincys had their weaknesses, but then they lay on the surface : there was never anything bad to be " found out " concerning them. Mrs. Bulstrode was vindicated from any resemblance to her husband. Harriet's faults were her own.

" She has always been showy," said Mrs. Hackbutt, making tea for a small party, " though she has got into the way of putting her religion forward, to conform to her husband ; she has tried to hold her head up above Middlemarch by making it known that she invites clergymen and heaven-knows-who from Riverston and those places."

"We can hardly blame her for that," said Mrs. Sprague; "because few of the best people in the town cared to associate with Bulstrode, and she must have somebody to sit down at her table."

"Mr. Thesiger has always countenanced him," said Mrs. Hackbutt. "I think he must be sorry now."

"But he was never fond of him in his heart—that every one knows," said Mrs. Tom Toller. "Mr. Thesiger never goes into extremes. He keeps to the truth in what is evangelical. It is only clergymen like Mr. Tyke, who want to use Dissenting hymn-books and that low kind of religion, who ever found Bulstrode to their taste."

"I understand Mr. Tyke is in great distress about him," said Mrs. Hackbutt. "And well he may be: they say the Bulstrodes have half kept the Tyke family."

"And of course it is a discredit to his doctrines," said Mrs. Sprague, who was elderly and old-fashioned in her opinions. "People will not make a boast of being methodistical in Middlemarch for a good while to come."

"I think we must not set down people's bad actions to their religion," said falcon-faced Mrs. Plymdale, who had been listening hitherto.

"Oh, my dear, we are forgetting," said Mrs. Sprague. "We ought not to be talking of this before you."

"I am sure I have no reason to be partial," said Mrs. Plymdale, colouring. "It's true Mr. Plymdale has always been on good terms with Mr. Bulstrode, and Harriet Vincy was my friend long before she married him. But I have always kept my own opinions and told her where she was wrong, poor thing. Still, in point of religion, I must say, Mr. Bulstrode might have done what he has, and worse, and yet have been a man of no religion. I don't say that there has not been a little too much of that—I like moderation myself. But truth is truth. The men tried at the assizes are not all over-religious, I suppose."

"Well," said Mrs. Hackbutt, wheeling adroitly, "all I can say is, that I think she ought to separate from him."

"I can't say that," said Mrs. Sprague. "She took him for better or worse, you know."

"But 'worse' can never mean finding out that your husband is fit for Newgate," said Mrs. Hackbutt. "Fancy living with such a man! I should expect to be poisoned."

" Yes, I think myself it is an encouragement to crime if such men are to be taken care of and waited on by good wives," said Mrs. Tom Toller.

" And a good wife poor Harriet has been," said Mrs. Plymdale. " She thinks her husband the first of men. It's true he has never denied her anything."

" Well, we shall see what she will do," said Mrs. Hackbutt. " I suppose she knows nothing yet, poor creature. I do hope and trust I shall not see her, for I should be frightened to death lest I should say anything about her husband. Do you think any hint has reached her ? "

" I should hardly think so," said Mrs. Tom Toller. " We hear that *he* is ill, and has never stirred out of the house since the meeting on Thursday ; but she was with her girls at church yesterday, and they had new Tuscan bonnets. Her own had a feather in it. I have never seen that her religion made any difference in her dress."

" She wears very neat patterns always," said Mrs. Plymdale, a little stung. " And that feather I know she got dyed a pale lavender on purpose to be consistent. I must say it of Harriet that she wishes to do right."

" As to her knowing what has happened, it can't be kept from her long," said Mrs. Hackbutt. " The Vincys know, for Mr. Vincy was at the meeting. It will be a great blow to him. There is his daughter as well as his sister."

" Yes, indeed," said Mrs. Sprague. " Nobody supposes that Mr. Lydgate can go on holding up his head in Middlemarch, things look so black about the thousand pounds he took just at that man's death. It really makes one shudder."

" Pride must have a fall," said Mrs. Hackbutt.

" I am not so sorry for Rosamond Vincy that was as I am for her aunt," said Mrs. Plymdale. " She needed a lesson."

" I suppose the Bulstrodes will go and live abroad somewhere," said Mrs. Sprague. " That is what is generally done when there is anything disgraceful in a family."

" And a most deadly blow it will be to Harriet," said Mrs. Plymdale. " If ever a woman was crushed, she will be. I pity her from my heart. And with all her faults, few women are better. From a girl she had the neatest ways, and was always good-hearted, and as open as the day. You might look into her drawers when you would—always the same. And so she has brought up Kate and Ellen. You may think how hard it will be for her to go among foreigners."

"The doctor says that is what he should recommend the Lydgates to do," said Mrs. Sprague. "He says Lydgate ought to have kept among the French."

"That would suit *her* well enough, I daresay," said Mrs. Plymdale; "there is that kind of lightness about her. But she got that from her mother; she never got it from her aunt Bulstrode, who always gave her good advice, and to my knowledge would rather have had her marry elsewhere."

Mrs. Plymdale was in a situation which caused her some complication of feeling. There had been not only her intimacy with Mrs. Bulstrode, but also a profitable business relation of the great Plymdale dyeing house with Mr. Bulstrode, which on the one hand would have inclined her to desire that the mildest view of his character should be the true one, but on the other, made her the more afraid of seeming to palliate his culpability. Again, the late alliance of her family with the Tollers had brought her in connection with the best circle, which gratified her in every direction except in the inclination to those serious views which she believed to be the best in another sense. The sharp little woman's conscience was somewhat troubled in the adjustment of these opposing "bests," and of her griefs and satisfactions under late events, which were likely to humble those who needed humbling, but also to fall heavily on her old friend whose faults she would have preferred seeing on a background of prosperity.

Poor Mrs. Bulstrode, meanwhile, had been no further shaken by the oncoming tread of calamity than in the busier stirring of that secret uneasiness which had always been present in her since the last visit of Raffles to The Shrubs. That the hateful man had come ill to Stone Court, and that her husband had chosen to remain there and watch over him, she allowed to be explained by the fact that Raffles had been employed and aided in earlier days, and that this made a tie of benevolence towards him in his degraded helplessness; and she had been since then innocently cheered by her husband's more hopeful speech about his own health and ability to continue his attention to business. The calm was disturbed when Lydgate had brought him home ill from the meeting, and in spite of comforting assurances during the next few days, she cried in private from the conviction that her husband was not suffering from bodily illness merely, but from something that afflicted his mind. He would not allow her to read to him, and scarcely to sit with him, alleging nervous susceptibility to sounds and movements;

yet she suspected that in shutting himself up in his private room he wanted to be busy with his papers. Something, she felt sure, had happened. Perhaps it was some great loss of money ; and she was kept in the dark. Not daring to question her husband, she said to Lydgate, on the fifth day after the meeting, when she had not left home except to go to church—

"Mr. Lydgate, pray be open with me : I like to know the truth. Has anything happened to Mr. Bulstrode ? "

"Some little nervous shock," said Lydgate, evasively. He felt that it was not for him to make the painful revelation.

"But what brought it on ? " said Mrs. Bulstrode, looking directly at him with her large dark eyes.

"There is often something poisonous in the air of public rooms," said Lydgate. "Strong men can stand it, but it tells on people in proportion to the delicacy of their systems. It is often impossible to account for the precise moment of an attack —or rather, to say why the strength gives way at a particular moment."

Mrs. Bulstrode was not satisfied with his answer. There remained in her the belief that some calamity had befallen her husband, of which she was to be kept in ignorance ; and it was in her nature strongly to object to such concealment. She begged leave for her daughters to sit with their father, and drove into the town to pay some visits, conjecturing that if anything were known to have gone wrong in Mr. Bulstrode's affairs, she should see or hear some sign of it.

She called on Mrs. Thesiger, who was not at home, and then drove to Mrs. Hackbutt's on the other side of the churchyard. Mrs. Hackbutt saw her coming from an up-stairs window, and remembering her former alarm lest she should meet Mrs. Bulstrode, felt almost bound in consistency to send word that she was not at home ; but against that, there was a sudden strong desire within her for the excitement of an interview in which she was quite determined not to make the slightest allusion to what was in her mind.

Hence Mrs. Bulstrode was shown into the drawing-room, and Mrs. Hackbutt went to her, with more tightness of lip and rubbing of her hands than was usually observable in her, these being precautions adopted against freedom of speech. She was resolved not to ask how Mr. Bulstrode was.

"I have not been anywhere except to church for nearly a week," said Mrs. Bulstrode, after a few introductory remarks.

" But Mr. Bulstrode was taken so ill at the meeting on Thursday that I have not liked to leave the house."

Mrs. Hackbutt rubbed the back of one hand with the palm of the other held against her chest, and let her eyes ramble over the pattern on the rug.

" Was Mr. Hackbutt at the meeting ? " persevered Mrs. Bulstrode.

" Yes, he was," said Mrs. Hackbutt, with the same attitude. " The land is to be bought by subscription, I believe."

" Let us hope that there will be no more cases of cholera to be buried in it," said Mrs. Bulstrode. " It is an awful visitation. But I always think Middlemarch a very healthy spot. I suppose it is being used to it from a child ; but I never saw the town I should like to live at better, and especially our end."

" I am sure I should be glad that you always should live at Middlemarch, Mrs. Bulstrode," said Mrs. Hackbutt, with a slight sigh. " Still, we must learn to resign ourselves, wherever our lot may be cast. Though I am sure there will always be people in this town who will wish you well."

Mrs. Hackbutt longed to say, " if you take my advice you will part from your husband," but it seemed clear to her that the poor woman knew nothing of the thunder ready to bolt on her head, and she herself could do no more than prepare her a little. Mrs. Bulstrode felt suddenly rather chill and trembling : there was evidently something unusual behind this speech of Mrs. Hackbutt's ; but though she had set out with the desire to be fully informed, she found herself unable now to pursue her brave purpose, and turning the conversation by an inquiry about the young Hackbutts, she soon took her leave saying that she was going to see Mrs. Plymdale. On her way thither she tried to imagine that there might have been some unusually warm sparring at the meeting between Mr. Bulstrode and some of his frequent opponents—perhaps Mr. Hackbutt might have been one of them. That would account for everything.

But when she was in conversation with Mrs. Plymdale that comforting explanation seemed no longer tenable. " Selina " received her with a pathetic affectionateness and a disposition to give edifying answers on the commonest topics, which could hardly have reference to an ordinary quarrel of which the most important consequence was a perturbation of Mr. Bulstrode's health. Beforehand Mrs. Bulstrode had thought that she would

sooner question Mrs. Plymdale than any one else ; but she found
to her surprise that an old friend is not always the person whom
it is easiest to make a confidant of : there was the barrier of
remembered communication under other circumstances—there
was the dislike of being pitied and informed by one who had been
long wont to allow her the superiority. For certain words of
mysterious appropriateness that Mrs. Plymdale let fall about
her resolution never to turn her back on her friends, convinced
Mrs. Bulstrode that what had happened must be some kind of
misfortune, and instead of being able to say with her native
directness, " What is it that you have in your mind ? " she
found herself anxious to get away before she had heard anything
more explicit. She began to have an agitating certainty that
the misfortune was something more than the mere loss of money,
being keenly sensitive to the fact that Selina now, just as Mrs.
Hackbutt had done before, avoided noticing what she said
about her husband, as they would have avoided noticing a
personal blemish.

She said good-bye with nervous haste, and told the coachman
to drive to Mr. Vincy's warehouse. In that short drive her
dread gathered so much force from the sense of darkness, that
when she entered the private counting-house where her brother
sat at his desk, her knees trembled and her usually florid face
was deathly pale. Something of the same effect was produced in him by the sight of her : he rose from his seat to
meet her, took her by the hand, and said, with his impulsive
rashness—

" God help you, Harriet ! you know all."

That moment was perhaps worse than any which came after.
It contained that concentrated experience which in great crises
of emotion reveals the bias of a nature, and is prophetic of the
ultimate act which will end an intermediate struggle. Without
that memory of Raffles she might still have thought only of
monetary ruin, but now along with her brother's look and words
there darted into her mind the idea of some guilt in her husband
—then, under the working of terror came the image of her husband exposed to disgrace—and then, after an instant of scorching
shame in which she felt only the eyes of the world, with one leap
of her heart she was at his side in mournful but unreproaching
fellowship with shame and isolation. All this went on within
her in a mere flash of time—while she sank into the chair, and
raised her eyes to her brother, who stood over her. " I know
nothing, Walter. What is it ? " she said faintly.

He told her everything, very inartificially, in slow fragments, making her aware that the scandal went much beyond proof, especially as to the end of Raffles.

"People will talk," he said. "Even if a man has been acquitted by a jury, they'll talk, and nod and wink—and as far as the world goes, a man might often as well be guilty as not. It's a breakdown blow, and it damages Lydgate as much as Bulstrode. I don't pretend to say what is the truth. I only wish we had never heard the name of either Bulstrode or Lydgate. You'd better have been a Vincy all your life, and so had Rosamond."

Mrs. Bulstrode made no reply.

"But you must bear up as well as you can, Harriet. People don't blame *you*. And I'll stand by you whatever you make up your mind to do," said the brother, with rough but well-meaning affectionateness.

"Give me your arm to the carriage, Walter," said Mrs. Bulstrode. "I feel very weak."

And when she got home she was obliged to say to her daughter, "I am not well, my dear; I must go and lie down. Attend to your papa. Leave me in quiet. I shall take no dinner."

She locked herself in her room. She needed time to get used to her maimed consciousness, her poor lopped life, before she could walk steadily to the place allotted her. A new searching light had fallen on her husband's character, and she could not judge him leniently: the twenty years in which she had believed in him and venerated him by virtue of his concealments came back with particulars that made them seem an odious deceit. He had married her with that bad past life hidden behind him and she had no faith left to protest his innocence of the worst that was imputed to him. Her honest ostentatious nature made the sharing of a merited dishonour as bitter as it could be to any mortal.

But this imperfectly-taught woman, whose phrases and habits were an odd patchwork, had a loyal spirit within her. The man whose prosperity she had shared through nearly half a life, and who had unvaryingly cherished her—now that punishment had befallen him it was not possible to her in any sense to forsake him. There is a forsaking which still sits at the same board and lies on the same couch with the forsaken soul, withering it the more by unloving proximity. She knew, when she locked her door, that she should unlock it ready to go down to her unhappy husband and espouse his sorrow, and say of his guilt, I will mourn and not reproach. But she needed time to gather up her strength ; she needed to sob out her farewell to all the gladness and pride of her life. When she had resolved to go down, she prepared herself by some little acts which might seem mere folly to a hard onlooker ; they were her way of expressing to all spectators visible or invisible that she had begun a new life in which she embraced humiliation. She took off all her ornaments and put on a plain black gown, and instead of wearing her much-adorned cap and large bows of hair, she brushed her hair down and out on a plain bonnet-cap, which made her look suddenly like an early Methodist.

Bulstrode, who knew that his wife had been out and had come in saying that she was not well, had spent the time in an agitation equal to hers. He had looked forward to her learning the truth from others, and had acquiesced in that probability, as something easier to him than any confession. But now that he imagined the moment of her knowledge come, he awaited the result in anguish. His daughters had been obliged to consent to leave him, and though he had allowed some food to be brought to him, he had not touched it. He felt himself perishing slowly in unpitied misery. Perhaps he should never see his wife's face with affection in it again. And if he turned to God there seemed to be no answer but the pressure of retribution.

It was eight o'clock in the evening before the door opened and his wife entered. He dared not look up at her. He sat with his eyes bent down, and as she went towards him she thought he looked smaller—he seemed so withered and shrunken. A movement of new compassion and old tenderness went through her like a great wave, and putting one hand on his which rested on the arm of the chair, and the other on his shoulder, she said, solemnly but kindly—

"Look up, Nicholas."

He raised his eyes with a little start and looked at her half amazed for a moment : her pale face, her changed, mourning dress, the trembling about her mouth, all said, "I know ;" and her hands and eyes rested gently on him. He burst out crying and they cried together, she sitting at his side. They could not yet speak to each other of the shame which she was bearing with him, or of the acts which had brought it down on them. His confession was silent, and her promise of faithfulness was silent. Open-minded as she was, she nevertheless shrank from the words which would have expressed their mutual consciousness as she would have shrunk from flakes of fire. She could not say, " How much is only slander and false suspicion ? " and he did not say, " I am innocent."

CHAPTER LXXV

" Le sentiment de la fausseté des plaisirs présents, et l'ignorance de la vanité des plaisirs absents, causent l'inconstance."—PASCAL.

ROSAMOND had a gleam of returning cheerfulness when the house was freed from the threatening figure, and when all the disagreeable creditors were paid. But she was not joyous : her married life had fulfilled none of her hopes, and had been quite spoiled for her imagination. In this brief interval of calm, Lydgate, remembering that he had often been stormy in his hours of perturbation, and mindful of the pain Rosamond had had to bear, was carefully gentle towards her ; but he, too, had lost some of his old spirit, and he still felt it necessary to refer to an economical change in their way of living as a matter of course, trying to reconcile her to it gradually, and repressing his anger when she answered by wishing that he would go to live in London. When she did not make this answer, she listened languidly, and wondered what she had that was worth living for. The hard and contemptuous words which had fallen from her husband in his anger had deeply offended that vanity which he had at first called into active enjoyment ; and what she regarded as his perverse way of looking at things, kept up a secret repulsion, which made her receive all his tenderness as a poor substitute for the happiness he had failed to give her. They were at a disadvantage with their neighbours, and there was no longer any outlook towards Quallingham—there was no outlook anywhere except in an occasional letter from Will Ladislaw. She had felt stung and disappointed by Will's resolution to quit Middlemarch, for in spite of what she knew and guessed about his admiration for Dorothea, she secretly cherished the belief that he had, or would necessarily come to have, much more admiration for herself ; Rosamond being one of those women who live much in the idea that each man they meet would have preferred them if the preference had not been hopeless. Mrs. Casaubon was all very well ; but Will's interest in her dated before he knew Mrs. Lydgate. Rosamond took his way of talking to herself, which was a mixture of playful fault-finding and hyperbolical gallantry, as the disguise of a deeper feeling ; and in his presence she felt that agreeable titillation of vanity and sense of romantic drama which Lydgate's presence had no longer the magic to create. She even fancied—what will not men and women fancy in these matters ?—that Will exaggerated his admiration for Mrs. Casaubon in order to pique herself. In this way poor Rosamond's brain had been busy before Will's departure. He would have made, she thought, a much more suitable husband for her than she had found in Lydgate. No notion could have been falser than this, for Rosamond's discontent in her marriage was due to the conditions of marriage itself, to its demand for self-suppression and tolerance, and not to the nature of her husband ; but the easy conception of an unreal Better had a sentimental charm which diverted her ennui. She constructed a little romance which was to vary the flatness of her life : Will Ladislaw was always to be a bachelor and live near her, always to be at her command, and have an understood though never fully expressed passion for her, which would be sending out lambent flames every now and then in interesting scenes. His departure had been a proportionate disappointment, and had sadly increased her weariness of Middlemarch ; but at first she had the alternative dream of pleasure in store from her intercourse with the family at Quallingham. Since then the troubles of her married life had deepened, and the absence of other relief encouraged her regretful rumination over that thin romance which she had once fed on. Men and women make sad mistakes about their own symptoms, taking their vague uneasy longings, sometimes for genius, sometimes for religion, and oftener still for a mighty love. Will Ladislaw had written chatty letters, half to her, and half to Lydgate, and she had replied : their separation, she felt, was not likely to be final, and the change she now most longed for was that Lydgate should go to live in London ; everything would be agreeable in London ; and she had set to work with quiet determination to win this result, when there came a sudden, delightful promise which inspirited her.

It came shortly before the memorable meeting at the town-hall, and was nothing less than a letter from Will Ladislaw to Lydgate, which turned indeed chiefly on his new interest in plans of colonisation, but mentioned incidentally, that he might find it necessary to pay a visit to Middlemarch within the next few weeks—a very pleasant necessity, he said, almost as good as holidays to a schoolboy. He hoped there was his old place on the rug, and a great deal of music in store for him. But he was quite uncertain as to the time. While Lydgate was reading the letter to Rosamond, her face looked like a reviving flower—it grew prettier and more blooming. There was nothing unendurable now : the debts were paid, Mr. Ladislaw was coming, and Lydgate would be persuaded to leave Middlemarch and settle in London, which was " so different from a provincial town."

That was a bright bit of morning. But soon the sky became black over poor Rosamond. The presence of a new gloom in her husband, about which he was entirely reserved towards her—for he dreaded to expose his lacerated feeling to her neutrality and misconception—soon received a painfully strange explanation, alien to all her previous notions of what could affect her happiness. In the new gaiety of her spirits, thinking that Lydgate had merely a worse fit of moodiness than usual, causing him to leave her remarks unanswered, and evidently to keep out of her way as much as possible, she chose, a few days after the meeting, and without speaking to him on the subject, to send out notes of invitation for a small evening party, feeling convinced that this was a judicious step, since people seemed to have been keeping aloof from them, and wanted restoring to the old habit of intercourse. When the invitations had been accepted, she would tell Lydgate, and give him a wise admonition as to how a medical man should behave to his neighbours ; for Rosamond had the gravest little airs possible about other people's duties. But all the invitations were declined, and the last answer came into Lydgate's hands.

"This is Chichely's scratch. What is he writing to you about ? " said Lydgate, wonderingly, as he handed the note to her. She was obliged to let him see it, and, looking at her severely, he said—

" Why on earth have you been sending out invitations without telling me, Rosamond ? I beg, I insist that you will not invite any one to this house. I suppose you have been inviting others, and they have refused too."

She said nothing.

" Do you hear me ? " thundered Lydgate.

" Yes, certainly I hear you," said Rosamond, turning her head aside with the movement of a graceful long-necked bird.

Lydgate tossed his head without any grace and walked out of the room, feeling himself dangerous. Rosamond's thought was, that he was getting more and more unbearable—not that there was any new special reason for this peremptoriness. His indisposition to tell her anything in which he was sure beforehand that she would not be interested was growing into an unreflecting habit, and she was in ignorance of everything connected with the thousand pounds except that the loan had come from her uncle Bulstrode. Lydgate's odious humours and their neighbours' apparent avoidance of them had an unaccountable date for her in their relief from money difficulties. If the invitations had been accepted she would have gone to invite her mamma and the rest, whom she had seen nothing of for several days; and she now put on her bonnet to go and inquire what had become of them all, suddenly feeling as if there were a conspiracy to leave her in isolation with a husband disposed to offend everybody. It was after the dinner hour, and she found her father and mother seated together alone in the drawing-room. They greeted her with sad looks, saying, "Well, my dear!" and no more. She had never seen her father look so downcast; and seating herself near him she said—

"Is there anything the matter, papa?"

He did not answer, but Mrs. Vincy, said, "Oh, my dear, have you heard nothing? It won't be long before it reaches you."

"Is it anything about Tertius?" said Rosamond, turning pale. The idea of trouble immediately connected itself with what had been unaccountable to her in him.

"Oh my dear, yes. To think of your marrying into this trouble. Debt was bad enough, but this will be worse."

"Stay, stay, Lucy," said Mr. Vincy. "Have you heard nothing about your uncle Bulstrode, Rosamond?"

"No, papa," said the poor thing, feeling as if trouble were not anything she had before experienced, but some invisible power with an iron grasp that made her soul faint within her.

Her father told her everything, saying at the end, "It's better for you to know, my dear. I think Lydgate must leave the town. Things have gone against him. I daresay he couldn't help it. I don't accuse him of any harm," said Mr. Vincy. He had always before been disposed to find the utmost fault with Lydgate.

The shock to Rosamond was terrible. It seemed to her that no lot could be so cruelly hard as hers—to have married a man who had become the centre of infamous suspicions. In many cases it is inevitable that the shame is felt to be the worst part of crime; and it would have required a great deal of disentangling reflection, such as had never entered into Rosamond's life, for her in these moments to feel that her trouble was less than if her husband had been certainly known to have done something criminal. All the shame seemed to be there. And she had innocently married this man with the belief that he and his family were a glory to her! She showed her usual reticence to her parents, and only said, that if Lydgate had done as she wished he would have left Middlemarch long ago.

"She bears it beyond anything," said her mother when she was gone.

"Ah, thank God!" said Mr. Vincy, who was much broken down.

But Rosamond went home with a sense of justified repugnance towards her husband. What had he really done—how had he really acted? She did not know. Why had he not told her everything? He did not speak to her on the subject, and of course she could not speak to him. It came into her mind once that she would ask her father to let her go home again; but dwelling on that prospect made it seem utter dreariness to her: a married woman gone back to live with her parents—life seemed to have no meaning for her in such a position: she could not contemplate herself in it.

The next two days Lydgate observed a change in her, and believed that she had heard the bad news. Would she speak to him about it, or would she go on for ever in the silence which seemed to imply that she believed him guilty? We must remember that he was in a morbid state of mind, in which almost all contact was pain. Certainly Rosamond in this case had equal reason to complain of reserve and want of confidence on his part; but in the bitterness of his soul he excused himself;—was he not justified in shrinking from the task of telling her, since now she knew the truth she had no impulse to speak to him? But a deeper-lying consciousness that he was in fault made him restless, and the silence between them became intolerable to him; it was as if they were both adrift on one piece of wreck and looked away from each other.

He thought, "I am a fool. Haven't I given up expecting anything? I have married care, not help." And that evening he said—

"Rosamond, have you heard anything that distresses you?"

"Yes," she answered, laying down her work, which she had been carrying on with a languid semi-consciousness, most unlike her usual self.

" What have you heard ? "

" Everything, I suppose.   Papa told me."

" That people think me disgraced ? "

" Yes," said Rosamond, faintly, beginning to sew again automatically.

There was silence.   Lydgate thought, " If she has any trust in me—any notion of what I am, she ought to speak now and say that she does not believe I have deserved disgrace."

But Rosamond on her side went on moving her fingers languidly.   Whatever was to be said on the subject she expected to come from Tertius.   What did she know ?   And if he were innocent of any wrong, why did he not do something to clear himself ?

This silence of hers brought a new rush of gall to that bitter mood in which Lydgate had been saying to himself that nobody believed in him—even Farebrother had not come forward. He had begun to question her with the intent that their conversation should disperse the chill fog which had gathered between them, but he felt his resolution checked by despairing resentment.   Even this trouble, like the rest, she seemed to regard as if it were hers alone.   He was always to her a being apart, doing what she objected to.   He started from his chair with an angry impulse, and thrusting his hands in his pockets, walked up and down the room.   There was an underlying consciousness all the while that he should have to master this anger, and tell her everything, and convince her of the facts. For he had almost learned the lesson that he must bend himself to her nature, and that because she came short in her sympathy, he must give the more.   Soon he recurred to his intention of opening himself : the occasion must not be lost.   If he could could bring her to feel with some solemnity that here was a slander which must be met and not run away from, and that the whole trouble had come out of his desperate want of money, it would be a moment for urging powerfully on her that they should be one in the resolve to do with as little money as possible, so that they might weather the bad time and keep themselves independent.   He would mention the definite measures which he desired to take, and win her to a willing spirit.   He was bound to try this—and what else was there for him to do ?

He did not know how long he had been walking uneasily backwards and forwards, but Rosamond felt that it was long, and wished that he would sit down.   She too had begun to think this an opportunity for urging on Tertius what he ought to do.

Whatever might be the truth about all this misery, there was one dread which asserted itself.

Lydgate at last seated himself, not in his usual chair, but in one nearer to Rosamond, leaning aside in it towards her, and looking at her gravely before he reopened the sad subject. He had conquered himself so far, and was about to speak with a sense of solemnity, as on an occasion which was not to be repeated. He had even opened his lips, when Rosamond, letting her hands fall, looked at him and said—

" Surely, Tertius——"

" Well ? "

" Surely now at last you have given up the idea of staying in Middlemarch. I cannot go on living here. Let us go to London. Papa, and every one else, says you had better go. Whatever misery I have to put up with, it will be easier away from here."

Lydgate felt miserably jarred. Instead of that critical outpouring for which he had prepared himself with effort, here was the old round to be gone through again. He could not bear it. With a quick change of countenance he rose and went out of the room.

Perhaps if he had been strong enough to persist in his determination to be the more because she was less, that evening might have had a better issue. If his energy could have borne down that check, he might still have wrought on Rosamond's vision and will. We cannot be sure that any natures, however inflexible or peculiar, will resist this effect from a more massive being than their own. They may be taken by storm and for the moment converted, becoming part of the soul which enwraps them in the ardour of its movement. But poor Lydgate had a throbbing pain within him, and his energy had fallen short of its task.

The beginning of mutual understanding and resolve seemed as far off as ever ; nay, it seemed blocked out by the sense of unsuccessful effort. They lived on from day to day with their thoughts still apart, Lydgate going about what work he had in a mood of despair, and Rosamond feeling, with some justification, that he was behaving cruelly. It was of no use to say anything to Tertius ; but when Will Ladislaw came, she was determined to tell him everything. In spite of her general reticence, she needed some one who would recognise her wrongs.

CHAPTER LXXVI

" To mercy, pity, peace, and love
  All pray in their distress,
And to these virtues of delight,
  Return their thankfulness."

   .   .   .   .

" For Mercy has a human heart,
  Pity a human face ;
And Love, the human form divine ;
  And Peace, the human dress."
      —WILLIAM BLAKE : *Songs of Innocence.*

SOME days later, Lydgate was riding to Lowick Manor, in consequence of a summons from Dorothea. The summons had not been unexpected, since it had followed a letter from Mr. Bulstrode, in which he stated that he had resumed his arrangements for quitting Middlemarch, and must remind Lydgate of his previous communications about the hospital, to the purport of which he still adhered. It had been his duty, before taking further steps, to reopen the subject with Mrs. Casaubon, who now wished, as before, to discuss the question with Lydgate. " Your views may possibly have undergone some change," wrote Mr. Bulstrode ; " but, in that case also, it is desirable that you should lay them before her."

Dorothea awaited his arrival with eager interest. Though, in deference to her masculine advisers, she had refrained from what Sir James had called " interfering in this Bulstrode business," the hardship of Lydgate's position was continually in her mind, and when Bulstrode applied to her again about the hospital, she felt that the opportunity was come to her which she had been hindered from hastening. In her luxurious home, wandering under the boughs of her own great trees, her thought was going out over the lot of others, and her emotions were imprisoned. The idea of some active good within her reach, " haunted her like a passion," and another's need having once come to her as a distinct image, preoccupied her desire with the yearning to give relief, and made her own ease tasteless. She was full of confident hope about this interview with Lydgate, never heeding what was said of his personal reserve ; never heeding that she was a very young woman. Nothing could have seemed more irrelevant to Dorothea than insistence on her youth and sex when she was moved to show her human fellowship.

As she sat waiting in the library, she could do nothing but live through again all the past scenes which had brought Lydgate into her memories. They all owed their significance to her marriage and its troubles—but no ; there were two occasions in which the image of Lydgate had come painfully in connection with his wife and some one else. The pain had been allayed for Dorothea, but it had left in her an awakening conjecture as to what Lydgate's marriage might be to him, a susceptibility to the slightest hint about Mrs. Lydgate. These thoughts were like a drama to her, and made her eyes bright, and gave an attitude of suspense to her whole frame, though she was only looking out from the brown library on to the turf and the bright green buds which stood in relief against the dark evergreens.

When Lydgate came in, she was almost shocked at the change in his face, which was strikingly perceptible to her who had not seen him for two months. It was not the change of emaciation, but that effect which even young faces will very soon show from the persistent presence of resentment and despondency. Her cordial look, when she put out her hand to him, softened his expression, but only with melancholy.

" I have wished very much to see you for a long while, Mr. Lydgate," said Dorothea when they were seated opposite each other ; " but I put off asking you to come until Mr. Bulstrode applied to me again about the hospital. I know that the advantage of keeping the management of it separate from that of the Infirmary depends on you, or, at least, on the good which you are encouraged to hope for from having it under your control. And I am sure you will not refuse to tell me exactly what you think."

" You want to decide whether you should give a generous support to the hospital," said Lydgate. " I cannot conscientiously advise you to do it in dependence on any activity of mine. I may be obliged to leave the town."

He spoke curtly, feeling the ache of despair as to his being able to carry out any purpose that Rosamond had set her mind against.

" Not because there is no one to believe in you ? " said Dorothea, pouring out her words in clearness from a full heart. " I know the unhappy mistakes about you. I knew them from the first moment to be mistakes. You have never done anything vile. You would not do anything dishonourable."

It was the first assurance of belief in him that had fallen on Lydgate's ears. He drew a deep breath, and said, " Thank you." He could say no more : it was something very new and strange in his life that these few words of trust from a woman should be so much to him.

" I beseech you to tell me how everything was," said Dorothea, fearlessly. " I am sure that the truth would clear you."

Lydgate started up from his chair and went towards the window, forgetting where he was. He had so often gone over in his mind the possibility of explaining everything without aggravating appearances that would tell, perhaps unfairly, against Bulstrode, and had so often decided against it—he had so often said to himself that his assertions would not change people's impressions—that Dorothea's words sounded like a temptation to do something which in his soberness he had pronounced to be unreasonable.

" Tell me, pray," said Dorothea, with simple earnestness ; " then we can consult together. It is wicked to let people think evil of any one falsely, when it can be hindered."

Lydgate turned, remembering where he was, and saw Dorothea's face looking up at him with a sweet trustful gravity. The presence of a noble nature, generous in its wishes, ardent in its charity, changes the lights for us : we begin to see things again in their larger, quieter masses, and to believe that we too can be seen and judged in the wholeness of our character. That influence was beginning to act on Lydgate, who had for many days been seeing all life as one who is dragged and struggling amid the throng. He sat down again, and felt that he was recovering his old self in the consciousness that he was with one who believed in it.

" I don't want," he said, " to bear hard on Bulstrode, who has lent me money of which I was in need—though I would rather have gone without it now. He is hunted down and miserable, and has only a poor thread of life in him. But I should like to tell you everything. It will be a comfort to me to speak where belief has gone beforehand, and where I shall not seem to be offering assertions of my own honesty. You will feel what is fair to another, as you feel what is fair to me."

" Do trust me," said Dorothea ; " I will not repeat anything without your leave. But at the very least, I could say that you have made all the circumstances clear to me, and that I know you are not in any way guilty. Mr. Farebrother would believe me, and my uncle, and Sir James Chettam. Nay, there are persons in Middlemarch to whom I could go ; although they don't know much of me, they would believe me. They would know that I could have no other motive than truth and justice.

I would take any pains to clear you. I have very little to do. There is nothing better that I can do in the world."

Dorothea's voice, as she made this childlike picture of what she would do, might have been almost taken as a proof that she could do it effectively. The searching tenderness of her woman's tones seemed made for a defence against ready accusers. Lydgate did not stay to think that she was Quixotic : he gave himself up, for the first time in his life, to the exquisite sense of leaning entirely on a generous sympathy, without any check of proud reserve. And he told her everything, from the time when, under the pressure of his difficulties, he unwillingly made his first application to Bulstrode ; gradually, in the relief of speaking, getting into a more thorough utterance of what had gone on in his mind—entering fully into the fact that his treatment of the patient was opposed to the dominant practice, into his doubts at the last, his ideal of medical duty, and his uneasy consciousness that the acceptance of the money had made some difference in his private inclination and professional behaviour, though not in his fulfilment of any publicly recognised obligation.

"It has come to my knowledge since," he added, "that Hawley sent some one to examine the housekeeper at Stone Court, and she said that she gave the patient all the opium in the phial I left, as well as a good deal of brandy. But that would not have been opposed to ordinary prescriptions, even of first-rate men. The suspicions against me had no hold there : they are grounded on the knowledge that I took money, that Bulstrode had strong motives for wishing the man to die, and that he gave me the money as a bribe to concur in some malpractices or other against the patient—that in any case I accepted a bribe to hold my tongue. They are just the suspicions that cling the most obstinately, because they lie in people's inclination and can never be disproved. How my orders came to be disobeyed is a question to which I don't know the answer. It is still possible that Bulstrode was innocent of any criminal intention— even possible that he had nothing to do with the disobedience, and merely abstained from mentioning it. But all that has nothing to do with the public belief. It is one of those cases on which a man is condemned on the ground of his character—it is believed that he has committed a crime in some undefined way, because he had the motive for doing it ; and Bulstrode's character has enveloped me, because I took his money. I am simply blighted—like a damaged ear of corn—the business is done and can't be undone."

"Oh, it is hard!" said Dorothea. "I understand the difficulty there is in your vindicating yourself. And that all this should have come to you who had meant to lead a higher life than the common, and to find out better ways—I cannot bear to rest in this as unchangeable. I know you meant that. I remember what you said to me when you first spoke to me about the hospital. There is no sorrow I have thought more about than that—to love what is great, and try to reach it, and yet to fail."

"Yes," said Lydgate, feeling that here he had found room for the full meaning of his grief. "I had some ambition. I meant everything to be different with me. I thought I had more strength and mastery. But the most terrible obstacles are such as nobody can see except oneself."

"Suppose," said Dorothea, meditatively. "Suppose we kept on the hospital according to the present plan, and you stayed here though only with the friendship and support of a few, the evil feeling towards you would gradually die out ; there would come opportunities in which people would be forced to acknowledge that they had been unjust to you, because they would see that your purposes were pure. You may still win a great fame like the Louis and Laennec I have heard you speak of, and we shall all be proud of you," she ended, with a smile.

"That might do if I had my old trust in myself," said Lydgate, mournfully. "Nothing galls me more than the notion of turning round and running away before this slander, leaving it unchecked behind me. Still, I can't ask any one to put a great deal of money into a plan which depends on me."

"It would be quite worth my while," said Dorothea, simply. "Only think. I am very uncomfortable with my money, because they tell me I have too little for any great scheme of the sort I like best, and yet I have too much. I don't know what to do. I have seven hundred a-year of my own fortune, and nineteen hundred a-year that Mr. Casaubon left me, and between three and four thousand of ready money in the bank. I wished to raise money and pay it off gradually out of my income which I don't want, to buy land with and found a village which should be a school of industry ; but Sir James and my uncle have convinced me that the risk would be too great. So you see that what I should most rejoice at would be to have something good to do with my money : I should like it to make other people's lives better to them. It makes me very uneasy—coming all to me who don't want it."

A smile broke through the gloom of Lydgate's face. The child-like grave-eyed earnestness with which Dorothea said all this was irresistible—blent into an adorable whole with her ready understanding of high experience. (Of lower experience such as plays a great part in the world, poor Mrs. Casaubon had a very blurred shortsighted knowledge, little helped by her imagination.) But she took the smile as encouragement of her plan.

"I think you see now that you spoke too scrupulously," she said, in a tone of persuasion. "The hospital would be one good ; and making your life quite whole and well again would be another."

Lydgate's smile had died away. "You have the goodness as well as the money to do all that ; if it could be done," he said. "But——"

He hesitated a little while, looking vaguely towards the window ; and she sat in silent expectation. At last he turned towards her and said impetuously—

"Why should I not tell you ?—you know what sort of bond marriage is. You will understand everything."

Dorothea felt her heart beginning to beat faster. Had he that sorrow too ? But she feared to say any word, and he went on immediately.

"It is impossible for me now to do anything—to take any step without considering my wife's happiness. The thing that I might like to do if I were alone, is become impossible to me. I can't see her miserable. She married me without knowing what she was going into, and it might have been better for her if she had not married me."

"I know, I know—you could not give her pain, if you were not obliged to do it," said Dorothea, with keen memory of her own life.

"And she has set her mind against staying. She wishes to go. The troubles she has had here have wearied her," said Lydgate, breaking off again, lest he should say too much.

"But when she saw the good that might come of staying——" said Dorothea, remonstrantly, looking at Lydgate as if he had forgotten the reasons which had just been considered. He did not speak immediately.

"She would not see it," he said at last, curtly, feeling at first that this statement must do without explanation. "And, indeed, I have lost all spirit about carrying on my life here." He paused a moment and then, following the impulse to let Dorothea see deeper into the difficulty of his life, he said, "The fact is, this trouble has come upon her confusedly. We have not been able to speak to each other about it. I am not sure what is in her mind about it : she may fear that I have really done something base. It is my fault ; I ought to be more open. But I have been suffering cruelly."

" May I go and see her ? " said Dorothea, eagerly. " Would she accept my sympathy ? I would tell her that you have not been blamable before any one's judgment but your own. I would tell her that you shall be cleared in every fair mind. I would cheer her heart. Will you ask her if I may go to see her ? I did see her once."

" I am sure you may," said Lydgate, seizing the proposition with some hope. " She would feel honoured—cheered, I think, by the proof that you at least have some respect for me. I will not speak to her about your coming—that she may not connect it with my wishes at all. I know very well that I ought not to have left anything to be told her by others, but——"

He broke off, and there was a moment's silence. Dorothea refrained from saying what was in her mind—how well she knew that there might be invisible barriers to speech between husband and wife. This was a point on which even sympathy might make a wound. She returned to the more outward aspect of Lydgate's position, saying cheerfully—

" And if Mrs. Lydgate knew that there were friends who would believe in you and support you, she might then be glad that you should stay in your place and recover your hopes— and do what you meant to do. Perhaps then you would see that it was right to agree with what I proposed about your continuing at the hospital. Surely you would, if you still have faith in it as a means of making your knowledge useful ? "

Lydgate did not answer, and she saw that he was debating with himself.

" You need not decide immediately," she said, gently. " A few days hence it will be early enough for me to send my answer to Mr. Bulstrode."

Lydgate still waited, but at last turned to speak in his most decisive tones.

" No ; I prefer that there should be no interval left for wavering. I am no longer sure enough of myself—I mean of what it would be possible for me to do under the changed circumstances of my life. It would be dishonourable to let others engage themselves to anything serious in dependence on me. I might be obliged to go away after all ; I see little chance of anything else. The whole thing is too problematic; I cannot consent to be the cause of your goodness being wasted. No—let the new hospital be joined with the old infirmary, and everything go on as it might have done if I had never come. I have kept a valuable register since I have been there; I shall send it to a man who will make use of it," he ended bitterly. "I can think of nothing for a long while but getting an income."

"It hurts me very much to hear you speak so hopelessly," said Dorothea. "It would be a happiness to your friends, who believe in your future, in your power to do great things, if you would let them save you from that. Think how much money I have; it would be like taking a burden from me if you took some of it every year till you got free from this fettering want of income. Why should not people do these things? It is so difficult to make shares at all even. This is one way."

"God bless you, Mrs. Casaubon!" said Lydgate, rising as if with the same impulse that made his words energetic, and resting his arm on the back of the great leather chair he had been sitting in. "It is good that you should have such feelings. But I am not the man who ought to allow himself to benefit by them. I have not given guarantees enough. I must not at least sink into the degradation of being pensioned for work that I never achieved. It is very clear to me that I must not count on anything else than getting away from Middlemarch as soon as I can manage it. I should not be able for a long while, at the very best, to get an income here, and—and it is easier to make necessary changes in a new place. I must do as other men do, and think what will please the world and bring in money; look for a little opening in the London crowd, and push myself; set up in a watering-place, or go to some southern town where there are plenty of idle English, and get myself puffed,—that is the sort of shell I must creep into and try to keep my soul alive in."

"Now that is not brave," said Dorothea,—"to give up the fight."

"No, it is not brave," said Lydgate, "but if a man is afraid of creeping paralysis?" Then, in another tone, "Yet you have made a great difference in my courage by believing in me. Everything seems more bearable since I have talked to you; and if you can clear me in a few other minds, especially in Farebrother's, I shall be deeply grateful. The point I wish you not to mention is the fact of disobedience to my orders. That would soon get distorted. After all, there is no evidence for

me but people's opinion of me beforehand. You can only
repeat my own report of myself."

"Mr. Farebrother will believe—others will believe," said
Dorothea. "I can say of you what will make it stupidity to
suppose that you would be bribed to do a wickedness."

"I don't know," said Lydgate, with something like a groan in
his voice. "I have not taken a bribe yet. But there is a pale
shade of bribery which is sometimes called prosperity. You
will do me another great kindness, then, and come to see my
wife?"

"Yes, I will. I remember how pretty she is," said Dorothea,
into whose mind every impression about Rosamond had cut
deep. "I hope she will like me."

As Lydgate rode away, he thought, "This young creature has
a heart large enough for the Virgin Mary. She evidently thinks
nothing of her own future, and would pledge away half her
income at once, as if she wanted nothing for herself but a chair
to sit in from which she can look down with those clear eyes at
the poor mortals who pray to her. She seems to have what I
never saw in any woman before—a fountain of friendship
towards men—a man can make a friend of her. Casaubon must
have raised some heroic hallucination in her? I wonder if she
could have any other sort of passion for a man? Ladislaw?—
there was certainly an unusual feeling between them. And
Casaubon must have had a notion of it. Well—her love might
help a man more than her money."

Dorothea on her side had immediately formed a plan of
relieving Lydgate from his obligation to Bulstrode, which she
felt sure was a part, though small, of the galling pressure he had
to bear. She sat down at once under the inspiration of their
interview, and wrote a brief note, in which she pleaded that she
had more claim than Mr. Bulstrode had to the satisfaction of
providing the money which had been serviceable to Lydgate—
that it would be unkind in Lydgate not to grant her the position
of being his helper in this small matter, the favour being entirely
to her who had so little that was plainly marked out for her to
do with her superfluous money. He might call her a creditor
or by any other name if it did but imply that he granted her
request. She enclosed a cheque for a thousand pounds, and
determined to take the letter with her the next day when she
went to see Rosamond.

CHAPTER LXXVII

" And thus thy fall hath left a kind of blot,
  To mark the full-fraught man and best indued
  With some suspicion."
                                —*Henry* V.

THE next day Lydgate had to go to Brassing, and told Rosamond that he should be away until the evening. Of late she had never gone beyond her own house and garden, except to church, and once to see her papa, to whom she said, " If Tertius goes away, you will help us to move, will you not, papa ? I suppose we shall have very little money. I am sure I hope some one will help us." And Mr. Vincy had said, " Yes, child, I don't mind a hundred or two. I can see the end of that." With these exceptions she had sat at home in languid melancholy and suspense, fixing her mind on Will Ladislaw's coming as the one point of hope and interest, and associating this with some new urgency on Lydgate to make immediate arrangements for leaving Middlemarch and going to London, till she felt assured that the coming would be a potent cause of the going, without at all seeing how. This way of establishing sequences is too common to be fairly regarded as a peculiar folly in Rosamond. And it is precisely this sort of sequence which causes the greatest shock when it is sundered : for to see how an effect may be produced is often to see possible missings and checks ; but to see nothing except the desirable cause, and close upon it the desirable effect, rids us of doubt and makes our minds strongly intuitive. That was the process going on in poor Rosamond, while she arranged all objects around her with the same nicety as ever, only with more slowness—or sat down to the piano, meaning to play, and then desisting, yet lingering on the music stool with her white fingers suspended on the wooden front, and looking before her in dreamy ennui. Her melancholy had become so marked that Lydgate felt a strange timidity before it, as a perpetual silent reproach, and the strong man, mastered by his keen sensibilities towards this fair fragile creature whose life he seemed somehow to have bruised, shrank from her look, and sometimes started at her approach, fear of her and fear for her rushing in only the more forcibly after it had been momentarily expelled by exasperation.

But this morning Rosamond descended from her room upstairs—where she sometimes sat the whole day when Lydgate was out—equipped for a walk in the town. She had a letter to post—a letter addressed to Mr. Ladislaw and written with charming discretion, but intended to hasten his arrival by a hint of trouble. The servant-maid, their sole house-servant now, noticed her coming down-stairs in her walking dress, and thought "there never did anybody look so pretty in a bonnet, poor thing."

Meanwhile Dorothea's mind was filled with her project of going to Rosamond, and with the many thoughts, both of the past and the probable future, which gathered round the idea of that visit. Until yesterday when Lydgate had opened to her a glimpse of some trouble in his married life, the image of Mrs. Lydgate had always been associated for her with that of Will Ladislaw. Even in her most uneasy moments—even when she had been agitated by Mrs. Cadwallader's painfully graphic report of gossip—her effort, nay, her strongest impulsive prompting, had been towards the vindication of Will from any sullying surmises ; and when, in her meeting with him after- wards, she had at first interpreted his words as a probable allusion to a feeling towards Mrs. Lydgate which he was determined to cut himself off from indulging, she had had a quick, sad, excusing vision of the charm there might be in his constant opportunities of companionship with that fair creature, who most likely shared his other tastes as she evidently did his delight in music. But there had followed his parting words— the few passionate words in which he had implied that she her- self was the object of whom his love held him in dread, that it was his love for her only which he was resolved not to declare but to carry away into banishment. From the time of that parting, Dorothea, believing in Will's love for her, believing with a proud delight in his delicate sense of honour and his determin- ation that no one should impeach him justly, felt her heart quite at rest as to the regard he might have for Mrs. Lydgate. She was sure that the regard was blameless.

There are natures in which, if they love us, we are conscious of having a sort of baptism and consecration : they bind us over to rectitude and purity by their pure belief about us ; and our sins become that worst kind of sacrilege which tears down the invisible altar of trust. "If you are not good, none is good"—those little words may give a terrific meaning to responsibility, may hold a vitriolic intensity for remorse.

Dorothea's nature was of that kind : her own passionate faults lay along the easily-counted open channels of her ardent character ; and while she was full of pity for the visible mistakes of others, she had not yet any material within her experience for subtle constructions and suspicions of hidden wrong. But that simplicity of hers, holding up an ideal for others in her believing conception of them, was one of the great powers of her woman-hood. And it had from the first acted strongly on Will Ladislaw. He felt, when he parted from her, that the brief words by which he had tried to convey to her his feeling about herself and the division which her fortune made between them, would only profit by their brevity when Dorothea had to interpret them : he felt that in her mind he had found his highest estimate.

And he was right there. In the months since their parting Dorothea had felt a delicious sad repose in their relation to each other, as one which was inwardly whole and without blemish. She had an active force of antagonism within her, when the antagonism turned on the defence either of plans or persons that she believed in ; and the wrongs which she felt that Will had received from her husband, and the external conditions which to others were grounds for slighting him, only gave the more tenacity to her affection and admiring judgment. And now with the disclosures about Bulstrode had come another fact affecting Will's social position, which roused afresh Doro-thea's inward resistance to what was said about him in that part of her world which lay within park palings.

"Young Ladislaw the grandson of a thieving Jew pawn-broker " was a phrase which had entered emphatically into the dialogues about the Bulstrode business, at Lowick, Tipton and Freshitt, and was a worse kind of placard on poor Will's back than the "Italian with white mice." Upright Sir James Chettam was convinced that his own satisfaction was righteous when he thought with some complacency that here was an added league to that mountainous distance between Ladislaw and Dorothea, which enabled him to dismiss any anxiety in that direction as too absurd. And perhaps there had been some pleasure in pointing Mr. Brooke's attention to this ugly bit of Ladislaw's genealogy, as a fresh candle for him to see his own folly by. Dorothea had observed the animus with which Will's part in the painful story had been recalled more than once ; but she had uttered no word, being checked now, as she had not been formerly in speaking of Will, by the consciousness of a deeper relation between them which must always remain in consecrated secrecy. But her silence shrouded her resistant emotion into a more thorough glow ; and this misfortune in Will's lot which, it seemed, others were wishing to fling at his back as an opprobrium, only gave something more of enthusiasm to her clinging thought.

She entertained no visions of their ever coming into nearer union, and yet she had taken no posture of renunciation. She had accepted her whole relation to Will very simply as part of her marriage sorrows, and would have thought it very sinful in her to keep up an inward wail because she was not completely happy, being rather disposed to dwell on the superfluities of her lot. She could bear that the chief pleasures of her tenderness should lie in memory, and the idea of marriage came to her solely as a repulsive proposition from some suitor of whom she at present knew nothing, but whose merits, as seen by her friends, would be a source of torment to her :—" somebody who will manage your property for you, my dear," was Mr. Brooke's attractive suggestion of suitable characteristics. " I should like to manage it myself, if I knew what to do with it," said Dorothea. No—she adhered to her declaration that she would never be married again, and in the long valley of her life, which looked so flat and empty of way-marks, guidance would come as she walked along the road, and saw her fellow-passengers by the way.

This habitual state of feeling about Will Ladislaw had been strong in all her waking hours since she had proposed to pay a visit to Mrs. Lydgate, making a sort of background against which she saw Rosamond's figure presented to her without hindrances to her interest and compassion. There was evidently some mental separation, some barrier to complete confidence which had arisen between this wife and the husband who had yet made her happiness a law to him. That was a trouble which no third person must directly touch. But Dorothea thought with deep pity of the loneliness which must have come upon Rosamond from the suspicions cast on her husband ; and there would surely be help in the manifestation of respect for Lydgate and sympathy with her.

" I shall talk to her about her husband," thought Dorothea, as she was being driven towards the town. The clear spring morning, the scent of the moist earth, the fresh leaves just showing their creased-up wealth of greenery from out their half-opened sheaths, seemed part of the cheerfulness she was feeling from a long conversation with Mr. Farebrother, who had joy-fully accepted the justifying explanation of Lydgate's conduct.

" I shall take Mrs. Lydgate good news, and perhaps she will like to talk to me and make a friend of me."

Dorothea had another errand in Lowick Gate : it was about a new fine-toned bell for the school-house, and as she had to get out of her carriage very near to Lydgate's, she walked thither across the street, having told the coachman to wait for some packages. The street door was open, and the servant was taking the opportunity of looking out at the carriage which was pausing within sight when it became apparent to her that the lady who " belonged to it " was coming towards her.

" Is Mrs. Lydgate at home ? " said Dorothea.

" I'm not sure, my lady ; I'll see, if you'll please to walk in," said Martha, a little confused on the score of her kitchen apron, but collected enough to be sure that " mum " was not the right title for this queenly young widow with a carriage and pair. " Will you please to walk in, and I'll go and see."

" Say that I am Mrs. Casaubon," said Dorothea, as Martha moved forward intending to show her into the drawing-room and then to go up-stairs to see if Rosamond had returned from her walk.

They crossed the broader part of the entrance-hall, and turned up the passage which led to the garden. The drawing-room door was unlatched, and Martha, pushing it without looking into the room, waited for Mrs. Casaubon to enter and then turned away, the door having swung open and swung back again without noise.

Dorothea had less of outward vision than usual this morning, being filled with images of things as they had been and were going to be. She found herself on the other side of the door without seeing anything remarkable, but immediately she heard a voice speaking in low tones which startled her as with a sense of dreaming in daylight, and advancing unconsciously a step or two beyond the projecting slab of a bookcase, she saw, in the terrible illumination of a certainty which filled up all outlines, something which made her pause motionless, without self-possession enough to speak.

Seated with his back towards her on a sofa which stood against the wall on a line with the door by which she had entered, she saw Will Ladislaw : close by him and turned towards him with a flushed tearfulness which gave a new brilliancy to her face sat Rosamond, her bonnet hanging back, while Will leaning towards her clasped both her upraised hands in his and spoke with low-toned fervour.

Rosamond in her agitated absorption had not noticed the silently advancing figure ; but when Dorothea, after the first immeasurable instant of this vision, moved confusedly backward and found herself impeded by some piece of furniture, Rosamond was suddenly aware of her presence, and with a spasmodic movement snatched away her hands and rose, looking at Dorothea who was necessarily arrested. Will Ladislaw, starting up, looked round also, and meeting Dorothea's eyes with a new lightning in them, seemed changing to marble. But she immediately turned them away from him to Rosamond and said in a firm voice—

"Excuse me, Mrs. Lydgate, the servant did not know that you were here. I called to deliver an important letter for Mr. Lydgate, which I wished to put into your own hands."

She laid down the letter on the small table which had checked her retreat, and then including Rosamond and Will in one distant glance and bow, she went quickly out of the room, meeting in the passage the surprised Martha, who said she was sorry the mistress was not at home, and then showed the strange lady out with an inward reflection that grand people were probably more impatient than others.

Dorothea walked across the street with her most elastic step and was quickly in her carriage again.

"Drive on to Freshitt Hall," she said to the coachman, and any one looking at her might have thought that though she was paler than usual she was never animated by a more self-possessed energy. And that was really her experience. It was as if she had drunk a great draught of scorn that stimulated her beyond the susceptibility to other feelings. She had seen something so far below her belief, that her emotions rushed back from it and made an excited throng without an object. She needed something active to turn her excitement out upon. She felt power to walk and work for a day, without meat or drink. And she would carry out the purpose with which she had started in the morning, of going to Freshitt and Tipton to tell Sir James and her uncle all that she wished them to know about Lydgate, whose married loneliness under his trial now presented itself to her with new significance, and made her more ardent in readiness to be his champion. She had never felt anything like this triumphant power of indignation in the struggle of her married life, in which there had always been a quickly subduing pang ; and she took it as a sign of new strength.

"Dodo, how very bright your eyes are !" said Celia, when

Sir James was gone out of the room. "And you don't see anything you look at, Arthur or anything. You are going to do something uncomfortable, I know. Is it all about Mr. Lydgate, or has something else happened?" Celia had been used to watch her sister with expectation.

"Yes, dear, a great many things have happened," said Dodo, in her full tones.

"I wonder what," said Celia, folding her arms cozily and leaning forward upon them.

"Oh, all the troubles of all people on the face of the earth," said Dorothea, lifting her arms to the back of her head.

"Dear me, Dodo, are you going to have a scheme for them?" said Celia, a little uneasy at this Hamlet-like raving.

But Sir James came in again, ready to accompany Dorothea to the Grange, and she finished her expedition well, not swerving in her resolution until she descended at her own door.

CHAPTER LXXVIII

Would it were yesterday and I i' the grave,
With her sweet faith above for monument.

ROSAMOND and Will stood motionless—they did not know how long—he looking towards the spot where Dorothea had stood, and she looking towards him with doubt. It seemed an endless time to Rosamond, in whose inmost soul there was hardly so much annoyance as gratification from what had just happened. Shallow natures dream of an easy sway over the emotions of others, trusting implicitly in their own petty magic to turn the deepest streams, and confident, by pretty gestures and remarks, of making the thing that is not as though it were. She knew that Will had received a severe blow, but she had been little used to imagining other people's states of mind except as a material cut into shape by her own wishes; and she believed in her own power to soothe or subdue. Even Tertius, that most perverse of men, was always subdued in the long-run : events had been obstinate, but still Rosamond would have said now, as she did before her marriage, that she never gave up what she had set her mind on.

She put out her arm and laid the tips of her fingers on Will's coat-sleeve.

"Don't touch me!" he said, with an utterance like the cut

of a lash, darting from her, and changing from pink to white and back again, as if his whole frame were tingling with the pain of the sting. He wheeled round to the other side of the room and stood opposite to her, with the tips of his fingers in his pockets and his head thrown back, looking fiercely not at Rosamond but at a point a few inches away from her.

She was keenly offended, but the signs she made of this were such as only Lydgate was used to interpret. She became suddenly quiet and seated herself, untying her hanging bonnet and laying it down with her shawl. Her little hands which she folded before her were very cold.

It would have been safer for Will in the first instance to have taken up his hat and gone away ; but he had felt no impulse to do this ; on the contrary, he had a horrible inclination to stay and shatter Rosamond with his anger. It seemed as impossible to bear the fatality she had drawn down on him without venting his fury as it would be to a panther to bear the javelin-wound without springing and biting. And yet—how could he tell a woman that he was ready to curse her ? He was fuming under a repressive law which he was forced to acknowledge : he was dangerously poised, and Rosamond's voice now brought the decisive vibration. In flute-like tones of sarcasm she said,

" You can easily go after Mrs. Casaubon and explain your preference."

" Go after her ! " he burst out, with a sharp edge in his voice. " Do you think she would turn to look at me, or value any word I ever uttered to her again at more than a dirty feather ?—Explain ! How can a man explain at the expense of a woman ! "

" You can tell her what you please," said Rosamond, with more tremor.

" Do you suppose she would like me better for sacrificing you ? She is not a woman to be flattered because I made myself despicable—to believe that I must be true to her because I was a dastard to you."

He began to move about with the restlessness of a wild animal that sees prey but cannot reach it. Presently he burst out again—

" I had no hope before—not much—of anything better to come. But I had one certainty—that she believed in me. Whatever people had said or done about me, she believed in me.—That's gone ! She'll never again think me anything but a paltry pretence—too nice to take heaven except upon flattering conditions, and yet selling myself for any devil's change by the sly. She'll think of me as an incarnate insult to her, from the first moment we . . ."

Will stopped as if he had found himself grasping something that must not be thrown and shattered. He found another vent for his rage by snatching up Rosamond's words again, as if they were reptiles to be throttled and flung off.

" Explain ! Tell a man to explain how he dropped into hell ! Explain my preference ! I never had a *preference* for her, any more than I have a preference for breathing. No other woman exists by the side of her. I would rather touch her hand if it were dead, than I would touch any other woman's living."

Rosamond, while these poisoned weapons were being hurled at her, was almost losing the sense of her identity, and seemed to be waking into some new terrible existence. She had no sense of chill resolute repulsion, of reticent self-justification such as she had known under Lydgate's most stormy displeasure ; all her sensibility was turned into a bewildering novelty of pain ; she felt a new terrified recoil under a lash never experienced before. What another nature felt in opposition to her own was being burnt and bitten into her consciousness. When Will had ceased to speak she had become an image of sickened misery : her lips were pale, and her eyes had a tearless dismay in them. If it had been Tertius who stood opposite to her, that look of misery would have been a pang to him, and he would have sunk by her side to comfort her, with that strong-armed comfort which she had often held very cheap.

Let it be forgiven to Will that he had no such movement of pity. He had felt no bond beforehand to this woman who had spoiled the ideal treasure of his life, and he held himself blameless. He knew that he was cruel, but he had no relenting in him yet.

After he had done speaking, he still moved about, half in absence of mind, and Rosamond sat perfectly still. At length Will, seeming to bethink himself, took up his hat, yet stood some moments irresolute. He had spoken to her in a way that made a phrase of common politeness difficult to utter ; and yet, now that he had come to the point of going away from her without further speech, he shrank from it as a brutality ; he felt checked and stultified in his anger. He walked towards the mantelpiece and leaned his arm on it, and waited in silence for —he hardly knew what. The vindictive fire was still burning in him, and he could utter no word of retractation; but it was nevertheless in his mind that having come back to this hearth where he had enjoyed a caressing friendship he had found calamity seated there—he had had suddenly revealed to him a trouble that lay outside the home as well as within it. And what seemed a foreboding was pressing upon him as with slow pincers :—that his life might come to be enslaved by this helpless woman who had thrown herself upon him in the dreary sadness of her heart. But he was in gloomy rebellion against the fact that his quick apprehensiveness foreshadowed to him, and when his eyes fell on Rosamond's blighted face it seemed to him that he was the more pitiable of the two : for pain must enter into its glorified life of memory before it can turn into compassion.

And so they remained for many minutes, opposite each other, far apart, in silence; Will's face still possessed by a mute rage, and Rosamond's by a mute misery. The poor thing had no force to fling out any passion in return; the terrible collapse of the illusion towards which all her hope had been strained was a stroke which had too thoroughly shaken her : her little world was in ruins, and she felt herself tottering in the midst as a lonely bewildered consciousness.

Will wished that she would speak and bring some mitigating shadow across his own cruel speech, which seemed to stand staring at them both in mockery of any attempt at revived fellowship. But she said nothing, and at last with a desperate effort over himself, he asked, " Shall I come in and see Lydgate this evening ? "

" If you like," Rosamond answered, just audibly.

And then Will went out of the house, Martha never knowing that he had been in.

After he was gone, Rosamond tried to get up from her seat, but fell back fainting. When she came to herself again, she felt too ill to make the exertion of rising to ring the bell, and she remained helpless until the girl, surprised at her long absence, thought for the first time of looking for her in all the down-stairs rooms. Rosamond said that she had felt suddenly sick and faint, and wanted to be helped up-stairs. When there she threw herself on the bed with her clothes on, and lay in apparent torpor, as she had done once before on a memorable day of grief.

Lydgate came home earlier than he had expected, about half-past five, and found her there. The perception that she was ill threw every other thought into the background. When he felt her pulse, her eyes rested on him with more persistence than they had done for a long while, as if she felt some content that he was there. He perceived the difference in a moment, and seating himself by her put his arm gently under her, and bending over her said, " My poor Rosamond ! has something agitated you ? " Clinging to him she fell into hysterical sobbings and cries, and for the next hour he did nothing but soothe and tend her. He imagined that Dorothea had been to see her, and that all this effect on her nervous system, which evidently involved some new turning towards himself, was due to the excitement of the new impressions which that visit had raised.

CHAPTER LXXIX

" Now, I saw in my dream, that just as they had ended their talk, they drew nigh to a very miry slough, that was in the midst of the plain ; and they, being heedless, did both fall suddenly into the bog. The name of the slough was Despond."—BUNYAN.

WHEN Rosamond was quiet, and Lydgate had left her, hoping that she might soon sleep under the effect of an anodyne, he went into the drawing-room to fetch a book which he had left there, meaning to spend the evening in his work-room, and he saw on the table Dorothea's letter addressed to him. He had not ventured to ask Rosamond if Mrs. Casaubon had called, but the reading of this letter assured him of the fact, for Dorothea mentioned that it was to be carried by herself.

When Will Ladislaw came in a little later, Lydgate met him with a surprise which made it clear that he had not been told of the earlier visit, and Will could not say, "Did not Mrs. Lydgate tell you that I came this morning ? "

" Poor Rosamond is ill," Lydgate added immediately on his greeting.

" Not seriously, I hope," said Will.

" No—only a slight nervous shock—the effect of some agitation. She has been overwrought lately. The truth is, Ladislaw, I am an unlucky devil. We have gone through several rounds of purgatory since you left, and I have lately got on to a worse ledge of it than ever. I suppose you are only just come down—you look rather battered—you have not been long enough in the town to hear anything ? "

"I travelled all night and got to the White Hart at eight o'clock this morning. I have been shutting myself up and resting," said Will, feeling himself a sneak, but seeing no alternative to this evasion.

And then he heard Lydgate's account of the troubles which Rosamond had already depicted to him in her way. She had not mentioned the fact of Will's name being connected with the public story—this detail not immediately affecting her—and he now heard it for the first time.

"I thought it better to tell you that your name is mixed up with the disclosures," said Lydgate, who could understand better than most men how Ladislaw might be stung by the revelation. "You will be sure to hear it as soon as you turn out into the town. I suppose it is true that Raffles spoke to you."

"Yes," said Will, sardonically. "I shall be fortunate if gossip does not make me the most disreputable person in the whole affair. I should think the latest version must be, that I plotted with Raffles to murder Bulstrode, and ran away from Middlemarch for the purpose."

He was thinking "Here is a new ring in the sound of my name to recommend it in her hearing; however—what does it signify now?"

But he said nothing of Bulstrode's offer to him. Will was very open and careless about his personal affairs, but it was among the more exquisite touches in nature's modelling of him that he had a delicate generosity which warned him into reticence here. He shrank from saying that he had rejected Bulstrode's money, in the moment when he was learning that it was Lydgate's misfortune to have accepted it.

Lydgate too was reticent in the midst of his confidence. He made no allusion to Rosamond's feeling under their trouble, and of Dorothea he only said, "Mrs. Casaubon has been the one person to come forward and say that she had no belief in any of the suspicions against me." Observing a change in Will's face, he avoided any further mention of her, feeling himself too ignorant of their relation to each other not to fear that his words might have some hidden painful bearing on it. And it occurred to him that Dorothea was the real cause of the present visit to Middlemarch.

The two men were pitying each other, but it was only Will who guessed the extent of his companion's trouble. When Lydgate spoke with desperate resignation of going to settle in

London, and said with a faint smile, " We shall have you again, old fellow," Will felt inexpressibly mournful, and said nothing. Rosamond had that morning entreated him to urge this step on Lydgate ; and it seemed to him as if he were beholding in a magic panorama a future where he himself was sliding into that pleasureless yielding to the small solicitations of circumstance, which is a commoner history of perdition than any single momentous bargain.

We are on a perilous margin when we begin to look passively at our future selves, and see our own figures led with dull consent into insipid misdoing and shabby achievement. Poor Lydgate was inwardly groaning on that margin, and Will was arriving at it. It seemed to him this evening as if the cruelty of his outburst to Rosamond had made an obligation for him, and he dreaded the obligation : he dreaded Lydgate's unsuspecting goodwill : he dreaded his own distaste for his spoiled life, which would leave him in motiveless levity.

CHAPTER LXXX

" Stern lawgiver ! yet thou dost wear
The Godhead's most benignant grace ;
Nor know we anything so fair
As is the smile upon thy face ;
Flowers laugh before thee on their beds,
And fragrance in thy footing treads ;
Thou dost preserve the Stars from wrong ;
And the most ancient Heavens, through thee, are fresh and strong."
—WORDSWORTH : *Ode to Duty.*

WHEN Dorothea had seen Mr. Farebrother in the morning, she had promised to go and dine at the parsonage on her return from Freshitt. There was a frequent interchange of visits between her and the Farebrother family, which enabled her to say that she was not at all lonely at the Manor, and to resist for the present the severe prescription of a lady companion. When she reached home and remembered her engagement, she was glad of it ; and finding that she had still an hour before she could dress for dinner, she walked straight to the schoolhouse and entered into a conversation with the master and mistress about the new bell, giving eager attention to their small details and repetitions, and getting up a dramatic sense that her life was very busy. She paused on her way back to talk to old Master Bunney who was putting in some garden-seeds, and discoursed wisely with that rural sage about the crops that would make the most return on a perch of ground, and the result of sixty years' experience as to soils—namely, that if your soil was pretty mellow it would do, but if there came wet, wet, wet to make it all of a mummy, why then——

Finding that the social spirit had beguiled her into being rather late, she dressed hastily and went over to the parsonage rather earlier than was necessary. That house was never dull, Mr. Farebrother, like another White of Selborne, having continually something new to tell of his inarticulate guests and *protégés*, whom he was teaching the boys not to torment ; and he had just set up a pair of beautiful goats to be pets of the village in general, and to walk at large as sacred animals. The evening went by cheerfully till after tea, Dorothea talking more than usual and dilating with Mr. Farebrother on the possible histories of creatures that converse compendiously with their antennæ, and for aught we know may hold reformed parliaments ; when suddenly some inarticulate little sounds were heard which called everybody's attention.

"Henrietta Noble," said Mrs. Farebrother, seeing her small sister moving about the furniture-legs distressfully, "what is the matter ? "

"I have lost my tortoise-shell lozenge-box. I fear the kitten has rolled it away," said the tiny old lady, involuntarily continuing her beaver-like notes.

"Is it a great treasure, aunt ? " said Mr. Farebrother, putting up his glasses and looking at the carpet.

"Mr. Ladislaw gave it me," said Miss Noble. "A German box—very pretty ; but if it falls it always spins away as far as it can."

"Oh, if it is Ladislaw's present," said Mr. Farebrother, in a deep tone of comprehension, getting up and hunting. The box was found at last under a chiffonier, and Miss Noble grasped it with delight, saying, "It was under a fender the last time."

"That is an affair of the heart with my aunt," said Mr. Farebrother, smiling at Dorothea, as he reseated himself.

"If Henrietta Noble forms an attachment to any one, Mrs. Casaubon," said his mother, emphatically,—"she is like a dog—she would take their shoes for a pillow and sleep the better."

"Mr. Ladislaw's shoes, I would," said Henrietta Noble.

Dorothea made an attempt at smiling in return. She was surprised and annoyed to find that her heart was palpitating violently, and that it was quite useless to try after a recovery of her former animation. Alarmed at herself—fearing some further betrayal of a change so marked in its occasion, she rose and said in a low voice with undisguised anxiety, " I must go ; I have overtired myself."

Mr. Farebrother, quick in perception, rose and said, " It is true ; you must have half-exhausted yourself in talking about Lydgate. That sort of work tells upon one after the excitement is over."

He gave her his arm back to the Manor, but Dorothea did not attempt to speak, even when he said good-night.

The limit of resistance was reached, and she had sunk back helpless within the clutch of inescapable anguish. Dismissing Tantripp with a few faint words, she locked her door, and turning away from it towards the vacant room she pressed her hands hard on the top of her head, and moaned out—

" Oh, I did love him ! "

Then came the hour in which the waves of suffering shook her too thoroughly to leave any power of thought. She could only cry in loud whispers, between her sobs, after her lost belief which she had planted and kept alive from a very little seed since the days in Rome—after her lost joy of clinging with silent love and faith to one who, misprized by others, was worthy in her thought— after her lost woman's pride of reigning in his memory—after her sweet dim perspective of hope, that along some pathway they should meet with unchanged recognition and take up the backward years as a yesterday.

In that hour she repeated what the merciful eyes of solitude have looked on for ages in the spiritual struggles of man—she besought hardness and coldness and aching weariness to bring her relief from the mysterious incorporeal might of her anguish : she lay on the bare floor and let the night grow cold around her ; while her grand woman's frame was shaken by sobs as if she had been a despairing child.

There were two images—two living forms that tore her heart in two, as if it had been the heart of a mother who seems to see her child divided by the sword, and presses one bleeding half to her breast while her gaze goes forth in agony towards the half which is carried away by the lying woman that has never known the mother's pang.

Here, with the nearness of an answering smile, here within the vibrating bond of mutual speech, was the bright creature whom she had trusted—who had come to her like the spirit of morning visiting the dim vault where she sat as the bride of a worn-out life ; and now, with a full consciousness which had never awakened before, she stretched out her arms towards him and cried with bitter cries that their nearness was a parting vision : she discovered her passion to herself in the unshrinking utterance of despair.

And there, aloof, yet persistently with her, moving wherever she moved, was the Will Ladislaw who was a changed belief exhausted of hope, a detected illusion—no, a living man towards whom there could not yet struggle any wail of regretful pity, from the midst of scorn and indignation and jealous offended pride. The fire of Dorothea's anger was not easily spent, and it flamed out in fitful returns of spurning reproach. Why had he come obtruding his life into hers, hers that might have been whole enough without him ? Why had he brought his cheap regard and his lip-born words to her who had nothing paltry to give in exchange ? He knew that he was deluding her—wished, in the very moment of farewell, to make her believe that he gave her the whole price of her heart, and knew that he had spent it half before. Why had he not stayed among the crowd of whom she asked nothing—but only prayed that they might be less contemptible ?

But she lost energy at last even for her loud-whispered cries and moans : she subsided into helpless sobs, and on the cold floor she sobbed herself to sleep.

In the chill hours of the morning twilight, when all was dim around her, she awoke—not with any amazed wondering where she was or what had happened, but with the clearest consciousness that she was looking into the eyes of sorrow. She rose, and wrapped warm things around her, and seated herself in a great chair where she had often watched before. She was vigorous enough to have borne that hard night without feeling ill in body, beyond some aching and fatigue ; but she had waked to a new condition : she felt as if her soul had been liberated from its terrible conflict ; she was no longer wrestling with her grief, but could sit down with it as a lasting companion and make it a sharer in her thoughts. For now the thoughts came thickly. It was not in Dorothea's nature, for longer than the duration of a paroxysm, to sit in the narrow cell of her calamity, in the besotted misery of a consciousness that only sees another's lot as an accident of its own.

She began now to live through that yesterday morning deliberately again, forcing herself to dwell on every detail and

its possible meaning. Was she alone in that scene? Was it
her event only? She forced herself to think of it as bound up
with another woman's life—a woman towards whom she had
set out with a longing to carry some clearness and comfort into
her beclouded youth. In her first outleap of jealous indignation
and disgust, when quitting the hateful room, she had flung away
all the mercy with which she had undertaken that visit. She
had enveloped both Will and Rosamond in her burning scorn,
and it seemed to her as if Rosamond were burned out of her sight
for ever. But that base prompting which makes a woman
more cruel to a rival than to a faithless lover, could have no
strength of recurrence in Dorothea when the dominant spirit
of justice within her had once overcome the tumult and had
once shown her the truer measure of things. All the active
thought with which she had before been representing to herself
the trials of Lydgate's lot, and this young marriage union which,
like her own, seemed to have its hidden as well as evident
troubles—all this vivid sympathetic experience returned to her
now as a power: it asserted itself as acquired knowledge asserts
itself and will not let us see as we saw in the day of our ignorance.
She said to her own irremediable grief, that it should make her
more helpful, instead of driving her back from effort.

And what sort of crisis might not this be in three lives whose
contact with hers laid an obligation on her as if they had been
suppliants bearing the sacred branch? The objects of her
rescue were not to be sought out by her fancy: they were
chosen for her. She yearned towards the perfect Right, that it
might make a throne within her, and rule her errant will.
" What should I do—how should I act now, this very day if
I could clutch my own pain, and compel it to silence, and think
of those three ! "

It had taken long for her to come to that question, and there
was light piercing into the room. She opened her curtains, and
looked out towards the bit of road that lay in view, with fields
beyond, outside the entrance-gates. On the road there was a
man with a bundle on his back and a woman carrying her baby ;
in the field she could see figures moving—perhaps the shepherd
with his dog. Far off in the bending sky was the pearly light ;
and she felt the largeness of the world and the manifold wakings
of men to labour and endurance. She was a part of that
involuntary, palpitating life, and could neither look out on it
from her luxurious shelter as a mere spectator, nor hide her
eyes in selfish complaining.

What she would resolve to do that day did not yet seem quite
clear, but something that she could achieve stirred her as with
an approaching murmur which would soon gather distinctness.
She took off the clothes which seemed to have some of the
weariness of a hard watching in them, and began to make her
toilet. Presently she rang for Tantripp, who came in her
dressing-gown.

"Why, madam, you've never been in bed this blessed night,"
burst out Tantripp, looking first at the bed and then at Dorothea's
face, which in spite of bathing had the pale cheeks and pink
eyelids of a *mater dolorosa.* "You'll kill yourself, you *will.*
Anybody might think now you had a right to give yourself
a little comfort."

"Don't be alarmed, Tantripp," said Dorothea, smiling.
"I have slept; I am not ill. I shall be glad of a cup of coffee
as soon as possible. And I want you to bring me my new
dress; and most likely I shall want my new bonnet to-day."

"They've lain there a month and more ready for you, madam,
and most thankful I shall be to see you with a couple o' pounds'
worth less of crape," said Tantripp, stooping to light the fire.
"There's a reason in mourning, as I've always said; and three
folds at the bottom of your skirt and a plain quilling in your
bonnet—and if ever anybody looked like an angel, it's you in
a net quilling—is what's consistent for a second year. At
least, that's *my* thinking," ended Tantripp, looking anxiously
at the fire; "and if anybody was to marry me flattering himself
I should wear those hijeous weepers two years for him, he'd
be deceived by his own vanity, that's all."

"The fire will do, my good Tan," said Dorothea, speaking as
she used to do in the old Lausanne days, only with a very low
voice; "get me the coffee."

She folded herself in the large chair, and leaned her head
against it in fatigued quiescence, while Tantripp went away
wondering at this strange contrariness in her young mistress—
that just the morning when she had more of a widow's face than
ever, she should have asked for her lighter mourning which she
had waived before. Tantripp would never have found the clue
to this mystery. Dorothea wished to acknowledge that she
had not the less an active life before her because she had buried
a private joy; and the tradition that fresh garments belonged
to all initiation, haunting her mind, made her grasp after even
that slight outward help towards calm resolve. For the resolve
was not easy.

Nevertheless at eleven o'clock she was walking towards Middlemarch, having made up her mind that she would make as quietly and unnoticeably as possible her second attempt to see and save Rosamond.

CHAPTER LXXXI

> " Du Erde warst auch diese Nacht beständig,
> Und athmest neu erquickt zu meinen Füssen,
> Beginnest schon mit Lust mich zu umgeben,
> Du regst und rührst ein kräftiges Beschliessen
> *Zum höchsten Dasein immerfort zu streben.*"
> —*Faust*: 2r Theil.

WHEN Dorothea was again at Lydgate's door speaking to Martha, he was in the room close by with the door ajar, preparing to go out.   He heard her voice, and immediately came to her.

" Do you think that Mrs. Lydgate can receive me this morning ? " she said, having reflected that it would be better to leave out all allusion to her previous visit.

" I have no doubt she will," said Lydgate, suppressing his thought about Dorothea's looks, which were as much changed as Rosamond's, " if you will be kind enough to come in and let me tell her that you are here.   She has not been very well since you were here yesterday, but she is better this morning, and I think it is very likely that she will be cheered by seeing you again."

It was plain that Lydgate, as Dorothea had expected, knew nothing about the circumstances of her yesterday's visit ; nay, he appeared to imagine that she had carried it out according to her intention.   She had prepared a little note asking Rosamond to see her, which she would have given to the servant if he had not been in the way, but now she was in much anxiety as to the result of his announcement.

After leading her into the drawing-room, he paused to take a letter from his pocket and put it into her hands, saying, " I wrote this last night, and was going to carry it to Lowick in my ride.   When one is grateful for something too good for common thanks, writing is less unsatisfactory than speech—one does not at least *hear* how inadequate the words are."

Dorothea's face brightened.   " It is I who have most to thank for, since you have let me take that place.   You *have* consented ? " she said, suddenly doubting.

" Yes, the cheque is going to Bulstrode to-day."

He said no more, but went up-stairs to Rosamond, who had but lately finished dressing herself, and sat languidly wondering what she should do next, her habitual industry in small things, even in the days of her sadness, prompting her to begin some kind of occupation, which she dragged through slowly or paused in from lack of interest. She looked ill, but had recovered her usual quietude of manner, and Lydgate had feared to disturb her by any questions. He had told her of Dorothea's letter containing the cheque, and afterwards he had said, " Ladislaw is come, Rosy ; he sat with me last night ; I daresay he will be here again to-day. I thought he looked rather battered and depressed." And Rosamond had made no reply.

Now, when he came up, he said to her very gently, " Rosy, dear, Mrs. Casaubon is come to see you again ; you would like to see her, would you not ? " That she coloured and gave rather a startled movement did not surprise him after the agitation produced by the interview yesterday—a beneficent agitation, he thought, since it seemed to have made her turn to him again.

Rosamond dared not say no. She dared not with a tone of her voice touch the facts of yesterday. Why had Mrs. Casaubon come again ? The answer was a blank which Rosamond could only fill up with dread, for Will Ladislaw's lacerating words had made every thought of Dorothea a fresh smart to her. Nevertheless, in her new humiliating uncertainty she dared do nothing but comply. She did not say yes, but she rose and let Lydgate put a light shawl over her shoulders, while he said, " I am going out immediately." Then something crossed her mind which prompted her to say, " Pray tell Martha not to bring any one else into the drawing-room." And Lydgate assented, thinking that he fully understood this wish. He led her down to the drawing-room door, and then turned away, observing to himself that he was rather a blundering husband to be dependent for his wife's trust in him on the influence of another woman.

Rosamond, wrapping her soft shawl around her as she walked towards Dorothea, was inwardly wrapping her soul in cold reserve. Had Mrs. Casaubon come to say anything to her about Will ? If so, it was a liberty that Rosamond resented ; and she prepared herself to meet every word with polite impassibility. Will had bruised her pride too sorely for her to feel any compunction towards him and Dorothea : her own injury seemed much the greater. Dorothea was not only the

" preferred " woman, but had also a formidable advantage in being Lydgate's benefactor ; and to poor Rosamond's pained confused vision it seemed that this Mrs. Casaubon—this woman who predominated in all things concerning her—must have come now with the sense of having the advantage, and with animosity prompting her to use it. Indeed, not Rosamond only, but any one else, knowing the outer facts of the case, and not the simple inspiration on which Dorothea acted, might well have wondered why she came.

Looking like the lovely ghost of herself, her graceful slimness wrapped in her soft white shawl, the rounded infantine mouth and cheek inevitably suggesting mildness and innocence, Rosamond paused at three yards' distance from her visitor and bowed. But Dorothea, who had taken off her gloves, from an impulse which she could never resist when she wanted a sense of freedom, came forward, and with her face full of a sad yet sweet openness, put out her hand. Rosamond could not avoid meeting her glance, could not avoid putting her small hand into Dorothea's, which clasped it with gentle mother-liness ; and immediately a doubt of her own prepossessions began to stir within her. Rosamond's eye was quick for faces ; she saw that Mrs. Casaubon's face looked pale and changed since yesterday, yet gentle, and like the firm softness of her hand. But Dorothea had counted a little too much on her own strength: the clearness and intensity of her mental action this morning were the continuance of a nervous exaltation which made her frame as dangerously responsive as a bit of finest Venetian crystal ; and in looking at Rosamond, she suddenly found her heart swelling, and was unable to speak—all her effort was required to keep back tears. She succeeded in that, and the emotion only passed over her face like the spirit of a sob ; but it added to Rosamond's impression that Mrs. Casaubon's state of mind must be something quite different from what she had imagined.

So they sat down without a word of preface on the two chairs that happened to be nearest, and happened also to be close together ; though Rosamond's notion when she first bowed was that she should stay a long way off from Mrs. Casaubon. But she ceased thinking how anything would turn out—merely wondering what would come. And Dorothea began to speak quite simply, gathering firmness as she went on.

" I had an errand yesterday which I did not finish ; that is why I am here again so soon. You will not think me too troublesome, when I tell you that I came to talk to you about the injustice that has been shown towards Mr. Lydgate. It will cheer you—will it not ?—to know a great deal about him, that he may not like to speak about himself just because it is in his own vindication and to his own honour. You will like to know that your husband has warm friends, who have not left off believing in his high character ? You will let me speak of this without thinking that I take a liberty ? "

The cordial, pleading tones which seemed to flow with generous heedlessness above all the facts which had filled Rosamond's mind as grounds of obstruction and hatred between her and this woman, came as soothingly as a warm stream over her shrinking fears. Of course Mrs. Casaubon had the facts in her mind, but she was not going to speak of anything connected with them. That relief was too great for Rosamond to feel much else at the moment. She answered prettily, in the new ease of her soul—

" I know you have been very good. I shall like to hear anything you will say to me about Tertius."

" The day before yesterday," said Dorothea, " when I had asked him to come to Lowick to give me his opinion on the affairs of the Hospital, he told me everything about his conduct and feelings in this sad event which has made ignorant people cast suspicions on him. The reason he told me was because I was very bold and asked him. I believed that he had never acted dishonourably, and I begged him to tell me the history. He confessed to me that he had never told it before, not even to you, because he had a great dislike to say, ' I was not wrong,' as if that were proof, when there are guilty people who will say so. The truth is, he knew nothing of this man Raffles, or that there were any bad secrets about him ; and he thought that Mr. Bulstrode offered him the money because he repented, out of kindness, of having refused it before. All his anxiety about his patient was to treat him rightly, and he was a little uncomfortable that the case did not end as he had expected ; but he thought then and still thinks that there may have been no wrong in it on any one's part. And I have told Mr. Farebrother, and Mr. Brooke, and Sir James Chettam : they all believe in your husband. That will cheer you, will it not ? That will give you courage ? "

Dorothea's face had become animated, and as it beamed on Rosamond very close to her, she felt something like bashful timidity before a superior, in the presence of this self-forgetful

ardour. She said, with blushing embarrassment, "Thank
you : you are very kind."

"And he felt that he had been so wrong not to pour out
everything about this to you. But you will forgive him. It
was because he feels so much more about your happiness than
anything else—he feels his life bound into one with yours, and
it hurts him more than anything, that his misfortunes must
hurt you. He could speak to me because I am an indifferent
person. And then I asked him if I might come to see you ;
because I felt so much for his trouble and yours. That is why
I came yesterday, and why I am come to-day. Trouble is so
hard to bear, is it not ?—How can we live and think that any
one has trouble—piercing trouble—and we could help them,
and never try ? "

Dorothea, completely swayed by the feeling that she was
uttering, forgot everything but that she was speaking from out
the heart of her own trial to Rosamond's. The emotion had
wrought itself more and more into her utterance, till the tones
might have gone to one's very marrow, like a low cry from some
suffering creature in the darkness. And she had unconsciously
laid her hand again on the little hand that she had pressed
before.

Rosamond, with an overmastering pang, as if a wound within
her had been probed, burst into hysterical crying as she had
done the day before when she clung to her husband. Poor
Dorothea was feeling a great wave of her own sorrow returning
over her—her thought being drawn to the possible share that
Will Ladislaw might have in Rosamond's mental tumult. She
was beginning to fear that she should not be able to suppress
herself enough to the end of this meeting, and while her hand
was still resting on Rosamond's lap, though the hand underneath
it was withdrawn, she was struggling against her own rising
sobs. She tried to master herself with the thought that this
might be a turning-point in three lives—not in her own ; no,
there the irrevocable had happened, but—in those three lives
which were touching hers with the solemn neighbourhood of
danger and distress. The fragile creature who was crying close
to her—there might still be time to rescue her from the misery
of false incompatible bonds ; and this moment was unlike any
other : she and Rosamond could never be together again with
the same thrilling consciousness of yesterday within them both.
She felt the relation between them to be peculiar enough to
give her a peculiar influence, though she had no conception

that the way in which her own feelings were involved was fully known to Mrs. Lydgate.

It was a newer crisis in Rosamond's experience than even Dorothea could imagine : she was under the first great shock that had shattered her dream-world in which she had been easily confident of herself and critical of others ; and this strange unexpected manifestation of feeling in a woman whom she had approached with a shrinking aversion and dread, as one who must necessarily have a jealous hatred towards her, made her soul totter all the more with a sense that she had been walking in an unknown world which had just broken in upon her.

When Rosamond's convulsed throat was subsiding into calm, and she withdrew the handkerchief with which she had been hiding her face, her eyes met Dorothea's as helplessly as if they had been blue flowers. What was the use of thinking about behaviour after this crying ? And Dorothea looked almost as childish, with the neglected trace of a silent tear. Pride was broken down between these two.

" We were talking about your husband," Dorothea said, with some timidity. " I thought his looks were sadly changed with suffering the other day. I had not seen him for many weeks before. He said he had been feeling very lonely in his trial ; but I think he would have borne it all better if he had been able to be quite open with you."

" Tertius is so angry and impatient if I say anything," said Rosamond, imagining that he had been complaining of her to Dorothea. " He ought not to wonder that I object to speak to him on painful subjects."

" It was himself he blamed for not speaking," said Dorothea. " What he said of you was, that he could not be happy in doing anything which made you unhappy—that his marriage was of course a bond which must affect his choice about everything ; and for that reason he refused my proposal that he should keep his position at the Hospital, because that would bind him to stay in Middlemarch, and he would not undertake to do anything which would be painful to you. He could say that to me, because he knows that I had much trial in my marriage, from my husband's illness, which hindered his plans and saddened him ; and he knows that I have felt how hard it is to walk always in fear of hurting another who is tied to us."

Dorothea waited a little ; she had discerned a faint pleasure stealing over Rosamond's face. But there was no answer, and she went on, with a gathering tremor, " Marriage is so unlike

everything else. There is something even awful in the nearness
it brings. Even if we loved some one else better than—than
those we were married to, it would be no use "—poor Dorothea,
in her palpitating anxiety, could only seize her language brokenly
—" I mean, marriage drinks up all our power of giving or
getting any blessedness in that sort of love. I know it may
be very dear—but it murders our marriage—and then the
marriage stays with us like a murder—and everything else is
gone. And then our husband—if he loved and trusted us, and
we have not helped him, but made a curse in his life . . ."

Her voice had sunk very low : there was a dread upon her of
presuming too far, and of speaking as if she herself were perfection addressing error. She was too much preoccupied with her
own anxiety, to be aware that Rosamond was trembling too ;
and filled with the need to express pitying fellowship rather than
rebuke, she put her hands on Rosamond's, and said with more
agitated rapidity,—" I know, I know that the feeling may be
very dear—it has taken hold of us unawares—it is so hard, it
may seem like death to part with it—and we are weak—I am
weak——"

The waves of her own sorrow, from out of which she was
struggling to save another, rushed over Dorothea with con-
quering force. She stopped in speechless agitation, not crying,
but feeling as if she were being inwardly grappled. Her face
had become of a deathlier paleness, her lips trembled, and
she pressed her hands helplessly on the hands that lay under
them.

Rosamond, taken hold of by an emotion stronger than her
own—hurried along in a new movement which gave all things
some new, awful, undefined aspect—could find no words, but
involuntarily she put her lips to Dorothea's forehead which was
very near her, and then for a minute the two women clasped
each other as if they had been in a shipwreck.

" You are thinking what is not true," said Rosamond, in an
eager half-whisper, while she was still feeling Dorothea's arms
round her—urged by a mysterious necessity to free herself from
something that oppressed her as if it were blood-guiltiness.

They moved apart, looking at each other.

" When you came in yesterday—it was not as you thought,"
said Rosamond in the same tone.

There was a movement of surprised attention in Dorothea
She expected a vindication of Rosamond herself.

" He was telling me how he loved another woman, that I

might know he could never love me," said Rosamond, getting more and more hurried as she went on. "And now I think he hates me because—because you mistook him yesterday. He says it is through me that you will think ill of him—think that he is a false person. But it shall not be through me. He has never had any love for me—I know he has not—he has always thought slightly of me. He said yesterday that no other woman existed for him besides you. The blame of what happened is entirely mine. He said he could never explain to you —because of me. He said you could never think well of him again. But now I have told you, and he cannot reproach me any more."

Rosamond had delivered her soul under impulses which she had not known before. She had begun her confession under the subduing influence of Dorothea's emotion ; and as she went on she had gathered the sense that she was repelling Will's reproaches, which were still like a knife-wound within her.

The revulsion of feeling in Dorothea was too strong to be called joy. It was a tumult in which the terrible strain of the night and morning made a resistant pain :—she could only perceive that this would be joy when she had recovered her power of feeling it. Her immediate consciousness was one of immense sympathy without check ; she cared for Rosamond without struggle now, and responded earnestly to her last words :

"No, he cannot reproach you any more."

With her usual tendency to over-estimate the good in others, she felt a great outgoing of her heart towards Rosamond for the generous effort which had redeemed her from suffering, not counting that the effort was a reflex of her own energy.

After they had been silent a little, she said—

"You are not sorry that I came this morning ? "

"No, you have been very good to me," said Rosamond. "I did not think that you would be so good. I was very unhappy. I am not happy now. Everything is so sad."

"But better days will come. Your husband will be rightly valued. And he depends on you for comfort. He loves you best. The worst loss would be to lose that—and you have not lost it," said Dorothea.

She tried to thrust away the too overpowering thought of her own relief, lest she should fail to win some sign that Rosamond's affection was yearning back towards her husband.

"Tertius did not find fault with me, then ? " said Rosamond, understanding now that Lydgate might have said anything to Mrs. Casaubon, and that she certainly was different from other women. Perhaps there was a faint taste of jealousy in the question. A smile began to play over Dorothea's face as she said—

"No, indeed! How could you imagine it?" But here the door opened, and Lydgate entered.

"I am come back in my quality of doctor," he said. "After I went away, I was haunted by two pale faces: Mrs. Casaubon looked as much in need of care as you, Rosy. And I thought that I had not done my duty in leaving you together; so when I had been to Coleman's I came home again. I noticed that you were walking, Mrs. Casaubon, and the sky has changed—I think we may have rain. May I send some one to order your carriage to come for you?"

"Oh no! I am strong: I need the walk," said Dorothea, rising with animation in her face. "Mrs. Lydgate and I have chatted a great deal, and it is time for me to go. I have always been accused of being immoderate and saying too much."

She put out her hand to Rosamond, and they said an earnest, quiet good-bye without kiss or other show of effusion: there had been between them too much serious emotion for them to use the signs of it superficially.

As Lydgate took her to the door she said nothing of Rosamond, but told him of Mr. Farebrother and the other friends who had listened with belief to his story.

When he came back to Rosamond, she had already thrown herself on the sofa, in resigned fatigue.

"Well, Rosy," he said, standing over her, and touching her hair, "what do you think of Mrs. Casaubon now you have seen so much of her?"

"I think she must be better than any one," said Rosamond, "and she is very beautiful. If you go to talk to her so often, you will be more discontented with me than ever!"

Lydgate laughed at the "so often." "But has she made you any less discontented with me"

"I think she has," said Rosamond, looking up in his face. "How heavy your eyes are, Tertius—and do push your hair back." He lifted up his large white hand to obey her, and felt thankful for this little mark of interest in him. Poor Rosamond's vagrant fancy had come back terribly scourged—meek enough to nestle under the old despised shelter. And the shelter was still there: Lydgate had accepted his narrowed lot with sad resignation. He had chosen this fragile creature, and had taken the burthen of her life upon his arms. He must walk as he could, carrying that burthen pitifully.

CHAPTER LXXXII

" My grief lies onward and my joy behind."
—SHAKESPEARE : *Sonnets.*

EXILES notoriously feed much on hopes, and are unlikely to stay in banishment unless they are obliged. When Will Ladislaw exiled himself from Middlemarch he had placed no stronger obstacle to his return than his own resolve, which was by no means an iron barrier, but simply a state of mind liable to melt into a minuet with other states of mind, and to find itself bowing, smiling, and giving place with polite facility. As the months went on, it had seemed more and more difficult to him to say why he should not run down to Middlemarch—merely for the sake of hearing something about Dorothea ; and if on such a flying visit he should chance by some strange coincidence to meet with her, there was no reason for him to be ashamed of having taken an innocent journey which he had beforehand supposed that he should not take. Since he was hopelessly divided from her, he might surely venture into her neighbourhood ; and as to the suspicious friends who kept a dragon watch over her—their opinions seemed less and less important with time and change of air.

And there had come a reason quite irrespective of Dorothea, which seemed to make a journey to Middlemarch a sort of philanthropic duty. Will had given a disinterested attention to an intended settlement on a new plan in the Far West, and the need for funds in order to carry out a good design had set him on debating with himself whether it would not be a laudable use to make of his claim on Bulstrode, to urge the application of that money which had been offered to himself as a means of carrying out a scheme likely to be largely beneficial. The question seemed a very dubious one to Will, and his repugnance to again entering into any relation with the banker might have made him dismiss it quickly, if there had not arisen in his imagination the probability that his judgment might be more safely determined by a visit to Middlemarch.

That was the object which Will stated to himself as a reason for coming down. He had meant to confide in Lydgate, and discuss the money question with him, and he had meant to amuse himself for the few evenings of his stay by having a great deal of music and badinage with fair Rosamond, without neglecting his friends at Lowick Parsonage :—if the Parsonage was close to the Manor, that was no fault of his. He had neglected the Farebrothers before his departure, from a proud resistance to the possible accusation of indirectly seeking interviews with Dorothea ; but hunger tames us, and Will had become very hungry for the vision of a certain form and the sound of a certain voice. Nothing had done instead—not the opera, or the converse of zealous politicians, or the flattering reception (in dim corners) of his new hand in leading articles.

Thus he had come down, foreseeing with confidence how almost everything would be in his familiar little world ; fearing, indeed, that there would be no surprises in his visit. But he had found that humdrum world in a terribly dynamic condition, in which even badinage and lyrism had turned explosive ; and the first day of this visit had become the most fatal epoch of his life. The next morning he felt so harassed with the nightmare of consequences—he dreaded so much the immediate issues before him—that seeing while he breakfasted the arrival of the Riverston coach, he went out hurriedly and took his place on it, that he might be relieved, at least for a day, from the necessity of doing or saying anything in Middlemarch. Will Ladislaw was in one of those tangled crises which are commoner in experience than one might imagine, from the shallow absoluteness of men's judgments. He had found Lydgate, for whom he had the sincerest respect, under circumstances which claimed his thorough and frankly-declared sympathy ; and the reason why, in spite of that claim, it would have been better for Will to have avoided all further intimacy, or even contact, with Lydgate, was precisely of the kind to make such a course appear impossible. To a creature of Will's susceptible temperament— without any neutral region of indifference in his nature, ready to turn everything that befell him into the collisions of a passionate drama—the revelation that Rosamond had made her happiness in any way dependent on him was a difficulty which his outburst of rage towards her had immeasurably increased for him. He hated his own cruelty, and yet he dreaded to show the fulness of his relenting : he must go to her again ; the friendship could not be put to a sudden end ; and her unhappiness was a power which he dreaded. And all the while there was no more foretaste of enjoyment in the life before him than if his limbs had been lopped off and he was making his fresh start on crutches. In the night he had debated whether he should not get on the coach, not for Riverston, but for London, leaving a note to Lydgate which would give a makeshift reason for his retreat. But there were strong cords pulling him back from that abrupt departure : the blight on his happiness in thinking of Dorothea, the crushing of that chief hope which had remained in spite of the acknowledged necessity for renunciation, was too fresh a misery for him to resign himself to it, and go straightway into a distance which was also despair.

Thus he did nothing more decided than taking the Riverston coach. He came back again by it while it was still daylight, having made up his mind that he must go to Lydgate's that evening. The Rubicon, we know, was a very insignificant stream to look at ; its significance lay entirely in certain invisible conditions. Will felt as if he were forced to cross his small boundary ditch, and what he saw beyond it was not empire, but discontented subjection.

But it is given to us sometimes even in our everyday life to witness the saving influence of a noble nature, the divine efficacy of rescue that may lie in a self-subduing act of fellowship. If Dorothea, after her night's anguish, had not taken that walk to Rosamond—why, she perhaps would have been a woman who gained a higher character for discretion, but it would certainly not have been as well for those three who were on one hearth in Lydgate's house at half-past seven that evening.

Rosamond had been prepared for Will's visit, and she received him with a languid coldness which Lydgate accounted for by her nervous exhaustion, of which he could not suppose that it had any relation to Will. And when she sat in silence bending over a bit of work, he innocently apologised for her in an indirect way by begging her to lean backward and rest. Will was miserable in the necessity for playing the part of a friend who was making his first appearance and greeting to Rosamond, while his thoughts were busy about her feeling since that scene of yesterday, which seemed still inexorably to enclose them both, like the painful vision of a double madness. It happened that nothing called Lydgate out of the room ; but when Rosamond poured out the tea, and Will came near to fetch it, she placed a tiny bit of folded paper in his saucer. He saw it and secured it quickly, but as he went back to his inn he had no eagerness to unfold the paper. What Rosamond had written to him would probably deepen the painful impressions of the evening. Still, he opened and read it by his bed-candle. There were only these few words in her neatly-flowing hand :—

"I have told Mrs. Casaubon. She is not under any mistake about you. I told her because she came to see me and was very kind. You will have nothing to reproach me with now. I shall not have made any difference to you."

The effect of these words was not quite all gladness. As Will dwelt on them with excited imagination, he felt his cheeks and ears burning at the thought of what had occurred between Dorothea and Rosamond—at the uncertainty how far Dorothea might still feel her dignity wounded in having an explanation of his conduct offered to her. There might still remain in her mind a changed association with him which made an irremediable difference—a lasting flaw. With active fancy he wrought himself into a state of doubt little more easy than that of the man who has escaped from wreck by night and stands on unknown ground in the darkness. Until that wretched yesterday —except the moment of vexation long ago in the very same room and in the very same presence—all their vision, all their thought of each other, had been as in a world apart, where the sunshine fell on tall white lilies, where no evil lurked, and no other soul entered. But now—would Dorothea meet him in that world again ?

CHAPTER LXXXIII

"And now good-morrow to our waking souls
Which watch not one another out of fear ;
For love all love of other sights controls,
And makes one little room, an everywhere."
—Dr. Donne.

On the second morning after Dorothea's visit to Rosamond, she had had two nights of sound sleep, and had not only lost all traces of fatigue, but felt as if she had a great deal of superfluous strength—that is to say, more strength than she could manage to concentrate on any occupation. The day before, she had taken long walks outside the grounds, and had paid two visits to the Parsonage ; but she never in her life told any one the reason why she spent her time in that fruitless manner, and this morning she was rather angry with herself for her childish restlessness. To-day was to be spent quite differently. What was there to be done in the village ? O dear ! nothing.

Everybody was well and had flannel; nobody's pig had died; and it was Saturday morning, when there was a general scrubbing of floors and door-stones, and when it was useless to go into the school. But there were various subjects that Dorothea was trying to get clear upon, and she resolved to throw herself energetically into the gravest of all. She sat down in the library before her particular little heap of books on political economy and kindred matters, out of which she was trying to get light as to the best way of spending money so as not to injure one's neighbours, or—what comes to the same thing—so as to do them the most good. Here was a weighty subject which, if she could but lay hold of it, would certainly keep her mind steady. Unhappily her mind slipped off it for a whole hour; and at the end she found herself reading sentences twice over with an intense consciousness of many things, but not of any one thing contained in the text. This was hopeless. Should she order the carriage and drive to Tipton? No; for some reason or other she preferred staying at Lowick. But her vagrant mind must be reduced to order: there was an art in self-discipline; and she walked round and round the brown library considering by what sort of manœuvre she could arrest her wandering thoughts. Perhaps a mere task was the best means—something to which she must go doggedly. Was there not the geography of Asia Minor, in which her slackness had often been rebuked by Mr. Casaubon? She went to the cabinet of maps and unrolled one: this morning she might make herself finally sure that Paphlagonia was not on the Levantine coast, and fix her total darkness about the Chalybes firmly on the shores of the Euxine. A map was a fine thing to study when you were disposed to think of something else, being made up of names that would turn into a chime if you went back upon them. Dorothea set earnestly to work, bending close to her map, and uttering the names in an audible, subdued tone, which often got into a chime. She looked amusingly girlish after all her deep experience—nodding her head and marking the names off on her fingers, with a little pursing of her lip, and now and then breaking off to put her hands on each side of her face and say, "Oh dear! oh dear!"

There was no reason why this should end any more than a merry-go-round; but it was at last interrupted by the opening of the door and the announcement of Miss Noble.

The little old lady, whose bonnet hardly reached Dorothea's shoulder, was warmly welcomed, but while her hand was being pressed she made many of her beaver-like noises, as if she had something difficult to say."

"Do sit down," said Dorothea, rolling a chair forward. "Am I wanted for anything? I shall be so glad if I can do anything."

"I will not stay," said Miss Noble, putting her hand into her small basket, and holding some article inside it nervously; "I have left a friend in the churchyard." She lapsed into her inarticulate sounds, and unconsciously drew forth the article which she was fingering. It was the tortoise-shell lozenge-box, and Dorothea felt the colour mounting to her cheeks.

"Mr. Ladislaw," continued the timid little woman. "He fears he has offended you, and has begged me to ask if you will see him for a few minutes."

Dorothea did not answer on the instant: it was crossing her mind that she could not receive him in this library, where her husband's prohibition seemed to dwell. She looked towards the window. Could she go out and meet him in the grounds? The sky was heavy, and the trees had begun to shiver as at a coming storm. Besides, she shrank from going out to him.

"Do see him, Mrs. Casaubon," said Miss Noble, pathetically; "else I must go back and say No, and that will hurt him."

"Yes, I will see him," said Dorothea. "Pray tell him to come."

What else was there to be done? There was nothing that she longed for at the moment except to see Will: the possibility of seeing him had thrust itself insistently between her and every other object; and yet she had a throbbing excitement like an alarm upon her—a sense that she was doing something daringly defiant for his sake.

When the little lady had trotted away on her mission, Dorothea stood in the middle of the library with her hands falling clasped before her, making no attempt to compose herself in an attitude of dignified unconsciousness. What she was least conscious of just then was her own body: she was thinking of what was likely to be in Will's mind, and of the hard feelings that others had had about him. How could any duty bind her to hardness? Resistance to unjust dispraise had mingled with her feeling for him from the very first, and now in the rebound of her heart after her anguish the resistance was stronger than ever. "If I love him too much it is because he has been used so ill:" there was a voice within her saying this to some imagined audience in the library, when the door was opened, and she saw Will before her.

She did not move, and he came towards her with more doubt and timidity in his face than she had ever seen before. He was in a state of uncertainty which made him afraid lest some look or word of his should condemn him to a new distance from her ; and Dorothea was afraid of her own emotion. She looked as if there were a spell upon her, keeping her motionless and hindering her from unclasping her hands, while some intense, grave yearning was imprisoned within her eyes. Seeing that she did not put out her hand as usual, Will paused a yard from her and said with embarrassment, " I am so grateful to you for seeing me."

" I wanted to see you," said Dorothea, having no other words at command. It did not occur to her to sit down, and Will did not give a cheerful interpretation to this queenly way of receiving him ; but he went on to say what he had made up his mind to say.

" I fear you think me foolish and perhaps wrong for coming back so soon. I have been punished for my impatience. You know—every one knows now—a painful story about my parentage. I knew of it before I went away, and I always meant to tell you of it if—if we ever met again."

There was a slight movement in Dorothea, and she unclasped her hands, but immediately folded them over each other.

" But the affair is matter of gossip now," Will continued. " I wished you to know that something connected with it— something which happened before I went away—helped to bring me down here again. At least I thought it excused my coming. It was the idea of getting Bulstrode to apply some money to a public purpose—some money which he had thought of giving me. Perhaps it is rather to Bulstrode's credit that he privately offered me compensation for an old injury : he offered to give me a good income to make amends ; but I suppose you know the disagreeable story ? "

Will looked doubtfully at Dorothea, but his manner was gathering some of the defiant courage with which he always thought of this fact in his destiny. He added, " You know that it must be altogether painful to me."

" Yes—yes—I know," said Dorothea, hastily.

" I did not choose to accept an income from such a source. I was sure that you would not think well of me if I did so," said Will. Why should he mind saying anything of that sort to her now ? She knew that he had avowed his love for her. " I felt that "—he broke off, nevertheless.

"You acted as I should have expected you to act," said Dorothea, her face brightening and her head becoming a little more erect on its beautiful stem.

"I did not believe that you would let any circumstance of my birth create a prejudice in you against me, though it was sure to do so in others," said Will, shaking his head backward in his old way, and looking with a grave appeal into her eyes.

"If it were a new hardship it would be a new reason for me to cling to you," said Dorothea, fervidly. "Nothing could have changed me but——" her heart was swelling, and it was difficult to go on ; she made a great effort over herself to say in a low tremulous voice, "but thinking that you were different—not so good as I had believed you to be."

"You are sure to believe me better than I am in everything but one," said Will, giving way to his own feeling in the evidence of hers. "I mean, in my truth to you. When I thought you doubted of that, I didn't care about anything that was left. I thought it was all over with me, and there was nothing to try for—only things to endure."

"I don't doubt you any longer," said Dorothea, putting out her hand ; a vague fear for him impelling her unutterable affection.

He took her hand and raised it to his lips with something like a sob. But he stood with his hat and gloves in the other hand, and might have done for the portrait of a Royalist. Still it was difficult to loose the hand, and Dorothea, withdrawing it in a confusion that distressed her, looked and moved away.

"See how dark the clouds have become, and how the trees are tossed," she said, walking towards the window, yet speaking and moving with only a dim sense of what she was doing.

Will followed her at a little distance, and leaned against the tall back of a leather chair, on which he ventured now to lay his hat and gloves, and free himself from the intolerable durance of formality to which he had been for the first time condemned in Dorothea's presence. It must be confessed that he felt very happy at that moment leaning on the chair. He was not much afraid of anything that she might feel now.

They stood silent, not looking at each other, but looking at the evergreens which were being tossed, and were showing the pale underside of their leaves against the blackening sky. Will never enjoyed the prospect of a storm so much : it delivered him from the necessity of going away. Leaves and little branches were hurled about, and the thunder was getting nearer. The light was more and more sombre, but there came a flash of lightning which made them start and look at each other, and then smile. Dorothea began to say what she had been thinking of.

"That was a wrong thing for you to say, that you would have had nothing to try for. If we had lost our own chief good, other people's good would remain, and that is worth trying for. Some can be happy. I seemed to see that more clearly than ever, when I was the most wretched. I can hardly think how I could have borne the trouble, if that feeling had not come to me to make strength."

"You have never felt the sort of misery I felt," said Will; "the misery of knowing that you must despise me."

"But I have felt worse—it was worse to think ill——" Dorothea had begun impetuously, but broke off.

Will coloured. He had the sense that whatever she said was uttered in the vision of a fatality that kept them apart. He was silent a moment, and then said passionately——

"We may at least have the comfort of speaking to each other without disguise. Since I must go away—since we must always be divided—you may think of me as one on the brink of the grave."

While he was speaking there came a vivid flash of lightning which lit each of them up for the other—and the light seemed to be the terror of a hopeless love. Dorothea darted instantaneously from the window; Will followed her, seizing her hand with a spasmodic movement; and so they stood, with their hands clasped, like two children, looking out on the storm, while the thunder gave a tremendous crack and roll above them, and the rain began to pour down. Then they turned their faces towards each other, with the memory of his last words in them, and they did not loose each other's hands.

"There is no hope for me," said Will. "Even if you loved me as well as I love you—even if I were everything to you—I shall most likely always be very poor : on a sober calculation, one can count on nothing but a creeping lot. It is impossible for us ever to belong to each other. It is perhaps base of me to have asked for a word from you. I meant to go away into silence, but I have not been able to do what I meant."

"Don't be sorry," said Dorothea, in her clear tender tones. "I would rather share all the trouble of our parting."

Her lips trembled, and so did his. It was never known which lips were the first to move towards the other lips; but they kissed tremblingly, and then they moved apart.

The rain was dashing against the window-panes as if an angry spirit were within it, and behind it was the great swoop of the wind ; it was one of those moments in which both the busy and the idle pause with a certain awe.

Dorothea sat down on the seat nearest to her, a long low ottoman in the middle of the room, and with her hands folded over each other on her lap, looked at the drear outer world. Will stood still an instant looking at her, then seated himself beside her, and laid his hand on hers, which turned itself upward to be clasped. They sat in that way without looking at each other, until the rain abated and began to fall in stillness. Each had been full of thoughts which neither of them could begin to utter.

But when the rain was quiet, Dorothea turned to look at Will. With passionate exclamation, as if some torture-screw were threatening him, he started up and said, " It is impossible ! "

He went and leaned on the back of the chair again, and seemed to be battling with his own anger, while she looked towards him sadly.

" It is as fatal as a murder or any other horror that divides people," he burst out again ; " it is more intolerable—to have our life maimed by petty accidents."

" No—don't say that—your life need not be maimed," said Dorothea, gently.

" Yes, it must," said Will, angrily. " It is cruel of you to speak in that way—as if there were any comfort. You may see beyond the misery of it, but I don't. It is unkind—it is throwing back my love for you as if it were a trifle, to speak in that way in the face of the fact. We shall never be married."

" Some time—we might," said Dorothea, in a trembling voice.

" When ? " said Will, bitterly. " What is the use of counting on any success of mine ? It is a mere toss up whether I shall ever do more than keep myself decently, unless I choose to sell myself as a mere pen and a mouthpiece. I can see that clearly enough. I could not offer myself to any woman, even if she had no luxuries to renounce."

There was silence. Dorothea's heart was full of something that she wanted to say, and yet the words were too difficult. She was wholly possessed by them : at that moment debate was mute within her. And it was very hard that she could not say what she wanted to say. Will was looking out of the window angrily. If he would have looked at her and not gone away from her side she thought everything would have been easier. At last he turned, still resting against the chair, and stretching his hand automatically towards his hat, said with a sort of exasperation, " Good-bye."

" Oh, I cannot bear it—my heart will break," said Dorothea, starting from her seat, the flood of her young passion bearing down all the obstructions which had kept her silent—the great tears rising and falling in an instant : " I don't mind about poverty—I hate my wealth."

In an instant Will was close to her and had his arms round her, but she drew her head back and held his away gently that she might go on speaking, her large tear-filled eyes looking at his very simply, while she said in a sobbing childlike way, " We could live quite well on my own fortune—it is too much—seven hundred a-year—I want so little—no new clothes—and I will learn what everything costs."

CHAPTER LXXXIV

" Though it be songe of old and yonge,
    That I sholde be to blame,
Theyrs be the charge, that spoke so large
    In hurtynge of my name."
                    —*The Not-browne Mayde.*

It was just after the Lords had thrown out the Reform Bill : that explains how Mr. Cadwallader came to be walking on the slope of the lawn near the great conservatory at Freshitt Hall, holding the " Times " in his hands behind him, while he talked with a trout-fisher's dispassionateness about the prospects of the country to Sir James Chettam. Mrs. Cadwallader, the Dowager Lady Chettam, and Celia were sometimes seated on garden-chairs, sometimes walking to meet little Arthur, who was being drawn in his chariot, and, as became the infantine Bouddha, was sheltered by his sacred umbrella with handsome silken fringe.

The ladies also talked politics, though more fitfully. Mrs. Cadwallader was strong on the intended creation of peers : she had it for certain from her cousin that Truberry had gone over to the other side entirely at the instigation of his wife, who had scented peerages in the air from the very first introduction of the Reform question, and would sign her soul away to take precedence of her younger sister, who had married a baronet. Lady Chettam thought that such conduct was very reprehensible, and

remembered that Mrs. Truberry's mother was a Miss Walsing-
ham of Melspring. Celia confessed it was nicer to be " Lady "
then " Mrs.," and that Dodo never minded about precedence if
she could have her own way. Mrs. Cadwallader held that it was a
poor satisfaction to take precedence when everybody about you
knew that you had not a drop of good blood in your veins ;
and Celia again, stopping to look at Arthur, said, " It would be
very nice, though, if he were a Viscount—and his lordship's little
tooth coming through ! He might have been, if James had
been an Earl."

" My dear Celia," said the Dowager, " James's title is worth far
more than any new earldom. I never wished his father to be
anything else than Sir James."

" Oh, I only meant about Arthur's little tooth," said Celia,
comfortably. " But see, here is my uncle coming."

She tripped off to meet her uncle, while Sir James and Mr.
Cadwallader came forward to make one group with the ladies.
Celia had slipped her arm through her uncle's, and he patted her
hand with a rather melancholy " Well, my dear ! " As they
approached, it was evident that Mr. Brooke was looking dejected,
but this was fully accounted for by the state of politics ; and as
he was shaking hands all round without more greeting than a
" Well, you're all here, you know," the Rector said, laughingly—

" Don't take the throwing out of the Bill so much to heart,
Brooke ; you've got all the riff-raff of the country on your
side."

" The Bill, eh ? ah ! " said Mr. Brooke, with a mild dis-
tractedness of manner. " Thrown out, you know, eh ? The
Lords are going too far, though. They'll have to pull up. Sad
news, you know. I mean, here at home—sad news. But you
must not blame me, Chettam."

" What is the matter ? " said Sir James. " Not another
gamekeeper shot, I hope ? It's what I should expect, when a
fellow like Trapping Bass is let off so easily."

" Gamekeeper ? No. Let us go in ; I can tell you all in the
house, you know," said Mr. Brooke, nodding at the Cadwalladers,
to show that he included them in his confidence. " As to
poachers like Trapping Bass, you know, Chettam," he continued,
as they were entering, " when you are a magistrate, you'll not
find it so easy to commit. Severity is all very well, but it's a
great deal easier when you've got somebody to do it for you.
You have a soft place in your heart yourself, you know—you're
not a Draco, a Jeffreys, that sort of thing."

Mr. Brooke was evidently in a state of nervous perturbation. When he had something painful to tell, it was usually his way to introduce it among a number of disjointed particulars, as if it were a medicine that would get a milder flavour by mixing. He continued his chat with Sir James about the poachers until they were all seated, and Mrs. Cadwallader, impatient of this drivelling, said—

"I'm dying to know the sad news. The gamekeeper is not shot ; that is settled. What is it, then ? "

"Well, it's a very trying thing, you know," said Mr. Brooke. " I'm glad you and the Rector are here ; it's a family matter— but you will help us all to bear it, Cadwallader. I've got to break it to you, my dear." Here Mr. Brooke looked at Celia— " You've no notion what it is, you know. And, Chettam, it will annoy you uncommonly—but, you see, you have not been able to hinder it, any more than I have. There's something singular in things : they came round, you know."

" It must be about Dodo," said Celia, who had been used to think of her sister as the dangerous part of the family machinery. She had seated herself on a low stool against her husband's knee.

" For God's sake let us hear what it is ! " said Sir James.

" Well, you know, Chettam, I couldn't help Casaubon's will : it was a sort of will to make things worse."

" Exactly," said Sir James, hastily. " But *what* is worse ? "

" Dorothea is going to be married again, you know," said Mr. Brooke, nodding towards Celia, who immediately looked up at her husband with a frightened glance, and put her hand on his knee.

Sir James was almost white with anger, but he did not speak.

" Merciful heaven ! " said Mrs. Cadwallader. " Not to young Ladislaw ? "

Mr. Brooke nodded, saying, " Yes ; to Ladislaw," and then fell into a prudential silence.

" You see, Humphrey ! " said Mrs. Cadwallader, waving her arm towards her husband. " Another time you will admit that I have some foresight ; or rather you will contradict me and be just as blind as ever. *You* supposed that the young gentleman was gone out of the country."

" So he might be, and yet come back," said the Rector, quietly.

" When did you learn this ? " said Sir James, not liking to hear any one else speak, though finding it difficult to speak himself.

"Yesterday," said Mr. Brooke, meekly. "I went to Lowick. Dorothea sent for me, you know. It had come about quite suddenly—neither of them had any idea two days ago—not any idea, you know. There's something singular in things. But Dorothea is quite determined—it is no use opposing. I put it strongly to her. I did my duty, Chettam. But she can act as she likes, you know."

"It would have been better if I had called him out and shot him a year ago," said Sir James, not from bloody-mindedness, but because he needed something strong to say.

"Really, James, that would have been very disagreeable," said Celia.

"Be reasonable, Chettam. Look at the affair more quietly," said Mr. Cadwallader, sorry to see his good-natured friend so overmastered by anger.

"That is not so very easy for a man of any dignity—with any sense of right—when the affair happens to be in his own family," said Sir James, still in his white indignation. "It is perfectly scandalous. If Ladislaw had had a spark of honour he would have gone out of the country at once, and never shown his face in it again. However, I am not surprised. The day after Casaubon's funeral I said what ought to be done. But I was not listened to."

"You wanted what was impossible, you know, Chettam," said Mr. Brooke. "You wanted him shipped off. I told you Ladislaw was not to be done as we liked with: he had his ideas. He was a remarkable fellow—I always said he was a remarkable fellow."

"Yes," said Sir James, unable to repress a retort, "it is rather a pity you formed that high opinion of him. We are indebted to that for him being lodged in this neighbourhood. We are indebted to that for seeing a woman like Dorothea degrading herself by marrying him." Sir James made little stoppages between his clauses, the words not coming easily. "A man so marked out by her husband's will, that delicacy ought to have forbidden her from seeing him again—who takes her out of her proper rank—into poverty—has the meanness to accept such a sacrifice—has always had an objectionable position—a bad origin—and, I *believe*, is a man of little principle and light character. That is my opinion," Sir James ended emphatically, turning aside and crossing his leg.

"I pointed everything out to her," said Mr. Brooke, apologetically—"I mean the poverty, and abandoning her position.

I said, ' My dear, you don't know what it is to live on seven hundred a-year, and have no carriage, and that kind of thing, and go amongst people who don't know who you are.' I put it strongly to her. But I advise you to talk to Dorothea herself. The fact is, she has a dislike to Casaubon's property. You will hear what she says, you know."

" No—excuse me—I shall not," said Sir James, with more coolness. " I cannot bear to see her again ; it is too painful. It hurts me too much that a woman like Dorothea should have done what is wrong."

" Be just, Chettam," said the easy, large-lipped Rector, who objected to all this unnecessary discomfort. " Mrs. Casaubon may be acting imprudently : she is giving up a fortune for the sake of a man, and we men have so poor an opinion of each other that we can hardly call a woman wise who does that. But I think you should not condemn it as a wrong action, in the strict sense of the word."

" Yes, I do," answered Sir James. " I think that Dorothea commits a wrong action in marrying Ladislaw."

" My dear fellow, we are rather apt to consider an act wrong because it is unpleasant to us," said the Rector, quietly. Like many men who take life easily, he had the knack of saying a home truth occasionally to those who felt themselves virtuously out of temper. Sir James took out his handkerchief and began to bite the corner.

" It is very dreadful of Dodo, though," said Celia, wishing to justify her husband. " She said she *never would* marry again— not anybody at all."

" I heard her say the same thing myself," said Lady Chettam, majestically, as if this were royal evidence.

" Oh, there is usually a silent exception in such cases," said Mrs. Cadwallader. " The only wonder to me is, that any of you are surprised. You did nothing to hinder it. If you would have had Lord Triton down here to woo her with his philanthropy, he might have carried her off before the year was over. There was no safety in anything else. Mr. Casaubon had prepared all this as beautifully as possible. He made himself disagreeable—or it pleased God to make him so—and then he dared her to contradict him. It's the way to make any trumpery tempting, to ticket it at a high price in that way."

" I don't know what you mean by wrong, Cadwallader," said Sir James, still feeling a little stung, and turning round in his chair towards the Rector. " He's not a man we can take into the family. At least, I must speak for myself," he continued, carefully keeping his eyes off Mr. Brooke. " I suppose others will find his society too pleasant to care about the propriety of the thing."

" Well, you know, Chettam," said Mr. Brooke, good-humouredly, nursing his leg, " I can't turn my back on Dorothea. I must be a father to her up to a certain point. I said, ' My dear, I won't refuse to give you away.' I had spoken strongly before. But I can cut off the entail, you know. It will cost money and be troublesome ; but I can do it, you know."

Mr. Brooke nodded at Sir James, and felt that he was both showing his own force of resolution and propitiating what was just in the Baronet's vexation. He had hit on a more ingenious mode of parrying than he was aware of. He had touched a motive of which Sir James was ashamed. The mass of his feeling about Dorothea's marriage to Ladislaw was due partly to excusable prejudice, or even justifiable opinion, partly to a jealous repugnance hardly less in Ladislaw's case than in Casaubon's. He was convinced that the marriage was a fatal one for Dorothea. But amid that mass ran a vein of which he was too good and honourable a man to like the avowal even to himself : it was undeniable that the union of the two estates —Tipton and Freshitt—lying charmingly within a ring-fence, was a prospect that flattered him for his son and heir. Hence when Mr. Brooke noddingly appealed to that motive, Sir James felt a sudden embarrassment ; there was a stoppage in his throat ; he even blushed. He had found more words than usual in the first jet of his anger, but Mr. Brooke's propitiation was more clogging to his tongue than Mr. Cadwallader's caustic hint.

But Celia was glad to have room for speech after her uncle's suggestion of the marriage ceremony, and she said, though with as little eagerness of manner as if the question had turned on an invitation to dinner, " Do you mean that Dodo is going to be married directly, uncle ? "

" In three weeks, you know," said Mr. Brooke, helplessly. " I can do nothing to hinder it, Cadwallader," he added, turning for a little countenance towards the Rector, who said—

" *I* should not make any fuss about it. If she likes to be poor, that is her affair. Nobody would have said anything if she had married the young fellow because he was rich. Plenty of beneficed clergy are poorer than they will be. Here is Elinor," continued the provoking husband ; " she vexed her friends by marrying me : I had hardly a thousand a-year—I was a lout—nobody could see anything in me—my shoes were not the right cut—all the men wondered how a woman could like me. Upon my word, I must take Ladislaw's part until I hear more harm of him."

"Humphrey, that is all sophistry, and you know it," said his wife. "Everything is all one—that is the beginning and end with you. As if you had not been a Cadwallader! Does any one suppose that I would have taken such a monster as you by any other name?"

"And a clergyman too," observed Lady Chettam with approbation. "Elinor cannot be said to have descended below her rank. It is difficult to say what Mr. Ladislaw is, eh, James?"

Sir James gave a small grunt, which was less respectful than his usual mode of answering his mother. Celia looked up at him like a thoughtful kitten.

"It must be admitted that his blood is a frightful mixture!" said Mrs. Cadwallader. "The Casaubon cuttle-fish fluid to begin with, and then a rebellious Polish fiddler or dancing-master, was it?—and then an old clo——"

"Nonsense, Elinor," said the Rector, rising. "It is time for us to go."

"After all, he is a pretty sprig," said Mrs. Cadwallader, rising too, and wishing to make amends. "He is like the fine old Crichley portraits before the idiots came in."

"I'll go with you," said Mr. Brooke, starting up with alacrity. "You must all come and dine with me to-morrow, you know— eh, Celia, my dear?"

"You will, James—won't you?" said Celia, taking her husband's hand.

"Oh, of course, if you like," said Sir James, pulling down his waistcoat, but unable yet to adjust his face good-humouredly. "That is to say, if it is not to meet anybody else."

"No, no, no," said Mr. Brooke, understanding the condition. "Dorothea would not come, you know, unless you had been to see her."

When Sir James and Celia were alone, she said, "Do you mind about my having the carriage to go to Lowick, James?"

"What, now, directly?" he answered, with some surprise.

"Yes, it is very important," said Celia.

"Remember, Celia, I cannot see her," said Sir James.

"Not if she gave up marrying?"

"What is the use of saying that?—however, I'm going to the stables. I'll tell Briggs to bring the carriage round."

Celia thought it was of great use, if not to say that, at least to take a journey to Lowick in order to influence Dorothea's mind. All through their girlhood she had felt that she could act on her sister by a word judiciously placed—by opening a little window for the daylight of her own understanding to enter among the strange coloured lamps by which Dodo habitually saw. And Celia the matron naturally felt more able to advise her childless sister. How could any one understand Dodo so well as Celia did, or love her so tenderly ?

Dorothea, busy in her boudoir, felt a glow of pleasure at the sight of her sister so soon after the revelation of her intended marriage. She had prefigured to herself, even with exaggeration, the disgust of her friends, and she had even feared that Celia might be kept aloof from her.

"O Kitty, I am delighted to see you !" said Dorothea, putting her hands on Celia's shoulder, and beaming on her. "I almost thought you would not come to me."

"I have not brought Arthur, because I was in a hurry," said Celia, and they sat down on two small chairs opposite each other, with their knees touching.

"You know, Dodo, it is very bad," said Celia, in her placid guttural, looking as prettily free from humours as possible. "You have disappointed us all so. And I can't think that it ever *will* be—you never can go and live in that way. And then there are all your plans ! You never can have thought of that. James would have taken any trouble for you, and you might have gone on all your life doing what you liked."

"On the contrary, dear," said Dorothea, "I never could do anything that I liked. I have never carried out any plan yet."

"Because you always wanted things that wouldn't do. But other plans would have come. And how *can* you marry Mr. Ladislaw, that we none of us ever thought you *could* marry ? It shocks James so dreadfully. And then it is all so different from what you have always been. You would have Mr. Casaubon because he had such a great soul, and was so old and dismal and learned ; and now, to think of marrying Mr. Ladislaw, who has got no estate or anything. I suppose it is because you must be making yourself uncomfortable in some way or other."

Dorothea laughed.

"Well, it is very serious, Dodo," said Celia, becoming more impressive. "How will you live ? and you will go away among queer people. And I shall never see you—and you won't mind about little Arthur—and I thought you always would——"

Celia's rare tears had got into her eyes, and the corners of her mouth were agitated.

"Dear Celia," said Dorothea, with tender gravity, "if you don't ever see me, it will not be my fault."

"Yes, it will," said Celia, with the same touching distortion of her small features. "How can I come to you or have you with me when James can't bear it ?—that is because he thinks it is not right—he thinks you are so wrong, Dodo. But you always were wrong ; only I can't help loving you. And nobody can think where you will live : where can you go ?"

"I am going to London," said Dorothea.

"How can you always live in a street ? And you will be so poor. I could give you half my things, only how can I, when I never see you ?"

"Bless you, Kitty," said Dorothea, with gentle warmth. "Take comfort : perhaps James will forgive me some time."

"But it would be much better if you would not be married," said Celia, drying her eyes, and returning to her argument ; "then there would be nothing uncomfortable. And you would not do what nobody thought you could do. James always said you ought to be a queen ; but this is not at all being like a queen. You know what mistakes you have always been making, Dodo, and this is another. Nobody thinks Mr. Ladislaw a proper husband for you. And you *said* you would never be married again."

"It is quite true that I might be a wiser person, Celia," said Dorothea, "and that I might have done something better, if I had been better. But this is what I am going to do. I have promised to marry Mr. Ladislaw ; and I am going to marry him."

The tone in which Dorothea said this was a note that Celia had long learned to recognise. She was silent a few moments, and then said, as if she had dismissed all contest, "Is he very fond of you, Dodo ?"

"I hope so. I am very fond of him."

"That is nice," said Celia, comfortably. "Only I would rather you had such a sort of husband as James is, with a place very near, that I could drive to."

Dorothea smiled, and Celia looked rather meditative. Presently she said, "I cannot think how it all came about." Celia thought it would be pleasant to hear the story.

"I daresay not," said Dorothea, pinching her sister's chin.
"If you knew how it came about, it would not seem wonderful
to you."

"Can't you tell me?" said Celia, settling her arms cozily.

"No, dear, you would have to feel with me, else you would
never know."

CHAPTER LXXXV

"Then went the jury out, whose names were Mr. Blindman, Mr. No-
good, Mr. Malice, Mr. Love-lust, Mr. Live-loose, Mr. Heady, Mr. High-
mind, Mr. Enmity, Mr. Liar, Mr. Cruelty, Mr. Hate-light, Mr. Implacable,
who every one gave in his private verdict against him among themselves,
and afterwards unanimously concluded to bring him in guilty before the
judge. And first among themselves, Mr. Blindman, the foreman, said, I
see clearly that this man is a heretic. Then said Mr. No-good, Away with
such a fellow from the earth! Ay, said Mr. Malice, for I hate the very
look of him. Then said Mr. Love-lust, I could never endure him. Nor
I, said Mr. Live-loose; for he would be always condemning my way.
Hang him, hang him, said Mr. Heady. A sorry scrub, said Mr. High-
mind. My heart riseth against him, said Mr. Enmity. He is a rogue, said
Mr. Liar. Hanging is too good for him, said Mr. Cruelty. Let us despatch
him out of the way, said Mr. Hate-light. Then said Mr. Implacable,
Might I have all the world given me, I could not be reconciled to him;
therefore let us forthwith bring him in guilty of death."—*Pilgrim's
Progress.*

WHEN immortal Bunyan makes his picture of the persecuting
passions bringing in their verdict of guilty, who pities Faithful?
That is a rare and blessed lot which some greatest men have not
attained, to know ourselves guiltless before a condemning crowd
—to be sure that what we are denounced for is solely the good
in us. The pitiable lot is that of the man who could not call
himself a martyr even though he were to persuade himself that
the men who stoned him were but ugly passions incarnate—
who knows that he is stoned, not for professing the Right, but
for not being the man he professed to be.

This was the consciousness that Bulstrode was withering
under while he made his preparations for departing from Middlemarch, and going to end his stricken life in that sad refuge,
the indifference of new faces. The duteous merciful constancy
of his wife had delivered him from one dread, but it could not
hinder her presence from being still a tribunal before which he
shrank from confession and desired advocacy. His equivoca-
tions with himself about the death of Raffles had sustained the
conception of an Omniscience whom he prayed to, yet he had a
terror upon him which would not let him expose them to

judgment by a full confession to his wife : the acts which he had washed and diluted with inward argument and motive, and for which it seemed comparatively easy to win invisible pardon— what name would she call them by ? That she should ever silently call his acts Murder was what he could not bear. He felt shrouded by her doubt : he got strength to face her from the sense that she could not yet feel warranted in pronouncing that worst condemnation on him. Some time, perhaps—when he was dying—he would tell her all : in the deep shadow of that time, when she held his hand in the gathering darkness, she might listen without recoiling from his touch. Perhaps : but concealment had been the habit of his life, and the impulse to confession had no power against the dread of a deeper humiliation.

He was full of timid care for his wife, not only because he deprecated any harshness of judgment from her, but because he felt a deep distress at the sight of her suffering. She had sent her daughters away to board at a school on the coast, that this crisis might be hidden from them as far as possible. Set free by their absence from the intolerable necessity of accounting for her grief or of beholding their frightened wonder, she could live unconstrainedly with the sorrow that was every day streaking her hair with whiteness and making her eyelids languid.

"Tell me anything that you would like to have me do, Harriet," Bulstrode had said to her ; " I mean with regard to arrangements of property. It is my intention not to sell the land I possess in this neighbourhood, but to leave it to you as a safe provision. If you have any wish on such subjects, do not conceal it from me."

A few days afterwards, when she had returned from a visit to her brother's, she began to speak to her husband on a subject which had for some time been in her mind.

"I *should* like to do something for my brother's family, Nicholas ; and I think we are bound to make some amends to Rosamond and her husband. Walter says Mr. Lydgate must leave the town, and his practice is almost good for nothing, and they have very little left to settle anywhere with. I would rather do without something for ourselves, to make some amends to my poor brother's family."

Mrs. Bulstrode did not wish to go nearer to the facts than in the phrase " make some amends ; " knowing that her husband must understand her. He had a particular reason, which she was not aware of, for wincing under her suggestion. He hesitated before he said—

"It is not possible to carry out your wish in the way you propose, my dear. Mr. Lydgate has virtually rejected any further service from me. He has returned the thousand pounds which I lent him. Mrs. Casaubon advanced him the sum for that purpose. Here is his letter."

The letter seemed to cut Mrs. Bulstrode severely. The mention of Mrs. Casaubon's loan seemed a reflection of that public feeling which held it a matter of course that every one would avoid a connection with her husband. She was silent for some time ; and the tears fell one after the other, her chin trembling as she wiped them away. Bulstrode, sitting opposite to her, ached at the sight of that grief-worn face, which two months before had been bright and blooming. It had aged to keep sad company with his own withered features. Urged into some effort at comforting her, he said—

"There is another means, Harriet, by which I might do a service to your brother's family, if you like to act in it. And it would, I think, be beneficial to you : it would be an advantageous way of managing the land which I mean to be yours."

She looked attentive.

"Garth once thought of undertaking the management of Stone Court in order to place your nephew Fred there. The stock was to remain as it is, and they were to pay a certain share of the profits instead of an ordinary rent. That would be a desirable beginning for the young man, in conjunction with his employment under Garth. Would it be a satisfaction to you ? "

"Yes, it would," said Mrs. Bulstrode, with some return of energy. "Poor Walter is so cast down ; I would try anything in my power to do him some good before I go away. We have always been brother and sister."

"You must make the proposal to Garth yourself, Harriet," said Mr. Bulstrode, not liking what he had to say, but desiring the end he had in view, for other reasons besides the consolation of his wife. "You must state to him that the land is virtually yours, and that he need have no transactions with me. Communications can be made through Standish. I mention this, because Garth gave up being my agent. I can put into your hands a paper which he himself drew up, stating conditions ; and you can propose his renewed acceptance of them. I think it is not unlikely that he will accept when you propose the thing for the sake of your nephew."

CHAPTER LXXXVI

" Le cœur se sature d'amour comme d'un sel divin qui le conserve ; de
là l'incorruptible adhérence de ceux qui se sont aimés dès l'aube de la vie,
et la fraîcheur des vielles amours prolongés.   Il existe un embaumement
d'amour.   C'est de Daphnis et Chlöe que sont faits Philémon et Baucis.
Cette vieillesse-là, ressemblance du soir avec l'aurore."
                            —Victor Hugo : *L'homme qui rit.*

MRS. GARTH, hearing Caleb enter the passage about tea-time,
opened the parlour-door and said, " There you are, Caleb.   Have
you had your dinner ? " (Mr. Garth's meals were much sub-
ordinated to " business.")

" Oh yes, a good dinner—cold mutton and I don't know what.
Where is Mary ? "

" In the garden with Letty, I think."

" Fred is not come yet ? "

" No.   Are you going out again without taking tea, Caleb ? "
said Mrs. Garth, seeing that her absent-minded husband was
putting on again the hat which he had just taken off.

" No, no ; I'm only going to Mary a minute."

Mary was in a grassy corner of the garden, where there was
a swing loftily hung between two pear-trees.   She had a pink
kerchief tied over her head, making a little poke to shade her
eyes from the level sunbeams, while she was giving a glorious
swing to Letty, who laughed and screamed wildly.

Seeing her father, Mary left the swing and went to meet him,
pushing back the pink kerchief and smiling afar off at him with
the involuntary smile of loving pleasure.

" I came to look for you, Mary," said Mr. Garth.   " Let us
walk about a bit."

Mary knew quite well that her father had something particular
to say : his eyebrows made their pathetic angle, and there was
a tender gravity in his voice : these things had been signs to her
when she was Letty's age.   She put her arm within his, and they
turned by the row of nut-trees.

" It will be a sad while before you can be married, Mary,"
said her father, not looking at her, but at the end of the stick
which he held in his other hand.

" Not a sad while, father—I mean to be merry," said Mary,
laughingly.   " I have been single and merry for four-and-
twenty years and more : I suppose it will not be quite as long
again as that."   Then, after a little pause, she said, more

gravely, bending her face before her father's, "If you are contented with Fred?"

Caleb screwed up his mouth and turned his head aside wisely.

"Now, father, you did praise him last Wednesday. You said he had an uncommon notion of stock, and a good eye for things."

"Did I?" said Caleb, rather slyly.

"Yes, I put it all down, and the date, *anno Domini*, and everything," said Mary. "You like things to be neatly booked. And then his behaviour to you, father, is really good; he has a deep respect for you; and it is impossible to have a better temper than Fred has."

"Ay, ay; you want to coax me into thinking him a fine match."

"No, indeed, father. I don't love him because he is a fine match."

"What for, then?"

"Oh, dear, because I have always loved him. I should never like scolding any one else so well; and that is a point to be thought of in a husband."

"Your mind is quite settled, then, Mary?" said Caleb, returning to his first tone. "There's no other wish come into it since things have been going on as they have been of late?" (Caleb meant a great deal in that vague phrase;) "because, better late than never. A woman must not force her heart—she'll do a man no good by that."

"My feelings have not changed, father," said Mary, calmly. "I shall be constant to Fred as long as he is constant to me. I don't think either of us could spare the other, or like any one else better, however much we might admire them. It would make too great a difference to us—like seeing all the old places altered, and changing the name for everything. We must wait for each other a long while; but Fred knows that."

Instead of speaking immediately, Caleb stood still and screwed his stick on the grassy walk. Then he said, with emotion in his voice, "Well, I've got a bit of news. What do you think of Fred going to live at Stone Court, and managing the land there?"

"How can that ever be, father?" said Mary, wonderingly.

"He would manage it for his aunt Bulstrode. The poor woman has been to me begging and praying. She wants to do the lad good, and it might be a fine thing for him. With saving, he might gradually buy the stock, and he has a turn for farming."

"Oh, Fred would be so happy? It is too good to believe."

"Ah, but mind you," said Caleb, turning his head warningly, "I must take it on *my* shoulders, and be responsible, and see after everything; and that will grieve your mother a bit, though she mayn't say so. Fred had need be careful."

"Perhaps it is too much, father," said Mary, checked in her joy. "There would be no happiness in bringing you any fresh trouble."

"Nay, nay; work is my delight, child, when it doesn't vex your mother. And then, if you and Fred get married," here Caleb's voice shook just perceptibly, "he'll be steady and saving; and you've got your mother's cleverness, and mine too, in a woman's sort of way; and you'll keep him in order. He'll be coming by-and-by, so I wanted to tell you first, because I think you'd like to tell *him* by yourselves. After that, I could talk it well over with him, and we could go into business and the nature of things."

"Oh, you dear good father!" cried Mary, putting her hands round her father's neck, while he bent his head placidly, willing to be caressed. "I wonder if any other girl thinks her father the best man in the world!"

"Nonsense, child; you'll think your husband better."

"Impossible," said Mary, relapsing into her usual tone; "husbands are an inferior class of men, who require keeping in order."

When they were entering the house with Letty, who had run to join them, Mary saw Fred at the orchard-gate, and went to meet him.

"What fine clothes you wear, you extravagant youth!" said Mary, as Fred stood still and raised his hat to her with playful formality. "You are not learning economy."

"Now that is too bad, Mary," said Fred. "Just look at the edges of these coat-cuffs! It is only by dint of good brushing that I look respectable. I am saving up three suits—one for a wedding-suit."

"How very droll you will look!—like a gentleman in an old fashion-book."

"Oh no, they will keep two years."

"Two years! be reasonable, Fred," said Mary, turning to walk. "Don't encourage flattering expectations."

"Why not? One lives on them better than on unflattering ones. If we can't be married in two years, the truth will be quite bad enough when it comes."

" I have heard a story of a young gentleman who once encouraged flattering expectations, and they did him harm."

" Mary, if you've got something discouraging to tell me, I shall bolt; I shall go into the house to Mr. Garth. I am out of spirits. My father is so cut up—home is not like itself. I can't bear any more bad news."

" Should you call it bad news to be told that you were to live at Stone Court, and manage the farm, and be remarkably prudent, and save money every year till all the stock and furniture were your own, and you were a distinguished agricultural character, as Mr. Borthrop Trumbull says—rather stout, I fear, and with the Greek and Latin sadly weather-worn ? "

" You don't mean anything except nonsense, Mary ? " said Fred, colouring slightly nevertheless.

" That is what my father has just told me of as what may happen, and he never talks nonsense," said Mary, looking up at Fred now, while he grasped her hand as they walked, till it rather hurt her; but she would not complain.

" Oh, I could be a tremendously good fellow then, Mary, and we could be married directly."

" Not so fast, sir; how do you know that I would not rather defer our marriage for some years ? That would leave you time to misbehave, and then if I liked some one else better, I should have an excuse for jilting you."

" Pray don't joke, Mary," said Fred, with strong feeling. " Tell me seriously that all this is true, and that you are happy because of it—because you love me best."

" It is all true, Fred, and I am happy because of it—because I love you best," said Mary, in a tone of obedient recitation.

They lingered on the door-step under the steep-roofed porch, and Fred almost in a whisper said,—

" When we were first engaged, with the umbrella-ring, Mary, you used to—— "

The spirit of joy began to laugh more decidedly in Mary's eyes, but the fatal Ben came running to the door with Brownie yapping behind him, and, bouncing against them, said—

" Fred and Mary ! are you ever coming in ?—or may I eat your cake ? "

FINALE

EVERY limit is a beginning as well as an ending. Who can quit young lives after being long in company with them, and not

desire to know what befell them in their after-years? For the
fragment of a life, however typical, is not the sample of an even
web: promises may not be kept, and an ardent outset may be
followed by declension; latent powers may find their long-
waited opportunity; a past error may urge a grand retrieval.

Marriage, which has been the bourne of so many narratives,
is still a great beginning, as it was to Adam and Eve, who kept
their honeymoon in Eden, but had their first little one among
the thorns and thistles of the wilderness. It is still the beginning
of the home epic—the gradual conquest or irremediable loss of
that complete union which makes the advancing years a climax,
and age the harvest of sweet memories in common.

Some set out, like Crusaders of old, with a glorious equipment
of hope and enthusiasm, and get broken by the way, wanting
patience with each other and the world.

All who have cared for Fred Vincy and Mary Garth will like
to know that these two made no such failure, but achieved a
solid mutual happiness. Fred surprised his neighbours in
various ways. He became rather distinguished in his side of
the county as a theoretic and practical farmer, and produced
a work on the "Cultivation of Green Crops and the Economy of
Cattle-Feeding" which won him high congratulations at agricultural meetings. In Middlemarch admiration was more
reserved: most persons there were inclined to believe that the
merit of Fred's authorship was due to his wife, since they had
never expected Fred Vincy to write on turnips and mangel-
wurzel.

But when Mary wrote a little book for her boys, called "Stories
of Great Men, taken from Plutarch," and had it printed and pub-
lished by Gripp & Co., Middlemarch, every one in the town was
willing to give the credit of this work to Fred, observing that
he had been to the University, "where the ancients were
studied," and might have been a clergyman if he had chosen.

In this way it was made clear that Middlemarch had never
been deceived, and that there was no need to praise anybody
for writing a book, since it was always done by somebody
else.

Moreover, Fred remained unswervingly steady. Some years
after his marriage he told Mary that his happiness was half
owing to Farebrother, who gave him a strong pull-up at the right
moment. I cannot say that he was never again misled by his
hopefulness: the yield of crops or the profits of a cattle sale
usually fell below his estimate; and he was always prone to

believe that he could make money by the purchase of a horse which turned out badly—though this, Mary observed, was of course the fault of the horse, not of Fred's judgment. He kept his love of horsemanship, but he rarely allowed himself a day's hunting; and when he did so, it was remarkable that he submitted to be laughed at for cowardliness at the fences, seeming to see Mary and the boys sitting on the five-barred gate, or showing their curly heads between hedge and ditch.

There were three boys: Mary was not discontented that she brought forth men-children only; and when Fred wished to have a girl like her, she said, laughingly, "That would be too great a trial to your mother." Mrs. Vincy in her declining years, and in the diminished lustre of her housekeeping, was much comforted by her perception that two at least of Fred's boys were real Vincys, and did not "feature the Garths." But Mary secretly rejoiced that the youngest of the three was very much what her father must have been when he wore a round jacket, and showed a marvellous nicety of aim in playing at marbles, or in throwing stones to bring down the mellow pears.

Ben and Letty Garth, who were uncle and aunt before they were well in their teens, disputed much as to whether nephews or nieces were more desirable; Ben contending that it was clear girls were good for less than boys, else they would not be always in petticoats, which showed how little they were meant for; whereupon Letty, who argued much from books, got angry in replying that God made coats of skins for both Adam and Eve alike—also it occurred to her that in the East the men too wore petticoats. But this latter argument, obscuring the majesty of the former, was one too many, for Ben answered contemptuously, "The more spooneys they!" and immediately appealed to his mother whether boys were not better than girls. Mrs. Garth pronounced that both were alike naughty, but that boys were undoubtedly stronger, could run faster, and throw with more precision to a greater distance. With this oracular sentence Ben was well satisfied, not minding the naughtiness; but Letty took it ill, her feeling of superiority being stronger than her muscles.

Fred never became rich—his hopefulness had not led him to expect that; but he gradually saved enough to become owner of the stock and furniture at Stone Court, and the work which Mr. Garth put into his hands carried him in plenty through those "bad times" which are always present with farmers.

Mary, in her matronly days, became as solid in figure as her mother ; but, unlike her, gave the boys little formal teaching, so that Mrs. Garth was alarmed lest they should never be well grounded in grammar and geography. Nevertheless, they were found quite forward enough when they went to school ; perhaps, because they had liked nothing so well as being with their mother. When Fred was riding home on winter evenings he had a pleasant vision beforehand of the bright hearth in the wainscoted parlour, and was sorry for other men who could not have Mary for their wife ; especially for Mr. Farebrother. " He was ten times worthier of you than I was," Fred could now say to her, magnanimously. "To be sure he was," Mary answered ; " and for that reason he could do better without me. But you—I shudder to think what you would have been —a curate in debt for horse-hire and cambric pocket-handkerchiefs ! "

On inquiry it might possibly be found that Fred and Mary still inhabit Stone Court—that the creeping plants still cast the foam of their blossoms over the fine stone-walls into the field where the walnut-trees stand in stately row—and that on sunny days the two lovers who were first engaged with the umbrella-ring may be seen in white-haired placidity at the open window from which Mary Garth, in the days of old Peter Featherstone, had often been ordered to look out for Mr. Lydgate.

Lydgate's hair never became white. He died when he was only fifty, leaving his wife and children provided for by a heavy insurance on his life. He had gained an excellent practice, alternating, according to the season, between London and a Continental bathing-place ; having written a treatise on Gout, a disease which has a good deal of wealth on its side. His skill was relied on by many paying patients, but he always regarded himself as a failure : he had not done what he once meant to do. His acquaintances thought him enviable to have so charming a wife, and nothing happened to shake their opinion. Rosamond never committed a second compromising indiscretion. She simply continued to be mild in her temper, inflexible in her judgment, disposed to admonish her husband, and able to frustrate him by stratagem. As the years went on he opposed her less and less, whence Rosamond concluded that he had learned the value of her opinion ; on the other hand, she had a more thorough conviction of his talents now that he gained a good income, and instead of the threatened cage in Bride Street provided one all flowers and gilding, fit for the bird of paradise that she resembled. In brief, Lydgate was what is called a successful man. But he died prematurely of diphtheria, and Rosamond afterwards married an elderly and wealthy physician, who took kindly to her four children. She made a very pretty show with her daughters, driving out in her carriage, and often spoke of her happiness as "a reward"—she did not say for what, but probably she meant that it was a reward for her patience with Tertius, whose temper never became faultless, and to the last occasionally let slip a bitter speech which was more memorable than the signs he made of his repentance. He once called her his basil plant; and when she asked for an explanation, said that basil was a plant which had flourished wonderfully on a murdered man's brains. Rosamond had a placid but strong answer to such speeches. Why then had he chosen her ? It was a pity he had not had Mrs. Ladislaw, whom he was always praising and placing above her. And thus the conversation ended with the advantage on Rosamond's side. But it would be unjust not to tell, that she never uttered a word in depreciation of Dorothea, keeping in religious remembrance the generosity which had come to her aid in the sharpest crisis of her life.

Dorothea herself had no dreams of being praised above other women, feeling that there was always something better which she might have done, if she had only been better and known better. Still, she never repented that she had given up position and fortune to marry Will Ladislaw, and he would have held it the greatest shame as well as sorrow to him if she had repented. They were bound to each other by a love stronger than any impulses which could have marred it. No life would have been possible to Dorothea which was not filled with emotion, and she had now a life filled also with a beneficent activity which she had not the doubtful pains of discovering and marking out for herself. Will became an ardent public man, working well in those times when reforms were begun with a young hopefulness of immediate good which has been much checked in our days, and getting at last returned to Parliament by a constituency who paid his expenses. Dorothea could have liked nothing better, since wrongs existed, than that her husband should be in the thick of a struggle against them, and that she should give him wifely help. Many who knew her, thought it a pity that so substantive and rare a creature should have been absorbed into the life of another, and be only known in a certain circle as a wife and mother. But no one stated exactly what else that was in her power she ought rather to have done—not even Sir James Chettam, who went no further than the negative prescription that she ought not to have married Will Ladislaw.

But this opinion of his did not cause a lasting alienation ; and the way in which the family was made whole again was characteristic of all concerned. Mr. Brooke could not resist the pleasure of corresponding with Will and Dorothea ; and one morning when his pen had been remarkably fluent on the prospects of Municipal Reform, it ran off into an invitation to the Grange, which, once written, could not be done away with at less cost than the sacrifice (hardly to be conceived) of the whole valuable letter. During the months of this correspondence Mr. Brooke had continually, in his talk with Sir James Chettam, been presupposing or hinting that the intention of cutting off the entail was still maintained ; and the day on which his pen gave the daring invitation, he went to Freshitt expressly to intimate that he had a stronger sense than ever of the reasons for taking that energetic step as a precaution against any mixture of low blood in the heir of the Brookes.

But that morning something exciting had happened at the Hall. A letter had come to Celia which made her cry silently as she read it ; and when Sir James, unused to see her in tears, asked anxiously what was the matter, she burst out in a wail such as he had never heard from her before.

" Dorothea has a little boy. And you will not let me go and see her. And I am sure she wants to see me. And she will not know what to do with the baby—she will do wrong things with it. And they thought she would die. It is very dreadful ! Suppose it had been me and little Arthur, and Dodo had been hindered from coming to see me ! I wish you would be less unkind, James ! "

" Good heavens, Celia ! " said Sir James, much wrought upon, " what do you wish ? I will do anything you like. I will take you to town to-morrow if you wish it." And Celia did wish it.

It was after this that Mr. Brooke came, and meeting the Baronet in the grounds, began to chat with him in ignorance of the news, which Sir James for some reason did not care to tell him immediately. But when the entail was touched on in the usual way, he said, " My dear sir, it is not for me to dictate to you, but for my part I would let that alone. I would let things remain as they are."

Mr. Brooke felt so much surprise that he did not at once find out how much he was relieved by the sense that he was not expected to do anything in particular.

Such being the bent of Celia's heart, it was inevitable that Sir James should consent to a reconciliation with Dorothea and her husband. Where women love each other, men learn to smother their mutual dislike. Sir James never liked Ladislaw, and Will always preferred to have Sir James's company mixed with another kind : they were on a footing of reciprocal tolerance which was made quite easy only when Dorothea and Celia were present.

It became an understood thing that Mr. and Mrs. Ladislaw should pay at least two visits during the year to the Grange, and there came gradually a small row of cousins at Freshitt who enjoyed playing with the two cousins visiting Tipton as much as if the blood of these cousins had been less dubiously mixed.

Mr. Brooke lived to a good old age, and his estate was inherited by Dorothea's son, who might have represented Middlemarch, but declined, thinking that his opinions had less chance of being stifled if he remained out of doors.

Sir James never ceased to regard Dorothea's second marriage as a mistake ; and indeed this remained the tradition concerning it in Middlemarch, where she was spoken of to a younger generation as a fine girl who married a sickly clergyman, old enough to be her father, and in little more than a year after his death gave up her estate to marry his cousin—young enough to have been his son, with no property, and not well-born. Those who had not seen anything of Dorothea usually observed that she could not have been " a nice woman," else she would not have married either the one or the other.

Certainly those determining acts of her life were not ideally beautiful. They were the mixed result of young and noble impulse struggling amidst the conditions of an imperfect social state, in which great feelings will often take the aspect of error, and great faith the aspect of illusion. For there is no creature whose inward being is so strong that it is not greatly determined by what lies outside it. A new Theresa will hardly have the opportunity of reforming a conventual life, any more than a new Antigone will spend her heroic piety in daring all for the sake of a brother's burial : the medium in which their ardent deeds took shape is for ever gone. But we insignificant people with our daily words and acts are preparing the lives of many Dorotheas, some of which may present a far sadder sacrifice than that of the Dorothea whose story we know.

Her finely-touched spirit had still its fine issues, though they were not widely visible. Her full nature, like that river of which Cyrus broke the strength, spent itself in channels which had no great name on the earth. But the effect of her being on those around her was incalculably diffusive : for the growing good of the world is partly dependent on unhistoric acts ; and that things are not so ill with you and me as they might have been, is half owing to the number who lived faithfully a hidden life, and rest in unvisited tombs.

THE END

EVERYMAN'S LIBRARY: A Selected List

This List covers a selection of volumes available in Everyman's Library. Those volumes marked with a * indicate that a paperback edition of this title is also available. Numbers only of hardback editions are given.

BIOGRAPHY

Brontë, Charlotte (1816–55). LIFE, 1857. By *Mrs Gaskell*.   318
Byron, Lord (1788–1824). LETTERS. Edited by *R. G. Howarth*, B.LITT.   931
Cellini, Benvenuto (1500–71). *THE LIFE OF BENVENUTO CELLINI, written by himself. 51
Evelyn, John (1620–1706). DIARY. Edited by *William Bray*, 1819.   2 vols. 220–1
Franklin, Benjamin (1706–90). AUTOBIOGRAPHY, 1817.   316
Goethe, Johann Wolfgang von (1749–1832). LIFE, 1855. By *G. H. Lewes*, 1817–78. 269
Hudson, William Henry (1841–1922). FAR AWAY AND LONG AGO, 1918.   956
Johnson, Dr Samuel (1709–84). LIVES OF THE ENGLISH POETS, 1781. 2 vols. 770–1.
  *BOSWELL'S LIFE OF JOHNSON, 1791. 2 vols. 1–2.
Keats, John (1795–1821). LIFE AND LETTERS, 1848. By *Lord Houghton* (1809–85). 801
Nelson, Horatio, Viscount (1758–1805). LIFE, 1813. By *Robert Southey* (1774–1843). 52
Pepys, Samuel (1633–1703). DIARY. Newly edited (1953), with modernized spelling.
    3 vols. 53–5
Plutarch (46?–120). LIVES OF THE NOBLE GREEKS AND ROMANS. Dryden's edition,
  1683–6. Revised by *A. H. Clough*, 1819–61.   3 vols. 407–9
Rousseau, Jean Jacques (1712–78). CONFESSIONS, 1782. Complete and unabridged.
    2 vols. 859–60
Scott, Sir Walter (1771–1832). LOCKHART'S LIFE OF SCOTT. An abridgment from the
  seven-volume work by *J. G. Lockhart* himself.   39
Sévigné, Marie de Rabutin-Chantal, Marquise de (1626–96). SELECTED LETTERS.   98
Vasari, Giorgio (1511–74). LIVES OF THE PAINTERS, SCULPTORS AND ARCHITECTS.
  Edited by *William Gaunt*.   4 vols. 784–7
Walpole, Horace (1717–97). SELECTED LETTERS. Edited, with an Introduction, by
  W. Hadley, M.A.   775

ESSAYS AND CRITICISM

An Everyman Anthology. Over a hundred authors from Everyman's Library
  represented.   663
Bacon, Francis, Lord Verulam (1561–1626). *ESSAYS. 1597–1626.   10
Belloc, Hilaire (1870–1953). *STORIES, ESSAYS AND POEMS.   948
Burke, Edmund (1729–97). REFLECTIONS ON THE FRENCH REVOLUTION, 1790. 460
Carlyle, Thomas (1795–1881). ESSAYS. Introduction by *J. R. Lowell*. Essays on men
  and affairs. 2 vols. 703–4. PAST AND PRESENT, 1843. 608. SARTOR RESARTUS,
  1838; and HEROES AND HERO-WORSHIP, 1841. 278
Castiglioni, Baldassare (1478–1529). THE BOOK OF THE COURTIER, 1528. *Sir Thomas
  Hoby's* translation, 1561.   807
Century. *A CENTURY OF ENGLISH ESSAYS FROM CAXTON TO BELLOC.   653
Chesterfield, Earl of (1694–1773). LETTERS TO HIS SON; AND OTHERS.   823
Chesterton, Gilbert Keith (1874–1936). *STORIES, ESSAYS AND POEMS.   913
Coleridge, Samuel Taylor (1772–1834). BIOGRAPHIA LITERARIA, 1817. 11. SHAKE-
  SPEAREAN CRITICISM, 1849. Edited by *Prof. T. M. Raysor* (1960). 2 vols. 162, 183.
De Quincey, Thomas (1785–1859). *CONFESSIONS OF AN ENGLISH OPIUM-EATER, 1822.
  223. THE ENGLISH MAIL-COACH AND OTHER WRITINGS. 609. REMINISCENCES
  OF THE ENGLISH LAKE POETS. 163. All edited by *Prof. John E. Jordan*.
Dryden, John (1631–1700). OF DRAMATIC POESY AND OTHER CRITICAL ESSAYS. The
  whole of Dryden's critical writings.   2 vols. 568–9
Elyot, Sir Thomas (1490?–1546). THE GOVERNOR, 1531. Edited by *S. E. Lehmberg*. 227
Emerson, Ralph Waldo (1803–82). ESSAYS, 1841–4.   12
Gray, Thomas (1716–71). ESSAYS. *(See Poetry and Drama Section.)*
Hamilton, Alexander (1757–1804), and Others. THE FEDERALIST, 1787–8.   519
Hazlitt, William (1778–1830). LECTURES ON THE ENGLISH COMIC WRITERS, 1819; and
  FUGITIVE WRITINGS. 411. LECTURES ON THE ENGLISH POETS, 1818; and THE
  SPIRIT OF THE AGE, 1825. 459. THE ROUND TABLE and CHARACTERS OF SHAKE-
  SPEAR'S PLAYS, 1817–18. 65. TABLE TALK, 1821–2, 1824. 321
Holmes, Oliver Wendell (1809–94). THE AUTOCRAT OF THE BREAKFAST-TABLE, 1858. 66

FICTION

Cooper, James Fenimore (1789–1851). THE LAST OF THE MOHICANS, 1826, A NARRA-TIVE OF 1757. 79. THE PATHFINDER, 1840. 78
Daudet, Alphonse (1840–97). TARTARIN OF TARASCON, 1872; and TARTARIN ON THE ALPS, 1885. 423
Defoe, Daniel (1661?–1731). ★THE FORTUNES AND MISFORTUNES OF MOLL FLANDERS, 1722. 837. ★JOURNAL OF THE PLAGUE YEAR, 1722. 289. ★THE LIFE, ADVENTURES AND PIRACIES OF THE FAMOUS CAPTAIN SINGLETON, 1720. 74. ★ROBINSON CRUSOE, and THE FARTHER ADVENTURES OF ROBINSON CRUSOE, 1719. Parts I and II complete. 59
De Rojas, Fernando (15th century). CELESTINA: OR THE TRAGI-COMEDY OF CALLISTO AND MELIBEA. Translation (1958) by Phyllis Hartnoll, M.A. 100
Dickens, Charles (1812–70). ★BARNABY RUDGE, 1841. 76. BLEAK HOUSE, 1852–3. 236. ★A CHRISTMAS CAROL and OTHER CHRISTMAS BOOKS, 1843–8. 239. CHRIST-MAS STORIES, 1850–67. 414. DAVID COPPERFIELD, 1849–50. 242. ★DOMBEY AND SON, 1846–6. 240. ★GREAT EXPECTATIONS, 1861. 234. ★HARD TIMES, 1854. 292. LITTLE DORRIT, 1857. 293. MARTIN CHUZZLEWIT, 1843–4. 241. NICHOLAS NICKLEBY, 1838–9. 238. THE OLD CURIOSITY SHOP, 1841. 173. ★OLIVER TWIST, 1838. 233. OUR MUTUAL FRIEND, 1864–5. 294. THE PICKWICK PAPERS, 1836–7. 235. ★A TALE OF TWO CITIES, 1859. 102. SKETCHES BY 'BOZ', 1835–6. 237
Dostoyevsky, Fyodor (1821–81). THE BROTHERS KARAMAZOV, 1879–80. Translated by Constance Garnett. 2 vols. 802–3. ★CRIME AND PUNISHMENT, 1866. Translated by Constance Garnett. 501. ★THE IDIOT, 1873. Translated by Eva M. Martin. 682. ★LETTERS FROM THE UNDERWORLD, 1864; and OTHER TALES. Translated by C. J. Hogarth. 654. ★POOR FOLK, 1845; and THE GAMBLER, 1867. Translated by C. J. Hogarth. 711. THE POSSESSED, 1871. Translated by Constance Garnett. 2 vols. 861–2
Dumas, Alexandre (1802–70). ★THE BLACK TULIP, 1850. The brothers De Witt in the Holland of 1672–5. 174. THE COUNT OF MONTE CRISTO, 1844. Napoleon's later phase. 2 vols. 393–4. THE THREE MUSKETEERS, 1844. The France of Cardinal Richelieu. 81. TWENTY YEARS AFTER, 1845. The execution of Charles the First. 175
Du Maurier, George Louis Palmella Busson (1834–96). TRILBY, 1894. 863
Edgeworth, Maria (1767–1849). CASTLE RACKRENT, 1800; and THE ABSENTEE, 1812. 410
Eliot, George. ★ADAM BEDE, 1859. 27. DANIEL DERONDA, 1876. 2 vols. 539–40. FELIX HOLT, 1866. 353. MIDDLEMARCH, 1872. 2 vols. 854–5. ★THE MILL ON THE FLOSS, 1860. 325. ROMOLA, 1863. The Florence of Savonarola. 231. ★SILAS MARNER, THE WEAVER OF RAVELOE, 1861. 121
★English Short Stories. Thirty-six stories from Middle Ages to present time. 743
Fielding, Henry (1707–54). AMELIA, 1751. Amelia is drawn from Fielding's first wife. 2 vols. 852–3. ★JONATHAN WILD, 1743; and JOURNAL OF A VOYAGE TO LISBON, 1755. 877. ★JOSEPH ANDREWS, 1742. A skit on Richardson's Pamela. 467. ★TOM JONES, 1749. The first great English novel of humour. 2 vols. 355–6
Flaubert, Gustave (1821–80). ★MADAME BOVARY, 1857. Translated by Eleanor Marx-Aveling. 808. SALAMMBÔ, 1862. Translated by J. C. Chartres, 869. ★SENTIMENTAL EDUCATION, 1869. Translation by Anthony Goldsmith. 969
Forster, Edward Morgan (b. 1879). A PASSAGE TO INDIA, 1924. Notes by the author. 972
Gaskell, Mrs Elizabeth (1810–65). ★CRANFORD, 1853. 83. ★MARY BARTON. 598
★Ghost Stories. Eighteen stories. 952
Gogol, Nikolay (1809–52). DEAD SOULS, 1842. 726. ★TARAS BULBA. 740
Goldsmith, Oliver (1728–74). ★THE VICAR OF WAKEFIELD, 1766. 295
Goncharov, Ivan (1812–91). OBLOMOV, 1857. Translated by Natalie Duddington. 878
Gorky, Maxim (1868–1936). ★THROUGH RUSSIA. 741
Grossmith, George (1847–1912), and Weedon (1853–1919). ★THE DIARY OF A NOBODY, 1894. 963
Hawthorne, Nathaniel (1804–64). THE HOUSE OF THE SEVEN GABLES, 1851. 176. ★THE SCARLET LETTER, 1850. 122. TWICE-TOLD TALES, 1837–42. 531
Hugo, Victor Marie (1802–85). LES MISÉRABLES, 1862. 2 vols. 363–4. ★NOTRE DAME DE PARIS, 1831. 422. TOILERS OF THE SEA, 1866. 509
James, Henry (1843–1916). ★THE AMBASSADORS, 1903. 987. ★THE TURN OF THE SCREW, 1898; and THE ASPERN PAPERS, 1888. 912
Jerome, Jerome K. (1859–1927). ★THREE MEN IN A BOAT, 1889, and THREE MEN ON THE BUMMEL, 1900. 118
Kingsley, Charles (1819–75). HEREWARD THE WAKE, 1866. 296. WESTWARD HO!, 1855. 20. HYPATIA, 1853. 230
Lamb, Charles (1775–1834), and Mary (1764–1847). ★TALES FROM SHAKESPEARE, 1807. Illustrated by Arthur Rackham. 8
Loti, Pierre (1850–1923). ICELAND FISHERMAN, 1886. 920
Lover, Samuel (1797–1868). HANDY ANDY, 1842. 178
Lytton, Edward Bulwer, Baron (1803–73). ★THE LAST DAYS OF POMPEII, 1834. 80
Mann, Thomas (1875–1955). STORIES AND EPISODES. 962
Manzoni, Alessandro (1785–1873). THE BETROTHED (I Promessi Sposi, 1840, rev. ed.). Translated (1951) by Archibald Colquhoun, with a Preface. 999
Marryat, Frederick (1792–1848). MR MIDSHIPMAN EASY. 82. THE SETTLERS IN CANADA, 1844. 370

3

REFERENCE

RELIGION AND PHILOSOPHY

SCIENCE

TRAVEL AND TOPOGRAPHY